THE UNIVERSE OF H. P. LOVECRAFT

16 SHORT STORIES OF MONSTERS AND TERROR FROM AN UNRIVALLED AUTHOR

British Library Cataloguing-in-Publication Data
A catalogue record for this book is available from
the British Library

Contents

H. P. LOVECRAFT

Howard Phillips Lovecraft was born in 1890 in Rhode Island, USA. Although a sickly boy, Lovecraft began writing at a very young age, quickly developing a deep and abiding interest in science. At just sixteen he was writing a monthly astronomy column for his local newspaper. However, in 1908, Lovecraft suffered a nervous breakdown and failed to get into university, sparking a period of five years in which he all but vanished.

In 1913, Lovecraft was invited to join the UAPA (United Amateur Press Association) – a development which re-invigorated his writing. In 1917, he began to focus on fiction, producing such well-known early stories as 'Dagon' and 'A Reminiscence of Dr. Samuel Johnson'. In 1924,

Lovecraft married and moved to New York, but he disliked life there intensely, and struggled to find work. A few years later, penniless and now divorced, he returned to Rhode Island. It was here, during the last decade of his life, that Lovecraft produced the vast majority of his best-known fiction, including 'The Dunwich Horror', 'The Shadow over Innsmouth', 'The Thing on the Doorstep' and arguably his most famous story, 'The Call of Cthulhu'. Having suffered from cancer of the small intestine for more than a year, Lovecraft died in March of 1937.

Witches' Hollow

District School Number Seven stood on the very edge of that wild country which lies west of Arkham. It stood in a little grove of trees, chiefly oaks and elms with one or two maples; in one direction the road led to Arkham, in the other it dwindled away into the wild, wooded country which always looms darkly on that western horizon. It presented a warmly attractive appearance to me when first I saw it on my arrival as the new teacher early in September, 1920, though it had no distinguishing architectural feature and was in every respect the replica of thousands of country schools scattered throughout New England, a compact, conservative building painted white, so that it shone forth from among the trees in the midst of which it stood.

It was an old building at that time, and no doubt has since been abandoned or torn down. The school district has now been consolidated, but at that time it supported this school in somewhat niggardly a manner, skimping and saving on every necessity. Its standard readers, when I came there to teach, were still *McGuffey's Eclectic Readers*, in editions published before the turn of the century. My charges added up to twenty-seven. There were Allens and Whateleys and Perkinses, Dunlocks and Abbotts and Talbots—and there was Andrew Potter.

I cannot now recall the precise circumstances of my especial notice of Andrew Potter. He was a large boy for his age, very dark of mien, with haunting eyes and a shock of tousselled black hair. His eyes brooded upon me with a kind of different quality which at first challenged me but ultimately left me strangely uneasy. He was in the fifth grade, and it did not take me long to discover that he could very easily advance into the seventh or eighth, but made no effort to do so. He seemed to have only a casual tolerance for his schoolmates, and for their part, they re-

5

spected him, but not out of affection so much as what struck me soon as fear. Very soon thereafter, I began to understand that this strange lad held for me the same kind of amused tolerance that he held for his schoolmates.

Perhaps it was inevitable that the challenge of this pupil should lead me to watch him as surreptitiously as I could, and as the circumstances of teaching a one-room school permitted. As a result, I became aware of a vaguely disquieting fact; from time to time, Andrew Potter responded to some stimulus beyond the apprehension of my senses, reacting precisely as if someone had called to him, sitting up, growing alert, and wearing the air of someone listening to sounds beyond my own hearing, in the same attitude assumed by animals hearing sounds beyond the pitch-levels of the human ear.

My curiosity quickened by this time, I took the first opportunity to ask about him. One of the eighth-grade boys, Wilbur Dunlock, was in the habit on occasion of staying after school and helping with the cursory cleaning that the room needed.

'Wilbur,' I said to him late one afternoon. 'I notice you don't seem to pay much attention to Andrew Potter, none of you. Why?'

He looked at me, a lttle distrustfully, and pondered his answer before he shrugged and replied, 'He's not like us.'

'In what way?'

He shook his head. 'He don't care if we let him play with us or not. He don't want to.'

He seemed reluctant to talk, but by dint of repeated questions I drew from him certain spare information. The Potters lived deep in the hills to the west along an all but abandoned branch of the main road that led through the hills. Their farm stood in a little valley locally known as Witches' Hollow which Wilbur described as 'a bad place.' There were only four of them — Andrew, an older sister, and their parents. They did not 'mix' with other people of the district, not even with the Dunlocks, who were their nearest neighbours, living but half a mile from the school itself, and thus, perhaps, four miles from Witches' Hollow, with woods separating the two farms.

More than this he could not—or would not—say.

About a week later, I asked Andrew Potter to remain after school. He offered no objection, appearing to take my request as a matter of course. As soon as the other children had gone, he came up to my desk and stood there waiting, his dark eyes fixed expectantly on me, and just the shadow of a smile on his full lips.

'I've been studying your grades, Andrew,' I said, 'and it seems

6

to me that with only a little effort you could skip into the sixth—perhaps even the seventh—grade. Wouldn't you like to make that effort?'

He shrugged.

'What do you intend to do when you get out of school?'

He shrugged again.

'Are you going to high school in Arkham?'

He considered me with eyes that seemed suddenly piercing in their keenness, all lethargy gone. 'Mr Williams, I'm here because there's a law says I have to be,' he answered. 'There's no law says I have to go to high school.'

'But aren't you interested?' I pressed him.

'What I'm interested in doesn't matter. It's what my folks want that counts.'

'Well, I'm going to talk to them.' I decided on the moment. 'Come along. I'll take you home.'

For a moment something like alarm sprang into his expression, but in seconds it diminished and gave way to that air of watchful lethargy so typical of him. He shrugged and stood waiting while I slipped my books and papers into the schoolbag I habitually carried. Then he walked docilely to the car with me and got in, looking at me with a smile that could only be described as superior.

We rode through the woods in silence, which suited the mood that came upon me as soon as we had entered the hills, for the trees pressed close upon the road, and the deeper we went, the darker grew the wood, perhaps as much because of the lateness of that October day as because of the thickening of the trees. From relatively open glades, we plunged into an ancient wood, and when at last we turned down the side road—little more than a lane—to which Andrew silently pointed, I found that I was driving through a growth of very old and strangely deformed trees. I had to proceed with caution; the road was so little used that underbrush crowded upon it from both sides, and, oddly, I recognized little of it, for all my studies in botany, though once I thought I saw saxifrage, curiously mutated. I drove abruptly, without warning, into the yard before the Potter house.

The sun was now lost behind the wall of trees, and the house stood on a kind of twilight. Beyond it stretched a few fields, strung out up the valley; in one, there were cornshocks, in another stubble, in yet another pumpkins. The house itself was forbidding, low to the ground, with half a second storey, gambrel-roofed, with shuttered windows, and the outbuildings stood gaunt and stark, looking as if they had never been used. The entire farm looked deserted; the only sign of life was in a few chickens that scratched at the earth behind the house.

Had it not been that the lane along which we had travelled ended here, I would have doubted that we had reached the Potter house. Andrew flashed a glance at me, as if he sought some expression on my face to convey to him what I thought. Then he jumped lightly from the car, leaving me to follow.

He went into the house ahead of me. I heard him announce me.

'Brought the teacher. Mr. Williams.'

There was no answer.

Then abruptly I was in the room, lit only by an old-fashioned kerosene lamp, and there were the other three Potters—the father, a tall, stoop-shouldered man, grizzled and greying, who could not have been more than forty but looked much, much older, not so much physically as psychically—the mother, an almost obscenely fat woman—and the girl, slender, tall, and with that same air of watchful waiting that I had noticed in Andrew.

Andrew made the brief introductions, and the four of them stood or sat, waiting upon what I had to say, and somewhat uncomfortably suggesting in their attitudes that I say it and get out.

'I wanted to talk to you about Andrew,' I said. 'He shows great promise, and he could be moved up a grade or two if he'd study a little more.'

My words were not welcomed.

'I believe he's smart enough for eighth grade,' I went on, and stopped.

'If he 'uz in eighth grade,' said his father, 'he's be havin' to go to high school 'fore he 'uz old enough to git outa goin' to school. That's the law. They told me.'

I could not help thinking of what Wilbur Dunlock had told me of the reclusiveness of the Potters, and as I listened to the elder Potter, and thought of what I had heard, I was suddenly aware of a kind of tension among them, and a subtle alteration in their attitude. The moment the father stopped talking, there was a singular harmony of attitude—all four of them seemed to be listening to some inner voice, and I doubt that they heard my protest at all.

'You can't expect a boy as smart as Andrew just to come back here,' I said.

'Here's good enough,' said old Potter. 'Besides, he's ours. And don't ye go talkin' 'bout us now, Mr. Williams.'

He spoke with so latently menacing an undercurrent in his

voice that I was taken aback. At the same time I was increasingly aware of a miasma of hostility, not proceeding so much from any one or all four of them, as from the house and its setting themselves.

'Thank you,' I said. 'I'll be going.'

I turned and went out, Andrew at my heels.

Outside, Andrew said softly, 'You shouldn't be talking about us, Mr. Williams. Pa gets mad when he finds out. You talked to Wilbur Dunlock.'

I was arrested at getting into the car. With one foot on the running board, I turned. 'Did he say so?' I asked.

He shook his head. 'You did, Mr. Williams,' he said, and backed away. 'It's not what he thinks, but what he might do.'

Before I could speak again, he had darted into the house.

For a moment I stood undecided. But my decision was made for me. Suddenly, in the twilight, the house seemed to burgeon with menace, and all the surrounding woods seemed to stand waiting but to bend upon me. Indeed, I was aware of a rustling, like the whispering of wind, in all the wood, though no wind stirred, and from the house itself came a malevolence like the blow of a fist. I got into the car and drove away, with that impression of malignance at my back like the hot breath of a ravaging pursuer.

I reached my room in Arkham at last, badly shaken. Seen in retrospect, I had undergone an unsettling psychic experience; there was no other explanation for it. I had the unavoidable conviction that, however blindly, I had thrust myself in far deeper waters than I knew, and the very unexpectedness of the experience made it the more chilling. I could not eat for the wonder of what went on in that house in Witches' Hollow, of what it was that bound the family together, chaining them to that place, preventing a promising lad like Andrew Potter even from the most fleeting wish to leave that dark valley and go out into a brighter world.

I lay for most of that night, sleepless, filled with a nameless dread for which all explanation eluded me, and when I slept at last my sleep was filled with hideously disturbing dreams, in which beings far beyond my mundane imagination held the stage, and cataclysmic events of the utmost terror and horror took place. And when I rose next morning, I felt that somehow I had touched upon a world totally alien to my kind.

I reached the school early that morning. But Wilbur Dunlock was there before me. His eyes met mine with sad reproach. I could not imagine what had happened to disturb this usually friendly pupil.

'You shouldn't a told Andrew Potter we talked about him,' he said with a kind of unhappy resignation.

'I didn't, Wilbur.'

'I know I didn't. So you must have,' he said. And then, 'Six of our cows got killed last night, and the shed where they were was crushed down on 'em.'

I was momentarily too startled to reply. 'A sudden windstorm,' I began, but he cut me off.

'Weren't no wind last night, Mr. Williams. And the cows were smashed.'

'You surely cannot think that the Potters had anything to do with this, Wilbur,' I cried.

He gave me a weary look—the look of one who knows, meeting the glance of one who should know but cannot understand, and said nothing more.

This was even more upsetting than my experience of the previous evening. He at least was convinced that there was a connection between our conversation about the Potter family and the Dunlocks' loss of half a dozen cows. And he was convinced with so deep a conviction that I knew without trying that nothing I could say would shake it.

When Andrew Potter came in, I looked in vain for any sign that anything out of the ordinary had taken place since last I had seen him.

Somehow I got through that day. Immediately after the close of the school session, I hastened into Arkham and went to the office of the *Arkham Gazette*, the editor of which had been kind enough, as a member of the local District Board of Education, to find my room for me. He was an elderly man, almost seventy, and might presumably know what I wanted to find out.

My appearance must have conveyed something of my agitation, for when I walked into his office, his eyebrows lifted, and he said, 'What's got your dander up, Mr. Williams ?'

I made some attempt to dissemble, since I could put my hand upon nothing tangible, and, viewed in the cold light of day, what I might have said would have sounded almost hysterical to an impartial listener. I said only, 'I'd like to know something about a Potter family that lives in Witches' Hollow, west of the school.'

He gave me an enigmatic glance. 'Never heard of old Wizard Potter?' he asked. And, before I could answer, he went on, 'No, of course, you're from Brattleboro. We could hardly expect Vermonters to know about what goes on in the Massachusetts back country. He lived there first. An old man when I first knew him. And these Potters were distant relatives, lived in Upper Michigan, inherited the property and came to live there when Wizard Potter died.'

'But what do you know about them?' I persisted.

'Nothing but what everybody else knows,' he said. 'When they came, they were nice friendly people. Now they talk to nobody, seldom come out—and there's all that talk about missing animals from the farms in the district. The people tie that all up.'

Thus begun, I questioned him at length.

I listened to a bewildering enigma of half-told tales, hints, legends and lore utterly beyond my comprehension. What seemed to be incontrovertible was a distant cousinship between Wizard Potter and one Wizard Whateley of nearby Dunwich—'a bad lot,' the editor called him; the solitary way of life of old Wizard Potter, and the incredible length of time he had lived; the fact that people generally shunned Witches' Hollow. What seemed to be sheer fantasy was the superstitious lore—that Wizard Potter had 'called something down from the sky, and it lived with him or in him until he died';—that a late traveller, found in a dying state along the main road, had gasped out something about 'that thing with the feelers—slimy, rubbery thing with the suckers on its feelers' that came out of the woods and attacked him—and a good deal more of the same kind of lore.

When he finished, the editor scribbled a note to the librarian at Miskatonic University in Arkham, and handed it to me. 'Tell him to let you look at that book. You may learn something.' He shrugged. 'And you may not. Young people now-days take the world with a lot of salt.'

I went supperless to pursue my search for the special knowledge I felt I needed, if I were to save Andrew Potter for a better life. For it was this rather than the satisfaction of my curiosity that impelled me. I made my way to the library of Miskatonic University, looked up the librarian, and handed him the editor's note.

The old man gave me a sharp look, said, 'Wait here, Mr. Williams,' and went off with a ring of keys. So the book, whatever it was, was kept under lock and key.

I waited for what seemed an interminable time. I was now beginning to feel some hunger, and to question my unseemly haste—and yet I felt that there was little time to be lost, though I could not define the catastrophe I hoped to avert. Finally the librarian came, bearing an ancient tome, and brought it around to a table within his range of vision. The book's title was in Latin—*Necronomicon*—though its author was evidently an Arabian, *Abdul Alhazred,* and its text was in somewhat archaic English.

I began to read with interest which soon turned to complete bewilderment. The book evidently concerned ancient, alien races, invaders of earth, great mythical beings called Ancient Ones and Elder Gods, with outlandish names like Cthulhu and Hastur, Shub-Niggurath and Azathoth, Dagon and Ithaqua and Wendigo and Cthugha, all involved in some kind of plan to dominate earth and served by some of its peoples—the Tcho-Tcho, and the Deep Ones, and the like. It was a book filled with cabbalistic lore, incantations, and what purported to be an account of a great interplanetary battle between the Elder Gods and the Ancient Ones and of the survival of cults and servitors in isolated and remote places on our planet as well as on sister planets. What this rigmarole had to do with my immediate problem, with the ingrown and strange Potter family and their longing for solitude and their anti-social way of life, was completely beyond me.

How long I would have gone on reading, I do not know. I was interrupted presently by the awareness of being studied by a stranger, who stood not far from me with his eyes moving from the book I was busy reading to me. Having caught my eye, he made so bold as to come over to my side.

'Forgive me,' he said, 'But what in this book interests a country school teacher?'

'I wonder now myself,' I said.

He introduced himself as Professor Martin Keane. 'I may say, sir,' he added, 'that I know this book practically by heart.'

'A farrago of superstition.'

'Do you think so?'

'Emphatically.'

'You have lost the quality of wonder, Mr. Williams. Tell me, if you will, what brought you to this book—'

I hesitated, but Professor Keane's personality was persuasive and inspired confidence.

'Let us walk, if you don't mind,' I said.

He nodded.

I returned the book to the librarian, and joined my new-found friend. Haltingly, as clearly as I could, I told him about Andrew Potter, the house in Witches' Hollow, my strange psychic experience—even the curious coincidence of Dunlock's cows. To all this he listened without interruption, indeed, with a singular absorption. I explained at last that my motive in looking into the background of Witches' Hollow was solely to do something for my pupil.

'A little research,' he said, 'would have informed you that many strange events have taken place in such remote places as Dunwich

12

and Innsmouth—even Arkham and Witches' Hollow,' he said when I finished. 'Look around you at these ancient houses with their shuttered rooms and ill-lit fanlights. How many strange events have taken place under those gambrel roofs! We shall never know. But let us put aside the question of belief! One may not need to see the embodiment of evil to believe in it, Mr. Williams. I should like to be of some small service to the boy in this matter. May I?'

'By all means!'

'It may be perilous—to you as well as to him.'

'I am not concerned about myself.'

'But I assure you, it cannot be any more perilous to the boy than his present position. Even death for him is less perilous.'

'You speak in riddles, Professor.'

'Let it be better so, Mr. Williams. But come—we are at my residence. Pray come in.'

We went into one of those ancient houses of which Professor Keane had spoken. I walked into the musty past, for the rooms were filled with books and all manner of antiquities. My host took me into what was evidently his sitting-room, swept a chair clear of books, and invited me to wait while he busied himself on the second floor.

He was not, however, gone very long—not even long enough for me to assimilate the curious atmosphere of the room in which I waited. When he came back he carried what I saw at once were objects of stone, roughly in the shape of five-pointed stars. He put five of them into my hands.

'Tomorrow after school — if the Potter boy is there — you must contrive to touch him with one of these, and keep it fixed upon him,' said my host. 'There are two other conditions. You must keep one of these at least on your person at all times, and you must keep all thought of the stone and what you are about to do out of your mind. These beings have a telepathic sense—an ability to read your thoughts.'

Startled, I recalled Andrew's charging me with having talked about them with Wilbur Dunlock.

'Should I not know what these are?' I asked.

'If you can abate your doubts for the time being,' my host answered with a grim smile. 'These stones are among the thousands bearing the Seal of R'lyeh which closed the prisons of the Ancient Ones. They are the seals of the Elder Gods.'

'Professor Keane, the age of superstition is past,' I protested.

'Mr. Williams—the wonder of life and its mysteries is never past,' he retorted. 'If the stone has no meaning, it has no power. If

13

it has no power, it cannot affect young Potter. And it cannot protect you.'

'From what?'

'From the power behind the malignance you felt at the house in Witches' Hollow,' he answered. 'Or was this too superstition?' He smiled. 'You need not answer. I know your answer. If something happens when you put the stone upon the boy, he cannot be allowed to go back home. You must bring him here to me. Are you agreed?'

'Agreed,' I answered.

That next day was interminable, not only because of the imminence of crisis, but because it was extremely difficult to keep my mind blank before the inquiring gaze of Andrew Potter. Moreover, I was conscious as never before of the wall of pulsing malignance at my back, emanating from the wild country there, a tangible menace hidden in a pocket of the dark hills. But the hours passed, however slowly, and just before dismissal I asked Andrew Potter to wait after the others had gone.

And again he assented with that casual air tantamount almost to insolence, so that I was compelled to ask myself whether he were worth 'saving' as I thought of saving him in the depths of my mind.

But I persevered. I had hidden the stone in my car, and, once the others were gone, I asked Andrew to step outside with me.

At this point I felt both helpless and absurd. I, a college graduate, about to attempt what for me seemed inevitably the kind of mumbo-jumbo that belonged to the African wilderness. And for a few moments, as I walked stiffly from the school house toward the car I almost flagged, almost simply invited Andrew to get into the car to be driven home.

But I did not. I reached the car with Andrew at my heels, reached in, seized a stone to slip into my own pocket, seized another, and turned with lightning rapidity to press the stone to Andrew's forehead.

Whatever I expected to happen, it was not what took place.

For, at the touch of the stone, an expression of the utmost horror shone in Andrew Potter's eyes; in a trice, his gave way to poignant anguish; a great cry of terror burst from his lips. He flung his arms wide, scattering his books, wheeled as far as he could with my hold upon him, shuddered, and would have fallen, had I not caught him and lowered him, foaming at the mouth, to the ground. And then I was conscious of a great, cold wind which whirled about us and was gone, bending the grasses and the flowers, rippling the edge of the wood, and tearing away the leaves at the outer band of trees.

14

Driven by my own terror, I lifted Andrew Potter into the car, laid the stone on his chest, and drove as fast as I could into Arkham, seven miles away. Professor Keane was waiting, no whit surprised at my coming. And he had expected that I would bring Andrew Potter, for he had made a bed ready for him, and together we put him into it, after which Keane administered a sedative.

Then he turned to me. 'Now then, there's no time to be lost. They'll come to look for him—the girl probably first. We must get back to the school house at once.'

But now the full meaning and horror of what had happened to Andrew Potter had dawned upon me, and I was so shaken that it was necessary for Keane to push me from the room and half drag me out of the house. And again, as I set down these words so long after the terrible events of that night, I find myself trembling with that apprehension and fear which seize hold of a man who comes for the first time face to face with the vast unknown and knows how puny and meaningless he is against that cosmic immensity. I knew in that moment that what I had read in that forbidden book at the Miskatonic Library was not a farrago of superstition, but the key to a hitherto unsuspected revelation perhaps far, far older than mankind in the universe. I did not dare to think of what Wizard Potter had called down from the sky.

I hardly heard Professor Keane's words as he urged me to discard my emotional reaction and think of what had happened in scientific, more clinical fashion. After all, I had now accomplished my objective—Andrew Potter was saved. But to insure it, he must be made free of the others, who would surely follow him and find him. I thought only of what waiting horror that quartet of country people from Michigan had walked into when they came to take up possession of the solitary farm in Witches' Hollow.

I drove blindly back to the school. There, at Professor Keane's behest, I put on the lights and sat with the door open to the warm night, while he concealed himself behind the building to wait upon their coming. I had to steel myself in order to blank out my mind and take up that vigil,

On the edge of night, the girl came . . .

And after she had undergone the same experience as her brother, and lay beside the desk, the star-shaped stone on her breast, their father showed up in the doorway. All was darkness now, and he carried a gun. He had no need to ask what had happened; he *knew*. He stood wordless, pointed to his daughter and the stone on her breast, and raised his gun. His inference was plain—if I did not remove the stone, he meant to shoot. Evidently this was the contingency the professor expected, for he came upon Potter from the rear and touched him with the stone.

Afterwards we waited for two hours—in vain, for Mrs. Potter.

'She isn't coming,' said Professor Keane at last. 'She harbours the seat of its intelligence—I had thought it would be the man. Very well—we have no choice—we must go to Witches' Hollow. These two can be left here.'

We drove through the darkness, making no attempt at secrecy, for the professor said the 'thing' in the house in the Hollow 'knew' we were coming but could not reach us past the talisman of the stone. We went through that close pressing forest, down the narrow lane where the queer undergrowth seemed to reach out toward us in the glow of the head lights, into the Potter yard.

The house stood dark save for a wan glow of lamplight in one room.

Professor Keane leaped from the car with his little bag of star-shaped stones, and went around sealing the house—with a stone at each of the two doors, and one at each of the windows, through one of which we could see the woman sitting at the kitchen table—stolid, watchful, *aware*, no longer dissembling, looking unlike that tittering woman I had seen in this house not long ago, but rather like some great sentient beast at bay.

When he had finished, my companion went around to the front and, by means of brush collected from the yard and piled against the door, set fire to the house heedless of my protests.

Then he went back to the window to watch the woman, explaining that only fire could destroy the elemental force, but that he hoped, still, to save Mrs. Potter. 'Perhaps you'd better not watch, Williams.'

I did not heed him. Would that I had—and so spared myself the dreams that invade my sleep even yet! I stood at the window behind him and watched what went on in that room — for the smell of smoke was now permeating the house. Mrs. Potter — or what animated her gross body—started up, went awkwardly to the back door, retreated, to the window, retreated from it, and came back to the centre of the room, between the table and the wood stove, not yet fired against the coming cold. There she fell to the floor, heaving and writhing.

The room filled slowly with smoke, hazing about the yellow lamp, making the room indistinct—but not indistinct enough to conceal completely what went on in the course of that terrible struggle on the floor, where Mrs. Potter threshed about as if in mortal convulsion and slowly, half visibly, something or other took shape—an incredible amorphous mass, only half glimpsed in the smoke, tentacled, shimmering, with a cold intelligence and a physical coldness that I could feel through the window. The thing rose like a cloud above the now motionless body of Mrs. Potter, and then fell upon the stove and drained into it like vapour!

'The stove!' cried Professor Keane, and fell back.

Above us, out of the chimney, came a spreading blackness, like smoke, gathering itself briefly there. Then it hurtled like a lightning bolt aloft, into the stars, in the direction of the Hyades, back to that place from which old Wizard Potter had called it into himself, away from where it had lain in wait for the Potters to come from Upper Michigan and afford it new host on the face of earth.

We managed to get Mrs. Potter out of the house, much shrunken now, but alive.

On the remainder of that night's events there is no need to to dwell—how the professor waited until fire had consumed the house to collect his store of star-shaped stones, of the reuniting of the Potter family—freed from the curse of Witches' Hollow and determined never to return to that haunted valley—of Andrew, who, when we came to waken him, was talking in his sleep of 'great winds that fought and tore' and a 'place by the Lake of Hali where they live in glory forever.'

What it was that old Wizard Potter had called down from the stars, I lacked the courage to ask, but I knew that it touched upon secrets better left unknown to the races of men, secrets I would never have become aware of had I not chanced to take District School Number Seven, and had among my pupils the strange boy who was Andrew Potter.

The Unnamable

WE WERE SITTING on a dilapidated seventeenth-century tomb in the late afternoon of an autumn day at the old burying ground in Arkham, and speculating about the unnamable. Looking toward the giant willow in the cemetery, whose trunk had nearly engulfed an ancient, illegible slab, I had made a fantastic remark about the spectral and unmentionable nourishment which the colossal roots must be sucking from that hoary, charnel earth; when my friend chided me for such nonsense and told me that since no interments had occurred there for over a century, nothing could possibly exist to nourish the tree in other than an ordinary manner. Besides, he added, my constant talk about 'unnamable' and 'unmentionable' things was a very puerile device, quite in keeping with my lowly standing as an author. I was too fond of ending my stories with sights or sounds which paralyzed my heroes' faculties and left them without courage, words, or associations to tell what they had experienced. We know things, he said, only through our five senses or our religious intuitions; wherefore it is quite impossible to refer to any object or spectacle which cannot be clearly depicted by the solid definitions of fact or the correct doctrines of theology – preferably those of the Congregationalists, with whatever modifications tradition and Sir Arthur Conan Doyle may supply.

With this friend, Joel Manton, I had often languidly disputed. He was principal of the East High School, born and bred in Boston and sharing New England's self-satisfied deafness to the delicate overtones of life. It was his view that only our normal, objective experiences possess any esthetic significance, and that it is the province of the artist not so much to rouse strong emotion by action, ecstasy, and astonishment, as to maintain a placid interest and appreciation by accurate, detailed transcripts of everyday affairs. Especially did he object to my preoccupation with the mystical and the unexplained; for although believing in the supernatural much more fully than I, he would not admit that it is sufficiently commonplace for literary treatment. That a mind can find its greatest pleasure in escapes from the daily treadmill, and in original and dramatic re-combinations of images usually thrown by habit and fatigue into the hackneyed patterns of actual existence, was something virtually incredible to his clear, practical, and logical intellect. With him all things and feelings had fixed dimensions, properties, causes, and effects; and although he vaguely knew that the mind sometimes holds visions and sensations of far less geometrical, classifiable, and workable nature, he believed himself justified in drawing an arbitrary line and ruling out of court all that cannot be experienced and understood by the average citizen. Besides, he was almost sure that nothing can be really 'unnamable.' It didn't sound sensible to him.

Though I well realized the futility of imaginative and metaphysical arguments against the complacency of an orthodox sun-dweller, something in the scene of this afternoon colloquy moved me to more than usual contentiousness. The crumbling slate slabs, the patriarchal trees, and the centuried gambrel roofs of the witch-haunted old town that stretched around, all combined to rouse my spirit in defense of my work; and I was soon carrying my thrusts into the enemy's own country. It was not, indeed, difficult to begin a counter-attack, for I knew that Joel Manton actually half clung to many old-wives' superstitions which sophisticated people had long outgrown; beliefs in the appearance of dying persons at distant places, and in the impressions left by old faces on the windows through which they had gazed all their lives. To credit these whisperings of rural grandmothers, I now insisted, argued a faith in the existence of spectral substances on the earth apart from and subsequent to their material counterparts. It argued a capability of believing in phenomena beyond all normal notions; for if a dead man can transmit his visible or tangible image half across the world, or down the stretch of the centuries, how can it be absurd to suppose that deserted houses are full of queer sentient things, or that old graveyards teem with the terrible, unbodied intelligence of generations? And since spirit, in order to cause all the manifestations attributed to it, cannot be limited by any of the laws of matter; why is it extravagant to imagine psychically living dead things in shapes – or absences of shapes – which must for human spectators be utterly and appallingly 'unnamable'? 'Common sense' in reflecting on these subjects, I assured my friend with some warmth, is merely a stupid absence of imagination and mental flexibility.

Twilight had now approached, but neither of us felt any wish to cease speaking. Manton seemed unimpressed by my arguments, and eager to refute them, having that confidence in his own opinions which had doubtless caused his success as a teacher; whilst I was too sure of my ground to fear defeat. The dusk fell, and lights faintly gleamed in some of the distant windows, but we did not move. Our seat on the tomb was very comfortable, and I knew that my prosaic friend would not mind the cavernous rift in the ancient, root-disturbed brickwork close behind us, or the utter blackness of the spot brought by the intervention of a tottering, deserted seventeenth-century house between us and the nearest lighted road. There in the dark, upon that riven tomb by the deserted house, we talked on about the 'unnamable,' and after my friend had finished his scoffing I told him of the awful evidence behind the story at which he had scoffed the most.

My tale had been called *The Attic Window*, and appeared in the January, 1922, issue of *Whispers*. In a good many places, especially the South and the Pacific coast, they took the magazines off the stands at the complaints of silly milksops; but New England didn't get the thrill and merely shrugged its shoulders at my extravagance. The thing, it was averred, was biologically impossible to start with; merely another of those crazy country mutterings which Cotton Mather had been gullible enough to dump into his chaotic *Magnalia Christi Americana*, and so poorly authenticated that even he had not ventured to name the locality where the horror occurred. And as to the way I amplified the bare jotting of the old mystic – that was quite impossible, and characteristic of a flighty and notional scribbler! Mather had indeed told of the thing as being born, but nobody but a cheap sensationalist would think of having it grow up, look into people's windows at night, and be hidden in the attic of a house, in flesh and in spirit, till someone saw it at the window centuries later and couldn't describe what it was that turned his hair gray. All this was flagrant trashiness, and my friend Manton was not slow to insist on that fact. Then I told him what I had found in an old diary kept between 1706 and 1723, unearthed among family papers not a mile from where we were sitting; that, and the certain reality of the scars on my ancestor's chest and back which the diary described. I told him, too, of the fears of others in that region, and how they were whispered down for generations; and how no mythical madness came to the boy who in 1793 entered an abandoned house to examine certain traces suspected to be there.

It had been an eldritch thing – no wonder sensitive students shudder at the Puritan age in Massachusetts. So little is known of what went on beneath the surface – so little, yet such a ghastly festering as it bubbles up putrescently in occasional ghoulish glimpses. The witchcraft terror is a horrible ray of light on what was stewing in men's crushed brains, but even that is a trifle. There was no beauty: no freedom – we can see that from the architectural and household remains, and the poisonous sermons of the cramped divines. And inside that rusted iron straitjacket lurked gibbering hideousness, perversion, and diabolism. Here, truly, was the apotheosis of the unnamable.

Cotton Mather, in that demoniac sixth book which no one should read after dark, minced no words as he flung forth his anathema. Stern as a Jewish prophet, and laconically unamazed as none since his day could be, he told of the beast that had brought forth what was more than beast but less than man – the thing with the blemished eye – and of the screaming drunken wretch that they hanged for having such an eye. This much he baldly told, yet without a hint of what came after. Perhaps he did not know, or perhaps he knew and did not dare to tell. Others knew, but did not dare to tell – there is no public hint of why they whispered about the lock on the door to the attic stairs in the house of a childless, broken, embittered old man who had put up a blank slate slab by an avoided grave, although one may trace enough evasive legends to curdle the thinnest blood.

It is all in that ancestral diary I found; all the hushed innuendoes and furtive tales of things with a blemished eye seen at windows in the night or in deserted meadows near the woods. Something had caught my ancestor on a dark valley road, leaving him with marks of horns on his chest and of apelike claws on his back; and when they looked for prints in the trampled dust they found the mixed marks of split hooves and vaguely anthropoid paws. Once a post-rider said he saw an old man chasing and calling to a frightful loping, nameless thing on Meadow Hill in the thinly moonlit hours before dawn, and many believed him. Certainly, there was strange talk one night in 1710 when the childless, broken old man was buried in the crypt behind his own house in sight of the blank slate slab. They never unlocked that attic door, but left the whole house as it was, dreaded and deserted. When noises came from it, they whispered and shivered; and hoped that the lock on that attic door was strong. Then they stopped hoping when the horror occurred at the parsonage, leaving not a soul alive or in one piece. With the years the legends take on a spectral character – I suppose the thing, if it was a living thing, must have died. The memory had lingered hideously – all the more hideous because it was so secret.

During this narration my friend Manton had become very silent, and I saw that my words had impressed him. He did not laugh as I paused, but asked quite seriously about the boy who went mad in 1793, and who had presumably been the hero of my fiction. I told him why the boy had gone to that shunned, deserted house, and remarked that he ought to be interested, since he believed that windows retained latent images of those who had sat at them. The boy had gone to look at the windows of that horrible attic, because of tales of things seen behind them, and had come back screaming maniacally.

Manton remained thoughtful as I said this, but gradually reverted to his analytical mood. He granted for the sake of argument that some unnatural monster had really existed, but reminded me that even the most morbid perversion of nature need not be *unnamable* or scientifically indescribable. I admired his clearness and persistence, and added some further revelations I had collected among the old people. Those later spectral legends, I made plain, related to monstrous apparitions more frightful than anything organic could be; apparitions of gigantic bestial forms sometimes visible and sometimes only tangible, which floated about on moonless nights and haunted the old house, the crypt behind it, and the grave where a sapling had sprouted beside an illegible slab. Whether or not such apparitions had ever gored or smothered people to death, as told in uncorroborated traditions, they had produced a strong and consistent impression; and were yet darkly feared by very aged natives, though largely forgotten by the last two generations – perhaps dying for lack of being thought about. Moreover, so far as esthetic theory was involved, if the psychic emanations of human creatures be grotesque distortions, what coherent representation could express or portray so gibbous and infamous a nebulosity as the specter of a malign, chaotic perversion, itself a morbid blasphemy against nature? Molded by the dead brain of a hybrid nightmare, would not such a vaporous terror constitute in all loathsome truth the exquisitely, the shriekingly *unnamable*?

The hour must now have grown very late. A singularly noiseless bat brushed by me, and I believe it touched Manton also, for although I could not see him I felt him raise his arm. Presently he spoke.

'But is that house with the attic window still standing and deserted?'

'Yes,' I answered. 'I have seen it.'

'And did you find anything there – in the attic or anywhere else?'

'There were some bones up under the eaves. They may have been what that boy saw – if he was sensitive he wouldn't have needed anything in the window-glass to unhinge him. If they all came from the same object it must have been an hysterical, delirious monstrosity. It would have been blasphemous to leave such bones in the world, so I went back with a sack and took them to the tomb behind the house. There was an opening where I could dump them in. Don't think I was a fool – you ought to have seen that skull. It had four-inch horns, but a face and jaw something like yours and mine.'

At last I could feel a real shiver run through Manton, who had moved very near. But his curiosity was undeterred.

'And what about the window-panes?'

'They were all gone. One window had lost its entire frame, and in all the others there was not a trace of glass in the little diamond apertures. They were that kind – the old lattice windows that went out of use before 1700. I don't believe they've had any glass for a hundred years or more – maybe the boy broke 'em if he got that far; the legend doesn't say.'

Manton was reflecting again.

'I'd like to see that house, Carter. Where is it? Glass or no glass, I must explore it a little. And the tomb where you put those bones, and the other grave without an inscription – the whole thing must be a bit terrible.'

'You did see it – until it got dark.'

My friend was more wrought upon than I had suspected, for at this touch of harmless theatricalism he started neurotically away from me and actually cried out with a sort of gulping gasp which released a strain of previous repression. It was an odd cry, and all the more terrible because it was answered. For as it was still echoing, I heard a creaking sound through the pitchy blackness, and knew that a lattice window was opening in that accursed old house beside us. And because all the other frames were long since fallen, I knew that it was the grisly glassless frame of that demoniac attic window.

Then came a noxious rush of noisome, frigid air from that same dreaded direction, followed by a piercing shriek just beside me on that shocking rifted tomb of man and monster. In another instant I was knocked from my gruesome bench by the devilish threshing of some unseen entity of titanic size but undetermined nature; knocked sprawling on the root-clutched mold of that abhorrent graveyard, while from the tomb came such a stifled uproar of gasping and whirring that my fancy peopled the rayless gloom with Miltonic legions of the misshapen damned. There was a vortex of withering, ice-cold wind, and then the rattle of loose bricks and plaster; but I had mercifully fainted before I could learn what it meant.

Manton, though smaller than I, is more resilient; for we opened our eyes at almost the same instant, despite his greater injuries. Our couches were side by side, and we knew in a few seconds that we were in St. Mary's Hospital. Attendants were grouped about in tense curiosity, eager to aid our memory by telling us how we came there, and we soon heard of the farmer who had found us at noon in a lonely field beyond Meadow Hill, a mile from the old burying ground, on a spot where an ancient slaughterhouse is reputed to have stood. Manton had two malignant wounds in the chest, and some less severe cuts or gougings in the back. I was not so seriously hurt, but was covered with welts and contusions of the most bewildering character, including the print of a split hoof. It was plain that Manton knew more than I, but he told nothing to the puzzled and interested physicians till he had learned what our injuries were. Then he said we were the victims of a vicious bull – though the animal was a difficult thing to place and account for.

After the doctors and nurses had left, I whispered an awe struck question:

'Good God, Manton, but *what was it*? Those scars – *was it like that?*'

And I was too dazed to exult when he whispered back a thing I had half expected—

'No – it wasn't that way at all. It was everywhere – a gelatin – a slime – yet it had shapes, a thousand shapes of horror beyond all memory. There were eyes – and a blemish. It was the pit – the maelstrom – the ultimate abomination. Carter, it was the *unnamable!*'

THE THING ON THE DOORSTEP

*   *   *

I

It is true that I have sent six bullets through the head of my best friend, and yet I hope to show by this statement that I am not his murderer. At first I shall be called a madman – madder than the man I shot in his cell at the Arkham Sanatorium. Later some of my readers will weigh each statement, correlate it with the known facts, and ask themselves how I could have believed otherwise than I did after facing the evidence of that horror – that thing on the doorstep.

Until then I also saw nothing but madness in the wild tales I have acted on. Even now I ask myself whether I was misled – or whether I am not mad after all. I do not know – but others have strange things to tell of Edward and Asenath Derby, and even the stolid police are at their wits' end to account for that last terrible visit. They have tried weakly to concoct a theory of a ghastly jest or warning by discharged servants, yet they know in their hearts that the truth is something infinitely more terrible and incredible.

So I say that I have not murdered Edward Derby. Rather have I avenged him, and in so doing purged the earth of a horror whose survival might have loosed untold terrors on all mankind. There are black zones of shadow close to our daily paths, and now and then some evil soul breaks a passage through. When that happens, the man who knows must strike before reckoning the consequences.

I have known Edward Pickman Derby all his life. Eight years my junior, he was so precocious that we had much in common from the time he was eight and I was sixteen. He was the most phenomenal child scholar I have ever known, and at seven was writing verse of a sombre, fantastic, almost morbid cast which astonished the tutors surrounding him. Perhaps his private education and coddled seclusion had something to do with his premature flowering. An only child, he had organic weaknesses which startled his doting

T-MOCL-B

27

parents and caused them to keep him closely chained to their side. He was never allowed out without his nurse, and seldom had a chance to play unconstrainedly with other children. All this doubtless fostered a strange secretive inner life in the boy, with imagination as his one avenue of freedom.

At any rate, his juvenile learning was prodigious and bizarre; and his facile writings such as to captivate me despite my greater age. About that time I had leanings towards art of a somewhat grotesque cast, and I found in this young child a rare kindred spirit. What lay behind our joint love of shadows and marvels was, no doubt, the ancient, mouldering, and subtly fearsome town in which we lived -- witch-cursed, legend-haunted Arkham, whose huddled, sagging gambrel roofs and crumbling Georgian balustrades brood out the centuries beside the darkly muttering Miskatonic.

As time went by I turned to architecture and gave up my design of illustrating a book of Edward's demoniac poems, yet our comradeship suffered no lessening. Young Derby's odd genius developed remarkably, and in his eighteenth year his collected nightmare-lyrics made a real sensation when issued under the title *Azathoth and Other Horrors*. He was a close correspondent of the notorious Baudelairean poet Justin Geoffrey, who wrote *The People of the Monolith* and died screaming in a madhouse in 1926 after a visit to a sinister, ill-regarded village in Hungary.

In self-reliance and practical affairs, however, Derby was greatly retarded because of his coddled existence. His health had improved, but his habits of childish dependence were fostered by over-careful parents, so that he never travelled alone, made independent decisions, or assumed responsibilities. It was early seen that he would not be equal to a struggle in the business or professional arena, but the family fortune was so ample that this formed no tragedy. As he grew to years of manhood he retained a deceptive aspect of boyishness. Blond and blue-eyed, he had the fresh complexion of a child; and his attempts to raise a moustache were discernible only with difficulty. His voice was soft and light, and his unexercised life gave him a juvenile chubbiness rather than the paunchiness of premature middle age. He was of good height, and his handsome face would have made him a notable gallant had not his shyness held him to seclusion and bookishness.

Derby's parents took him abroad every summer, and he was quick to seize on the surface aspects of European thought and expression. His Poe-like talents turned more and more towards the decadent, and other artistic sensitivenesses and yearnings were half-aroused in him. We had great discussions in those days. I had been through Harvard, had studied in a Boston architects' office, had married, and had finally returned to Arkham to practise my profession – settling in the family homestead in Saltonstall Street since my father had moved to Florida for his health. Edward used to call almost every evening, till I came to regard him as one of the household. He had a characteristic way of ringing the doorbell or sounding the knocker that grew to be a veritable code signal, so that after dinner I always listened for the familiar three brisk strokes followed by two more after a pause. Less frequently I would visit at his house and note with envy the obscure volumes in his constantly growing library.

Derby went through Miskatonic University in Arkham since his parents would not let him board away from them. He entered at sixteen and completed his course in three years, majoring in English and French literature and receiving high marks in everything but mathematics and the sciences. He mingled very little with the other students, though looking enviously at the 'daring' or 'Bohemian' set – whose superficially 'smart' language and meaningless ironic pose he aped, and whose dubious conduct he wished he dared adopt.

What he did do was to become an almost fanatical devotee of subterranean magical lore, for which Miskatonic's library was and is famous. Always a dweller on the surface of phantasy and strangeness, he now delved deep into the actual runes and riddles left by a fabulous past for the guidance or puzzlement of posterity. He read things like the frightful *Book of Eibon*, the *Unaussprechlichen Kulten* of von Junzt, and the forbidden *Necronomicon* of the mad Arab Abdul Alhazred, though he did not tell his parents he had seen them. Edward was twenty when my son and only child was born, and seemed pleased when I named the newcomer Edward Derby Upton, after him.

By the time he was twenty-five Edward Derby was a prodigiously learned man and a fairly well-known poet and fantaisiste, though his lack of contacts and responsibilities had slowed down his literary growth by making his products derivative and over-bookish. I was perhaps his closest friend – finding him an inexhaustible mine of vital theoretical topics, while he relied on me for advice in whatever matters he did not wish to refer to his parents. He remained single – more through shyness, inertia, and parental protectiveness than through inclination – and moved in society only to the slightest and most perfunctory extent. When the war came both health and ingrained timidity kept him at home. I went to Plattsburg for a commission, but never got overseas.

So the years wore on. Edward's mother died when he was thirty-four, and for months he was incapacitated by some odd psychological malady. His father took him to Europe, however, and he managed to pull out of his trouble without visible effects. Afterwards he seemed to feel a sort of grotesque exhilaration, as if of partial escape from some unseen bondage. He began to mingle in the more 'advanced' college set despite his middle age, and was present at some extremely wild doings – on one occasion paying heavy blackmail (which he borrowed of me) to keep his presence at a certain affair from his father's notice. Some of the whispered rumours about the wild Miskatonic set were extremely singular. There was even talk of black magic and of happenings utterly beyond credibility.

II

Edward was thirty-eight when he met Asenath Waite. She was, I judge, about twenty-three at the time; and was taking a special course in mediaeval metaphysics at Miskatonic. The daughter of a friend of mine had met her before – in the Hall School at Kingsport – and had been inclined to shun her because of her odd reputation. She was dark, smallish, and very good-looking except for over-protuberant eyes; but something in her expression alienated extremely sensitive people. It was, however, largely her origin and conversation which caused average folk to avoid her. She was one of the Innsmouth Waites, and dark legends have clustered for generations about crumbling, half-deserted Innsmouth and its people. There are tales of horrible bargains about the year 1850, and of a strange element 'not quite human' in the ancient families of the run-down fishing port – tales such as only old-time Yankees can devise and repeat with proper awesomeness.

Asenath's case was aggravated by the fact that she was Ephraim Waite's daughter – the child of his old age by an unknown wife who always went veiled. Ephraim lived in a half-decayed mansion in Washington Street, Innsmouth, and those who had seen the place (Arkham folk avoid going to Innsmouth whenever they can) declared that the attic windows were always boarded, and that strange sounds sometimes floated from within as evening drew on. The old man was known to have been a prodigious magical student in his day, and legend averred that he could raise or quell storms at sea according to his whim. I had seen him once or twice in my youth as he came to Arkham to consult forbidden tomes at the college library, and had hated his wolfish, saturnine face with its tangle of iron-grey beard. He had died insane – under rather queer circumstances – just before his daughter (by his will made a nominal ward of the principal) entered the Hall School, but she had been his morbidly avid pupil and looked fiendishly like him at times.

The friend whose daughter had gone to school with Asenath Waite repeated many curious things when the news of Edward's acquaintance with her began to spread about. Asenath, it seemed, had posed as a kind of magician at school; and had really seemed able to accomplish some highly baffling marvels. She professed to be able to raise thunderstorms, though her seeming success was generally laid to some uncanny knack at prediction. All animals markedly disliked her, and she could make any dog howl by certain motions of her right hand. There were times when she displayed snatches of knowledge and language very singular – and very shocking – for a young girl; when she would frighten her schoolmates with leers and winks of an inexplicable kind, and would seem to extract an obscene zestful irony from her present situation.

Most unusual, though, were the well-attested cases of her influence over other persons. She was, beyond question, a genuine hypnotist. By gazing peculiarly at a fellow-student she would often give the latter a distinct feeling of *exchanged personality* – as if the subject were placed momentarily in the magician's body and able to stare half across the room at her real body, whose eyes blazed and protruded with an alien expression. Asenath often made wild claims about the nature of consciousness and about its independence of the physical frame – or at least from the life-processes of the physical frame. Her crowning rage, however, was that she was not a man; since she believed a male brain had certain unique and far-reaching cosmic powers. Given a man's brain, she declared, she could not only equal but surpass her father in mastery of unknown forces.

Edward met Asenath at a gathering of 'intelligentsia' held in one of the students' rooms, and could talk of nothing else when he came to see me the next day. He had found her full of the interests and erudition which engrossed him most, and was in addition wildly taken with her appearance. I had never seen the young woman, and recalled casual references only faintly, but I knew who she was. It seemed rather regrettable that Derby should become so upheaved about her; but I said nothing to discourage him, since infatuation thrives on opposition. He was not, he said, mentioning her to his father.

In the next few weeks I heard of very little but Asenath from young Derby. Others now remarked Edward's autumnal gallantry, though they agreed that he did not look even nearly his actual age, or seem at all inappropriate as an escort for his bizarre divinity. He was only a trifle paunchy despite his indolence and self-indulgence, and his face was absolutely without lines. Asenath, on the other hand, had the premature crow's feet which come from the exercise of an intense will.

About this time Edward brought the girl to call on me, and I at once saw that his interest was by no means one-sided. She eyed him continually with an almost predatory air, and I perceived that their intimacy was beyond untangling. Soon afterwards I had a visit from old Mr. Derby, whom I had always admired and respected. He had heard the tales of his son's new friendship, and had wormed the whole truth out of 'the boy'. Edward meant to marry Asenath, and had even been looking at houses in the suburbs. Knowing my usually great influence with his son, the father wondered if I could help to break the ill-advised affair off; but I regretfully expressed my doubts. This time it was not a question of Edward's weak will but of the woman's strong will. The perennial child had transferred his dependence from the parental image to a new and stronger image, and nothing could be done about it.

The wedding was performed a month later – by a justice of the peace, according to the bride's request. Mr. Derby, at my advice, offered no opposition, and he, my wife, my son, and I attended the brief ceremony – the other guests being wild young people from the college. Asenath had bought the old Crowninshield place in the country at the end of High

Street, and they proposed to settle there after a short trip to Innsmouth, whence three servants and some books and household goods were to be brought. It was probably not so much consideration for Edward and his father as a personal wish to be near the college, its library, and its crowd of 'sophisticates', that made Asenath settle in Arkham instead of returning permanently home.

When Edward called on me after the honeymoon I thought he looked slightly changed. Asenath had made him get rid of the undeveloped moustache, but there was more than that. He looked soberer and more thoughtful, his habitual pout of childish rebelliousness being exchanged for a look almost of genuine sadness. I was puzzled to decide whether I liked or disliked the change. Certainly he seemed for the moment more normally adult than ever before. Perhaps the marriage was a good thing – might not the *change* of dependence form a start towards actual *neutralization*, leading ultimately to responsible independence? He came alone, for Asenath was very busy. She had brought a vast store of books and apparatus from Innsmouth (Derby shuddered as he spoke the name), and was finishing the restoration of the Crowninshield house and grounds.

Her home – in that town – was a rather disgusting place, but certain objects in it had taught him some surprising things. He was progressing fast in esoteric lore now that he had Asenath's guidance. Some of the experiments she proposed were very daring and radical – he did not feel at liberty to describe them – but he had confidence in her powers and intentions. The three servants were very queer – an incredibly aged couple who had been with old Ephraim and referred occasionally to him and to Asenath's dead mother in a cryptic way, and a swarthy young wench who had marked anomalies of feature and seemed to exude a perpetual odour of fish.

III

For the next two years I saw less and less of Derby. A fortnight would sometimes slip by without the familiar three-and-two strokes at the front door; and when he did call – or when, as happened with increasing infrequency, I called on him – he was very little disposed to converse on vital topics. He had become secretive about those occult studies which he used to describe and discuss so minutely, and preferred not to talk of his wife. She had aged tremendously since her marriage, till now – oddly enough – she seemed the elder of the two. Her face held the most concentratedly determined expression I had ever seen, and her whole aspect seemed to gain a vague, unplaceable repulsiveness. My wife and son noticed it as much as I, and we all ceased gradually to call on her – for which, Edward admitted in one of his boyishly tactless moments, she was unmitigatedly grateful. Occasionally the Derbys would go on long trips – ostensibly to Europe, though Edward sometimes hinted at obscurer destinations.

It was after the first year that people began talking about the change in Edward Derby. It was very casual talk, for the change was purely psychological; but it brought up some interesting points. Now and then, it seemed Edward was observed to wear an expression and to do things wholly incompatible with his usual flabby nature. For example – although in the old days he could not drive a car, he was now seen occasionally to dash into or out of the old Crowninshield driveway with Asenath's powerful Packard, handling it like a master, and meeting traffic entanglements with a skill and determination utterly alien to his accustomed nature. In such cases he seemed always to be just back from some trip or just starting on one – what sort of trip, no one could guess, although he mostly favoured the Innsmouth road.

Oddly, the metamorphosis did not seem altogether pleasing. People said he looked too much like his wife, or like old Ephraim Waite himself, in these moments – or perhaps these moments seemed unnatural because they were so rare. Sometimes, hours after starting out in this way, he would return listlessly sprawled on the rear seat of the car while an obviously hired chauffeur or mechanic drove. Also, his preponderant aspect on the streets during his decreasing round of social contacts (including, I may say, his calls on me) was the old-time indecisive one – its irresponsible childishness even more marked than in the past. While Asenath's face aged, Edward's – aside from those exceptional occasions – actually relaxed into a kind of exaggerated immaturity, save when a trace of the new sadness or understanding would flash across it. It was really very puzzling. Meanwhile the Derbys almost dropped out of the gay college circle – not through their own disgust, we heard, but because something about their present studies shocked even the most callous of the other decadents.

It was in the third year of the marriage that Edward began to hint openly to me of a certain fear and dissatisfaction. He would let fall remarks about things 'going too far', and would talk darkly about the need of 'gaining his identity'. At first I ignored such references, but in time I began to question him guardedly, remembering what my friend's daughter had said about Asenath's hypnotic influence over the other girls at school – the cases where students had thought they were in her body looking across the room at themselves. This questioning seemed to make him at once alarmed and grateful, and once he mumbled something about having a serious talk with me later.

About this time old Mr. Derby died, for which I was afterwards very thankful. Edward was badly upset, though by no means disorganized. He had seen astonishingly little of his parent since his marriage, for Asenath had concentrated in herself all his vital sense of family linkage. Some called him callous in his loss – especially since those jaunty and confident moods in the car began to increase. He now wished to move back into the old family mansion, but Asenath insisted on staying in the Crowninshield house to which she had become well adjusted.

Not long afterwards my wife heard a curious thing from a friend – one of the few who had not dropped the Derbys. She had been out to the end of High Street to call on the couple, and had seen a car shoot briskly out of the drive with Edward's oddly confident and almost sneering face above the wheel. Ringing the bell, she had been told by the repulsive wench that Asenath was also out; but had chanced to look at the house in leaving. There, at one of Edward's library windows, she had glimpsed a hastily withdrawn face – a face whose expression of pain, defeat, and wistful hopelessness was poignant beyond description. It was – incredibly enough in view of its usual domineering cast – Asenath's; yet the caller had vowed that in that instant the sad, muddled eyes of poor Edward were gazing out from it.

Edward's calls now grew a trifle more frequent, and his hints occasionally became concrete. What he said was not to be believed, even in centuried and legend-haunted Arkham; but he threw out his dark lore with a sincerity and convincingness which made one fear for his sanity. He talked about terrible meetings in lonely places, of cyclopean ruins in the heart of the Maine woods beneath which vast staircases led down to abysses of nighted secrets, of complex angles that led through invisible walls to other regions of space and time, and of hideous exchanges of personality that permitted explorations in remote and forbidden places, on other worlds and in different space-time continua.

He would now and then back up certain crazy hints by exhibiting objects which utterly nonplussed me – elusively coloured and bafflingly textured objects like nothing ever heard of on earth, whose insane curves and surfaces answered no conceivable purpose and followed no conceivable geometry. These things, he said, came 'from outside'; and his wife knew how to get them. Sometimes – but always in frightened and ambiguous whispers – he would suggest things about old Ephraim Waite, whom he had seen occasionally at the college library in the old days. These adumbrations were never specific, but seemed to evolve around some especially horrible doubt as to whether the old wizard were really dead – in a spiritual as well as corporeal sense.

At times Derby would halt abruptly in his revelations, and I wondered whether Asenath could possibly have divined his speech at a distance and cut him off through some unknown sort of telepathic mesmerism – some power of the kind she had displayed at school. Certainly, she suspected that he told me things, for as the weeks passed she tried to stop his visits with words and glances of a most inexplicable potency. Only with difficulty could he get to see me, for although he would pretend to be going somewhere else, some invisible force would generally clog his motions or make him forget his destination for the time being. His visits usually came when Asenath was away – 'away in her own body', as he once oddly put it. She always found out later – the servants watched his goings and comings – but evidently she thought it inexpedient to do anything drastic.

IV

Derby had been married more than three years on that August day when I got that telegram from Maine. I had not seen him for two months, but had heard he was away 'on business'. Asenath was supposed to be with him, though watchful gossip declared there was someone upstairs in the house behind the doubly curtained windows. They had watched the purchases made by the servants. And now the town marshal of Chesuncook had wired of the draggled madman who stumbled out of the woods with delirious ravings and screamed to me for protection. It was Edward – and he had been just able to recall his own name and address.

Chesuncook is close to the widest, deepest, and least explored forest belt in Maine, and it took a whole day of feverish jolting through fantastic and forbidding scenery to get there in a car. I found Derby in a cell at the town farm vacillating between frenzy and apathy. He knew me at once, and began pouring out a meaningless, half-incoherent torrent of words in my direction.

'Dan – for God's sake! The pit of the shaggoths! Down the six thousand steps ... the abomination of abominations ... I never would let her take me, and then I found myself there – Iä! Shub-Niggurath! – The shape rose up from the altar, and there were five hundred that howled – The Hooded Thing bleated "Kamog! Kamog!" – that was old Ephraim's secret name in the coven – I was there, where she promised she wouldn't take me – A minute before I was locked in the library, and then I was there, where she had gone with my body – in the place of utter blasphemy, the unholy pit where the black realm begins and the watcher guards the gate – I saw a shaggoth – it changed shape – I can't stand it – I'll kill her if she ever sends me there again – I'll kill that entity – her, him, it – I'll kill it with my own hands!'

It took me an hour to quiet him, but he subsided at last. The next day I got him decent clothes in the village, and set out with him for Arkham. His fury of hysteria was spent, and he was inclined to be silent, though he began muttering darkly to himself when the car passed through Augusta – as if the sight of a city aroused unpleasant memories. It was clear that he did not wish to go home; and considering the fantastic delusions he seemed to have about his wife – delusions undoubtedly springing from some actual hypnotic ordeal to which he had been subjected – I thought it would be better if he did not. I would, I resolved, put him up myself for a time; no matter what unpleasantness it would make with Asenath. Later I would help him get a divorce, for most assuredly there were mental factors which made this marriage suicidal for him. When we struck open country again

Derby's muttering faded away, and I let him nod and drowse on the seat beside me as I drove.

During our sunset dash through Portland the muttering commenced again, more distinctly than before, and as I listened I caught a stream of utterly insane drivel about Asenath. The extent to which she had preyed on Edward's nerves was plain, for he had woven a whole set of hallucinations around her. His present predicament, he mumbled furtively, was only one of a long series. She was getting hold of him, and he knew that some day she would never let go. Even now she probably let him go only when she had to, because she couldn't hold on long at a time. She constantly took his body and went to nameless places for nameless rites, leaving him in her body and locking him upstairs – but sometimes she couldn't hold on, and he would find himself suddenly in his own body again in some far-off, horrible, and perhaps unknown place. Sometimes she'd get hold of him again and sometimes she couldn't. Often he was left stranded somewhere as I had found him – time and again he had to find his way home from frightful distances, getting somebody to drive the car after he found it.

The worst thing was that she was holding on to him longer and longer at a time. She wanted to be a man – to be fully human – that was why she got hold of him. She had sensed the mixture of fine-wrought brain and weak will in him. Some day she would crowd him out and disappear with his body – disappear to become a great magician like her father and leave him marooned in the female shell that wasn't even quite human. Yes, he knew about the Innsmouth blood now. There had been traffic with things from the sea – it was horrible. ... And old Ephraim – he had known the secret, and when he grew old did a hideous thing to keep alive – he wanted to live forever – Asenath would succeed – one successful demonstration had taken place already.

As Derby muttered on I turned to look at him closely, verifying the impression of change which an earlier scrutiny had given me. Paradoxically, he seemed in better shape than usual – harder, more normally developed, and without the trace of sickly flabbiness caused by his indolent habits. It was as if he had been really active and properly exercised for the first time in his coddled life, and I judged that Asenath's force must have pushed him into unwonted channels of motion and alertness. But just now his mind was in a pitiable state; for he was mumbling wild extravagances about his wife, about black magic, about old Ephraim, and about some revelation which would convince even me. He repeated names which I recognized from bygone browsings in forbidden volumes, and at times made me shudder with a certain thread of mythological consistency – or convincing coherence – which ran through his maundering. Again and again he would pause, as if to gather courage for some final and terrible disclosure.

'Dan, Dan, don't you remember him – wild eyes and the unkempt beard that never turned white? He glared at me once, and I never forgot it. Now *she* glares that way. *And I know why!* He found it in the *Necronomicon* – the formula. I don't dare tell you the page yet, but when I do you can read and understand. Then you will know what has engulfed me. On, on, on, on – body to body to body – he means never to die. The lifeglow – he knows how to break the link . . . it can flicker on a while even when the body is dead. I'll give you hints and maybe you'll guess. Listen, Dan – do you know why my wife always takes such pains with that silly backhand writing? Have you ever seen a manuscript of old Ephraim's? Do you want to know why I shivered when I saw some hasty notes Asenath had jotted down?

'Asenath – *is there such a person?* Why did they half-think there was poison in old Ephraim's stomach? Why do the Gilmans whisper about the way he shrieked – like a frightened child – when he went mad and Asenath locked him up in the padded attic room where – the other – had been? *Was it old Ephraim's soul that was locked in? Who locked in whom?* Why had he been looking for months for someone with a fine mind and a weak will? – Why did he curse that his daughter wasn't a son? Tell me, Daniel Upton – *what devilish exchange was perpetrated in the house of horror where that blasphemous monster had his trusting, weak-willed half-human child at his mercy?* Didn't he make it permanent – as she'll do in the end with me? Tell me why that thing that calls itself Asenath writes differently off guard, *so that you can't tell its script from—*'

Then the thing happened. Derby's voice was rising to a thin treble scream as he raved, when suddenly it was shut off with an almost mechanical click. I thought of those other occasions at my home when his confidences had abruptly ceased – when I had half-fancied that some obscure tele-pathic wave of Asenath's mental force was intervening to keep him silent. This, though, was something altogether different – and, I felt, infinitely more horrible. The face beside me was twisted almost unrecognizably for a moment, while through the whole body there passed a shivering motion – as if all the bones, organs, muscles, nerves, and glands were readjusting themselves to a radically different posture, set of stresses, and general personality.

Just where the supreme horror lay, I could not for my life tell; yet there swept over me such a swamping wave of sickness and repulsion – such a freezing, petrifying sense of utter alienage and abnormality – that my grasp of the wheel grew feeble and uncertain. The figure beside me seemed less like a life-long friend than like some monstrous intrusion from outer space – some damnable, utterly accursed focus of unknown and malign cosmic forces.

I had faltered only a moment, but before another moment was over my companion had seized the wheel and forced me to change places with him. The dusk was now very thick, and the lights of Portland far behind, so I could not see much of his face. The blaze of his eyes, though, was phenomenal; and I knew that he must now be in that queerly energized state – so unlike his usual self – which so many people had noticed. It seemed odd and incredible that listless Edward Derby – he who could never assert himself, and who had never learned to drive – should be ordering me about and taking the wheel of my own car, yet that was precisely what had happened. He did not speak for some time, and in my inexplicable horror I was glad he did not.

In the light of Biddeford and Saco I saw his firmly set mouth, and shivered at the blaze of his eyes. The people were right – he did look damnably like his wife and like old Ephraim when in these moods. I did not wonder that the moods were disliked – there was certainly something unnatural in them, and I felt the sinister element all the more because of the wild ravings I had been hearing. This man, for all my lifelong knowledge of Edward Pickman Derby, was a stranger – an intrusion of some sort from the black abyss.

He did not speak until we were on a dark stretch of road, and when he did his voice seemed utterly unfamiliar. It was deeper, firmer, and more decisive than I had ever known it to be; while its accent and pronunciation were altogether changed – though vaguely, remotely, and rather disturbingly recalling something I could not quite place. There was, I thought, a trace of very profound and very genuine irony in the timbre – not the flashy, meaninglessly jaunty pseudo-irony of the callow 'sophisticate', which Derby had habitually affected, but something grim, basic, pervasive, and potentially evil. I marvelled at the self-possession so soon following the spell of panic-struck muttering.

'I hope you'll forget my attack back there, Upton,' he was saying. 'You know what my nerves are, and I guess you can excuse such things. I'm enormously grateful, of course, for this lift home.

'And you must forget, too, any crazy things I may have been saying about my wife – and about things in general. That's what comes from overstudy in a field like mine. My philosophy is full of bizarre concepts, and when the mind gets worn out it cooks up all sorts of imaginary concrete applications. I shall take a rest from now on – you probably won't see me for some time, and you needn't blame Asenath for it.

'This trip was a bit queer, but it's really very simple. There are certain Indian relics in the north woods – standing stones and all that – which mean a good deal in folklore, and Asenath and I are following that stuff up. It was a hard search, so I seem to have gone off my head. I must send somebody for the car when I get home. A month's relaxation will put me on my feet.'

I do not recall just what my own part of the conversation was, for the baffling alienage of my seatmate filled all my consciousness. With every moment my feeling of elusive cosmic horror increased, till at length I was in a virtual delirium of longing for the end of the drive. Derby did not offer to relinquish the wheel, and I was glad of the speed with which Portsmouth and Newburyport flashed by.

At the junction where the main highway runs inland and avoids Innsmouth, I was half-afraid my driver would take the bleak shore road that goes through that damnable place. He did not, however, but darted rapidly past Rowley and Ipswich towards our destination. We reached Arkham before midnight, and found the lights still on at the old Crowninshield house. Derby left the car with a hasty repetition of his thanks, and I drove home alone with a curious feeling of relief. It had been a terrible drive – all the more terrible because I could not quite tell why – and I did not regret Derby's forecast of a long absence from my company.

The next two months were full of rumours. People spoke of seeing Derby more and more in his new energized state, and Asenath was scarcely ever in to her callers. I had only one visit from Edward, when he called briefly in Asenath's car – duly reclaimed from wherever he had left it in Maine – to get some books he had lent me. He was in his new state, and paused only long enough for some evasively polite remarks. It was plain that he had nothing to discuss with me when in this condition – and I noticed that he did not even trouble to give the old three-and-two signal when ringing the doorbell. As on that evening in the car, I felt a faint, infinitely deep horror which I could not explain; so that his swift departure was a prodigious relief.

In mid-September Derby was away for a week, and some of the decadent college set talked knowingly of the matter – hinting at a meeting with a notorious cult-leader, lately expelled from England, who had established headquarters in New York. For my part I could not get that strange ride from Maine out of my head. The transformation I had witnessed had affected me profoundly, and I caught myself again and again trying to account for the the thing – and for the extreme horror it had inspired in me.

But the oddest rumours were those about the sobbing in the old Crowninshield house. The voice seemed to be a woman's, and some of the younger people thought it sounded like Asenath's. It was heard only at rare intervals, and would sometimes be choked off as if by force. There was talk of an investigation, but this was dispelled one day when Asenath appeared in the street and chatted in a sprightly way with a large number of acquaintances – apologizing for her recent absence and speaking incidentally about the nervous breakdown and hysteria of a guest from Boston. The guest was never seen, but Asenath's appearance left nothing to be said. And then someone complicated matters by whispering that the sobs had once or twice been in a man's voice.

One evening in mid-October, I heard the familiar three-and-two ring at the front door. Answering it myself I found Edward on the steps, and saw in a moment that his personality was the old one which I had not encountered since the day of his ravings on that terrible ride from Chesuncook. His face was twitching with a mixture of odd emotions in which fear and triumph seemed to share dominion, and he looked furtively over his shoulder as I closed the door behind him.

Following me clumsily to the study, he asked for some whisky to steady his nerves. I forbore to question him, but waited till he felt like beginning whatever he wanted to say.

At length he ventured some information in a choking voice.

'Asenath has gone, Dan. We had a long talk last night while the servants were out, and I made her promise to stop preying on me. Of course I had certain – certain occult defences I never told you about. She had to give in, but got frightfully angry. Just packed up and started for New York – walked right out to catch the eight-twenty in to Boston. I suppose people will talk, but I can't help that. You needn't mention that there was any trouble – just say she's gone on a long research trip.

'She's probably going to stay with one of her horrible groups of devotees. I hope she'll go west and get a divorce – anyhow, I've made her promise to keep away and let me alone. It was horrible, Dan – she was stealing my body – crowding me out – making a prisoner of me. I lay low and pretended to let her do it, but I had to be on the watch. I could plan if I was careful, for she can't read my mind literally, or in detail. All she could read of my planning was a sort of general mood of rebellion – and she always thought I was helpless. Never thought I could get the best of her ... but I had a spell or two that worked.'

Derby looked over his shoulder and took some more whisky.

'I paid off those damned servants this morning when they got back. They were ugly about it, and asked questions, but they went. They're her kind – Innsmouth people – and were hand and glove with her. I hope they'll let me alone – I didn't like the way they laughed when they walked away. I must get as many of Dad's old servants again as I can. I'll move back home now.

'I suppose you think I'm crazy, Dan – but Arkham history ought to hint at things that back up what I've told you – and what I'm going to tell you. You've seen one of the changes, too – in your car after I told you about Asenath that day coming home from Maine. That was when she got me – drove me out of my body. The last thing I remember was when I was all worked up trying to tell you *what that she-devil is*. Then she got me, and in a flash I was back at the house – in the library where those damned servants had me locked up – and in that cursed fiend's body . . . that isn't even human. . . . You know it was she you must have ridden home with – that preying wolf in my body – you ought to have known the difference!'

I shuddered as Derby paused. Surely, I *had* known the difference – yet could I accept an explanation as insane as this? But my distracted caller was growing even wilder.

'I had to save myself – I had to, Dan! She'd have got me for good at Hallowmass – they hold a Sabbat up there beyond Chesuncook, and the sacrifice would have clinched things. She'd have got me for good – she'd have been I, and I'd have been she – forever – too late – My body'd have been hers for good— She'd have been a man, and fully human, just as she wanted to be – I suppose she'd have put me out of the way – killed her own ex-body with me in it, damn her, *just as she did before* – just as she, he, or it did before—' Edward's face was now atrociously distorted, and he bent it uncomfortably close to mine as his voice fell to a whisper.

'You must know what I hinted in the car – *that she isn't Asenath at all, but really old Ephraim himself.* I suspected it a year and a half ago, and I know it now. Her handwriting shows it when she goes off guard – sometimes she jots down a note in writing that's just like her father's manuscripts, stroke for stroke – and sometimes she says things that nobody but an old man like Ephraim could say. He changed forms with her when he felt death coming – she was the only one he could find with the right kind of brain and a weak enough will – he got her body permanently, just as she almost got mine, and then poisoned the old body he'd put her into. Haven't you seen old Ephraim's soul glaring out of that she-devil's eyes dozens of times – and out of mine when he has control of my body?'

The whisperer was panting and paused for breath. I said nothing; and when he resumed his voice was nearer normal. This, I reflected, was a case for the asylum, but I would not be the one to send him there. Perhaps time and freedom from Asenath would do its work. I could see that he would never wish to dabble in morbid occultism again.

'I'll tell you more later – I must have a long rest now. I'll tell you something of the forbidden horrors she led me into – something of the age-old horrors that even now are festering in out-of-the-way corners with a few monstrous priests to keep them alive. Some people know things about the universe that nobody ought to know, and can do things that nobody ought to be able to do. I've been in it up to my neck, but that's the end. Today I'd burn that damned *Necronomicon* and all the rest if I were librarian at Miskatonic.

'But she can't get me now. I must get out of that accursed house as soon as I can, and settle down at home. You'll help me, I know, if I need help. Those devilish servants, you know – and if people should get too inquisitive about Asenath. You see, I can't give them her address. . . . Then there are certain groups of searchers – certain cults, you know – that might misunderstand our breaking up . . . some of them have damnably curious ideas and methods. I know you'll stand by me if anything happens – even if I have to tell you a lot that will shock you. . . .'

I had Edward stay and sleep in one of the guest-chambers that night, and in the morning he seemed calmer. We discussed certain possible arrangements for his moving back into the Derby mansion, and I hoped he would lose no time in making the change. He did not call the next evening, but I saw him frequently during the ensuing weeks. We talked as little as possible about strange and unpleasant things, but discussed the renovation of the old Derby house, and the travels which Edward promised to take with my son and me the following summer.

Of Asenath we said almost nothing, for I saw that the subject was a peculiarly disturbing one. Gossip, of course, was rife; but that was no novelty in connection with the strange menage at the old Crowninshield house. One thing I did not like was what Derby's banker let fall in an over-expansive mood at the Miskatonic Club – about the cheques Edward was sending regularly to a Moses and Abigail Sargent and a Eunice Babson in Innsmouth. That looked as if those evil-faced servants were extorting some kind of tribute from him – yet he had not mentioned the matter to me.

I wished that the summer – and my son's Harvard vacation – would come, so that we could get Edward to Europe. He was not, I soon saw, mending as rapidly as I had hoped he would; for there was something a bit hysterical in his occasional exhilaration, while his moods of fright and depression were altogether too frequent. The old Derby house was ready by December, yet Edward constantly put off moving. Though he hated and seemed to fear the Crowninshield place, he was at the same time queerly enslaved by it. He could not seem to begin dismantling things, and invented every kind of excuse to postpone action. When I pointed this out to him he appeared unaccountably frightened. His father's old butler – who was there with other reacquired servants – told me one day that Edward's occasional prowlings about the house, and especially down in the cellar, looked odd and unwholesome to him. I wondered if Asenath had been writing disturbing letters, but the butler said there was no mail which could have come from her.

It was about Christmas that Derby broke down one evening while calling on me. I was steering the conversation towards next summer's travels when he suddenly shrieked and leaped up from his chair with a look of shocking, uncontrollable fright – a cosmic panic and loathing such as only the nether gulfs of nightmare could bring to any sane mind.

'My brain! My brain! God, Dan – it's tugging – from beyond – knocking – clawing – that she-devil – even now – Ephraim – Kamog! Kamog! The pit of the shaggoths – Iä! Shub-Niggurath! The Goat with a Thousand Young! . . .

'The flame – the flame – beyond body, beyond life – in the earth – oh, God! . . .'

I pulled him back to his chair and poured some wine down his throat as his frenzy sank to a dull apathy. He did not resist, but kept his lips moving as if talking to himself. Presently I realized that he was trying to talk to me, and bent my ear to his mouth to catch the feeble words.

'– Again, again – she's trying – I might have known – nothing can stop that force; not distance nor magic, nor death – it comes and comes, mostly in the night – I can't leave – it's horrible – oh, God, Dan, *if you only knew as I do just how horrible it is. . . .*'

When he had slumped down into a stupor I propped him with pillows and let normal sleep overtake him. I did not call a doctor, for I knew what would be said of his sanity, and wished to give nature a chance if I possibly could. He waked at midnight, and I put him to bed upstairs, but he was gone by morning. He had let himself quietly out of the house – and his butler, when called on the wire, said he was at home pacing about the library.

Edward went to pieces rapidly after that. He did not call again, but I went daily to see him. He would always be sitting in his library, staring at nothing and having an air of abnormal *listening*. Sometimes he talked rationally, but always on trivial topics. Any mention of his trouble, of future plans, or of Asenath would send him into a frenzy. His butler said he had frightful seizures at night, during which he might eventually do himself harm.

I had a long talk with his doctor, banker, and lawyer, and finally took the physician with two specialist colleagues to visit him. The spasms that resulted from the first questions were violent and pitiable – and that evening a closed car took his poor struggling body to the Arkham Sanatorium. I was made his guardian, and called on him twice weekly – almost weeping to hear his wild shrieks, awesome whispers, and dreadful, droning repetitions of such phrases as 'I had to do it – I had to do it – it'll get me – it'll get me – down there – down there in the dark – Mother! Mother! Dan! Save me – save me—'

How much hope of recovery there was, no one could say, but I tried my best to be optimistic. Edward must have a home if he emerged, so I transferred his servants to the Derby mansion, which would surely be his sane choice. What to do about the Crowninshield place with its complex arrangements and collections of utterly inexplicable objects I could not decide, so left it momentarily untouched – telling the Derby household to go over and dust the chief rooms once a week, and ordering the furnace man to have a fire on those days.

The final nightmare came before Candlemas – heralded, in cruel irony, by a false gleam of hope. One morning late in January the sanatorium telephoned to report that Edward's reason had suddenly come back. His continuous memory, they said, was badly impaired; but sanity itself was certain. Of course he must remain some time for observation, but there could be little doubt of the outcome. All going well, he would surely be free in a week.

I hastened over in a flood of delight, but stood bewildered when a nurse took me to Edward's room. The patient rose to greet me, extending his hand with a polite smile, but I saw in an instant that he bore the strangely energized personality which had seemed so foreign to his own nature – the competent personality I had found so vaguely horrible, and which Edward himself had once vowed was the intruding soul of his wife. There was the same blazing vision – so like Asenath's and old Ephraim's – and the same firm mouth; and when he spoke I could sense the same grim, pervasive irony in his voice – the deep irony so redolent of potential evil. This was the person who had driven my car through the night five months before – the person I had not seen since that brief call when he had forgotten the old time doorbell signal and stirred such nebulous fears in me – and now he filled me with the same dim feeling of blasphemous alienage and ineffable cosmic hideousness.

He spoke affably of arrangements for release – and there was nothing for me to do but assent, despite some remarkable gaps in his recent memories. Yet I felt that something was terribly, inexplicably wrong and abnormal. There were horrors in this thing that I could not reach. This was a sane person – but was it indeed the Edward Derby I had known? If not, who or what was it – and where was Edward? Ought it to be free or confined – or ought it to be extirpated from the face of the earth? There was a hint of the abysmally sardonic in everything the creature said – the Asenath-like eyes lent a special and baffling mockery to certain words about the early liberty earned by an *especially close confinement*! I must have behaved very awkwardly, and was glad to beat a retreat.

All that day and the next I racked my brain over the problem. What had happened? What sort of mind looked out through those alien eyes in Edward's face? I could think of nothing but this dimly terrible enigma, and gave up all efforts to perform my usual work. The second morning the hospital called up to say that the recovered patient was unchanged, and by evening I was close to a nervous collapse – a state I admit, though others will vow it coloured my subsequent vision. I have nothing to say on this point except that no madness of mine could account for *all* the evidence.

V

It was in the night – after that second evening – that stark, utter horror burst over me and weighed my spirit with a black clutching panic from which it can never shake free. It began with a telephone call just before midnight. I was the only one up, and sleepily took down the receiver in the library. No one seemed to be on the wire, and I was about to hang up and go to bed when my ear caught a very faint suspicion of sound at the other end. Was someone trying under great difficulties to talk? As I listened I thought I heard a sort of half-liquid bubbling noise – 'glub . . . glub . . . glub' – which had an odd suggestion of inarticulate, unintelligible word and syllable divisions. I called 'Who is it?' But the only answer was 'glub . . . glub . . . glub-glub.' I could only assume that the noise was mechanical, but fancying that it might be a case of a broken instrument able to receive but not to send, I added, 'I can't hear you. Better hang up and try Information.' Immediately I heard the receiver go on the hook at the other end.

This, I say, was just about midnight. When the call was traced afterwards it was found to come from the old Crowninshield house, though it was fully half a week from the housemaid's day to be there. I shall only hint what was found at that house – the upheaval in a remote cellar storeroom, the tracks, the dirt, the hastily rifled wardrobe, the baffling marks on the telephone, the clumsily used stationery, and the detestable stench lingering over everything. The police, poor fools, have their smug little theories, and are still searching for those sinister discharged servants – who have dropped out of sight amidst the present furore. They speak of a ghoulish revenge for things that were done, and say I was included because I was Edward's best friend and adviser.

Idiots! Do they fancy those brutish clowns could have forged that handwriting? Do they fancy they could have brought what later came? Are they blind to the changes in that body that was Edward's? As for me, *I now believe all that Edward Derby ever told me.* There are horrors beyond life's edge that we do not suspect, and once in a while man's evil prying calls them just within our range. Ephraim – Asenath – that devil called them in, and they engulfed Edward as they are engulfing me.

Can I be sure that I am safe? Those powers survive the life of the physical form. The next day – in the afternoon, when I pulled out of my prostration and was able to walk and talk coherently – I went to the madhouse and shot him dead for Edward's and the world's sake, but can I be sure till he is cremated? They are keeping the body for some silly autopsies by different doctors – but I say he must be cremated. *He must be cremated – he who was not Edward Derby when I shot him.* I shall go mad if he is not, for I may be the next. But my will is not weak – and I shall not let it be undermined by the terrors I know are seething around it. One life – Ephraim, Asenath, and Edward – who now? I *will not* be driven out of my body . . . I *will not* change souls with that bullet-ridden lich in the madhouse!

But let me try to tell coherently of that final horror. I will not speak of what the police persistently ignored – the tales of that dwarfed, grotesque, malodorous thing met by at least three wayfarers in High Street just before two o'clock, and the nature of the single footprints in certain places. I will say only that just about two the doorbell and knocker waked me – doorbell and knocker both, plied alternately and uncertainly in a kind of weak desperation, *and each trying to keep to Edward's old signal of three-and-two strokes.*

Roused from sound sleep, my mind leaped into a turmoil. Derby at the door – and remembering the old code! That new personality had not remembered it . . . was Edward suddenly back in his rightful state? Why was he here in such evident stress and haste? Had he been released ahead of time, or had he escaped? Perhaps, I thought as I flung on a robe and bounded downstairs, his return to his own self had brought raving and violence, revoking his discharge and driving him to a desperate dash for freedom. Whatever had happened, he was good old Edward again, and I would help him!

When I opened the door into the elm-arched blackness a gust of insufferably foetid wind almost flung me prostrate. I choked in nausea, and for a second scarcely saw the dwarfed humped figure on the steps. The summons had been Edward's, but who was this foul, stunted parody? Where had Edward had time to go? His ring had sounded only a second before the door opened.

The caller had on one of Edward's overcoats – its bottom almost touching the ground, and its sleeves rolled back yet still covering the hands. On the head was a slouch hat pulled low, while a black silk muffler concealed the face. As I stepped unsteadily forward, the figure made a semi-liquid sound like that I had heard over the telephone – 'glub . . . glub . . .' – and thrust at me a large, closely written paper impaled on the end of a long pencil. Still reeling from the morbid and unaccountable foetor, I seized the paper and tried to read it in the light from the doorway.

Beyond question, it was in Edward's script. But why had he written when he was close enough to ring – and why was the script so awkward, coarse and shaky? I could make out nothing in the dim half light, so edged back into the hall, the dwarf figure clumping mechanically after but pausing on the inner door's threshold. The odour of this singular messenger was really appalling, and I hoped (not in vain, thank God!) that my wife would not wake up and confront it.

Then, as I read the paper, I felt my knees give under me and my vision go black. I was lying on the floor when I came to, that accursed sheet still clutched in my fear-rigid hands. This is what it said:

'Dan – go to the sanatorium and kill it. Exterminate it. It isn't Edward Derby any more. She got me – it's Asenath – *and she has been dead three months and a half*. I lied when I said she had gone away. I killed her. I had to. It was sudden, but we were alone and I was in my right body. I saw a candlestick and smashed her head in. She would have got me for good at Hallowmass.

'I buried her in the farther cellar storeroom under some old boxes and cleaned up all the traces. The servants suspected next morning, but they have such secrets that they dare not tell the police. I sent them off, but God knows what they – and others of the cult – will do.

'I thought for a while I was all right, and then I felt the tugging at my brain. I knew what it was – I ought to have remembered. A soul like hers – or Ephraim's – is half detached, and keeps right on after death as long as the body lasts. She was getting me – making me change bodies with her – *seizing my body and putting me in that corpse of hers buried in the cellar*.

'I knew what was coming – that's why I snapped and had to go to the asylum. Then it came – I found myself choked in the dark – in Asenath's rotting carcass down there in the cellar under the boxes where I put it. And I knew she must be in my body at the sanatorium – permanently for it was after Hallowmass, and the sacrifice would work even without her being there – sane, and ready for release as a menace to the world. I was desperate, *and in spite of everything I clawed my way out.*

'I'm gone too far to talk – I couldn't manage to telephone – but I can still write. I'll get fixed up somehow and bring this last word and warning. *Kill that fiend* if you value the peace and comfort of the world. *See that it is cremated.* If you don't, it will live on and on, body to body for ever, and I can't tell you what it will do. Keep clear of black magic, Dan, it's the devil's business. Goodbye – you've been a great friend. Tell the police whatever they'll believe – and I'm damnably sorry to drag all this on you. I'll be at peace before long – this thing won't hold together much more. Hope you can read this. *And kill that thing – kill it.*

Yours – Ed.'

It was only afterwards that I read the last half of this paper, for I had fainted at the end of the third paragraph. I fainted again when I saw and smelled what cluttered up the threshold where the warm air had struck it. The messenger would not move or have consciousness any more.

The butler, tougher-fibred than I, did not faint at what met him in the hall in the morning. Instead, he telephoned the police. When they came I had been taken upstairs to bed but the – other mass – lay where it had collapsed in the night. The men put handkerchiefs to their noses.

What they finally found inside Edward's oddly-assorted clothes was mostly liquescent horror. There were bones, too – and a crushed-in skull. Some dental work positively identified the skull as Asenath's.

THE SURVIVOR

By H. P. Lovecraft and August Derleth

I had never intended to speak or write again of the Charriere house, once I had fled Providence on that shocking night of discovery—there are memories which every man would seek to suppress, to disbelieve, to wipe out of existence—but I am forced to set down now the narrative of my brief acquaintance with the house on Benefit Street, and my precipitate flight there-from, lest some innocent person be subjected to indignity by the police in an effort to explain the horrible discovery the police have made at last—that same ghastly horror it was my lot to look upon before any other human eye—and what I saw was surely far more terrible than what remained to be seen after all these years, the house having reverted to the city, as I had known it would.

While it is true that an antiquarian might be expected to know considerably less about some ancient avenues of human research than about old houses, it is surely conceivable that one who is steeped in the processes of research among the habita-tions of the human race might occasionally encounter a more abstruse mystery than the date of an ell or the source of a gambrel roof and find it possible to come to certain conclu-sions about it, no matter how incredible, how horrible or frightening or even—yes, damnable! In those quarters where antiquarians gather, the name of Alijah Atwood is not entirely unknown; modesty forbids me to say more, but it is surely permissible to point out that anyone sufficiently interested to look up references will find more than a few paragraphs about me in those directories devoted to information for the antiquary.

I came to Providence, Rhode Island, in 1930, intending to make only a brief visit and then to go on to New Orleans. But I saw the Charriere house on Benefit Street, and was drawn to it as only an antiquarian would be drawn to any unusual house isolated in a New England street of a period not its own, a house clearly of some age, and with an indefinable aura that both attracted and repelled.

What was said about the Charriere house—that it was haunted—was no more than what was said about many an old, abandoned dwelling in the old world as well as in the new, and even, if I can depend on the solemn articles in the *Journal of American Folklore*, about the primitive dwellings of American Indians, Australian bush-people, the Polynesians, and many others. Of ghosts I do not wish to write ; suffice it to say that there have been within the circle of my experience certain manifestations which have lent themselves to no scientific explanation, though I am rational enough to believe that there is such explanation to be found, once man chances upon the proper interpretation through the correct scientific approach.

In that sense, surely the Charriere house was not haunted. No spectre passed among its rooms rattling its chain, no voice moaned at midnight, no sepulchral figure appeared at the witching hour to warn of approaching doom. But that there was an aura about the house—one of evil? of terror? of hideous, eldritch things?—none could deny ; and had I been born a less insensitive clod, I have no doubt that the house would have driven me forth raving out of mind. Its aura was less tangible than others I have known, but it suggested that the house concealed unspeakable secrets, long hidden from human perception. Above all else, it conveyed an overpowering sense of age—of centuries not alone of its own being, but far, far in the past, when the world was young, which was curious indeed, for the house, however old, was less than three centuries of age.

I saw it first as an antiquarian, delighted to discover set in a row of staid New England houses a house which was manifestly of a seventeenth-century Quebec style, and thus so different from its neighbors as to attract immediately the eye of any passerby. I had made many visits to Quebec, as well as to other old cities of the North American continent, but on this first visit to Providence, I had not come primarily in search of ancient dwellings, but to call upon a fellow antiquarian of note, and it was on my way to his home on Barnes Street that I passed the Charriere house, observed that it was not tenanted, and resolved to lease it for my own. Even so, I might not have done so, had it not been for the curious reluctance of my friend to speak of the house, and, indeed, his seeming unwillingness that I go near the place. Perhaps I do him an injustice in retrospect, for he, poor fellow, was even then on his deathbed, though neither of us knew it; so it was at his bedside I sat, and not in his study, and it was there that I asked about the house, describing it unmistakably, for, of course, I did not then know its name or anything about it.

A man named Charriere had owned it—a French surgeon, who had come down from Quebec. But who had built it, Gamwell did not know; it was Charriere he had known. "A tall, rough-skinned man—I saw little of him, but no one saw more. He had retired from practice," said Gamwell. He had lived there—and presumably older members of his family, though Gamwell could not say as to this—for as long as Gamwell had known the house. Dr. Charriere had lived a reclusive life, and had died, according to notice duly published in the Providence *Journal*, in 1927, three years ago. Indeed, the date of Dr. Charriere's death was the only date that Gamwell could give me; all else was shrouded in vagueness. The house had not been rented more than once; there had been a brief occupation by a professional man and his family, but they had left it after a month, complaining of its dampness and the smells of the old house; since then it had stood empty, but it could not be torn down, for Dr. Charriere had left in his will a considerable sum of money to keep the property off the tax-delinquent list for a long enough time—some said twenty years—to guarantee that the house would be standing there if and when heirs of the surgeon appeared to lay claim to it, the doctor having written vaguely of a nephew in French Indo-China, on military service. All attempts to find the nephew had proved futile, and now the house was being permitted to stand until the period specified in the will of Dr. Charriere had expired.

"I think of leasing it," I told Gamwell.

Ill though he was, my fellow antiquarian raised himself up on one elbow in protest. "A passing whim, Atwood—let it pass. I have heard disquieting things of the house."

"What things?" I asked him bluntly.

But of these things he would not speak ; he only shook his head feebly and closed his eyes.

"I hope to examine it tomorrow," I went on.

"It offers nothing you could not find in Quebec, believe me," said Gamwell.

But, as I have set forth, his curious opposition served only to augment my desire to examine the house at close range. I did not mean to spend a lifetime there, but only to lease it for a half year or so, and make it a base of operations, while I went about the countryside around the city as well as the lanes and byways of Providence in search of the antiquities of that region. Gamwell did surrender at last the name of the firm of lawyers in whose hands the Charriere will had been placed, and when I made application to them, and overcame their own lack of enthusiasm, I became master of the old Charriere house for a period of not more than six months, and less, if I so chose.

I took possession of the house at once, though I was somewhat nonplussed to discover that, while running water had been put in, electricity had not. I found among the furnishings of the house—these had been left in each room, exactly as at the death of Dr. Charriere—a half dozen lamps of various shapes and ages, some of them apparently dating back a century or more, with which to light my way. I had expected to find the house cobwebbed and dusty, but I was surprised to learn that this was not the case, though I had not understood that the lawyers—the firm of Baker & Greenbaugh—had undertaken to care for the house during the half century it was to stand, short of someone's appearing to lay claim to it as the sole survivor of Dr. Charriere and his line.

The house was all I had hoped for. It was heavily timbered, and in some of the rooms paper had begun to peel from the plaster, while in others the plaster itself had never been covered with paper, and shone yellow with age on the wall. Its rooms were irregular—appearing to be either quite large or very small. It was of two storeys, but the upper floor had not been much used. The lower or ground floor, however, abounded in evidence of its one-time occupant, the surgeon, for one room of it had manifestly served him as a laboratory of some kind, and an adjoining room as a study, for both had the look of having been but recently abandoned in the midst of some inquiry or research, quite as if the occupation of the house by its brief tenant—*post-mortem* Charriere—had not touched

60

upon these rooms. And perhaps it had not, for the house was large enough to permit of habitation without disturbing them, both laboratory and study being at the back of the house, opening out upon a garden, now much overgrown with shrubs and trees, a garden of some size, since the house occupied a frontage of over three lots in width, and in depth reached to a high stone wall which was but a lot removed from the street in its rear.

Dr. Charriere had evidently been in the midst of some work when his hour had struck, and I confess its nature intrigued me at once, for it was plainly no ordinary one. The inquiry was not alone a study of man, for there were strange, almost cabalistic drawings, resembling physiological charts, of various kinds of saurians, though the most prominent among them were of the order *Loricata* and the genera *Crocodylus* and *Osteolaemus*, though there were also recognizable drawings of *Gavialis, Tomistoma, Gaiman,* and *Alligator,* with a lesser number being speculative sketches of earlier members of this reptilian order reaching back to the Jurassic period. Yet even this fascinating glimpse of the surgeon's odd vein of inquiry would not have stimulated any really genuine delving into his affairs had it not been for the antiquarian mystery of the house.

The Charriere house impressed me at once as having been the product of its age, save for the later introduction of water-works. I had all along assumed that Dr. Charriere himself had built it; Gamwell had nowhere in our somewhat elliptical conversation given me to understand otherwise; nor had he, for that matter, mentioned the surgeon's age at his death. Presuming it to be a well-rounded eighty years, then it was certainly not he who had built the house, for internal evidence spoke clearly of its origin in the vicinity of the year 1700!—or over two centuries before Dr. Charriere's death. It seemed to me, therefore, that the house only bore the name of its most recent long-time tenant, and not that of its builder; it was the pursuit of this problem which brought me to several disturbing facts which bore no relationship, seemingly, to credible facts.

For one thing, the year of Dr. Charriere's birth was nowhere in evidence. I sought out his grave—it was, strangely, on his own property; he had obtained permission to be buried in his garden, not far from a gracious old well which stood, roofed over, with bucket and all still as it had stood, doubtless, for almost as long as the house had been standing—with a view to examine its headstone for the date of his birth, but, to my

disappointment and chagrin, his stone bore only his name—
Jean-François Charriere—his calling: Surgeon—his places of
residence of professional occupation—Bayonne: Paris: Pondicherry: Quebec: Providence—and the year of his death:
1927. No more. This was enough only to further me on my
quest, and forthwith I started to make inquiry by letter of
acquaintances in various places where research might be done.

Within a fortnight, the results of my inquiries were at hand.
But, far from being in any way satisfied, I was more perplexed
than ever. I had made my first inquiry of a correspondent in
Bayonne, presuming that, since this was first mentioned on the
stone, Charriere might have been born in that vicinity. I had
next inquired in Paris, then of a friend in London, who might
have access to information in British archives pertaining to
India, and then in Quebec. What did I glean from all this correspondence but a riddling sequence of dates? A Jean-François
Charriere had indeed been born in Bayonne—but in the year
1636! The name was not unknown in Paris, either, for a seven-
teen-year old lad of that name had studied under the Royalist
exile, Richard Wiseman, in 1653 and for three years thereafter.
At Pondicherry—and later, too, on the Coromandel Coast
of India—one Dr. Jean-François Charriere, surgeon in the
French army, had been on duty from 1674 onward. And in
Quebec, the earliest record of Dr. Charriere was in 1691; he
had practiced in that city for six years, and had then left the
city for an unknown destination.

I was left, patently, with but one conclusion: that the said
Dr. Jean-François Charriere, born in Bayonne, 1636, last
known to have been in Quebec the very year of the erection of
the Charriere house on Benefit Street, was a forebear of the
same name as the late surgeon who had last occupied the
house. But if so, there was an absolute lacuna between that
time in 1697 and the lifetime of the last occupant of the house,
for there was nowhere any account of the family of that earlier
Jean-François Charriere; if there had been a Madame Charriere, if there had been children—as assuredly there must have
been for the line to continue to the present century—there was
no record of them. It was not impossible that the elderly gentle-
man who had come down from Quebec might have been of
single status upon his arrival in Providence, and might have
married thereafter. He would then have been sixty-one years
of age. Yet a search of the appropriate registry failed to reveal
any record of such a marriage, and I was left more bewildered

than ever, though, as an antiquarian, I was fully aware of the difficulties of discovering facts and I was not at that time too discouraged to continue my inquiries.

I took a new line, and approached the firm of Baker & Greenbaugh for information about the late Dr. Charriere. Here an even more curious rebuff awaited me, for when I inquired about the appearance of the French surgeon, both the lawyers were forced to admit that they had never laid eyes on him. All their instructions had come by letter, together with cheques of generous figures; they had acted for Dr. Charriere approximately six years before his death, and thereafter; before that time, they had not been retained by Dr. Charriere.

I inquired then about his "nephew," since the existence of a nephew implied, at least, that there had at one time been a sister or brother to Charriere. But here, too, I was rebuffed; Gamwell had misinformed me, for Charriere had not specifically identified him as a nephew, but only as "the sole male survivor of my line"; this survivor had only been presumed to have been a nephew, and all search for him had come to naught, though there was that in Dr. Charriere's will which implied that the said "sole male survivor" would not need to be sought, but would make application to the firm of Baker & Greenbaugh either in person or by letter in such terms as to be unmistakable. Mystery there was, certainly; the lawyers did not deny it, but it was understood, also, that they had been well rewarded for their trust, too well to permit of any betrayal of it save in such casual terms as they had related to me. After all, as one of the lawyers sensibly pointed out, only three years had elapsed since the death of Dr. Charriere, and there was still ample time for the survivor to present himself.

Failing in this line of inquiry, I again called on my old friend, Gamwell, who was still abed, and now noticeably weaker. His attending physician, whom I encountered on the way out, now for the first time intimated that old Gamwell might not rise again, and cautioned me not to excite him, or to tire him with too many questions. Nevertheless, I was determined to ferret out what I could about Charriere, though I was not entirely prepared for the keen scrutiny to which I was subjected by Gamwell, quite as if he had expected that less than three weeks' residence in the Charriere house should have altered my very appearance.

After the amenities had been exchanged, I turned to the subject about which I had come; explaining that I had found the house so interesting, I desired to know more of its late tenant. Gamwell had mentioned seeing him.

"But that was years ago," said Gamwell. "He's been dead three years. Let me see—1907, I think."

I was astounded. "But that was twenty years before he died!" I protested.

Nevertheless, Gamwell insisted, that was the year.

And how had he looked? I pressed the question upon him.

Disappointingly, senility and illness had encroached upon the old man's once fine mind.

"Take a newt, grow him a little, teach him to walk on his hind legs, and dress him in elegant clothes," Gamwell said. "I give you Dr. François Charriere. Except that his skin was rough, almost horny. A cold man. He lived in another world."

"How old was he?" I asked then. "Eighty?"

"Eighty?" He was contemplative. "When first I saw him—I was but twenty, then—he looked no older. And twenty years ago—my good Atwood—he had not changed a jot. He seemed eighty the first time. Was it the perspective of my youth? Perhaps. He seemed eighty in 1907. And died twenty years later."

"A hundred, then."

"It might well have been."

But Gamwell, too, was dissatisfying. Once again there was nothing definite, nothing concrete, no single fact—only an impression, a memory, of someone, I felt, Gamwell had disliked for no reason he could name. Perhaps some professional jealousy he did not care to name biased his judgment.

I next sought the neighbors, but I found them for the most part younger people who had little memory of Dr. Charriere, except as someone whom they wished elsewhere, for he had an abominable traffic in lizards and the like, and none knew what diabolic experiments he performed in his laboratory. Only one among them was of advanced age ; this was an old woman, a Mrs. Hepzibah Cobbett, who lived in a little two-storey house directly behind the Charriere garden wall, and I found her much enfeebled, in a wheel chair, guarded over by her daughter, a hawk-nosed woman whose cold blue eyes looked at me askance from behind her pince-nez. Yet the old woman spoke, starting to life at mention of Dr. Charriere's name, realizing that I lived in the house.

"Ye'll not live there long, mark my words. It's a devil's house," she said with some spirit that degenerated rapidly into a senile cackling. "Many's the time I've laid eyes on him. A tall

man, bent like a sickle, with a wee tuft of beard like a goat's
whisker on his chin. And what was it that crawled about at his
feet I could not see? A long, black thing, too big for a snake—
though 'twas snakes I thought of every time I set eyes on Dr.
Charriere. And what was it screamed that night? And what
barked at the well?—a fox, indeed, I know a fox and a dog,
too. Like the yawping of a seal. I've seen things, I tell ye, but
nobody'll believe a poor old woman with one foot in her grave.
And ye—ye won't either, for none does."

What was I to make of this? Perhaps the daughter was
right when she said, as she showed me out, "You must over-
look mother's ramblings. She has an arteriosclerotic condition
which occasionally makes her sound quite weak-minded." But
I did not think old Mrs. Cobbett weak-minded, for her eyes
snapped and sparkled when she talked, quite as if she were en-
joying a secret joke of proportions so vast that its very outlines
escaped her keeper, the grim daughter who hovered ever near.

Disappointment seemed to await me at every turn. All
avenues of information yielded little more together than any
one had yielded. Newspaper files, library, records—all that was
to be found was the date of the erection of the house: 1697,
and the date of the death of Dr. Jean-François Charriere. If
any other Charriere had died in the city's history, there was no
mention of him. It was inconceivable that death had stricken
all the other members of the Charriere family, predeceasing
the late tenant of the house on Benefit Street, away from Providence, and yet it must have been so, for there was no other
feasible explanation.

Yet there was one additional fact—a likeness of Dr. Charriere which I discovered in the house; though no name was
appended to it where it hung in a remote and almost inacces-
sible corner of an upstairs room, the initials J. F. C. identified
it beyond reasonable doubt. It was the likeness of a thin-faced
ascetic, wearing a straggly goatee; his face was distinguished
by high cheek-bones, sunken cheeks, and dark, blazing eyes.
His aspect was gaunt and sepulchral.

Thus, in the absence of other avenues of information, I was
driven once again to the papers and books left in Dr. Charriere's study and laboratory. Hitherto, I had been much away
from the house, in the pursuit of my inquiry into Dr. Charriere's background; but now I was as much confined to the
house as I had previously been away from it. Perhaps it was
because of this confinement that I began to grow more keenly

aware of the aura of the house—both in a psychic and a physical sense. That unhappy professional man and his family who had remained here but a month and then left because of the smells abounding had perhaps conditioned me to *smell* the house, and now, for the first time, I did indeed become sharply cognizant of various aromas and musks, some of them typical of old houses, but others completely alien to me. The dominant one, however, was identifiable; it was a musk I had encountered several times before—in zoos, swamps, along stagnant pools—almost a miasma which suggested most strongly the presence of reptiles. It was not impossible that reptiles had found their way through the city to the haven of the garden behind the Charriere house, but it was incredible that they should have persisted in such numbers as to taint the very air of the place. Yet, seek as I might, I could find no source of this reptilian musk, inside or out, though I fancied once that it emanated from the well, which was doubtless a result of an allusory conviction.

The musk persisted, and it was especially strong whenever rain fell, or fog formed, or dew lay on the grass, as might have been expected, moisture heightening all odors. The house was moist, too; its short-lived tenantry had been explained in part by this, and in this, certainly, the renter had not been in error. I found it often unpleasant, but not disturbing—not half so disturbing as other aspects of the house.

Indeed, it was as if my invasion of the study and laboratory had stirred the old house to protest, for certain hallucinations began to occur with annoying regularity. There was, for one, the curious barking sound which seemed to emanate from the garden late at night. And, for another, the illusion that an oddly bent, reptilian figure haunted the darkness of the garden outside the study windows. These and other illusions persisted—and I, in turn, persisted in looking upon them as hallucinatory—until that fateful night when, after hearing a distinct sound as of someone bathing in the garden, I woke from my sleep convinced that I was not alone in the house, and, putting on my dressing-robe and slippers, I lit a lamp and hurried to the study.

What I saw there must certainly have been inspired by the nature of my inquiry into the late Dr. Charriere's papers; that it was a figment of a nightmare, I could not doubt at the moment, though I caught but a faint glimpse of the invader; for there was an invader in the study, and he made off with certain papers belonging to the Charriere estate, but as I saw him in the brief glimpse I had of him in the wan yellow light of the lamp held overhead and partially blinding me he seemed to glisten, he shone blackly, and he seemed to be wearing a skin-tight suit of some rough, black material. I saw him for only an instant, before he leapt through the open window into the darkness of the garden ; I would have followed then, had it not been for the disquieting things I saw in the light of the lamp.

Where the invader had stood there were the irregular marks of feet—of wet feet—and more, of feet which were oddly broad, the toes of which were so long-nailed as to leave the marks of those nails before each toe ; and where he had bent above the papers there was the same wetness ; and over all there hung the powerful reptilian musk I had begun to accept as an integral part of the house, so powerful, indeed, that I almost reeled and fainted.

But my interest in the papers transcended fear or curiosity. At that time, the only rational explanation which occurred to me was that one of the neighbors, who had some animus against the Charriere house and were constantly agitating to have it torn down, must have come from swimming to invade the study. Far-fetched, yes, certainly. But could any other explanation readily account for what I saw? I am inclined to think not.

As for the papers, certain of them were undeniably gone. Fortunately, these were the very ones I had finished with ; I had put them into a neat pile, though many were not consecutive. I could not imagine why anyone would have wanted to take them, unless someone other than myself were interested in Dr. Charriere, perhaps with a view to laying claim to the house and property ; for these papers were painstaking notes about the longevity of crocodiles and alligators, as well as of related reptiles. It had already begun to be plainly evident to me that the late doctor had been studying reptilian longevity with almost obsessive devotion, and with a view, clearly, to learning how man might lengthen his own life. If the secrets of reptilian longevity had been revealed to Dr. Charriere, there was nothing in his papers thus far to show that it had, though I had upon two or three disquieting suggestions of "operations" performed—on whom was not set down—with a view to increasing the life span of the subject.

True, there was one variant vein of notes in what I assumed to be Dr. Charriere's handwriting, treated as a related subject, but, to me, one at variance from the more or less scientific inquiry into the long life of reptiles. This was a sequence of cryptic references to certain mythological creatures, particularly one named "Cthulhu," and another named "Dagon," who were evidently deities of the sea in some ancient mythology completely unknown to me; and suggestions of long-lived creatures (or people?) who served these ancient Gods, named the "Deep Ones," evidently amphibious creatures living in the depths of the seas. Among these notes were photographs of a singularly hideous monolithic statue, of a distinctly saurian cast of feature, labeled "E. coast Hivaoa Is., Marquesas. Object of worship?", and of a totem pole of the North-west Coast Indians of a disturbingly similar workmanship, also reptilian in aspect, this one being marked, "Kwakiutl Indian totem. Quatsino Sound. Sim. t. erected by Tlingit Inds." These curious notes existed as if to show that Dr. Charriere was not averse to examining rites of ancient sorceries and primitive religious beliefs in an effort to bring about some earnestly desired goal.

What that goal might be was soon evident enough. Dr. Charriere had not been interested in the study of longevity for its sake alone; no, he had also wished to prolong his own life. And there were certain upsetting hints in the writings he had left behind him to suggest that in part, at least, he had succeeded beyond his wildest dreams. This was a disturbing discovery to make because it recalled again the curious history of that first Jean-François Charriere, also a surgeon, about whose later years and death there was fully as much mystery as there was about the birth and early years of the late Dr. Jean-François Charriere, who died in Providence in 1927.

The events of that night, though not frightening me too badly, did result in my purchasing a powerful Luger pistol in a second-hand shop, as well as a new flashlight; the lamp had impeded me in the night, which a flashlight would not do in similar circumstances. If indeed I had a visitor from among the neighbors, I could be sure that the papers he had taken would no more than whet his appetite, and sooner or later he would return. Against that contingency I meant to be fully prepared, and if again I caught a marauder in the study of the house I had leased, I would not hesitate to shoot if my demand to stop where he was were not heeded. I hoped, however, that I would not have occasion to use the weapon in such a manner.

On the next night I resumed my study of Dr. Charriere's books and papers. The books had surely at one time belonged to his forebears, for many of them dated back through the centuries; among them was a book translated into the French from the English of R. Wiseman, testifying to some connection between the Dr. Jean-François Charriere who had studied in Paris under Wiseman, and that other surgeon of similar name who had, until recently, lived in Providence, Rhode Island.

They were en masse a singular hodge-podge of books. They seemed to be in every known language, from French to Arabic. Indeed, I could not hope to translate a majority of the titles, though I could read French and had some smattering of the other Romance languages. I had at that time no understanding of the meaning of such a title as *Unaussprechlichen Kulten,* by von Junzt, though I suspected that it was akin to the Count d'Erlette's *Cules des Goules,* since it stood next to that book on the shelf. But then, books on zoological subjects stood beside weighty tomes about ancient cultures; they bore such titles as *An Inquiry Into the Relationship of the Peoples of Polynesia and the Indian Cultures of the South American Continent, with Special Reference to Peru ; The Pnakotic Manuscripts, De Furtivis Literarum Notis,* by Giambattista Porta ; Thicknesse's *Kryptographik* ; the *Daemonolatreia* of Remigius ; Banfort's *The Saurian Age* ; a file of the Aylesbury, Massachusetts, *Transcript* ; another of the Arkham, Massachusetts, *Gazette*— and the like. Some of these books were certainly of immense value, for many of them dated as far back as from 1670 to 1820, and, though all showed much wear from use, all were still in relatively good condition.

These books, however, meant comparatively little to me. In retrospect, I am constrained to believe that, had I examined them more attentively, I might have learned even more than I did ; but there is a saying that too much knowledge of matters men are better off without knowing is even more damning than too little. I soon gave over my examination of the books because I discovered, pressed in among them on the shelves, what seemed at first glance to be a diary or journal, but was, on closer examination, manifestly a notebook, for the entries dated too far back to have encompassed Dr. Carriere's span of years. Yet all were written in a crabbed, tiny script, which was most certainly the late surgeon's, and, despite the age of the first pages, all had been written by the same hand, suggesting that Dr. Charriere had set down these notes in a kind of rough chronology, very probably from some earlier draft. Nor were they jottings alone ; some were illustrated with crude drawings which were nevertheless effective, as are on many occasions the primitive paintings of untutored artists.

Thus, upon the very first page of the hand-bound manuscript, I came upon this entry: "1851. Arkham. Aseph Goade, D.O." and with it a drawing, presumably of the said Aseph Goade, emphasizing certain aspects of his features, which were batrachian in essence, for they were distinguished by an abnormally wide mouth, with peculiar leathery lips, a very low brow, strangely webbed eyes, and a generally squat physiognomy, giving them a distinctly and unmistakably froglike appearance. This drawing took up the majority of the page, and the jotting accompanying it I assumed to be a notation of an encounter—evidently in research, for it could hardly have been in the flesh—with a sub-human type—(could the "D.O." have been a reference to the "Deep Ones," mention of which I had previously encountered?), which, doubtless, Dr. Charriere looked upon as a verification of the trend of his research, a trend to support a belief he probably held that some kinship with batrachia, and hence very probably also saurians, could be traced.

To that end, too, there were other jottings. Most of them were so vague—perhaps purposely so—as to seem to me at that first examination of them virtually meaningless. What was I to make of a page like this, for instance?

"1857. St Augustine. Henry Bishop. Skin very scaly, but not ichthyic. Said to be 107 years old. No deteriorative process. All senses still keen. Ancestry uncertain, but Polynesian trade in background.

"1861. Charleston. Balacz family. Crusted hands. Double jaw construction. Entire family manifesting similar stigmata. Anton 117 years old. Anna 109. Unhappy away from water.

"1863. Innsmouth. Marsh, Waite, Eliot, Gilman families. Captain Obed Marsh a trader in Polynesia, married to a Polynesian woman. All bearing facial characteristics similar to Aseph Goade's. Much secretive living. Women seldom seen in streets, but at night much swimming—entire families, all the rest of the town keeping to their houses, swimming out to Devil Reef. Relationship to D. O. very marked. Considerable traffic between Innsmouth and Ponape. Some dark religious worship.

"1871. Jed Price, carnival entertainer. Billed as 'Alligator Man.' Appears in pool of alligators. Saurian look. Long lantern jaw. Said to have pointed teeth, but whether real or filed unable to determine."

This was the general tenor of the jottings in the book. Their range was continental—there were notes referring to Canada and Mexico as well as the eastern seaboard of North America. From then, Dr. Jean-François Charriere began to emerge as a man obsessed with a strange compulsion—to establish proof of the longevity of certain human beings seemingly bearing some kinship to saurian or batrachian ancestors.

Admittedly, the weight of the evidence gathered, could one have accepted it all as fact, rather than as wishfully colored accounts of people with some marked physical defect, seemed to lend to Dr. Charriere and his belief a strange and provocative corroboration. Yet the surgeon had not often gone beyond the realm of pure conjecture. What he sought seemed to be the connecting link among the various instances which had come to his notice. He had sought this link in three bodies of lore. The most familiar of these was the *Vodu* legendry of Negro culture. Next to it, in familiarity, stood the animal worship of ancient Egypt. Finally, and most important, according to the surgeon's notes, was a completely alien culture which was as old as earth, nay, older, involving ancient Elder Gods and their terrible, unceasing conflict with equally primeval Old Ones who bore such names as Cthulhu, Hastur, Yog-Sothoth, Shub-Niggurath, and Nyarlathotep, and who were served in turn by such curious beings as the Tcho-Tcho People, the Deep Ones, the Shantaks, the Abominable Snow Men, and others, some of whom appeared to have been a sub-order of human being, but others of which were either definite mutations or not human at all. All this fruit of Dr. Charriere's research was fascinating, but in no case had he adduced a definite, provable link. There were certain saurian references in the *Vodu* cult; there were similar connections to the religious culture of ancient Egypt; and there were many obscure and tantalizing suggestions connecting the saurians to the Cthulhu myth-pattern, ranging far deeper into the past than *Crocodylus* and *Gavialis*, embracing *Tyrannosaurus* and *Brontosaurus, Megalosaurus* and other Mesozoic reptilia.

In addition to these interesting notes, there were diagrams of what seemed to be very odd operations, the nature of which I did not fully comprehend at that time. These were apparently copied out of ancient texts, particularly one given frequently as source, entitled *De Vermis Myteriis*, by Ludvig Prinn, another of those obscure references completely foreign to me. The operations themselves suggested a *raison d'être* too astounding to accept on face ; one of them, for instance, was designed to stretch the skin, consisting of many incisions made to "permit growth." Yet another was a simple cross-incision made at the base of the spine for the purpose of "extension of the tail-bone." What these fantastic diagrams suggested was too horrible to contemplate, yet it was part and parcel, surely, of the strange research conducted for so many years by Dr. Charriere, whose seclusion was thus readily explicable, since his was a project which could only be conducted in secret lest it bring down upon him the scorn and laughter of his fellow scientists.

Among these papers there were also certain references set down in such a manner that I could not doubt they were the experiences of the narrator. Yet, for all that these antedated 1850, in some cases by decades, they were unmistakably in Dr. Charriere's handwriting, so that—excepting always the possibility that he had transcribed the experiences of someone else— it was evident that he was more than an octogenarian at the time of his death, indeed, far more, so much more that the very anticipation of it made me uneasy, and cast my thoughts back to that other Dr. Charriere who had gone before him.

The sum total of Dr Charriere's credo amounted to a strongly hypothetical conviction that a human being could, by means of certain operations, together with other unusual practices of a macabre nature, take upon himself something of the logevity that characterized the sauria ; that as much as a century and a half, perhaps even two centuries, could be added to a man's life span ; and, beyond that, given a period of semiconscious torpor in some moist place, which would amount to a kind of gestation, the individual could emerge again, somewhat altered in aspect, true, to begin another lengthy span of life, which would, by virtue of the physiological *changes* which had taken place in him, be of necessity somewhat altered from his previous mode of existence. To support this conviction, Dr. Charriere had amassed only a number of legendary tales, certain data of a kindred nature, and highly speculative accounts of curious human mutations known to have existed in the past two hundred and ninety-one years—a figure which later assumed far more meaning, when I realized that this was the exact span of time from the year of the birth of that earlier Dr. Charriere to the date of the later surgeon's death. Nowhere in all this material was there anything resembling a concrete line of scientific research, with adducible proof—only hints, vague intimations, hideous suggestions—sufficient, in truth, to fill a casual reader with horrible doubts and terrible, half-formed convictions, but not nearly enough to warrant the sober interest of any genuine scholar.

How much farther I would have gone into Dr. Charriere's research, I do not know.

Had it not been for the occurrence of *that* which sent me screaming in horror from that house on Benefit Street, it was possible that I would have gone much farther instead of leaving house and contents to be claimed by a survivor who, I know now, will never come, thus leaving the house to fall to its ultimate destruction by the city.

It was while I was contemplating these "findings" of Dr. Charriere that I became aware of being under scrutiny, that manifestation people are fond of calling the "sixth sense." Unwilling to turn, I did the next best thing ; I opened my pocketwatch, set it up before me, and used the inside of the highly polished case as a kind of mirror to reflect the windows behind me. And there I saw, dimly reflected, a horrible travesty of a human face, which so startled me that I turned to view for myself that which I had seen mirrored. But there was nothing at the pane, save the shadow of movement. I rose, put out the light, and hastened to the window. Did I then see a tall, curiously bent figure, crouched and shuffling in an awkward gait into the darkness of the garden? I believed that I did, but I was not given to folly enough to venture out in pursuit. Whoever it was would come again, even as he had come the previous night.

Accordingly, I settled back to watch, a score of possible explanations crowding upon my mind. As the source of my nocturnal visitor, I confess I put at the head of the list the neighbors who had long opposed the continued standing of the house of Dr. Charriere. It was possible that they meant to frighten me away, unaware of the shortness of my lease ; it was also possible that there was something in the study they wanted, though this was far-fetched, in view of the time they had had to search the house during its long period of unoccupancy. Certainly the truth of the matter never once occurred to me ; I am not by nature any more skeptical than an antiquarian might be expected to be ; but the true identity of my visitor did not, I confess, suggest itself to me despite all the curious inter-locking circumstances which might have conveyed a greater meaning to a less scientific mind than my own.

As I sat there in the dark, I was more than ever impressed with the aura of the old house. The very darkness seemed alive, but incredibly remote from the life of Providence which swirled all around it. The interior darkness was filled instead with the psychic residue of years—the persistent smell of moisture, ac-companied by that musk so commonly associated with reptilian quarters at the zoo; the smell of old wood, old limestone, of which the cellar walls were composed, the odor of decay, for the centuries had begun to deteriorate both wood and stone. And there was something more—the vaporous hint of an ani-mal presence, which seemed indeed to grow stronger with every passing moment.

I sat there well over an hour, before I heard any untoward sound.

Then it was indistinguishable. At first I thought it a bark, akin to that sound made by alligators; but then I thought it rather less a figment of my perfervid imagination than the actual sound of a door closing. Yet it was some time before another sound smote upon my ears—a rustling of papers. As-tonishing as it was, an intruder had actually found his way into the study before my very eyes without being seen! I turned on the flashlight, which was directed at the desk I had left.

What I saw was incredible, horrible. It was not a man who stood there, but a travesty of a man. I know that for one cata-clysmic moment I thought consciousness would leave me; but a sense of urgency coupled with an awareness of acute danger swept over me, and without a moment's hesitation, I fired four times, at such a range that I knew each shot had found harbor in the body of the bestial thing that leaned over Dr. Charriere's desk in that darkened study.

Of what followed I have, mercifully, only the vaguest memory. A wild thrashing about—the escape of the invader—my own uncertain pursuit. I had struck him, certainly, for a trail of blood led from the study to the windows through which he had gone, tearing away glass and frame in one. Outside, the light of my flash gleamed on the drops of blood, so that I had no difficulty following them. Even without this to follow, the strong musk pervading the night air would have enabled me to trace whoever had gone ahead.

I was led—not away from the house—but deeper into the garden, straight to the curb of the well behind the house. And over the curb *into the well,* where I saw for the first time in the glow of the flashlight the cunningly fashioned steps which led down into that dark maw. So great was the discharge of blood at the well-curb, that I was confident I had mortally wounded the intruder. It was that confidence which impelled me to follow, despite the manifest danger.

Would that I had turned at the well-curb and gone away from that accursed place! For I followed down the rungs of the ladder set into the well-wall—not to the water below, as I had first thought I might be led—but to an aperture opening into a tunnel in the well-wall, leading even deeper into the garden. Compelled now by a burning desire to know the nature of my victim, I pushed into this tunnel, unmindful of the damp earth which stained my clothes, with my light thrust before me, and my weapon in instant readiness. Up ahead I could see a kind of hollowed out cavern—not any larger than enough to permit a man to kneel upright—and in the center of my flashlight's glow stood a casket, at sight of which I hesitated momentarily, for I recognized the direction of the tunnel away from the well led toward the grave of Dr. Charriere.

But I had come too far to retreat.

The smell in this narrow opening was almost indescribable. Pervading every part of the tunnel was the nauseatingly strong musk of reptiles; indeed, it lay so thickly in the air that I had to force myself to press on toward the casket. I came up to it and saw that it lay uncovered. The trail of blood led to the edge of the casket and into it. Impelled by burning curiosity and a half-formed fear of what I might find, I rose to my knees and forced the light tremblingly into the casket....

It may well be charged that after so many years my memory is no longer to be relied upon. But what I saw there was imprinted indelibly on my memory. For there, in the glow of my light, lay a newly-dead being, the implications of whose existence overwhelmed me with horror. This was the thing I had killed. Half-man, half-saurian, it was a ghastly travesty upon what had once been a human being. Its clothes were split and torn by the horrible mutations of the flesh, by the crusted skin which had burst its bonds, its hands and unshod feet were flat, powerful in appearance, claw-like. I gazed in speechless terror at the shuddersome tail-like appendage which pushed bluntly out from the base of the spine, at the terribly elongated, crocodilian jaw, to which still grew a tuft of hair, like a goat's beard. . . .

All this I saw before a merciful unconsciousness overcame me,—*for I had seen enough to recognize what lay in that coffin —him who had lain there in a cataleptic torpor since 1927, waiting his turn to come back in frightfully altered form to live again—Dr. Jean-François Charriere, surgeon, born in Bayonne in 1636, "died" in Providence in 1927—and I knew that the survivor of whom he had written in his will was none other than himself, born again, renewed by a hellish knowledge of long-forgotten, eldritch rites more ancient than mankind, as old as that early vernal earth on which great beasts fought and tore!*

THE ANCESTOR

By H. P. Lovecraft and August Derleth

1

When my cousin, Ambrose Perry, retired from the active practice of medicine, he was still a comparatively young man, ruddy and vigorous and in his fifties. He had had a very lucrative practice in Boston, and, though he was fond of his work, he was somewhat more given to the development of certain of his theories, which—and he was an individualist in this—he did not inflict upon his colleagues, whom, truth to tell, he was inclined to look down upon as too bound by the most orthodox methods, and too timid to venture forth upon experiments of their own without the sanction of the American Medical Association. He was a cosmopolitan in every sense of the word, for he had studied extensively in Europe—in Vienna, at the Sorbonne, at Heidelberg—and he had traveled widely, but for all that he was content to lose himself in wild country in Vermont, when at last he chose retirement to climax his brilliant career.

He went into virtual seclusion at his home, which he had built in the middle of a dense wood, and outfitted with as complete a laboratory as money could buy. No one heard from him, and for three years not a word of his activities reached the public prints or the private correspondence of his relatives and friends. It was thus with considerable surprise that I received a letter from him—I found it waiting on my return from a sojourn in Europe—asking me to come and spend some time with him, if possible. I replied regretfully that I had now to set about finding a position for myself, and expressed my pleasure at hearing from him and the hope that some day I might be able to avail myself of his invitation, which was as kind as it was unexpected. His answer came by return mail, offering me a handsome emolument if I would accept the position of secretary—by which, I was certain, he meant me to do everything about the house as well as take notes.

Perhaps my motivation was as much curiosity as the attractiveness of the remuneration, which was generous ; I accepted as quickly, almost fearful lest he withdraw his offer, and within a week I presented myself at my cousin's rambling house, built in the Pennsylvania Dutch farm manner, though of but one storey with sharply pointed gables and deeply pitched roofs. I had had some difficulty finding it, even after receiving my cousin's explicit instructions, for he was at least ten miles from the nearest village, which was a hamlet called Tyburn, and his house was set so far back from the little-traveled road, and had so slight a lane leading up to it, that I was constrained to believe for some time that I had traveled past it in my eagerness to arrive at the hour I had promised.

An alert German shepherd dog guarded the premises, but, though he was chained, he was not at all vicious, for apart from watching me intently, he neither growled nor made any move in my direction when I went up to the door and rang the bell. My cousin's appearance, however, shocked me, for he was thin and gaunt ; the hale, ruddy man I had last seen almost four years ago had vanished, and in his place stood a mere travesty of his former self. His hearty vigor, too, seemed sadly diminished, though his handshake was firm and strong, and his eyes no less keen.

"Welcome, Henry," he cried at sight of me. "Even Ginger seems to have accepted you without so much as a bark."

At the mention of his name, the dog came bounding forward as far as his long chain would reach, tail wagging.

"But come in. You can always put your car up later on."

I did as I was bidden and found the interior of his house very masculine, almost severe in its appointments. A meal was on the table, and I learned that, far from expecting me to do other than serve as his "secretary", my cousin had a cook and a handyman, who lived above his garage, and had no intention whatsoever that I should do more than take down such notes as he intended to give me, and to file the results of his experiments. For he was experimenting ; he made so much clear at once, though he said nothing of the nature of his experiments, and all during our meal, in the course of which I met both Edward and Meta Reed, the couple who took care of the house and grounds, he asked only about myself, what I had been doing, what I hoped to do—at thirty, he reminded me, there was considerably less time to dawdle about deciding on one's future—and occasionally, though only as my own answers to his questions brought up their names, about other members of the family, who were, as always, widely scattered.

Yet I felt that he asked about me only to satisfy the amenities of the situation, and without any real interest, though he did once hint that if only I could turn to medicine for a career, he might be persuaded to see me through college in pursuit of my degree. But all this, I felt sure, was only the superficiality, the politeness of the moment, representing those aspects of our first meeting in some years which were to be got over with at the earliest opportunity; there was, moreover, that in his manner which suggested a suppressed impatience at this subject he himself had initiated, an impatience with me for my preoccupation with his questions, and at himself for having so far yielded to the conventionalities of the situation as to have asked questions about matters in which he was plainly not interested at all.

The Reeds, man and wife, who were both in their sixties, were subdued. They made little conversation, not only because Mrs. Reed both cooked and served her dinner, but because they were plainly accustomed to carrying on an existence apart from their employer's, for all that they ate at his table. They were both greying, yet they managed to look far more youthful than Ambrose, and they showed none of the signs of the physical deterioration which had come upon my cousin. The meal went on with only the dialogue between Ambrose and myself to break the silence; the Reeds partook of the meal not in subservience, but with a mask of indifference, though I did notice, two or three times, that quick, sharp glances passed from one to the other of them at something my cousin said, but that was all.

It was not until we had retired to Ambrose's study that he touched upon that subject closest to his thoughts. My cousin's study adjoined his laboratory, which was at the rear of the house; the kitchen and large dining and living room combination came next, and the bedrooms, curiously, were at the front of the house; once in the cozy study, Ambrose relaxed, his voice filled with the tremor of excitement.

"You will never guess the direction my experiments have taken since I left practice, Henry," he began, "and I dare to wonder at my temerity in telling you. Were it not, indeed, that I need someone to set down these amazing facts, I would not do so. But now that I am on the road to success, I must think of posterity. I have, in short, made successful efforts to recapture all my past, down to the most minute nooks and crannies of human memory, and I am now further convinced that, by the same methods, I can extend this perceptive process to *hereditary* memory and recreate the events of man's heredity. I see your expression—you doubt me."

"On the contrary, I am astounded at the possibilities in it," I answered, quite truthfully—though I failed to admit that a stab of alarm possessed me simultaneously.

"Ah, good, good! I sometimes think that, because of the means I must use to induce the state of mind necessary to this ceaseless probing of past time, I have gravely disappointed the Reeds, for they look upon all experimentation on human beings as fundamentally un-Christian and treading upon forbidden ground."

I wanted to ask what means he had reference to, but I knew that in good time he would tell me if he had a mind to ; if he had not, no question of mine would bring the answer. And presently he came to it.

"I have found that a combination of drugs and music, taken at a time when the body is half-starved, induces the mood and makes it possible to cast back in time and sharpen all the faculties to such a degree that memory is regained. I can tell you, Henry, I have achieved the most singular and remarkable results ; I have actually gone back to memory of the womb, incredible as it may seem."

He spoke with great intensity ; his eyes shone, his voice trembled. Plainly, he was exhilarated beyond ordinary stimulation by his dreams of success. This had been one of his goals when he was still in practice ; now he had used his considerable means to further his ambition to achieve success in this, and he seemed to have accomplished something. So much I was ready to admit, however cautiously, for his experiments explained his appearance—drugs and starvation could easily account for his gauntness, which was in fact a kind of emaciation—he had starved himself so frequently and so steadily that he had not only lost his excess weight but had reduced beyond the point of wisdom and health. Furthermore, as I sat listening to him, I could not help observing that he had all the aspects of fanaticism, and I knew that no demur I could offer would effect him in the slightest or bring about any deviation whatsoever in his direction. He had his eyes fixed on this strange goal, and he would permit nothing and no one to deflect him from it.

"But you will have the task of transcribing my shorthand notes, Henry," he went on, less intensely. "For, of course, I have kept them—some of them written in a trance-like state, quite as if I were possessed by some spirit guide, which is an

80

absurdity, naturally. They range backward in time to just before my birth, and I am now engaged in probing ancestral
memory. You shall see how far I have got when you have had
time to examine and transcribe such data as I have set down."

With that, my cousin turned to other matters, and soon ex-
cused himself, vanishing into his laboratory.

2

It took me fully a fortnight to assimilate and copy Ambrose's notes, which were more extensive than he had led me to
believe, and also disturbingly revelatory. I had already come to
look upon Ambrose as extremely quixotic, but now I was convinced that a strong vein of aberration was manifest in his
make-up as well, for the relentless driving of himself to achieve
an end which was incapable of proof, for the most part, and
promised no boon to mankind even if his goal were reached,
seemed to me to border on irrational fanaticism. He was not
interested so much for the information he might obtain in this
incessant probing of memory as he was in the experiment for
its sake alone, and what was most disturbing about it was the
patent evidence that his experiment, which might at first have
had only the proportions of a hobby, was becoming obsessive,
to such an extent that all other matters were relegated to
second place—not excluding his health.

At the same time, I was forced to admit that the material the
notes contained was often deeply surprising. There was no
question but that my cousin had found some way to tap the
stream of memory; he had established beyond doubt that
everything that happened to a human being was registered in
some compartment of the brain, and that it needed but the
proper bridge to its place of storage in memory to bring it to
consciousness once more. By recourse to drugs and music, he
had gone back into the past to such a degree that his notes, as
finally put together, constituted an exact biography which was
in no way complicated by the glossing over of wish-fulfillment
dreams, the enchantment of distance, or the ego-gratifications
which always play a part in adjustment of the individual personality to life's disappointments which have dealt blows to the
ego.

My cousin's course so far was undeniably fascinating. For
the immediately past years, his notes mentioned many people
we knew in common; but soon the two decades between us

began to become obvious and his memory concerned strangers to me and events in which I had no part, even indirectly. The notes were especially revealing in what they conveyed of my cousin's dominant thoughts during his youth and early manhood—in their cryptic references to the themes which were constantly uppermost in his thoughts.

"Argued vehemently with de Lesseps about the primal source. The chimpanzee linkage too recent. Primal fish?" So he wrote of his days at the Sorbonne. And, at Vienna—" 'Man did not always live in trees'—so says von Wiedersen. Agreed. Presumably he swam. What role, if any, did man's ancestors have in the age of the brontosaur?" Such notes as these, including many far more detailed, were interspersed with the daily record of his years, mingling with accounts of parties, romances, an adolescent duel, differences with his parents, and the like—all the assorted trivia of one man's life. This subject appeared to hold my cousin's interest with an astonishing consistency; his more recent years, of course, were filled with it, but it recurred all the way through his life from the age of nine onward, when on one occasion he had asked our grandfather to explain the family tree and demanded to know what was beyond the registered beginnings of the line.

There was, too, in these notes, certain evidence of how much he was taxing himself in this obsessive experiment, for his handwriting had undergone a marked decrease in legibility from the time he had first begun to chronicle his memories to the present; that is, as he went backward through time to his earliest years—and indeed, into the place of darkness which was the womb, for he had accomplished this return, if his notes were not a skillful fabrication—his script grew steadily more illegible, quite as if there were a change in degrees with the change in the age of his memories, which was as fantastic a concept as, I felt then, my cousin's belief that he could reach back into ancestral and hereditary memory, both involving the memory of his forebears for many generations, and presumably transmitted in the genes and chromosomes from which he had sprung.

To a very large extent, however, I suspended judgment while I was putting his notes in order, and there was no mention of the notes, except for the help I asked once or twice when I could not decipher a word in Ambrose's script. Read over, when at last it was completed, the transcript was impressive and cogent, and I handed it to my cousin at last with mixed feelings and not without some suspension of belief.

"Are you convinced?" he asked me.

"As far as you've gone, yes," I admitted.

"You shall see," he replied imperturbably.

I undertook to remonstrate with him about the diligence with which he pursued this dream of his. In the two weeks it had taken me to assimilate and copy his notes, he had plainly driven himself beyond the bounds of reason. He had taken so little food and had slept so little that he had grown noticeably thinner and more haggard than he had been on the day of my arrival. He had been secluded in his laboratory day and night, for long hours at a time; indeed, on many occasions in that fortnight there were but three of us at the table for meals— Ambrose had not come out of the laboratory. His hands had a tendency to tremble, and there was a hint of palsy too about his mouth, while his eyes burned with the fire of the fanatic, to whom all else but the goal of his fanaticism had ceased to exist.

The laboratory was out of bounds for me. Though my cousin had no objection to showing me about the extensive laboratory, he required the utmost solitude when he was conducting his experiments. Nor had he any intention of setting down exactly what drugs he had recourse to—though I had reason to believe that *Cannabis indica*, or Indian hemp, commonly known as hashish, was one of them—in the punishment he inflicted on his body in pursuit of his wild dream to recapture his ancestral and hereditary memory, a goal he sought daily and often nightly, as well, without surcease, so much so that I saw him with increasing rarity, though he sat for a long time with me on the night I finally gave him the transcript of his notes tracing the course of his life through his recaptured memory, going over each page with me, making certain small corrections and additions, striking out a few passages here and there, and, in general, improving the narrative as I had transcribed it. A retyping was obviously necessary, but what then, if I were not to attend him in the actual course of his experiments?

But my cousin had yet another sheaf of notes ready for me when the retyping was finished. And this time the notes were not of his own memories, but ranged back through time; they were the memories of his parents, his grandparents, of his forebears even before them—not specific, as were his own, but only general, yet enough to convey an amazing picture of the family before his own generation. They were memories of great cataclysms, of major events of history, of the earth in its youth; they were such recreations of time past as I would have thought impossible for one man to set down. Yet here they were, undeniably, impressive and unforgettable: an accomplishment by any standard. I was convinced that they were a skillful fabrication, yet I dared not pass judgement on Ambrose, whose fanatical belief brooked no doubt. I copied them as carefully as I copied his earlier notes, and in but a few days I finished and handed the new transcript to him.

"You need not doubt me, Henry," he said, smiling grimly. "I see it in your eyes. What would I have to gain by making a false record? I am not prone to self-deception."

"I am not qualified to judge, Ambrose. Perhaps not even to believe or disbelieve."

"That is well enough put," agreed my cousin.

I pressed him to tell me what I must do next, but he suggested that I wait on his pleasure. I might take the time to explore the woods or roam the fields on the far side of the road, until he had more work ready for me. I planned to take his suggestion and explore the adjoining woods, but this was never to be done, for other events intervened. That very night I was set in a different direction, providing a decided change from the routine of my cousin's increasingly difficult notes, for in the middle of the night Reed came to awaken me and tell me that Ambrose wanted me in his laboratory.

I dressed and went down at once.

I found Ambrose stretched out on an operating table, clad in the worn mouse-colored dressing-gown he usually wore. He was in a semi-stuporous state, yet not so far gone that he failed to recognize me.

"Something's happened to my hands," he said with effort. "I'm going under. Will you take down anything I may say?"

"What is it?" I asked.

"A temporary nerve block, perhaps. A muscular cramp. I don't know. They'll be all right tomorrow."

"All right," I said. "I'll take down anything you may say."

I took his pad and pencil and sat waiting.

The atmosphere of the laboratory, ill-lit with but one low red light near the operating table, was eerie. My cousin looked far more like a corpse than a man under the influence of drugs. Moreover, there was playing in one corner an electric phonograph, so that the low, discordant strains of Stravinsky's *Le Sacre du Printemps* flowed through the room and took possession of it. My cousin lay perfectly still, and for a long time not a sound escaped him ; he had sunk into the deep drugged sleep in which he carried on his experiement, and I could not have awakened him had I tried.

Perhaps an hour elapsed before he began to speak, and then he spoke so disjointedly that I was hard put to it to catch his words.

"Forest sunk into earth," he said. "Great ones fighting, tearing. Run, run. . . ." And again, "New trees for old. Footprint ten feet across. We live in cave, cold, damp, fire. . . ."

I put down everything he said insofar as I could catch his muttered words. Incredibly, he seemed to be dreaming of the saurian age, for his hints were of great beasts that roamed the face of his land and fought and tore, walking through forests as though they were of grass, seeking out and devouring mankind, the dwellers in caves and holes under the surface of the earth.

But the effort of driving himself back so far into the past was a singular strain on my cousin Ambrose, and, when at last he came back to consciousness that night, he shuddered, directing me to turn off the phonograph, and muttered something about "degenerative tissues" curiously allied to "my dreams—my memories," and announced that we would all rest for a while before he resumed his experiments.

3

It is possible that if my cousin could have been persuaded to rest his experiment on the admitted probability of ultimate success, and taken care of himself, he might have avoided the consequences of pushing himself beyond the boundaries mortal man was meant to go. But he did not do so ; indeed, he scorned my every suggestion, and reminded me that he was the doctor, not I. My retort that like all doctors, he was more careless of himself as patient than he would have been of anyone else fell on deaf ears. Yet even I could not have foreseen what was to take place, though Ambrose's vague hint about "degenerative tissues" ought to have lent direction to my contemplation of the harm he was doing to himself by the addiction to drugs which had made him their victim.

For a week he rested.

Then he resumed his experiments, and soon I was once more putting his notes into typescript. But this time his notes were increasingly difficult to decipher ; his script was indeed deteriorating, even as he had hinted, and, moreover, their subject was often very difficult to follow, though it was evident that Ambrose had gone far back in time. The possibility remained, of course, and was strong, that my cousin had fallen victim to a kind of self-hypnosis, and that, far from experiencing any such memory as he chronicled, he was reproducing from the memory of books he had read the salient aspects of the lives of anciet cave- and tree-dwellers; yet there were disturbingly clear indications from time to time that the observations he made were not made from any printed text or the memory of such a text, though I had no way of seeking out such possible sources for my cousin's bizarre chroniclings.

I saw Ambrose increasingly seldom, but on the rare occasions when I did see him, I could not avoid noticing the alarming degree to which he had yielded to drugs and starvation ; his emaciation was complicated by certain repellent signs of degeneration. He tended to slaver at his food and his eating habits became so deplorable that Mrs. Reed was pointedly absent from the table at more than one occasion ; though, because of Ambrose's growing dislike of leaving his laboratory, we were not often more than three at table.

I do not remember just when the drastic alteration in Ambrose's habits came about, but I believe I had been at the house just over two months. Now that I think back to it, it seems to my that events were signalled by Ginger, my cousin's dog, which began to act up most restlessly. Whereas hitherto he had been a singularly well-behaved dog, now he began to bark often at night, and by day he whined and moved about house and yard with an air of alarm. Mrs. Reed said of him, "That dog smells or hears something he don't like." Perhaps she spoke truly, for all that I paid little attention.

It was about this time that my cousin elected to remain in his laboratory all together, instructing me to leave his food on a tray outside the laboratory door. I took issue with him, but he would neither open the door nor come out, and very often he left his food stand for some time before he took it in, so that Mrs. Reed made ever less attempts to serve him hot food, for most of the time it had grown cold by the time he took it in. Curiously, none of us ever saw Ambrose take his food ; the tray might stand for an hour, two hours, even three—then suddenly it would be gone, only to be replaced later by an empty tray.

His eating habits also underwent a change; though he had formerly been a heavy coffee drinker, he now spurned it, returning his cup untouched so many times that Mrs. Reed no longer troubled to serve it. He seemed to grow ever more partial to simpler foods—meat, potatoes, lettuce, bread—and was not attracted to salads or most casserole dishes. Sometimes his empty tray contained notes, but these were growing fewer and farther between, and such as there were I found almost impossible to transcribe, for in his handwriting now, as well as in the content of his notes, there was the same distressing deterioration. He seemed to have difficulty properly holding a pencil, and his lines were scrawled in large letters over all the sheets of paper without any sense of order, though this was not entirely unexpected in one heavily dosed with drugs.

The music which welled forth from the laboratory was even more primitive. Ambrose had obtained certain records of ethnic music—Polynesian, ancient Indian, and the like—and it was these he now played to the exclusion of all else. These were weird sounds, indeed, and peculiarly trying in endless repetition, however interesting they were at first hearing, and they prevailed with monotonous insistence, night and day, for over a week, when one night the phonograph began to manifest every indication of having run down or worn out, and then abruptly stopped, it was not thereafter heard again.

It was at about this time that the notes ceased to appear, and, concomitant with this development, there were two others. The dog, Ginger, erupted into frantic barking during the night, at fairly regular intervals, as if someone were invading the property; I got up once or twice, and once I did think I saw some unpleasantly large animal scuttling into the woods, but nothing came of this; it was gone by the time I had got outside, and, however wild this portion of Vermont was, it was not bear county, nor, for that matter, was there any likelihood of encountering in the woods anything larger or more dangerous than a deer. The other development was more disturbing; Mrs. Reed noticed it first, and called my attention to it—a pervasive and highly repellent musk, clearly an animal odor, which seemed emanate from the laboratory.

Could my cousin somehow have brought an animal in from the woods through the back door of the laboratory, which opened out upon the woods? This was always a possibility, but, in truth, I knew of no animal which might give out so powerful a musk. Efforts to question Ambrose from this side of the door were of no avail; he resolutely refused to make any answer, and even the threat of the Reeds that they would leave, unable any longer to work in such a stench, did not move him. After three days of it, the Reeds departed with their belongings, and I was left alone to take care of Ambrose and his dog.

In the shock of discovery, the exact sequence of events thereafter is no longer very clear. I know that I determined to reach my cousin by one way or other, though all my pleadings remained unanswered. I lightened my burdens as much as possible by unchaining the dog that morning, and letting him roam. I made no attempt to undertake the various tasks Reed had performed, but spent my time going to and from the laboratory door. I had long ago given up trying to look into the laboratory from the outside, for its windows were high rectangles parallel to the roof, and, like the single window in the door, they were covered over so as to make it impossible to look in upon any experiment under way inside.

Though my cajolery and pleadings had no effect on Ambrose, I knew that ultimately he must eat, and that, if I withheld food from him, he would finally be forced to come out of the laboratory. So for all of one day I set no food before his door ; I sat grimly watching for him to appear, despite the almost nauseating animal musk which invaded the house from behind the laboratory door. But he did not appear. Determinedly, I continued to keep my vigil at the door, fighting sleep, which was not difficult, for in the quiet of the night I was aware of peculiarly disturbing movements within the laboratory—awkward, shuffling sounds, as if some large creature were crawling about, —combined with a guttural mewing sound, as if some mute animal were trying to speak. Several times I called out, and as often I tried the laboratory door anew, but it still resisted my efforts, being not only locked, but also barred by some heavy object.

I decided that, if this refusal to serve my cousin the food to which he had become accustomed did not bring him out, I would tackle the outer door of the laboratory in the morning, and force it by whatever means I could devise. I was now in a state of high alarm, since Ambrose's persistent silence seemed wholly unlike him.

But this decision had hardly been made, when I was aware of the frantic excitement of the dog. This time, unhampered by the chain which had hitherto bound him, he streaked along one side of the house and made for the woods, and in a moment I heard the furious snarling and growling which always accompanied an attack.

Momentarily forgetting my cousin, I made for the nearest door, snatching up my flashlight as I ran, and, running outside, I was on my way to the woods when I stopped short, I had come around the corner of the house, in view of the back of the laboratory—and I saw that the door to the laboratory stood open.

Instantly I turned and ran into the laboratory.

All was dark inside. I called my cousin's name. There was no response. With the flashlight I found the switch and turned up the light.

The sight that met my eyes startled me profoundly. When last I had been in the laboratory, it had been a conspicuously neat and trim room—yet now it was in a shocking state. Not only were the impedimenta of my cousin's experiments tipped over and broken, but there were scattered over instruments and floor fragments of partly decayed food—some that was clearly recognizable as having come prepared, but also a disturbing amount of wild food—remains of partially-consumed rabbits, squirrels, skunks, woodchucks, and birds. Above all, the laboratory bore the nauseatingly repellent odor of a primal animal's abode—the scattered instruments bespoke civilization, but the smell and sight of the place were of subhuman life.

Of my cousin Ambrose there was no sign.

I recalled the large animal I had seen faintly in the woods, and the first thought that came to mind was that somehow the creature had broken into the laboratory and made off with Ambrose, the dog in pursuit. I acted on the thought, and ran from the laboratory to the place in the woods from which still came the throaty, animal sounds of a lethal battle which ended only as I came running up, Ginger stepped back, panting, and my light fell upon the kill.

I do not know how I managed to return to the house, to call the authorities, even to think coherently for five minutes at a time, so great was the shock of discovery. For in that one cataclysmic moment, I understood everything that had taken place —I knew why the dog barked so frantically in the night when the "thing" had gone to feed, I understood the source of that horrible animal musk. I realized that what had happened to my cousin was inevitable.

For the thing that lay below Ginger's bloody jaws was a sub-human caricature of a man, a hellish parody of primal growth, with horrible malformations of face and body, giving off an all-pervasive and wholly charnel musk—but it was clad in the rags of my cousin's mouse-colored dressing-gown, and it wore on its wrist my cousin's watch.

By some unknown primal law of nature, in sending his memory back to that prehuman era, into man's hereditary past, Ambrose had been trapped in that period of evolution, and his body had retrograded to the level of man's pre-human existence on the earth. He had gone nightly to forage for food in the woods, maddening the already alarmed dog; and it was by my hand that he had come to this horrible end—for I had un-chained Ginger and made it possible for Ambrose to come to his death at the jaws of his own dog!

The Peabody Heritage

I NEVER KNEW my great-grandfather Asaph Peabody, though I was five years old when he died on his great old estate north-east of the town of Wilbraham, Massachusetts. There is a childhood memory of once visiting there, at a time when the old man was lying ill; my father and mother mounted to his bed-room, but I remained below with my nurse, and never saw him. He was reputed to be wealthy, but time whittles away at wealth as at all things, for even stone is mortal, and surely mere money could not be expected to withstand the ravages of the ever-increas-ing taxation, dwindling a little with each death. And there were many deaths in our family, following my great-grandfather's in 1907. Two of my uncles died after – one was killed on the Western front, and another went down on the *Lusitania*. Since a third uncle had died before them, and none of them had ever married, the estate fell to my father on my grandfather's death in 1919.

My father was not a provincial, though most of his forbears had been. He was little inclined to life in the country, and made no effort to take an interest in the estate he had inherited, beyond spending my great-grandfather's money on various investments in Boston and New York. Nor did my mother share any of my own interest in rural Massachusetts. Yet neither of them would consent to sell it, though on one occasion, when I was home from college, my mother did propose that the property be sold, and my father coldly dismissed the subject; I remember his sudden freezing – there is no more fitting word to describe his reaction – and his curious reference to 'the Peabody heritage' – as well as his carefully phrased words: 'Grandfather predicted that one of his blood would recover the heritage.' My mother had asked scornfully: 'What heritage? Didn't your father just about spend it all?' to which my father made no reply, resting his case in his icy inference that there were certain good reasons why the property could not be sold, as if it were entailed beyond any process of law. Yet he never went near the property; the taxes were paid regularly by one Ahab Hopkins, a lawyer in Wilbraham, who made reports on the property to my parents, though they always ignored them, dismissing any suggestion of 'keeping up' the property by saying it would be like 'throwing good money after bad'.

The property was abandoned, to all intent and purpose; and abandoned it remained. The lawyer had once or twice made a half-hearted attempt to rent it, but even a brief boom in Wilbraham had not brought more than transient renters to the old homestead, and the Peabody place yielded inexorably to time and the weather. It was thus in a sad state of disrepair when I came into the property on the sudden death by motor-car accident of both my parents in the autumn of 1929. Nevertheless, what with the decline in property values which took place subsequent to the inauguration of the depression that year, I determined to sell my Boston property and refurbish the house outside of Wilbraham for my own use. I had enough of a competence on my parents' death so that I could afford to retire from the practice of law, which had always demanded of me greater preciseness and attention than I wished to give to it.

Such a plan, however, could not be implemented until at least part of the old house had been got ready for occupation once more. The dwelling itself was the product of many generations. It had been built originally in 1787, at first as a simple colonial house, with severe lines, an unfinished second storey, and four impressive pillars at the front. But, in time, this had become the basic part of the house, the heart, as it were. Subsequent generations had altered and added to it – at first by the addition of a floating stairway and a second storey; then by various ells and wings, so that at the time I was preparing to make it my residence, it was a large, rambling structure, which occupied over an acre of land, adding to the house itself the lawn and gardens, which were in as great a state of disuse as the house.

The severe colonial lines had been softened by age and less regardful builders, and the architecture was no longer pure, for gambrel roof vied with mansard roof, small-paned windows with large, figured and elaborately sculptured cornices with plain, dormers with unbroken roof. Altogether the impression the old house conveyed was not displeasing, but to anyone of architectural sensibilities, it must have appeared a woeful and unhappy conglomeration of architectural styles and kinds of ornament. Any such impression, however, must surely have been softened by the tremendously spreading ancient elms and oaks which crowded upon the house from all sides save the garden, which had been taken over among the roses, so long grown untended, by young poplar and birch trees. The whole effect of the house, therefore, despite the accretions of time and

differing tastes, was of faded magnificence, and even its un-
painted walls were in harmony with the great-girthed trees all
around.

The house had no less than twenty-seven rooms. Of these, I
selected a trio in the south-east corner to be rehabilitated, and
all that autumn and early winter, I drove up from Boston to keep
an eye on the progress of the venture. Cleaning and waxing the
old wood brought out its beautiful colour, installing electricity
removed the dark gloom of the rooms, and only the waterworks
delayed me until late winter; but by February the twenty-
fourth, I was able to take up my residence in the ancestral Peabody home. Then for a month I was occupied with plans for the
rest of the house, and, though I had initially thought of having
some of the additions torn down and the oldest parts of the
structure retained, I soon abandoned this project in favour of
the decision to keep the house as it was, for it had a pervasive
charm born, no doubt, of the many generations which had lived
there, as well as of the essence of the events which had taken
place within its walls.

Within that month, I was quite taken with the place, and
what had been primarily a temporary move was gladly embraced
as a lifelong ideal. But alas, this ideal grew to such proportions
that it soon brought about a grandiose departure which subtly
altered my direction and threw me off the track on a course I had
never wished to take. This scheme was the determination to move
to the family vault, which had been cut into a hillside within
sight of the house, though away a little from the highway which
passed in front of the estate, the remains of my parents, who had
been decently interred in a Boston plot. This was in addition to
my resolve to make an attempt also to bring back to the United
States the bones of my dead uncle, which reposed somewhere in
France, and thus re-unite the family, as far as possible, on the
ancestral acres near Wilbraham. It was just such a plan as might
occur to a bachelor who was also a reclusive solitary, which I

had become in the short space of that month, surrounded by the architect's drawings and the lore of the old house which was about to begin a new lease of life in a new era far, far removed from that of its simple beginnings.

It was in pursuit of this plan that I made my way one day in March to the family vault, with the keys the lawyer for the estate had delivered into my hands. The vault was not obtrusive; indeed, no part of it was ordinarily visible except the massive door, for it had been built into a natural slope, and was almost concealed by the trees which had grown without pruning for decades. The door and the vault, as well, had been built to last for centuries; it dated back almost as far as the house, and for many generations every member of the Peabody family from old Jedediah, the first to occupy the house, onward, had been interred here. The door offered me some resistance, since it had not been opened for years, but at length it yielded to my efforts and the vault lay open to me.

The Peabody dead lay in their coffins – thirty-seven of them, some in cubicles, some outside. Some of the cubicles where the earliest Peabodies had lain held only the remains of coffins, while that reserved for Jedediah was completely empty, with not even the dust to show that coffin and body had once reposed in that place. They were in order, however, save for the casket which bore the body of my great-grandfather Asaph Peabody; this seemed curiously disturbed, standing out of line with the others, among those more recent ones – my grandfather's and my one uncle's – which had no cubicles of their own but were simply on a ledge extended outward from the cubicled wall. Moreover, it seemed as if someone had lifted or attempted to lift the cover, for one of the hinges was broken, and the other loosened.

My attempt to straighten my great-grandfather's coffin was instinctive, but in so doing the cover was still further jostled and slipped partially off, revealing to my startled gaze all that remained of Asaph Peabody. I saw that through some hideous error, he had been buried face downward – I did not want to think, even at so long a time after his death, that the old man might have been buried in a cataleptic state and so suffered a painful death in that cramped, airless space. Nothing but bones survived, bones and portions of his garments. Nevertheless, I was constrained to alter mistake or accident, whichever it might be; so I removed the cover of the coffin, and reverently turned skull and bones over so that the skeleton of my great-grand-father lay in its rightful position. This act, which might have seemed grisly in other circumstances, seemed only wholly nat-ural, for the vault was aglow with the sunlight and shadows that speckled the floor through the open door, and it was not at that hour a cheerless place. But I had come, after all, to ascertain how much room remained in the vault, and I was gratified to note that there was ample room for both my parents, my uncle – if his remains could be found and brought thither from France – and, finally, myself.

I prepared, therefore, to carry on with my plans, left the vault well locked behind me, and returned to the house ponder-ing ways and means of bringing my uncle's remains back to the country of his birth. Without delay, I wrote to the authorities in Boston on behalf of the disinterment of my parents, and to those of the county in which I now resided for permission to re-inter my parents in the family vault.

The singular chain of events which seemed to centre about the old Peabody homestead began, as nearly as I can recall, on that very night. True, I had had an oblique kind of warning that something might be amiss with the old house, for old Hopkins, on surrendering his keys, had asked me insistently when I came to take possession whether I was sure I wanted to take this step, and had seemed equally intent upon pointing out that the house was 'a lonely sort of place', that the farming neighbours 'never looked kindly on the Peabodys', and that there had always been a 'kind of difficulty keeping renters there'. It was one of those places, he said, almost with relish at making a distinct point, 'to which nobody ever goes for a picnic. You'll never find paper plates or napkins *there!*' – a plethora of ambiguities which nothing could persuade the old man to reduce to facts, since, evidently, there were no facts, but that the neighbours frowned upon an estate of such magnitude in the midst of what was otherwise good farming land. This, in truth, stretched out on all sides of my property of but forty acres, most of it woods – a land of neat fields, stone walls, rail fences, along which trees grew and shrubbery made adequate cover for birds. An old man's talk, I thought it, given rise by his kinship with the farmers who surrounded me: solid, sturdy Yankee stock, no whit different from the Peabodys, save that they toiled harder and perhaps longer.

But on that night, one on which the winds of March howled and sang among the trees about the house, I became obsessed with the idea that I was not alone in the house. There was a sound not so much of footsteps as of *movement* from somewhere upstairs, one that defies description, save that it was as of someone moving about in a narrow space, forward and back, forward and back. I remember that I went out in the great dark space into which the floating stairway descended, and listened to the darkness above; for the sound seemed to drift down the stairs, sometimes unmistakable, sometimes a mere whisper; and I stood there listening, listening, listening, trying to identify its source, trying to conjure up from my rationalisation some explanation for it, since I had not heard it before, and concluded at last that in some fashion a limb of a tree must be driven by the wind to brush against the house, forward and back. Settled on this, I returned to my quarters, and was no more disturbed by it – not that it ceased, for it did not, but that I had given it a rational excuse for existence.

I was less able to rationalise my dreams that night. Though ordinarily not at all given to dreams, I was literally beset by the most grotesque phantasms of sleep, in which I played a passive role and was subjected to all manner of distortions of time and space, sensory illusions, and several frightening glimpses of a shadowy figure in a conical black hat with an equally shadowy creature at his side. These I saw as through a glass, darkly, and the twilit landscape as through a prism. Indeed, I suffered not so much dreams as fragments of dreams, none of them having either beginning or ending, but inviting me into an utterly bizarre and alien world, as through another dimension of which I was not aware in the mundane world beyond sleep. But I survived that restless night, if somewhat haggardly.

On the very next day I learned a most interesting fact from the architect who came out to discuss my plans for further renovation, a young man not given to the quaint beliefs about old houses common to isolated, rural areas. 'One who came to look at the house would never think,' he said, 'that it had a secret room – well hidden – would you?' he said, spreading his drawings before me.

'And has it?' I asked.

'Perhaps a "priest's hole",' he guessed. 'For runaway slaves.'

'I've never seen it.'

'Nor I. But look here . . .' And he showed me on the plans he had reconstructed from the foundations and the rooms as we knew them, that there was a space unaccounted for along the north wall upstairs, in the oldest part of the house. No priest's hole, certainly; there were no Papists among the Peabodys. But runaway slaves – perhaps. If so, however, how came it there so early, before there were enough slaves to make the run for Canada to justify the room's coming into being? No, not that either.

'Can you find it, do you think?' I asked.

'It has to be there.'

And so indeed it was. Cleverly concealed, though the absence of a window in the north wall of the bedroom ought to have warranted an earlier examination. The door to it was hidden in the finely-wrought carvings which decorated that entire wall, which was of red cedar; had one not known the room must have been there, one would hardly have seen the door which had no knob and worked only by pressure upon one of the carvings, which the architect found, not I, for I have never had an adeptness at things of that kind. However it lay rather within the province of an architect than my own and I paused only long enough to study the rusty mechanism of the door before stepping into the room.

It was a small confining space. Yet it was not as small as a priest's hole; a man could walk upright in it for a distance of ten feet or so, though the slant of the roof would cut off any walking in the direction opposed to it. The long way, yes; across to the wall, no. What was more, the room bore every sign of having been occupied in past time, for it was left undisturbed, there were still books and papers about, as well as chairs which had been used at a small desk against one wall.

The room presented the most singular appearance. Though it was small, its angles seemed to be awry, as if the builder were subtly determined to confound its owner. Moreover, there were curious designs drawn upon the floor, some of them actually cut into the planking in a crudely barbarous fashion, roughly circular in plan, with all manner of oddly repellent drawings around the outer and inner edges. There was a similar repulsiveness about the desk, for it was black, rather than brown, and it had the surprising appearance of having been burned; it looked, indeed, as if it served in more than the capacity of a desk. On it, moreover, was a stack of what looked at first glance to be very ancient books, bound in some sort of leather, as well as a manuscript of some kind, likewise bound.

There was little time for any examination, however, for the

architect was with me and, having seen all he wished, which was just sufficient to verify his suspicion of the room's existence, he was eager to be off.

'Shall we plan to eliminate it, cut in a window?' he asked, and added, 'Of course, you won't want to keep it.'

'I don't know,' I answered. 'I'm not sure. It depends on how old it is.'

If the room were as ancient as I thought it to be, then I would be quite naturally hesitant to destroy it. I wanted a chance to poke around it a little, to examine the old books. Besides, there was no haste; this decision did not need to be made at once; there were other things the architect could do before either of us need think about the hidden room upstairs. It was there that the matter rested.

I had fully intended to return to the room next day, but certain events intervened. In the first place, I spent another very troubled night, the victim of recurrent dreams of a most disturbing nature, for which I could not account, since I had never been given to dreams except as a concomitant of illness. These dreams were, perhaps not unnaturally, of my ancestors, particularly of one long-bearded old fellow, wearing a conical black hat of strange design, whose face, unfamiliar to me in dream, was in actuality that of my great-grandfather Asaph, as a row of family portraits in the lower hall verified next morning. This ancestor seemed to be involved in an extraordinary progression through the air, quite as if he were flying. I saw him walking through walls, walking on the air, silhouetted among treetops. And wherever he went, he was accompanied by a large black cat which had the same ability to transcend the laws of time and space. Nor did my dreams have any progression or even, each within itself, any unity; they were a mixed-up sequence of scenes in which my great-grandfather, his cat, his house, and his property took part as in unrelated tableaux. They were distinctly related to my dreams of the previous night, and accompanied again by all the extra-dimensional trappings of those first nocturnal experiences, differing only in that they possessed greater clarity. These dreams insistently disturbed me throughout the night.

I was thus in no mood to learn from the architect that there would be some further delay in the resumption of work at the Peabody place. He seemed reticent or reluctant to explain, but I pressed him to do so, until at last he admitted that the workmen he had hired had all notified him early this morning that none of them wished to work on this 'job'. Nevertheless, he assured me, he would have no difficulty hiring some inexpensive Polish or Italian labourers from Boston, if I would be a little patient with him. I had no alternative, but, in fact, I was not as much annoyed as I pretended to be, for I began to have certain doubts about the wisdom of making all the alterations I had intended. After all, a part of the old house must necessarily stand with no more than re-inforcement, for much of the charm of the old place lay in its age; I adjured him, therefore, to take his time, and went out to make such purchases as I had intended to make when I came into Wilbraham.

I had hardly begun to do so before I was aware of a most sullen attitude on the part of the natives. Whereas, heretofore, they had either paid me no attention at all, since many of them did not know me, or they had greeted me perfunctorily, if they had made my acquaintance, I found them on that morning of one mind – no one wished to speak to me or to be seen speaking to me. Even the storekeepers were unnecessarily short, if not downright unpleasant, their manner suggesting plainly that they would appreciate my taking my trade elsewhere. It was possible, I reflected, that they had learned of my plans to renovate the old Peabody house, and might be opposed to it on twin grounds – either that the renovation would contribute to the destruction of its charm, or that it would, on the other hand, give another and longer lease of life to a piece of property that surrounding farmers would much have preferred to cultivate, once the house and the woods were gone.

My first thoughts, however, soon gave way to indignation. I was not a pariah, and I did not deserve to be shunned like one, and when, finally, I stopped in at the office of Ahab Hopkins, I unburdened myself to him rather more volubly than was my custom, even though, as I could see, I made him uneasy.

'Ah, well, Mr Peabody,' he said, seeking to soothe my ruffled composure, 'I would not take that too seriously. After all, these people have had a grievous shock, and they are in an ugly, suspicious mood. Besides, they are basically a superstitious lot. I am an old man, and I have never known them to be otherwise.'

Hopkins's gravity gave me pause. 'A shock, you say. You must forgive me – I've heard nothing.'

He favoured me with a most curious look, at which I was quite taken aback. 'Mr Peabody, two miles up the road from your place lives a family by the name of Taylor. I know George well. They have ten children. Or perhaps I had better say "had". Last night, their second youngest, a child of slightly over two years of age, was taken from his bed and carried off without a trace.'

'I am sorry to hear it. But what has that got to do with me?'

'Nothing, I'm sure, Mr Peabody. But you're a comparative stranger here, and, well – you must know it sooner or later – the name of Peabody is not looked on with pleasure – in fact, I may say it is hated – by many people of the community.'

I was astounded and did not attempt to hide it. 'But why?'

'Because there are many people who believe every kind of gossip and muttered talk, no matter how ridiculous it is,' Hopkins answered. 'You are an old enough man to realise that it is so, even if you're unfamiliar with our rural countryside, Mr Peabody. There were all manner of stories common about your great-grandfather, when I was a child, and, since during the years of his incumbency of the homestead, there were certain ugly disappearances of little children, of whom no trace was ever found, there is possibly a natural inclination to connect these two events – a new Peabody on the homestead, and a recurrence of a kind of event associated with another Peabody's residence there.'

'Monstrous!' I cried.

'Undoubtedly,' Hopkins agreed with an almost perverse amiability, 'but so it is. Besides, it is now April. Walpurgis Night is scarce a month away.'

I fear my face must have been so blank as to disconcert him.

'Oh, come, Mr Peabody,' said Hopkins with false joviality, 'you are surely aware that your great-grandfather was considered to be a warlock!'

I took my leave of him, gravely disturbed. Despite my shock and outrage, despite my indignation at the manner in which the natives showed their scorn and – yes, fear – of me, I was even more upset by the nagging suspicion that there was a disquieting logic to the events of the previous night and this day. I had dreamed of my great-grandfather in strange terms indeed, and now I heard him spoken of in far more significant terms. I knew only enough to know that the natives had looked upon my great-grandfather superstitiously as the male counterpart of a witch – a warlock or wizard; by whatever name they called him, so they had seen him. I made no further attempt to be even decently courteous to the natives who turned their heads when I came walking toward them, but got into my car and drove out to the homestead. There my patience was still further tried, for I found nailed to my front door a crude warning – a sheet of tablet paper upon which some illiterate, ill-intentioned neighbour had scrawled in pencil: '*Git out – or els.*'

Possibly because of these distressing events, my sleep that night was far more troubled by dreams than it had been on previous nights. Save for one major difference – there was more continuity in the scenes I saw while I tossed in restless slumber. Again it was my great-grandfather, Asaph Peabody, who occupied them, but he seemed now to have grown so sinister in appearance as to be threatening, and his cat moved with him with the hair of its neck ruffled, its pointed ears forward, and tail erect – a monstrous creature, which glided or floated along beside or behind him. He carried something – something white, or flesh-coloured, but in the murkiness of my dream would not permit me to recognise it. He went through woods, over countryside, among trees; he travelled in narrow passageways, and once, I was certain, he was in a tomb or vault. I recognised, too, certain parts of the house. But he was not alone in his dreams – lingering always in the background was a shadowy, but monstrous Black Man – not a Negro, but a man of such vivid blackness as to be literally darker than night, but with flaming eyes which seemed to be of living fire. There were all manner of lesser creatures about the old man – bats, rats, hideous little beings which were half human, half rat. Moreover, I was given to auditory hallucinations simultaneously, for from time to time, I seemed to hear muffled crying, as if a child were in pain, and, at the same time, a hideous, cackling laughter, and a chanting voice saying: 'Asaph will *be* again. Asaph will *grow* again.'

Indeed, when at last I woke from this continuing nightmare, just as the dawn light was making itself manifest in the room, I could have sworn that the crying of a child still sounded in my ears, as if it came from within the very walls itself. I did not sleep again, but lay wide-eyed, wondering what the coming night would bring, and the next, and the next after that.

The coming of the Polish workmen from Boston put my dreams temporarily from my mind. They were a stolid, quiet lot. Their foreman, a thick-set man named Jon Cieciorka, was matter-of-fact and dictatorial with the men under him; he was a well-muscled fellow of fifty or thereabouts, and the three men whom he directed moved in haste at his command, as if they

feared his wrath. They had told the architect that they could no
come for a week, the foreman explained, but another job had
been postponed, and here they were; they had driven up from
Boston after sending the architect a telegram. But they had his
plans, and they knew what must be done.

Their very first act was to remove the plaster from the north
wall of the room immediately beneath the hidden room. They
had to work carefully, for the studding which supported the
second storey could not be disturbed, nor need it be. Plaster and
lathing, which, I saw as they began, was of that old-fashioned
kind made by hand, had to be taken off and replaced; the plaster
had begun to discolour and to break loose years before, so that
the room was scarcely habitable. It had been so, too, with that
corner of the house which I now occupied, but, since I had made
greater changes there, the alterations had taken longer.

I watched the men work for a little while, and had just become accustomed to the sounds of their pounding, when suddenly, they ceased. I waited a moment, and then started up and
went out into the hall. I was just in time to see all four of them,
clustered near the wall, cross themselves superstitiously, back
away a little, and then break and run from the house. Passing
me, Cieciorka flung an epithet at me in horror and anger. Then
they were out of the house, and while I stood as if rooted to the
spot, I heard their car start and leap away from my property.

Utterly bewildered, I turned towards where they had been
working. They had removed a considerable section of the plaster
and lathing; indeed, several of their tools were still scattered
about. In their work, they had exposed that section of the wall
which lay behind the baseboard, and all the accumulated de-
tritus of the years which had come to rest in that place. It was
not until I drew close to the wall that I saw what they must have
seen and understood what had sent these superstitious louts
running in fear and loathing from the house.

For at the base of the wall, behind the baseboard, there lay, among long yellowed papers half gnawed away by mice, yet still bearing on their surfaces the unmistakably cabalistic designs of some bygone day, among wicked implements of death and destruction – short, dagger-like knives rusted by what must surely have been blood – *the small skulls and bones of at least three children*!

I stared unbelievingly, for the superstitious nonsense I had heard only a day before from Ahab Hopkins now took on a more sinister cast. So much I realised on the instant. Children had disappeared during my great-grandfather's aegis; he had been suspected of wizardry, of witchcraft, of playing roles in which the sacrifice of little children was an integral part; now here, within the walls of his house, were such remains as lent weight to the native suspicions of his nefarious activities!

Once my initial shock had passed, I knew I must act with despatch. If this discovery were made known, then indeed my tenure here would be bitterly unhappy, made so by the god-fearing natives of the neighbourhood. Without hesitating further, I ran for a cardboard box and, returning to the wall with it, gathered up every vestige of bone I could find, and carried this gruesome burden to the family vault, where I emptied the bones into the cubicle which had once held the remains of Jedediah Peabody, now long since gone to dust. Fortunately, the small skulls disintegrated, so that anyone searching there would find only the remains of someone long dead, and only an expert would have been able to determine the origin of the bones which remained sufficiently unimpaired to offer any key. By the time any report from the Polish workmen came back to the architect, I would be able to deny the truth of them, though for this report I was destined to wait in vain, for the fear-ridden **Poles** never revealed to the architect a word of their real reason **for deserting** their job.

I did not wait to learn this from the architect, who was bound eventually to find someone who would undertake such alteration as I wished made, but guided by an instinct I did not know I possessed, I made my way to the hidden room, carrying a powerful flashlight, determined to subject it to the most painstaking examination. Almost at once upon entering it, however, I made a spine-chilling discovery; though the marks the architect and I had made in our brief foray into the room were still identifiably evident, there were other, more recent marks which suggested that someone – or something – had been in this room since I had last entered it. The marks were plain to be seen – of a man, bare of foot, and, equally unmistakably, the prints of a cat. But these were not the most terrifying evidences of some sinister occupation – they began out of the north-east corner of the curiously angled room, at a point where it was impossible for a man to stand, and scarcely high enough for a cat; yet it was here that they materialised in the room, and from this point that they came forward, proceeding in the direction of the black desk – where there was something far worse, though I did not notice it until I was almost upon the desk in following the footsteps.

The desk had been freshly stained. A small pool of some viscous fluid lay there, as if it had boiled up out of the wood – scarcely more than three inches in diameter, next to a mark in the dust as if the cat or a doll or a bundle of some kind had lain there. I stared at it, trying to determine what it might be in the glow of my flashlight, sending my light ceiling-ward to detect, if possible, any opening through which rain might have come, until I remembered that there had been no rainfall since my first and only visit to this strange secret room. Then I touched my index finger to the pool and held it in the light. The colour was red – the colour of blood – and simultaneously I knew without being told that this was what it was. Of how it came there I dared not think.

By this time the most terrifying conclusions were crowding to mind, but without any logic. I backed away from the desk, pausing only long enough to snatch up some of the leather-bound books, and the manuscript which reposed there; and with these in my possession, I retreated from the room into the more prosaic surroundings outside – where the rooms were not constructed of seemingly impossible angles, suggesting dimensions beyond the knowledge of mankind. I hastened almost guiltily to my quarters below, hugging the books carefully to my bosom.

Curiously, as soon as I opened the books, I had an uncanny conviction that I knew their contents. Yet I had never seen them before, nor, to the best of my knowledge, had I ever encountered such titles as *Malleus Maleficarum* and the *Daemonialitas* of Sinistrari. They dealt with witch-lore and wizardry, with all manner of spells and legends, with the destruction of witches and warlocks by fire, with their methods of travel – 'Among their chief operations are being bodily transported from place to place . . . seduced by the illusions and phantasms of devils, do actually, as they believe and profess, ride in the night-time on certain beasts . . . or simply walk upon the air out of the openings built for them and for none other. Satan himself deludes in dreams the mind which he holds captive, leading it through devious ways. . . . They take the unguent, which they made at the devil's instruction from the limbs of children, particularly of those whom they have killed, and anoint with it a chair or a broomstick; whereupon they are immediately carried up into the air, either by day or by night, and either visibly or, if they wish, invisibly . . .' But I read no more of this, and turned to Sinistrari.

Almost at once my eye fell upon this disturbing passage – '*Promittunt Diabolo statis temporibus sacrificia, et oblationes; singulis quindecim diebus, vel singulo mense saltem, necem alicujus infantis, aut mortale veneficium, et singulis hebdomadis alia mala in damnum humani generis, ut grandines, tempestates, incendia, mortem animalium . . .*' setting forth how warlocks and witches must bring about, at stated intervals, the murder of a child, or some other homicidal act of sorcery, the mere reading of which filled me with an indescribable sense of alarm, as a result of which I did no more than glance at the other books I had brought down, the *Vitae sophistrarum* of Eunapius, Anania's *De Natura Daemonum*, Stampa's *Fuga Satanae*, Bouget's *Discours des Sorciers*, and that untitled work by Olaus Magnus, bound in a smooth black leather, which only later I realised was human skin.

The mere possession of these books betokened a more than ordinary interest in the lore of witchcraft and wizardry; indeed, it was such manifest explanation for the superstitious beliefs about my great-grandfather which abounded in and about Wilbraham, that I understood at once why they should have persisted for so long. Yet there must have been something more, for few people could have known about these books. What more? The bones in the wall beneath the hidden chamber spoke damningly for some hideous connection between the Peabody house and the unsolved crimes of other years. Even so, this was surely not a public one. There must have been some overt feature of my great-grandfather's life which established the connection in their minds, other than his reclusiveness and his reputation for parsimony, of which I knew. There was not likely to be any key to the riddle among these things from the hidden room, but there might well be some clue in the files of the Wilbraham *Gazette*, which were available in the public library.

Accordingly, half an hour later found me in the stacks of that institution, searching through the back issues of the *Gazette*. This was a time-consuming effort, since it involved a blind search of issue after issue during the later years of my great-grandfather's life, and not at all certain to be rewarding, though the newspapers of his day were less hampered and bound by legal restrictions than those of my own time. I searched for over an hour without coming upon a single reference to Asaph Peabody, though I did pause to read accounts of the 'outrages' perpetrated upon people – primarily children – of the countryside in the vicinity of the Peabody place, invariably accompanied by editorial queries about the 'animal' which was 'said to be a large black creature of some kind, and it has been reported to be of different sizes – sometimes as large as a cat, and sometimes as big as a lion' – which was a circumstance no doubt due solely to the imagination of the reporting witnesses, who were principally children under ten, victims of mauling or biting, from which they had made their escape, happily more fortunate in this than younger children who had vanished without trace at intervals during the year in which I read: 1905. But throughout all this, there was no mention of my great-grandfather; and, indeed, there was nothing until the year of his death.

Then, and only then, did the editor of the *Gazette* put into print what must have represented the current belief about Asaph Peabody. 'Asaph Peabody is gone. He will long be remembered. There are those among us who have attributed to him powers which belonged rather more to an era in the past than to our own time. There was a Peabody among those charged at Salem; indeed, it was from Salem that Jedediah Peabody removed when he came to build his home near Wilbraham. The pattern of superstition knows no reason. It is perhaps mere coincidence that Asaph Peabody's old black cat has not been seen since his death, and it is undoubtedly mere ugly rumour that the Peabody coffin was not opened before interment because there was some alteration in the body tissues or in the conventions of burial to make such opening unwise. This is again lending credence to old wives' tales – that a warlock must be buried face downward and never thereafter disturbed, save by fire. . . .'

This was a strange, oblique method of writing. Yet it told me much, perhaps uncomfortably more than I had anticipated. My great-grandfather's cat had been looked upon as his familiar – for every witch or warlock has his personal devil in any shape it might care to assume. What more natural than my great-grandfather's cat should be mistaken for his familiar, for it had evidently in life been as constant a companion to him as it was in my dreams of the old man? The one disturbing note struck by the editorial comment lay in the reference to his interment, for I knew what the editor could have not have known – that Asaph Peabody had indeed been buried face downward. I knew more – that he had been disturbed, and should not have been. And I suspected yet more – that something other than myself walked at the old Peabody homestead, walking in my dreams and over the countryside and in the air!

That night, once more, the dreams came, accompanied by that same exaggerated sense of hearing, which made it seem as if I were attuned to cacophonous sound from other dimensions. Once again my great-grandfather went about his hideous business, but this time it seemed that his familiar, the cat, stopped several times and turned to face squarely at me, with a wickedly triumphant grin on its evil face. I saw the old man in a conical black hat and a long black robe walking from woodland seemingly through the wall of a house, coming forth into a darkened room, spare of furnishings, appearing then before a black altar, where the Black Man stood waiting for the sacrifice which was too horrible to watch, yet I had no alternative, for the power of my dreams was such that I must look upon this hellish deed. And I saw him and his cat and the Black Man again, this time in the midst of a deep forest, far from Wilbraham, together with many others, before a large outdoors altar, to celebrate the Black Mass and the orgies that followed upon it. But they were not always so clear; sometimes the dreams were only arrow-swift descents through unlimited chasms of strangely coloured twilight and bafflingly cacophonous sound, where gravity had no meaning, chasms utterly alien to nature, but in which I was always singularly perceptive on an extra-sensory plane, able to hear and see things I would never have been aware of while waking. Thus I heard the eldritch chants of the Black Mass, the screams of a dying child, the discordant music of pipes, the inverted prayers of homage, the orgiastic cries of celebrants, though I could not always see them. And on occasion, too, my dreams conveyed portions of conversations, snatches of words, meaningless of themselves, but capable of dark and disquieting explication.

'Shall he be chosen?'

'By Belial, by Beelzebub, by Sathanus . . .

'Of the blood of Jedediah, of the blood of Asaph, companioned by Balor.'

'Bring him to the Book!'

Then there were those curious figments of dreams in which I myself appeared to be taking part, particularly one in which I was being led, alternately by my great-grandfather and by the cat, to a great black-bound book in which were written names in glowing fire, countersigned in blood, and which I was instructed to sign, my great-grandfather guiding my hand, while the cat, whom I heard Asaph Peabody call Balor, having clawed at my wrist to produce blood into which to dip the pen, capered and danced about. There was about this dream one aspect which had a more disturbing bond to reality. In the course of the way through the woods to the meeting place of the coven, the path led beside a marsh where we walked in the black mud of the sedge, near to foetid slough in a place where there was a charnel odour of decay; I sank into the mud repeatedly in that place, though neither the cat nor great-grandfather seemed to more than float upon its surface.

And in the morning, when at last I awoke after sleeping over long, I found upon my shoes, which had been clean when I went to bed, a drying black mud which was the substance of my dream. I started from bed at the sight of them, and followed the tracks they had made easily enough, tracing them backwards, out of the room, up the stairs, into the hidden room on the second storey – and, once there, inexorably, to that same bewitched corner of peculiar angle from which the footprints in the dust had led into the room! I stared in disbelief, yet my eyes did not deceive me. This was madness, but it could not be denied. Nor could the scratch on my wrist be wished out of existence.

I literally reeled from the hidden room, beginning at last vaguely to understand why my parents had been loath to sell the Peabody homestead; something had come down to them of its lore from my grandfather, for it must have been he who had had great-grandfather buried with his face downward in the family crypt. And, however much they may have scorned the superstitious lore they had inherited, they were unwilling to chance its defiance. I understood, too, why periods of rental had failed, for the house itself was a sort of focal point for forces beyond the comprehension or control of any one person, if indeed any human being; and I knew that I was already infected with the aura of the habitation, that, indeed, in a sense I was a prisoner of the house and its evil history.

I now sought the only avenue of further information open to me. The manuscript of the journal kept by my great-grandfather. I hastened to it directly, without pausing for breakfast, and found it to be a sequence of notes, set down in his flowing script, together with clippings from letters, newspapers, magazines, and even books, which had seemed to him pertinent, though these were peculiarly unconnected, yet all dealing with inexplicable events – doubtless, in great-grandfather's eyes, sharing a common origin in witchcraft. His own notes were spare, yet revealing.

'Did what had to be done today. J taking on flesh, incredibly. But this is part of the lore. Once turned over, all begins again. The familiar returns, and the clay takes shape again a little more with each sacrifice. To turn him back would be futile now. There is only the fire.'

And again:

'Something in the house. A cat? I see him, but cannot catch him.'

'Definitely a black cat. Where he came from, I do not know. Disturbing dreams. Twice at a Black Mass.'

'In dream the cat led me to the Black Book. Signed.'

'In dream an imp called Balor. A handsome fellow. Explained the bondage.'

And soon after:

'Balor came to me today. I would not have guessed him the same. He is as handsome a cat as he was a young imp. I asked him whether this was the same form in which he had served J. He indicated that it was. Led the way to the corner with a strange and extra-dimensional angle which is the door to outside. J had so constructed it. Showed me how to walk through it . . .

I could bear to read no further. Already I had read far too much.

I knew now what had happened to the remains of Jedediah Peabody. And I knew what I must do. However fearful I was of what I must find, I went without delay to the Peabody crypt, entered it, and forced myself to go to the coffin of my great-grandfather. There, for the first time, I noticed the bronze plate attached beneath the name of Asaph Peabody, and the engraving upon it: 'Woe betide him who disturbs his rest!'

Then I raised the lid.

Though I had every reason to expect what I saw, I was horrified no less. For the bones I had last seen were terribly altered. What had been but bone and fragments, dust and tatters of clothing, had begun a shocking alteration. Flesh was beginning to grow once again on the remains of my great-grandfather, Asaph Peabody – flesh that took its origin from the evil upon which he had begun to live anew when I had so witlessly turned over his mortal remains – and from that other thing within his coffin – the poor, shrivelling body of that child which, though it had vanished from the home of George Taylor less than ten days ago, already had a leathern, parchment appearance, as if it were drained of all substance, and partially mummified!

I fled the vault, numb with horror, but only to build the pyre I knew I must gather together. I worked feverishly, in haste lest someone surprise me at my labours, though I knew that the people had shunned the Peabody homestead for decades. And then, this done, I laboured alone to drag Åsaph Peabody's coffin and its hellish contents to the pyre, just as, decades before, Asaph himself had done to Jedediah's coffin and what it had contained! Then I stood by, while the holocaust consumed coffin and contents, so that I alone heard the high shrill wail of rage which rose from the flames like the ghost of a scream.

All that night the diminishing ashes of that pyre still glowed. I saw it from the windows of the house.

And inside, I saw something else.

A black cat which came to the door of my quarters and leered wickedly in at me.

And I remembered the path through the marsh I had taken, the muddied footprints, the mud on my shoes. I remembered the scratch on my wrist, and the Black Book I had signed. Even as Asaph Peabody had signed it.

I turned to where the cat lurked in the shadows and called it gently. 'Balor!'

It came and sat on its haunches just inside the door.

I took my revolver from the drawer of my desk and deliberately shot it.

It kept right on regarding me. Not so much as a whisker twitched.

Balor. One of the lesser devils.

This, then, was the Peabody heritage. The house, the grounds, the woods – these were only the superficial, material aspects of

the extra-dimensional angles in the hidden room, the path
through the marsh to the coven, the signatures in the Black
Book....

*Who, I wonder, after I am dead, if I am buried as the others
were, will turn me over?*

THE OUTSIDER

UNHAPPY is he to whom the memories of childhood bring only
fear and sadness. Wretched is he who looks back upon lone
hours in vast and dismal chambers with brown hangings and
maddening rows of antique books, or upon awed watches in
twilight groves of grotesque, gigantic, and vine-encumbered
trees that silently wave twisted branches far aloft. Such a lot
the gods gave to me – to me, the dazed, the disappointed; the
barren, the broken. And yet I am strangely content and cling
desperately to those withered memories, when my mind momentarily threatens to reach beyond to *the other*.

I know not where I was born, save that the castle was infinitely old and infinitely horrible, full of dark passages and having high ceilings where the eye could find only cobwebs and

shadows. The stones in the crumbling corridors seemed always hideously damp, and there was an accursed smell everywhere, as of the piled-up corpses of dead generations. It was never light, so that I used sometimes to light candles and gaze steadily at them for relief, nor was there any sun outdoors, since the terrible trees grew high above the topmost accessible tower. There was one black tower which reached above the trees into the unknown outer sky, but that was partly ruined and could not be ascended save by a well-nigh impossible climb up the sheer wall, stone by stone.

I must have lived years in this place, but I cannot measure the time. Beings must have cared for my needs, yet I cannot recall any person except myself, or anything alive but the noiseless rats and bats and spiders. I think that whoever nursed me must have been shockingly aged, since my first conception of a living person was that of something mockingly like myself, yet distorted, shrivelled, and decaying like the castle. To me there was nothing grotesque in the bones and skeletons that strewed some of the stone crypts deep down among the foundations. I fantastically associated these things with everyday events, and thought them more natural than the coloured pictures of living beings which I found in many of the mouldy books. From such books I learned all that I know. No teacher urged or guided me, and I do not recall hearing any human voice in all those years – not even my own; for although I had read of speech, I had never thought to try to speak aloud. My aspect was a matter equally unthought of, for there were no mirrors in the castle, and I merely regarded myself by instinct as akin to the youthful figures I saw drawn and painted in the books. I felt conscious of youth because I remembered so little.

Outside, across the putrid moat and under the dark mute trees, I would often lie and dream for hours about what I read in the books; and would longingly picture myself amidst gay crowds in the sunny world beyond the endless forests. Once I tried to escape from the forest, but as I went further from the castle the shade grew denser and the air more filled with brooding fear; so that I ran frantically back lest I lose my way in a labyrinth of nighted silence.

So through endless twilights I dreamed and waited, though I knew not what I waited for. Then in the shadowy solitude my longing for light grew so frantic that I could rest no more, and I lifted entreating hands to the single black ruined tower that reached above the forest into the unknown outer sky. And at last I resolved to scale that tower, fall though I might; since it were better to glimpse the sky and perish, than to live without ever beholding day.

In the dank twilight I climbed the worn and aged stone stairs till I reached the level where they ceased, and thereafter clung perilously to small footholds leading upwards. Ghastly and terrible was that dead, stairless cylinder of rock; black, ruined, and deserted, and sinister with startled bats whose wings made no noise. But more ghastly and terrible still was the slowness of my progress; for climb as I might, the darkness overhead grew no thinner, and a new chill as of haunted and venerable mould assailed me. I shivered as I wondered why I did not reach the light, and would have looked down had I dared. I fancied that night had come suddenly upon me, and vainly groped with one free hand for a window embrasure, that I might peer out and above, and try to judge the height I had attained.

All at once, after an infinity of awesome, sightless crawling up that concave and desperate precipice, I felt my head touch a solid thing, and I knew I must have gained the roof, or at least some kind of floor. In the darkness I raised my free hand and tested the barrier, finding it stone and immovable. Then came a deadly circuit of the tower, clinging to whatever holds the slimy wall could give; till finally my testing hand found the barrier yielding, and I turned upwards again, pushing the slab or door with my head as I used both hands in my fearful ascent. There was no light revealed above, and as my hands went higher I knew that my climb was for the nonce ended;

since the slab was the trap-door of an aperture leading to a level stone surface of greater circumference than the lower tower, no doubt the floor of some lofty and capacious observation chamber. I crawled through carefully, and tried to prevent the heavy slab from falling back into place, but failed in the latter attempt. As I lay exhausted on the stone floor I heard the eerie echoes of its fall, but hoped when necessary to pry it up again.

Believing I was now at prodigious height, far above the accursed branches of the wood, I dragged myself up from the floor and fumbled about for windows, that I might look for the first time upon the sky, and the moon and stars of which I had read. But on every hand I was disappointed; since all that I found were vast shelves of marble, bearing odious oblong boxes of disturbing size. More and more I reflected, and wondered what hoary secrets might abide in this high apartment so many eons cut off from the castle below. Then unexpectedly my hands came upon a doorway, where hung a portal of stone, rough with strange chiselling. Trying it, I found it locked; but with a supreme burst of strength I overcame all obstacles and dragged it open inwards. As I did so there came to me the purest ecstasy I have ever known; for shining tranquilly through an ornate grating of iron, and down a short stone passageway of steps that ascended from the newly found doorway, was the radiant full moon, which I had never before seen save in dreams and in vague visions I dared not call memories.

Fancying now that I had attained the very pinnacle of the castle, I commenced to rush up the few steps beyond the door; but the sudden veiling of the moon by a cloud caused me to stumble, and I felt my way more slowly in the dark. It was still very dark when I reached the grating – which I tried carefully and found unlocked, but which I did not open for fear of falling from the amazing height to which I had climbed. Then the moon came out.

Most demoniacal of all shocks is that of the abysmally unexpected and grotesquely unbelievable. Nothing I had before undergone could compare in terror with what I now saw; with the bizarre marvels that sight implied. The sight itself was as simple as it was stupefying, for it was merely this: instead of a dizzying prospect of treetops seen from a lofty eminence, there stretched around me on the level through the grating nothing less than *the solid ground*, decked and diversified by marble slabs and columns, and overshadowed by an ancient stone church, whose ruined spire gleamed spectrally in the moonlight.

Half unconscious, I opened the grating and staggered out upon the white gravel path that stretched away in two directions. My mind, stunned and chaotic as it was, still held the frantic craving for light; and not even the fantastic wonder which had happened could stay my course. I neither knew nor cared whether my experience was insanity, dreaming, or magic; but was determined to gaze on brilliance and gaiety at any cost. I knew not who I was nor what I was, nor what my surroundings might be; though as I continued to stumble along I became conscious of a kind of fearsome latent memory that made my progress not wholly fortuitous. I passed under an arch out of that region of slabs and columns, and wandered through the open country; sometimes following the visible road, but sometimes leaving it curiously to tread across meadows where only occasional ruins bespoke the ancient presence of a forgotten road. Once I swam across a swift river where crumbling, mossy masonry told of a bridge long vanished.

Over two hours must have passed before I reached what seemed to be my goal, a venerable ivied castle in a thickly wooded park, maddeningly familiar, yet full of perplexing strangeness to me. I saw that the moat was filled in, and that some of the well-known towers were demolished; whilst new wings existed to confuse the beholder. But what I observed with chief interest and delight were the open windows – gorgeously ablaze with light and sending forth sound of the gayest revelry. Advancing to one of these I looked in and saw an oddly dressed company, indeed; making merry, and speaking brightly to one another. I had never, seemingly, heard human speech before and could guess only vaguely what was said. Some of the faces seemed to hold expressions that brought up incredibly remote recollections, others were utterly alien.

I now stepped through the low windows into the brilliantly lighted room, stepping as I did so from my single bright moment of hope to my blackest convulsion of despair and realisation. The nightmare was quick to come, for as I entered, there occurred immediately one of the most terrifying demonstrations I had ever conceived. Scarcely had I crossed the sill when there descended upon the whole company a sudden and unheralded fear of hideous intensity, distorting every face and evoking the most horrible screams from nearly every throat. Flight was universal, and in the clamour and panic several fell in a swoon and were dragged away by their madly fleeing companions. Many covered their eyes with their hands, and plunged blindly and awkwardly in their race to escape, over-turning furniture and stumbling against the walls before they managed to reach one of the many doors.

The cries were shocking; and as I stood in the brilliant apartment alone and dazed, listening to their vanishing echoes, I trembled at the thought of what might be lurking near me unseen. At a casual inspection the room seemed deserted, but when I moved towards one of the alcoves I thought I detected a presence there – a hint of motion beyond the golden-arched doorway leading to another and somewhat similar room. As I approached the arch I began to perceive the presence more clearly; and then, with the first and last sound I ever uttered – a ghastly ululation that revolted me almost as poignantly as its noxious cause – I beheld in full, frightful vividness the inconceivable, indescribable, and unmentionable monstrosity which had by its simple appearance changed a merry company to a herd of delirious fugitives.

I cannot even hint what it was like, for it was a compound of all that is unclean, uncanny, unwelcome, abnormal, and detestable. It was the ghoulish shade of decay, antiquity, and desolution, the putrid, dripping eidolon of unwholesome revelation, the awful baring of that which the merciful earth should always hide. God knows it was not of this world – or no longer of this world – yet to my horror I saw in its eaten-away and bone-revealing outlines a leering abhorrent travesty of the human shape; and in its mouldy, disintergrating apparel an unspeakable quality that chilled me even more.

I was almost paralysed, but not too much so to make a feeble effort towards flight; a backward stumble which failed to break the spell in which the nameless, voiceless monster held me. My eyes bewitched by the glassy orbs which stared loathsomely into them refused to close; though they were mercifully blurred and showed the terrible object but indistinctly after the first shock. I tried to raise my hand to shut out the sight, yet so stunned were my nerves that my arm could not fully obey my will. The attempt, however, was enough to disturb my balance, so that I had to stagger forward several steps to avoid falling. As I did so I became suddenly and agonisingly aware of the *nearness* of the carrion thing, whose hideous hollow breathing I half fancied I could hear. Nearly mad, I found myself yet able to throw out a hand to ward off the fetid apparition which pressed so close; when in one cataclysmic second of cosmic nightmarishness and hellish accident *my fingers touched the rotting outstretched paw of the monster beneath the golden arch.*

I did not shriek, but all the fiendish ghouls that ride the nightwind shrieked for me as in that same second there crashed down upon my mind a single and fleeting avalanche of soul-annihilating memory. I knew in that second all that had been; I remembered beyond the frightful castle and the trees, and recognized the altered edifice in which I now stood; I recognised, most terrible of all, the unholy abomination that stood leering before me as I withdrew my sullied fingers from its own.

But in the cosmos there is balm as well as bitterness, and

that balm is nepenthe. In the supreme horror of that second I forgot what had horrified me, and the burst of black memory vanished in the chaos of echoing images. In a dream I fled from that haunted and accursed pile, and ran swiftly and silently in the moonlight. When I returned to the churchyard place of marble and went down the steps I found the stone trap-door immovable; but I was not sorry, for I had hated the antique castle and the trees. Now I ride with the mocking and friendly ghouls on the night wind, and play by day amongst the catacombs of Nephren-Ka in the sealed and unknown valley of Hadoth by the Nile. I know that light is not for me, save that of the moon over the rock tombs of Neb, nor any gaiety save the unnamed feasts of Nitokris beneath the Great Pyramid; yet in my new wildness and freedom I almost welcome the bitterness of alienage.

For although nepenthe has calmed me, I know always that I am an outsider; a stranger in this century and among those who are still men. This I have known ever since I stretched out my fingers to the abomination within that great gilded frame; stretched out my fingers and touched *a cold and unyielding surface of polished glass.*

THE NAMELESS CITY

WHEN I drew nigh the nameless city I knew it was accursed. I was travelling in a parched and terrible valley under the moon, and afar I saw it protruding uncannily above the sands as parts of a corpse may protrude from an ill-made grave. Fear spoke from the age-worn stones of this hoary survivor of the deluge, this great-grandmother of the oldest pyramid; and a viewless aura repelled me and bade me retreat from antique and sinister secrets that no man should see, and no man else had ever dared to see.

Remote in the desert of Araby lies the nameless city, crumbling and inarticulate, its low walls nearly hidden by the sands of uncounted ages. It must have been thus before the first stones of Memphis were laid, and while the bricks of Babylon were yet unbaked. There is no legend so old as to give it a name, or to recall that it was ever alive; but it is told of in whispers around campfires and muttered about by grandmas in the tents of sheiks so that all the tribes shun it without wholly knowing why. It was of this place that Abdul Alhazred, the mad poet, dreamed on the night before he sang his unexplainable couplet :

"That is not dead which can eternal lie,
And with strange aeons even death may die."

I should have known that the Arabs had good reason for

shunning the nameless city, the city told of in strange tales but seen by no living man, yet I defied them and went into the untrodden waste with my camel. I alone have seen it, and that is why no other face bears such hideous lines of fear as mine; why no other man shivers so horribly when the night wind rattles the windows. When I came upon it in the ghastly stillness of unending sleep it looked at me, chilly from the rays of a cold moon amidst the desert's heat. And as I returned its look I forgot my triumph at finding it, and stopped still with my camel to wait for the dawn.

For hours I waited, till the east grew grey and the stars faded, and the grey turned to roseate light edged with gold. I heard a moaning and saw a storm of sand stirring among the antique stones though the sky was clear and the vast reaches of the desert still. Then suddenly above the desert's far rim came the blazing edge of the sun, seen through the tiny sandstorm which was passing away, and in my fevered state I fancied that from some remote depth there came a crash of musical metal to hail the fiery disc as Memnon hails it from the banks of the Nile. My ears rang and my imagination seethed as I led my camel slowly across the sand to that unvocal stone place; that place too old for Egypt and Meroe to remember; that place which I alone of living men had seen.

In and out amongst the shapeless foundations of houses and places I wandered, finding never a carving or inscription to tell of these men, if men they were, who built this city and dwelt therein so long ago. The antiquity of the spot was unwholesome, and I longed to encounter some sign or device to prove that the city was indeed fashioned by mankind. There were certain *proportions* and *dimensions* in the ruins which I did not like. I had with me many tools, and dug much within the walls of the obliterated edifices; but progress was slow, and nothing significant was revealed. When night and the moon returned I felt a chill wind which brought new fear, so that I did not dare to remain in the city. And as I went outside the antique walls to sleep, a small sighing sandstorm gathered behind me, blowing over the grey stones though the moon was bright and most of the desert still.

I awakened just at dawn from a pageant of horrible dreams, my ears ringing as from some metallic peal. I saw the sun peering redly through the last gusts of a little sandstorm that hovered over the nameless city, and marked the quietness of the rest of the landscape. Once more I ventured within those brooding ruins that swelled beneath the sand like an ogre under a coverlet, and again dug vainly for relics of the forgotten race. At noon I rested, and in the afternoon I spent much time tracing the walls and bygone streets, and the outlines of the nearly vanished buildings. I saw that the city had been mighty indeed, and wondered at the sources of its greatness. To myself I pictured all the splendours of an age so distant that Chaldaea could not recall it, and thought of Sarnath the Doomed, that stood in the land Mnar when mankind was young, and of Ib, that was carven of grey stone before mankind existed.

All at once I came upon a place where the bed rock rose stark through the sand and formed a low cliff; and here I saw with joy what seemed to promise further traces of the antediluvian people. Hewn rudely on the face of the cliff were the unmistakable façades of several small, squat rock houses or temples; whose interiors may preserve many secrets of ages too remote for calculation, though sandstorms had long since effaced any carvings which may have been outside.

Very low and sand-choked were all of the dark apertures near me, but I cleared one with my spade and crawled through it, carrying a torch to reveal whatever mysteries it might hold. When I was inside I saw that the cavern was indeed a temple, and beheld plain signs of the race that had lived and worshipped before the desert was a desert. Primitive altars, pillars, and niches, all curiously low, were not absent; and though I saw no sculptures nor frescoes, there were many singular stones clearly shaped into symbols by artificial means. The lowness of the chiselled chamber was very strange, for I could hardly kneel upright; but the area was so great that my torch showed only part of it at a time. I shuddered oddly in some of the far corners; for certain altars and stones suggested forgotten rites of terrible, revolting, and inexplicable nature and made me wonder what manner of men could have made and frequented such a temple. When I had seen all that the place contained, I crawled out again, avid to find what the other temples might yield.

Night had now approached, yet the tangible things I had seen made curiosity stronger than fear, so that I did not flee from the long moon-cast shadows that had daunted me when first I saw the nameless city. In the twilight I cleared another aperture and with a new torch crawled into it, finding more vague stones and symbols, though nothing more definite than the other temple had contained. The room was just as low, but much less broad, ending in a very narrow passage crowded with obscure and cryptical shrines. About these shrines I was prying when the noise of a wind and my camel outside broke through the stillness and drew me forth to see what could have frightened the beast.

The moon was gleaming vividly over the primitive ruins, lighting a dense cloud of sand that seemed blown by a strong but decreasing wind from some point along the cliff ahead of me. I knew it was this chilly, sandy wind which had disturbed the camel, and was about to lead him to a place of better shelter when I chanced to glance up and saw that there was no wind atop the cliff. This astonished me and made me fearful again, but I immediately recalled the sudden local winds that I had seen and heard before at sunrise and sunset, and judged it was a normal thing. I decided it came from some rock fissure leading to a cave, and watched the troubled sand to trace it to its source; soon perceiving that it came from the black orifice of a temple a long distance south of me, almost out of sight. Against the choking sand-cloud I plodded towards this temple, which as I neared it loomed larger than the rest, and showed a doorway far less clogged with caked sand. I would have entered had not the terrific force of the icy wind almost quenched my torch. It poured madly out of the dark door, sighing uncannily as it ruffled the sand and spread among the weird ruins. Soon it grew fainter and the sand grew more and more still, till finally all was at rest again; but a presence seemed stalking among the spectral stones of the city, and when I glanced at the moon it seemed to quiver as though mirrored in unquiet water. I was more afraid than I could explain, but not enough to dull my thirst for wonder; so as soon as the wind was quite gone I crossed into the dark chamber from which it had come.

This temple, as I had fancied from the outside, was larger than either of those I had visited before; and was presumably a natural cavern since it bore winds from some region beyond. Here I could stand quite upright, but saw that the stones and altars were as low as those in the other temples. On the walls and roof I beheld for the first time some traces of the pictorial art of the ancient race, curious curling streaks of paint that had almost faded or crumbled away; and on two of the altars I saw with rising excitement a maze of well-fashioned curvilinear carvings. As I held my torch aloft it seemed to me that the shape of the roof was too regular to be natural, and I wondered what the prehistoric cutters of stone had first worked upon. Their engineering skill must have been vast.

Then a brighter flare of the fantastic flame showed that for which I had been seeking, the opening to those remoter abysses whence the sudden wind had blown; and I grew faint when I saw that it was a small and plainly artificial door chiselled in the solid rock. I thrust my torch within, beholding a black tunnel with the roof arching low over a rough flight of very small, numerous and steeply descending steps. I shall always see those steps in my dreams, for I came to learn what they meant. At the time I hardly knew whether to call them steps or mere footholds in a precipitous descent. My mind was whirling with mad thoughts, and the words and warnings of Arab prophets seemed to float across the desert from the land that men know to the nameless city that men dare not know. Yet I hesitated only a moment before advancing through the portal and commencing to climb cautiously down the steep passage, feet first, as though on a ladder.

It is only in the terrible phantasms of drugs of delirium that any other man can have such a descent as mine. The narrow passage led infinitely down like some hideous haunted well, and the torch I held about my head could not light the unknown depths towards which I was crawling. I lost track of the hours and forgot to consult my watch, thought I was frightened when I thought of the distance I must be traversing. There were changes of direction and of steepness; and once I came to a long, low, level passage where I had to wriggle feet first along the rocky floor, holding the torch at arm's length beyond my head. The place was not high enough for kneeling. After that were more of the steep steps, and I was still scrambling down interminably when my failing torch died out. I do not think I noticed it at the time, for when I did notice it I was still holding it above me as if it were ablaze. I was quite unbalanced with that instinct for the strange and the unknown which had made me a wanderer upon earth and a haunter of far, ancient, and forbidden places.

In the darkness there flashed before my mind fragments of my cherished treasury of daemoniac lore; sentences from Alhazred the mad Arab, paragraphs from the apocryphal nightmares of Damascius, and infamous lines from the delirious "Image du Monde" of Gauthier de Metz. I repeated queer extracts, and muttered of Afrasiab and the daemons that floated with him down the Oxus; later chanting over and over again a phrase from one of Lord Dunsany's tales – "The unreverberate blackness of the abyss." Once when the descent grew amazingly steep I recited something in sing-song from Thomas Moore until I feared to recite more :

"A reservoir of darkness, black
As witches' cauldrons are, when fill'd
With moon-drugs in th' eclipse distill'd.
Leaning to look if foot might pass
Down thro' that chasm, I saw, beneath,
As far as vision could explore,
The jetty sides as smooth as glass,
Looking as if just varnished o'er
With that dark pitch the Seat of Death
Throws out upon its slimy shore."

Time had quite ceased to exist when my feet again felt a level floor, and I found myself in a place slightly higher than the rooms in the two smaller temples now so incalculably far above my head. I could not quite stand, but could kneel upright, and in the dark I shuffled and crept hither and thither at random. I soon knew that I was in a narrow passage whose walls were lined with cases of wood having glass fronts. As in that Palaeozoic and abysmal place I felt of such things as polished wood and glass I shuddered at the possible implications. The cases were apparently ranged along each side of the passage at regular intervals, and were oblong and horizontal, hideously like coffins in shape and size. When I tried to move two or three for further examination, I found that they were firmly fastened.

I saw that the passage was a long one, so floundered ahead rapidly in a creeping run that would have seemed horrible had any eye watched me in the blackness; crossing from side to side occasionally to feel of my surroundings and be sure the walls and rows of cases still stretched on. Man is so used to thinking visually that I almost forgot the darkness and pictured the endless corridor of wood and glass in its low-studded monotony as though I saw it. And then in a moment of indescribable emotion I did see it.

Just when my fancy merged into real sight I cannot tell : but there came a gradual glow ahead, and all at once I knew that I saw the dim outlines of the corridor and the cases, revealed by some unknown subterranean phosphorescence. For a little while all was exactly as I had imagined it, since the glow was very faint; but as I mechanically kept stumbling ahead into the stronger light I realized that my fancy had been but feeble. This hall was no relic of crudity like the temples in the city above, but a monument of the most magnificent and exotic art. Rich, vivid, and daringly fantastic designs and pictures formed a continuous scheme of mural painting whose lines and colours were beyond description. The cases were of a strange golden wood, with fronts of exquisite glass, and containing the mummified forms of creatures outreaching in grotesqueness the most chaotic dreams of man.

To convey any idea of these monstrosities is impossible. They were of the reptile kind, with body lines suggesting sometimes the crocodile, sometimes the seal, but more often nothing of which either the naturalist or the palaeontologist ever heard. In size they approximated a small man, and their fore-legs' bore delicate and evident feet curiously like human hands and fingers. But strangest of all were their heads, which presented a contour violating all known biological principles. To nothing can such things be well compared – in one flash I thought of comparisons as varied as the cat, the bulldog, the mythic Satyr, and the human being. Not Jove himself had had so colossal and protuberant a forehead, yet the horns and the noselessness and the alligator-like jaw placed the things outside all established categories. I debated for a time on the reality of the mummies, half-suspecting they were artificial idols; but soon decided they were indeed some palaeogean species which had lived when the nameless city was alive. To crown their grotesqueness, most of them were gorgeously enrobed in the costliest of fabrics, and lavishly laden with ornaments of gold, jewels, and unknown shining metals.

The importance of these crawling creatures must have been vast, for they held first place among the wild designs on the frescoed walls and ceiling. With matchless skill had the artist drawn them in a world of their own, wherein they had cities and gardens fashioned to suit their dimensions; and I could not help but think that their pictured history was allegorical, perhaps showing the progress of the race that worshipped them. These creatures, I said to myself, were to the men of the nameless city what the she-wolf was to Rome, or some totem-beast is to a tribe of Indians.

Holding this view, I could trace roughly a wonderful epic of the nameless city; the tale of a mighty sea-coast metropolis that ruled the world before Africa rose out of the waves, and of its struggles as the sea shrank away, and the desert crept into the fertile valley that held it. I saw its wars and triumphs, its troubles and defeats, and afterwards its terrible fight against the desert when thousands of its people – here represented in allegory by the grotesque reptiles – were driven to chisel their way down through the rocks in some marvellous manner to another world whereof their prophets had told them. It was all vividly weird and realistic, and its connection with the awesome descent I had made was unmistakable. I even recognized the passages.

As I crept along the corridor toward the brighter light I saw later stages of the painted epic – the leave-taking of the race that had dwelt in the nameless city and the valley around for ten million years; the race whose souls shrank from quitting scenes their bodies had known so long where they had settled as nomads in the earth's youth, hewing in the virgin rock those primal shrines at which they had never ceased to worship. Now that the light was better I studied the pictures more closely and, remembering that the strange reptiles must represent the unknown men, pondered upon the customs of the nameless city. Many things were peculiar and inexplicable. The civilization, which included a written alphabet, had seemingly risen to a higher order than those immeasurably later civilizations of Egypt and Chaldea, yet there were curious omissions. I could, for example, find no pictures to represent deaths or funeral customs, save such as were related to wars, violence, and plagues; and I wondered at the reticence shown concerning natural death. It was as though an ideal of immortality had been fostered as a cheering illusion.

Still nearer the end of the passage were painted scenes of the utmost picturesqueness and extravagance : contrasted views of the nameless city in its desertion and growing ruin, and of the strange new realm of paradise to which the race had hewed its way through the stone. In these views the city and the desert valley were shown always by moonlight, a golden nimbus hovering over the fallen walls and half-revealing the splendid perfection of former times, shown spectrally and elusively by the artist. The paradisal scenes were almost too extravagant to be believed; portraying a hidden world of eternal day filled with glorious cities and ethereal hills and valleys. At the very last I thought I saw signs of an artistic anticlimax. The paintings were less skilful, and much more bizarre than even the wildest of the earlier scenes. They seemed to record a slow decadence of the ancient stock, coupled with a growing ferocity towards the outside world from which it was driven by the desert. The forms of the people – always represented by the sacred reptiles – appeared to be gradually wasting away, though their spirit was shewn hovering about the ruins by moonlight gained in proportion. Emaciated priests, displayed as reptiles in ornate robes, cursed the upper air and all who breathed it; and one terrible final scene showed a primitive-looking man, perhaps a pioneer of ancient Irem, the City of Pillars, torn to pieces by members of the elder race. I remember how the Arabs fear the nameless city, and was glad that beyond this place the grey walls and ceiling were bare.

As I viewed the pageant of mural history I had approached very closely the end of the low-ceilinged hall, and was aware of a gate through which came all of the illuminating phosphorescence. Creeping up to it, I cried aloud in transcendent amazement at what lay beyond; for instead of other and brighter chambers there was only an illimitable void of uniform radiance, such as one might fancy when gazing down from the peak of Mount Everest upon a sea of sunlit mist. Behind me was a passage so cramped that I could not stand upright in it; before me was an infinity of subterranean effulgence.

Reaching down from the passage into the abyss was the head of a steep flight of steps – small numerous steps like those of the black passages I had traversed – but after a few feet the glowing vapours concealed everything. Swung back open against the left-hand wall of the passage was a massive door of brass, incredibly thick and decorated with fantastic bas-reliefs, which could if closed shut the whole inner world of light away from the vaults and passages of rock. I looked at the steps, and for the nonce dared not try them. I touched the open brass door, and could not move it. Then I sank prone to the stone floor, my mind aflame with prodigious reflections which not even a death-like exhaustion could banish.

As I lay still with closed eyes, free to ponder, many things I had lightly noted in the frescoes came back to me with new and terrible significance – scenes representing the nameless city in its heyday – the vegetation of the valley around it, and the distant lands with which its merchants traded. The allegory of the crawling creatures puzzled me by its universal prominence, and I wondered that it would be so closely followed in a pictured history of such importance.

In the frescoes the nameless city had been shown in proportions fitted to the reptiles. I wondered what its real proportions and magnificence had been, and reflected a moment on certain oddities I had noticed in the ruins. I thought curiously of the lowness of the primal temples and of the underground corridor, which were doubtless hewn thus out of deference to the reptiles deities there honoured; though it perforce reduced the worshippers to crawling. Perhaps the very rites here involved a crawling in imitation of the creatures. No religious theory, however, could easily explain why the level passages in that awesome descent should be as low as the temples – or lower, since one could not even kneel in it. As I thought of the crawling creatures, whose hideous mummified forms were so close to me, I felt a new throb of fear. Mental associations are curious, and I shrank from the idea that except for the poor primitive man torn to pieces in the last painting, mine was the only human form amidst the many relics and symbols of primordial life.

But as always in my strange and roving existence, wonder soon drove out fear; for the luminous abyss and what it might contain presented a problem worthy of the greatest explorer. That a weird world of mystery lay far down that flight of peculiarly small steps I could not doubt, and I hoped to find there those human memorials which the painted corridor had failed to give. The fescoes had pictured unbelievable cities, and valleys in this lower realm, and my fancy dwelt on the rich and colossal ruins that awaited me.

My fears, indeed, concerned the past rather than the future. Not even the physical horror of my position in that cramped corridor of dead reptiles and antediluvian frescoes, miles below the world I knew and faced by another world of eerie light and mist, could match the lethal dread I felt at the abysmal antiquity of the scene and its soul. An ancientness so vast that measurement is feeble seemed to leer down from the primal stones and rock-hewn temples of the nameless city, while the very latest of the astounding maps in the frescoes showed oceans and continents that man has forgotten, with only here and there some vaguely familiar outline. Of what could have happened in the geological ages since the paintings ceased and the death-hating race resentfully succumbed to decay, no man might say. Life had once teemed in these caverns and in the luminous realm beyond; now I was alone with vivid relics, and I trembled to think of the countless ages through which these relics had kept a silent deserted vigil.

Suddenly there came another burst of that acute fear which had intermittently seized me ever since I first saw the terrible valley and the nameless city under a cold moon, and despite my exhaustion I found myself starting frantically to a sitting posture and gazing back along the black corridor toward the tunnels that rose to the outer world. My sensations were like those which had made me shun the nameless city at night, and were as inexplicable as they were poignant. In another moment, however, I received a still greater shock in the form of a definite sound – the first which had broken the utter silence of these tomb-like depths. It was a deep, low moaning, as of a distant throng of con-demned spirits, and came from the direction in which I was staring. Its volume rapidly grew, till soon it reverberated frightfully through the low passage, and at the same time I became conscious of an increasing draught of cold air, likewise flowing from the tunnels and the city above. The touch of this air seemed to restore my balance, for I instantly recalled the sudden gusts which had risen around the mouth of the abyss each sunset and sunrise, one of which had indeed revealed the hidden tunnels to me. I looked at my watch and saw that sunrise was near, so braced myself to resist the gale that was sweeping down to its cavern home as it had swept forth at evening. My fear again waned low, since a natural phenomenon tends to dispel broodings over the unknown.

More and more madly poured the shrieking, moaning

night wind into that gulf of the inner earth. I dropped prone again and clutched vainly at the floor for fear of being swept bodily through the open gate into the phosphorescent abyss. Such fury I had not expected, and as I grew aware of an actual slipping of my form toward the abyss I was beset by a thousand new terrors of apprehension and imagination. The malignancy of the blast awakened incredible fancies; once more I compared myself shudderingly to the only human image in that frightful corridor, the man who was torn to pieces by the nameless race, for in the fiendish clawing of the swirling currents there seemed to abide a vindictive rage all the stronger because it was largely impotent. I think I screamed frantically near the last – I was almost mad – but if I did so my cries were lost in the hell-born babel of the howling wind-wraiths. I tried to crawl against the murderous invisible torrent, but I could not even hold my own as I was pushed slowly and inexorably towards the unknown world. Finally reason must have wholly snapped; for I fell to babbling over and over that unexplainable couplet of the mad Arab Alhazred, who dreamed of the nameless city :

"That is not dead which can eternal lie,
And with strange aeons even death may die."

Only the grim brooding desert gods know what really took place – what indescribable struggles and scrambles in the dark I endured or what Abaddon guided me back to life, where I must always remember and shiver in the night wind till oblivion – or worse – claims me. Monstrous, unnatural, colossal, was the thing – too far beyond all the ideas of man to be believed except in the silent damnable small hours of the morning when one cannot sleep.

I have said that the fury of the rushing blast was infernal – cacodaemoniacal – and that its voices were hideous with the pent-up viciousness of desolate eternities. Presently these voices, while still chaotic before me, seemed to my beating brain to take articulate form behind me; and down there in the grave of unnumbered aeon-dead antiquities, leagues below the dawn-lit world of men, I heard the ghastly cursing and snarling of strange-tongued fiends. Turning, I saw outlined against the luminous aether of the abyss that could not be seen against the dusk of the corridor – a nightmare horde of rushing devils; hate-distorted, grotesquely panoplied, half-transparent devils of a race no man might mistake – the crawling reptiles of the nameless city.

And as the wind died away I was plunged into the ghoul-pooled darkness of earth's bowels; for behind the last of the creatures the great brazen door clanged shut with a deafening peal of metallic music whose reverberations swelled out to the distant world to hail the rising sun as Memnon hails it from the banks of the Nile.

THE MOON-BOG

Somewhere, to what remote and fearsome region I know not, Denys Barry has gone. I was with him the last night he lived among men, and heard his screams when the thing came to him; but all the peasants and police in County Meath could never find him, or the others, though they searched long and far. And now I shudder when I hear the frogs piping in swamps, or see the moon in lonely places.

I had known Denys Barry well in America, where he had grown rich, and had congratulated him when he bought back the old castle by the bog at sleepy Kilderry. It was from Kilderry that his father had come, and it was there that he wished to enjoy his wealth among ancestral scenes. Men of his blood had once ruled over Kilderry and built and dwelt in the castle, but those days were very remote, so that for generations the castle had been empty and decaying. After he went to Ireland Barry wrote me often, and told me how under his care the grey castle was rising tower by tower to its ancient splendour, how the ivy was climbing slowly over the restored walls as it had climbed so many centuries ago, and how the peasants blessed him for bringing back the old days with his gold from over the sea. But in time there came troubles, and the peasants ceased to bless him, and fled away instead as from a doom. And then he sent a letter and asked me to visit him, for he was lonely in the castle with no one to speak to save the new servants and labourers he had brought from the North.

The bog was the cause of all these troubles, as Barry told me the night I came to the castle. I had reached Kilderry in the summer sunset, as the gold of the sky lighted the green of the hills and groves and the blue of the bog, where on a far islet a strange olden ruin glistened spectrally. That sunset was very beautiful, but the peasants at Ballylough had warned me against it and said that Kilderry had become accursed, so that I almost shuddered to see the high turrets of the castle gilded with fire. Barry's motor had met me at the Ballylough station, for Kilderry is off the railway. The villagers had shunned the car and the driver from the North, but had whispered to me with pale faces when they saw I was going to Kilderry. And that night, after our reunion, Barry told me why.

The peasants had gone from Kilderry because Denys Barry was to drain the great bog. For all his love of Ireland, America had not left him untouched, and he hated the beautiful wasted space where peat might be cut and land opened up. The legends and superstitions of Kilderry did not move him, and he laughed when the peasants first refused to help, and then cursed him and went away to Ballylough with their few belongings as they saw his determination. In their place he sent for labourers from the North, and when the servants left he replaced them likewise. But it was lonely among strangers, so Barry had asked me to come.

When I heard the fears which had driven the people from Kilderry I laughed as loudly as my friend had laughed, for these fears were of the vaguest, wildest, and most absurd character. They had to do with some preposterous legend of the bog, and of a grim guardian spirit that dwelt in the strange olden ruin on the far islet I had seen in the sunset. There were tales of dancing lights in the dark of the moon, and of chill winds when the night was warm; of wraiths in white hovering over the waters, and of an imagined city of stone deep down below the swampy surface. But foremost among the weird fancies, and alone in its absolute unanimity, was that of the curse awaiting him who should dare to touch or drain the vast reddish morass. There were secrets, said the peasants, which must not be uncovered; secrets that had lain hidden since the plague came to the children of Partholan in the fabulous years beyond history. In the *Book Of Invaders* it is told that these sons of the Greeks were all buried at Tallaght, but old men in Kilderry said that one city was overlooked, saved by its patron moon-goddess; so that only the wooded hills buried it when the men of Nemed swept down from Scythia in their thirty ships.

Such were the idle tales which had made the villagers leave Kilderry, and when I heard them I did not wonder that Denys Barry had refused to listen. He had, however, a great interest in antiquities, and proposed to explore the bog thoroughly when it was drained. The white ruins on the islet he had often visited, but though their age was plainly great, and their contour very little like that of most ruins in Ireland, they were too dilapidated to tell the days of their glory. Now the work of drainage was ready to begin, and the labourers from the North were soon to strip the forbidden bog of its green moss and red heather, and kill the tiny shell-paved streamlets and quiet blue pools fringed with rushes.

After Barry had told me these things I was very drowsy, for the travels of the day had been wearying and my host had talked late into the night. A man-servant showed me to my room, which was in a remote tower overlooking the village, and the plain at the edge of the bog, and the bog itself; so that I could see from my windows in the moonlight the silent roofs from which the peasants had fled and which now sheltered the labourers from the North, and too, the parish church with its antique spire, and far out across the brooding bog the remote olden ruin on the islet gleaming white and spectral. Just as I dropped to sleep I fancied I heard faint sounds from the distance; sounds that were wild and half musical, and stirred me with a weird excitement which coloured my dreams. But when I awaked next morning I felt it had all been a dream, for the visions I had seen were more wonderful than any sound of wild pipes in the night. Influenced by the legends that Barry had related, my mind had in slumber hovered around a stately city in a green valley, where marble streets and statues, villas and temples, carvings and inscriptions, all spoke in certain tones the glory that was Greece. When I told this dream to Barry we both laughed; but I laughed the louder, because he was perplexed about his labourers from the North. For the sixth time they had all over-slept, waking very slowly and dazedly, and acting as if they had not rested, although they were known to have gone early to bed the night before.

That morning and afternoon I wandered alone through the sun-gilded village and talked now and then with idle labourers, for Barry was busy with the final plans for beginning his work of drainage. The labourers were not as happy as they might have been, for most of them seemed uneasy over some dream which they had had, yet which they tried in vain to remember. I told them of my dream, but they were not interested till I spoke of the weird sounds I thought I had heard. Then they looked oddly at me, and said that they seemed to remember weird sounds, too.

In the evening Barry dined with me and announced that he would begin the drainage in two days. I was glad, for although I disliked to see the moss and the heather and the little streams and lakes depart, I had a growing wish to discern the ancient secrets the deep-matted peat might hide. And that night my dreams of piping flutes and marble peristyles came to a sudden and dis-quieting end; for upon the city in the valley I saw a pestilence descend, and then a frightful avalanche of wooded slopes that covered the dead bodies in the streets and left unburied only the temple of Artemis on the high peak, where the aged moon-priestess Cleis lay cold and silent with a crown of ivory on her silver head.

I have said that I awaked suddenly and in alarm. For some time I could not tell whether I was waking or sleeping, for the sound of flutes still rang shrilly in my ears; but when I saw on the floor the icy moonbeams and the outlines of a latticed gothic window I decided I must be awake and in the castle of Kilderry. Then I heard a clock from some remote landing below strike the hour of two, and knew I was awake. Yet still there came that monotonous piping from afar; wild, weird airs that made me think of some dance of fauns on distant Maenalus. It would not let me sleep, and in impatience I sprang up and paced the floor. Only by chance did I go to the north window and look out upon the silent village and the plain at the edge of the bog. I had no wish to gaze abroad, for I wanted to sleep; but the flutes tormented me, and I had to do or see something. How could I have suspected the thing I was to behold?

There in the moonlight that flooded the spacious plain was a spectacle which no mortal, having seen it, could ever forget. To the sound of reedy pipes that echoed over the bog there glided silently and eerily a mixed throng of swaying figures, reeling through such a revel as the Sicilians may have danced to Demeter in the old days under the harvest moon beside the Cyane. The wide plain, the golden moonlight, the shadowy moving forms, and above all the shrill monotonous piping, produced an effect which almost paralysed me; yet I noted amidst my fear that half of these tireless, mechanical dancers were the labourers whom I had thought asleep, whilst the other half were strange airy beings in white, half-indeterminate in nature, but suggesting pale wistful naiads from the haunted fountains of the bog. I do not know how long I gazed at this sight from the lonely turret window before I dropped suddenly in a dreamless swoon, out of which the high sun of morning aroused me.

My first impulse on awaking was to communicate all my fears and observations to Denys Barry, but as I saw the sunlight glowing through the latticed east window I became sure that there was no reality in what I thought I had seen. I am given to strange fantasms, yet am never weak enough to believe in them; so on this occasion contented myself with questioning the labourers, who slept very late and recalled nothing of the previous night save misty dreams of shrill sounds. This matter of the spectral piping harassed me greatly, and I wondered if the crickets of autumn had come before their time to vex the night and haunt the visions of men. Later in the day I watched Barry in the library poring over his plans for the great work which was to begin on the morrow, and for the first time felt a touch of the same kind of fear that had driven the peasants away. For some unknown reason I dreaded the thought of disturbing the ancient bog and its sunless secrets, and pictured terrible sights lying black under the unmeasured depth of age-old peat. That these secrets should be brought to light seemed injudicious, and I began to wish for an excuse to leave the castle and the village. I went so far as to talk casually to Barry on the subject, but did not dare continue after he gave his resounding laugh. So I was silent when the sun set gently over the far hills, and Kilderry blazed all red and gold in a flame that seemed a portent.

Whether the events of that night were of reality or illusion I shall never ascertain. Certainly they transcend anything we dream of in nature and the universe; yet in no normal fashion can I explain those disappearances which were known to all men after it was over. I retired early and full of dread, and for a long time could not sleep in the uncanny silence of the tower. It was very dark, for although the sky was clear the moon was now well in the wane, and would not rise till the small hours. I thought as I lay there of Denys Barry, and of what would befall that bog when the day came, and found myself almost frantic with an impulse to rush out into the night, take Barry's car, and drive madly to Ballylough out of the menaced lands. But before my fears could crystallise into action I had fallen asleep, and gazed in dreams upon the city in the valley, cold and dead under a shroud of hideous shadow.

Probably it was the shrill piping that awaked me, yet that piping was not what I noticed first when I opened my eyes. I was lying with my back to the east window overlooking the bog, where the waning moon would rise, and therefore expected to see light cast on the opposite wall before me; but I had not looked for such a sight as now appeared. Light indeed glowed on the panels ahead, but it was not any light that the moon gives. Terrible and piercing was the shaft of ruddy refulgence that streamed through the gothic window, and the whole chamber was brilliant with a splendour intense and unearthly. My immediate actions were peculiar for such a situation, but it is only in tales that a man does the dramatic and foreseen thing. Instead of looking out across the bog toward the source of the new light, I kept my eyes from the window in panic fear, and clumsily drew on my clothing with some dazed idea of escape. I remember seizing my revolver and hat, but before it was over I had lost them both without firing the one or donning the other. After a time the fascination of the red radiance overcame my fright, and I crept to the east window and looked out whilst the maddening, incessant piping whined and reverberated through the castle and over all the village.

Over the bog was a deluge of flaring light, scarlet and sinister, and pouring from the strange olden ruin on the far islet. The aspect of that ruin I cannot describe—I must have been mad, for it seemed to rise majestic and undecayed, splendid and column-cinctured, the flame-reflecting marble of its entablature piercing the sky like the apex of a temple on a mountain-top. Flutes shrieked and drums began to beat, and as I watched in awe and terror I thought I saw dark saltant forms silhoutted grotesquely against the vision of marble and effulgence. The effect was titanic—altogether unthinkable—and I might have stared indefinitely had not the sound of the piping seemed to grow stronger at my left. Trembling with a terror oddly mixed with ecstasy I crossed the circular room to the north window from which I could see the village and the plain at the edge of the bog. There my eyes dilated again with a wild wonder as great as if I had just turned from a scene beyond the pale of nature, for on the ghastly red-litten plain was moving a procession of beings in such a manner as none ever saw before save in nightmares.

Half gliding, half floating in the air, the white-clad bog-wraiths were slowly retreating toward the still waters and the island ruin in fantastic formations suggesting some ancient and solemn ceremonial dance. Their waving translucent arms, guided by the detestable piping of those unseen flutes, beckoned in uncanny rhythm to a throng of lurching labourers who followed doglike with blind, brainless, floundering steps as if dragged by a clumsy but resistless demon-will. As the naiads neared the bog, without altering their course, a new line of stumbling stragglers zigzagged drunkenly out of the castle from some door far below my window, groped sightlessly across the courtyard and through the intervening bit of village, and joined the floundering column of labourers on the plain. Despite their distance below me I at once knew they were the servants brought from the North, for I recognised the ugly and unwieldly form of the cook, whose very absurdness had now become unutterably tragic. The flutes piped horribly, and again I heard the beating of the drums from the direction of the island ruin. Then silently and gracefully the naiads reached the water and melted one by one into the ancient bog; while the line of followers, never checking their speed, splashed awkwardly after them and vanished amidst a tiny vortex of unwholesome bubbles which I could barely see in the scarlet light. And as the last pathetic straggler, the fat cook, sank heavily out of sight in that sullen pool, the flutes and the drums grew silent, and the blinding red rays from the ruins snapped instantaneously out, leaving the village of doom lone and desolate in the wan beams of a new-risen moon.

My condition was now one of indescribable chaos. Not knowing whether I was mad or sane, sleeping or waking, I was saved only by a merciful numbness. I believe I did ridiculous things such as offering prayers to Artemis, Latona, Demeter, Persephone, and Plouton. All that I recalled of a classic youth came to my lips as the horrors of the situation roused my deepest superstitions. I felt that I had witnessed the death of a whole village, and knew I was alone in the castle with Denys Barry, whose boldness had brought down a doom. As I thought of him new terrors convulsed me, and I fell to the floor; not fainting, but physically helpless. Then I felt the icy blast from the east window where the moon had risen, and began to hear the shrieks in the castle far below me. Soon those shrieks had attained a magnitude and quality which cannot be written of, and which make me faint as I think of them. All I can say is that they came from something I had known as a friend.

At some time during this shocking period the cold wind and the screaming must have roused me, for my next impression is of racing madly through inky rooms and corridors and out across the courtyard into the hideous night. They found me at dawn wandering mindless near Ballylough, but what unhinged me utterly was not any of the horrors I had seen or heard before. What I muttered about as I came slowly out of the shadows was a pair of fantastic incidents which occurred in my flight: incidents of no significance, yet which haunt me unceasingly when I am alone in certain marshy places or in the moonlight.

As I fled from the accursed castle along the bog's edge I heard a new sound: common, yet unlike any I had heard before at Kilderry. The stagnant waters, lately quite devoid of animal life, now teemed with a horde of slimy enormous frogs which piped shrilly and incessantly in tones strangely out of keeping with their size. They glistened bloated and green in the moonbeams, and seemed to gaze up at the fount of light. I followed the gaze of one very fat and ugly frog, and saw the second of the things which drove my senses away.

Stretching directly from the strange olden ruin on the far islet to the waning moon, my eyes seemed to trace a beam of faint quivering radiance having no reflection in the waters of the bog. And upward along that pallid path my fevered fancy pictured a thin shadow slowly writhing; a vague contorted shadow struggling as if drawn by unseen demons. Crazed as I was, I saw in that awful shadow a monstrous resemblance—a nauseous, unbelievable caricature—a blasphemous effigy of him who had been Denys Barry.

The Festival

I was far from home, and the spell of the eastern sea was upon me. In the twilight I heard it pounding on the rocks, and I knew it lay just over the hill where the twisting willows writhed against the clearing sky and the first stars of evening. And because my fathers had called me to the old town beyond, I pushed on through the shallow, new-fallen snow along the road that soared lonely up to where Aldebaran twinkled among the trees; on toward the very ancient town I had never seen but often dreamed of.

It was the Yuletide, that men call Christmas though they know in their hearts it is older than Bethlehem and Babylon, older than Memphis and mankind. It was the Yuletide, and I had come at last to the ancient sea town where my people had dwelt and kept festival in the elder time when festival was forbidden; where also they had commanded their sons to keep festival once every century, that the memory of primal secrets might not be forgotten. Mine were an old people, and were old even when this land was settled three hundred years before. And they were strange, because they had come as dark furtive folk from opiate southern gardens of orchids, and spoken another tongue before they learnt the tongue of the blue-eyed fishers. And now they were scattered, and shared only the rituals of mysteries that none living could understand. I was the only one who came back that night to the old fishing town as legend bade, for only the poor and the lonely remember.

Then beyond the hill's crest I saw Kingsport outspread

frostily in the gloaming; snowy Kingsport with its ancient vanes and steeples, ridge-poles and chimney-pots, wharves and small bridges, willow-trees and graveyards; endless labyrinths of steep, narrow, crooked streets, and dizzy church-crowned central peak that time durst not touch; ceaseless mazes of colonial houses piled and scattered at all angles and levels like a child's disordered blocks; antiquity hovering on grey wings over winter-whitened gables and gambrel roofs; fanlights and small-paned windows one by one gleaming out in the cold dusk to join Orion and the archaic stars. And against the rotting wharves the sea pounded; the secretive, immemorial sea out of which the people had come in the elder time.

Beside the road at its crest a still higher summit rose, bleak and wind-swept, and I saw that it was a burying-ground where black gravestones stuck ghoulishly through the snow like the decayed fingernails of a gigantic corpse. The printless road was very lonely, and sometimes I thought I heard a distant horrible creaking as of a gibbet in the wind. They had hanged four kinsmen of mine for witchcraft in 1692, but I did not know just where.

As the road wound down the seaward slope I listened for the merry sounds of a village at evening, but did not hear them. Then I thought of the season, and felt that these old Puritan folk might well have Christmas customs strange to me, and full of silent hearthside prayer. So after that I did not listen for merriment or look for wayfarers, kept on down past the hushed lighted farmhouses and shadowy stone walls to where the signs of ancient shops and sea taverns creaked in the salt breeze, and the grotesque knockers of pillared doorways glistened along deserted unpaved lanes in the light of little, curtained windows.

I had seen maps of the town, and knew where to find the home of my people. It was told that I should be known and welcomed, for village legend lives long; so I hastened through Back Street to Circle Court, and across the fresh snow on the one full flagstone pavement in the town, to where Green Lane leads off behind the Market House. The old maps still held good, and I had no trouble; though at Arkham they must have lied when they said the trolleys ran to this place, since I saw not a wire overhead. Snow would have hid the rails in any case. I was glad I had chosen to walk, for the white village had seemed very beautiful from the hill; and now I was eager to knock at the door of my people, the seventh house on the left in Green Lane, with an ancient peaked roof and jutting second story, all built before 1650.

There were lights inside the house when I came upon it, and I saw from the diamond window-panes that it must have been kept very close to its antique state. The upper part over-hung the narrow grass-grown street and nearly met the over-hanging part of the house opposite, so that I was almost in a tunnel, with the low stone doorstep wholly free from snow. There was no sidewalk, but many houses had high doors reached by double flights of steps with iron railings. It was an odd scene, and because I was strange to New England I had never known its like before. Though it pleased me, I would have relished it better if there had been footprints in the snow, and people in the streets, and a few windows without drawn curtains.

When I sounded the archaic iron knocker I was half afraid. Some fear had been gathering in me, perhaps because of the strangeness of my heritage, and the bleakness of the evening, and the queerness of the silence in that aged town of curious customs. And when my knock was answered I was fully afraid, because I had not heard any footsteps before the door creaked open. But I was not afraid long, for the gowned, slippered old man in the doorway had a bland face that reassured me; and though he made signs that he was dumb, he wrote a quaint and ancient welcome with the stylus and wax tablet he carried.

He beckoned me into a low, candle-lit room with massive exposed rafters and dark, stiff, sparse furniture of the seven-teenth century. The past was vivid there, for not an attribute was missing. There was a cavernous fireplace and a spinning-wheel at which a bent old woman in loose wrapper and deep poke-bonnet sat back toward me, silently spinning despite the festive season. An indefinite dampness seemed upon the place, and I marvelled that no fire should be blazing. The high-backed settle faced the row of curtained windows at the left, and seemed to be occupied, though I was not sure. I did not like everything about what I saw, and felt again the fear I had had. This fear grew stronger from what had before lessened it, for the more I looked at the old man's face the more its very blandness terrified me. The eyes never moved, and the skin was too much like wax. Finally I was sure it was not a face at all, but a fiendishly cunning mask. But the flabby hands, curiously gloved, wrote genially on the tablet and told me I must wait a while before I could be led to the place of the festival.

Pointing to a chair, table, and pile of books, the old man now left the room; and when I sat down to read I saw that the books were hoary and mouldy, and that they included old Morryster's wild *Marvells of Science*, the terrible *Saducismus Triumphatus* of Joseph Glanvil, published in 1681, the shocking *Daemonolatreia* of Remigius, printed in 1595 at Lyons, and worst of all, the unmentionable *Necronomicon* of the mad Arab Abdul Alhazred, in Olaus Wormius' forbidden Latin translation; a book which I had never seen, but of which I had heard monstrous things whispered. No one spoke to me, but I could hear the creaking of signs in the wind outside, and the whir of the wheel as the bonneted old woman continued her silent spinning, spinning. I thought the room and the books and the people very morbid and disquieting, but because an old tradition of my fathers had summoned me to strange feastings, I resolved to expect queer things. So I tried to read, and soon became tremblingly absorbed by something I found in that accursed *Necronomicon*; a thought and a legend too hideous for sanity or consciousness, but I disliked it when I fancied I heard the closing of one of the windows that the settle faced, as if it had been stealthily opened. It had seemed to follow a whirring that was not of the old woman's spinning-wheel. This was not much, though, for the old woman was spinning very hard, and the aged clock had been striking. After that I lost the feeling that there were persons on the settle, and was reading intently and shudderingly when the old man came back booted and dressed in a loose antique costume, and sat down on that very bench, so that I could not see him. It was certainly nervous waiting, and the blasphemous book in my hands made it doubly so. When eleven struck, however, the old man stood up, glided to a massive carved chest in a corner, and got two hooded cloaks; one of which he donned, and the other of which he draped round the old woman, who was ceasing her monotonous spinning. Then they both started for the outer door; the woman lamely creeping, and the old man, after picking up the very book I had been reading, beckoning me as he drew his hood over that unmoving face or mask.

We went out into the moonless and tortuous network of that incredibly ancient town; went out as the lights in the curtained windows disappeared one by one, and the Dog Star leered at the throng of cowled, cloaked figures that poured silently from every doorway and formed monstrous processions up this street and that, past the creaking signs and antediluvian gables, the thatched roofs and diamond-paned windows; threading precipitous lanes where decaying houses overlapped and crumbled together, gliding across open courts and churchyards where the bobbing lanthorns made eldritch drunken constellations.

Amid these hushed throngs I followed my voiceless guides; jostled by elbows that seemed preternaturally soft, and pressed by chests and stomachs that seemed abnormally pulpy; but seeing never a face and hearing never a word. Up, up, up, the eery columns slithered, and I saw that all the travellers were converging as they flowed near a sort of focus of crazy alleys at the top of a high hill in the centre of the town, where perched a great white church. I had seen it from the road's crest when I looked at Kingsport in the new dusk, and it had made me shiver because Aldebaran had seemed to balance itself a moment on the ghostly spire.

There was an open space around the church; partly a churchyard with spectral shafts, and partly a half-paved square swept nearly bare of snow by the wind, and lined with unwholesomely archaic houses having peaked roofs and overhanging gables. Death-fires danced over the tombs, revealing vistas, though queerly failing to cast any shadows. Past the churchyard, where there were no houses, I could see over the hill's summit and watch the glimmer of stars on the harbour, though the town was invisible in the dark. Only once in a while a lanthorn bobbed horribly through serpentine alleys on its way to overtake the throng that was now slipping speechlessly into the church. I waited till the crowd had oozed into the black doorway, and till all the stragglers had followed. The old man was pulling at my sleeve, but I was determined to be the last. Crossing the threshold into the swarming temple of unknown darkness, I turned once to look at the outside world as the churchyard phosphorescence cast a sickly glow on the hilltop pavement. And as I did so I shuddered. For though the wind had not left much snow, a few patches did remain on the path near the door; and in that fleeting backward look it seemed to my troubled eyes that they bore no mark of passing feet, nor even mine.

The church was scarce lighted by all the lanthorns that had entered it, for most of the throng had already vanished. They had streamed up the aisle between the high pews to the trapdoor of the vaults which yawned loathsomely open just before the pulpit, and were now squirming noiselessly in. I followed dumbly down the footworn steps and into the dark, suffocating crypt. The tail of that sinuous line of night-marchers seemed very horrible, and as I saw them wriggling into a venerable tomb they seemed more horrible still. Then I noticed that the tomb's floor had an aperture down which the throng was sliding, and in a moment we were all descending an ominous staircase of rough-hewn stone; a narrow spiral staircase damp and peculiarly odorous, that wound endlessly down into the bowels of the hill past monotonous walls of dripping stone blocks and crumbling mortar. It was a silent, shocking descent, and I observed after a horrible interval that the walls and steps were changing in nature, as if chiselled out of the solid rock. What mainly troubled me was that the myriad footfalls made no sound and set up no echoes. After more aeons of descent I saw some side passages or burrows leading from unknown recesses of blackness to this shaft of nighted mystery. Soon they became excessively numerous, like impious catacombs of nameless menace; and their pungent odour of decay grew quite unbearable. I knew we must have passed down through the mountain and beneath the earth of Kingsport itself, and I shivered that a town should be so aged and maggoty with subterraneous evil.

Then I saw the lurid shimmering of pale light, and heard the insidious lapping of sunless waters. Again I shivered, for I did not like the things that the night had brought, and wished bitterly that no forefather had summoned me to this primal rite. As the steps and the passage grew broader, I heard another sound, the thin, whining mockery of a feeble flute; and suddenly there spread out before me the boundless vista of an inner world—a vast fungous shore lit by a belching column of sick greenish flame and washed by a wide oily river that flowed from abysses frightful and unsuspected to join the blackest gulfs of immemorial ocean.

Fainting and gasping, I looked at that unhallowed Erebus of titan toadstools, leprous fire and slimy water, and saw the cloaked throngs forming a semicircle around the blazing pillar. It was the Yule-rite, older than man and fated to survive him; . the primal rite of the solstice and of spring's promise beyond the snows; the rite of fire and evergreen, light and music. And in the stygian grotto I saw them do the rite, and adore the sick pillar of flame, and throw into the water handfuls gouged out of the viscous vegetation which glittered green in the chlorotic glare. I saw this, and I saw something amorphously squatted far away from the light, piping noisomely on a flute; and as the thing piped I thought I heard noxious muffled flutterings in the foetid darkness where I could not see. But what frightened me most was that flaming column; spouting volcanically from depths profound and inconceivable, casting no shadows as healthy flame should, and coating the nitrous stone with a nasty, venomous verdigris. For in all that seething combustion no warmth lay, but only the clamminess of death and corruption.

The man who had brought me now squirmed to a point directly beside the hideous flame, and made stiff ceremonial motions to the semicircle he faced. At certain stages of the ritual they did grovelling obeisance, especially when he held above his head that abhorrent *Necronomicon* he had taken with him; and I shared all the obeisances because I had been summoned to this festival by the writings of my forefathers. Then the old man made a signal to the half-seen flute-player in the darkness, which player thereupon changed its feeble drone to a scarce louder drone in another key; precipitating as it did so a horror unthinkable and unexpected. At this horror I sank nearly to the lichened earth, transfixed with a dread not of this or any world, but only of the mad spaces between the stars.

Out of the unimaginable blackness beyond the gangrenous glare of that cold flame, out of the tartarean leagues through which that oily river rolled uncanny, unheard, and unsuspected, there flopped rhythmically a horde of tame, trained, hybrid winged things that no sound eye could ever wholly grasp, or sound brain ever wholly remember. They were not altogether crows, nor moles, nor buzzards, nor ants, nor vampire bats, nor decomposed human beings; but something I cannot and must not recall. They flopped limply along, half with their webbed feet and half with their membranous wings; and as they reached the throng of celebrants the cowled figures seized and mounted them, and rode off one by one along the reaches of that unlighted river, into pits and galleries of panic where poison springs feed frightful cataracts.

The old spinning woman had gone with the throng, and the old man remained only because I had refused when he motioned me to seize an animal and ride like the rest. I saw when I staggered to my feet that the amorphous flute-player had rolled out of sight, but that two of the beasts were patiently standing by. As I hung back, the old man produced his stylus and tablet and wrote that he was the true deputy of my fathers who had founded the Yule worship in this ancient place; that it had been decreed I should come back, and that the most secret mysteries were yet to be performed. He wrote this in a very ancient hand, and when I still hesitated he pulled from his loose robe a seal ring and a watch, both with my family arms, to prove that he was what he said. But it was a hideous proof, because I knew from old papers that that watch had been buried with my great-great-great-great-grandfather in 1698.

Presently the old man drew back his hood and pointed to the family resemblance in his face, but I only shuddered, because I was sure that the face was merely a devilish waxen mask. The flopping animals were now scratching restlessly at the lichens, and I saw that the old man was nearly as restless himself. When one of the things began to waddle and edge away, he turned quickly to stop it; so that the suddenness of his motion dislodged the waxen mask from what should have been his head. And then, because that nightmare's position barred me from the stone staircase down which we had come, I flung myself into the oily underground river that bubbled somewhere to the caves of the sea; flung myself into that putrescent juice of earth's inner horrors before the madness of my screams could bring down upon me all the charnel legions these pest-gulfs might conceal . . .

At the hospital they told me I had been found half-frozen in Kingsport Harbour at dawn, clinging to the drifting spar that accident sent to save me. They told me I had taken the wrong fork of the hill road the night before, and fallen over the cliffs at Orange Point; a thing they deduced from prints found in the snow. There was nothing I could say, because everything was wrong. Everything was wrong, with the broad windows showing a sea of roofs in which only about one in five was ancient, and the sound of trolleys and motors in the streets below. They insisted that this was Kingsport, and I could not deny it. When I went delirious at hearing that the hospital stood near the old churchyard on Central Hill, they sent me to St. Mary's Hospital in Arkham, where I could have better care. I liked it there, for the doctors were broad-minded, and even lent me their influence in obtaining the carefully sheltered copy of Alhazred's objectionable *Necronomicon* from the library of Miskatonic University. They said something about a 'psychosis', and agreed I had better get any harassing obsessions off my mind.

So I read that hideous chapter, and shuddered doubly because it was indeed not new to me. I had seen it before, let footprints tell what they might; and where it was I had seen it were best forgotten. There was no one—in waking hours—who could remind me of it; but my dreams are filled with terror, because of phrases I dare not quote. I dare quote only one paragraph, put into such English as I can make from the awkward Low Latin.

'The nethermost caverns,' wrote the mad Arab, 'are not for the fathoming of eyes that see; for their marvels are strange and terrific. Cursed the ground where dead thoughts live new and oddly bodied, and evil the mind that is held by no head. Wisely did Ibn Schacabao say, that happy is the tomb where no wizard hath lain, and happy the town at night whose wizards are all ashes. For it is of old rumour that the soul of the devil-bought hastes not from his charnel clay, but fats and instructs *the very worm that gnaw*; till out of corruption horrid life springs, and the dull scavengers of earth wax crafty to vex it and swell monstrous to plague it. Great holes secretly are digged where earth's pores ought to suffice, and things have learnt to walk that ought to crawl.'

THE DIARY OF ALONZO TYPER
by H. P. Lovecraft and William Lumley

Editor's note: Alonzo Hasbrouck Typer of Kingston, New York, was last seen and recognised on April 17, 1908, around noon, at the Hotel Richmond in Batavia. He was the only survivor of an ancient Ulster County family, and was fifty-three years old at the time of his disappearance.

Mr Typer was educated privately and at Columbia and Heidelberg universities. All his life was spent as a student, the field of his researches including many obscure and generally feared borderlands of human knowledge. His papers on vampirism, ghouls, and poltergeist phenomena were privately printed after rejection by many publishers. He resigned from the Society for Psychical Research in 1920 after a series of peculiarly bitter controversies.

163

At various times Mr Typer travelled extensively, sometimes dropping out of sight for long periods. He is known to have visited obscure spots in Nepal, India, Tibet, and Indo-China, and passed most of the year 1899 on mysterious Easter Island. The extensive search for Mr Typer after his disappearance yielded no results, and his estate was divided among distant cousins in New York City.

The diary herewith presented was allegedly found in the ruins of a large country house near Attica, N.Y., which had borne a curiously sinister reputation for generations before its collapse. The edifice was very old, antedating the general white settlement of the region, and had formed the home of a strange and secretive family named van der Heyl, which had migrated from Albany in 1746 under a curious cloud of witchcraft suspicion. The structure probably dated from about 1760.

Of the history of the van der Heyls very little is known. They remained entirely aloof from their normal neighbours, employed negro servants brought directly from Africa and speaking little English, and educated their children privately and at European colleges. Those of them who went out into the world were soon lost to sight, though not before gaining evil repute for association with Black Mass groups and cults of even darker significance.

Around the dreaded house a straggling village arose, populated by Indians and later by renegades from the surrounding country, which bore the dubious name of Chorazin. Of the singular hereditary strains which afterwards appeared in the mixed Chorazin villagers, several monographs have been written by ethnologists. Just behind the village, and in sight of the van der Heyl house, is a steep hill crowned with a peculiar ring of ancient standing stones which the Iroquois always regarded with fear and loathing. The origin and nature of the stones, whose date, according to archaeological and climatological evidence, must be fabulously early, is a problem still unsolved.

From about 1795 onward, the legends of the incoming pioneers and later population have much to say about strange cries and chants proceeding at certain seasons from Chorazin and from the great house and hill of standing stones; though there is reason to suppose that the noises ceased about 1872, when the entire van der Heyl household—servants and all—suddenly and simultaneously disappeared.

Thenceforward the house was deserted; for other disastrous

events—including three unexplained deaths, five disappearances, and four cases of sudden insanity—occurred when later owners and interested visitors attempted to stay in it. The house, village, and extensive rural areas on all sides reverted to the state and were auctioned off in the absence of discoverable van der Heyl heirs. Since about 1890 the owners (successively the late Charles A. Shields and his son Oscar S. Shields, of Buffalo) have left the entire property in a state of absolute neglect, and have warned all inquirers not to visit the region.

Of those known to have approached the house during the last forty years, most were occult students, police officers, newspaper men, and odd characters from abroad. Among the latter was a mysterious Eurasian, probably from Cochin-China, whose later appearance with blank mind and bizarre mutilations excited wide press notice in 1903.

Mr Typer's diary—a book about 6 by $3\frac{1}{2}$ inches in size, with tough paper and an oddly durable binding of thin sheet metal—was discovered in the possession of one of the decadent Chorazin villagers on November 16, 1935, by a state policemen sent to investigate the rumoured collapse of the deserted van der Heyl mansion. The house had indeed fallen, obviously from sheer age and decrepitude, in the severe gale of November 12. Disintegration was peculiarly complete, and no thorough search of the ruins could be made for several weeks. John Eagle, the swarthy, simian-faced, Indian-like villager who had the diary, said that he found the book quite near the surface of the debris, in what must have been an upper front room.

Very little of the contents of the house could be identified, though an enormous and astonishingly solid brick vault in the cellar (whose ancient iron door had to be blasted open because of the strangely figured and perversely tenacious lock) remained intact and presented several puzzling features. For one thing, the walls were covered with still undeciphered hieroglyphs roughly incised in the brickwork. Another peculiarity was a huge circular aperture in the rear of the vault, blocked by a cave-in evidently caused by the collapse of the house.

But strangest of all was the apparently *recent* deposit of some fetid, slimy, pitch-black substance on the flagstoned floor, extending in a yard-board, irregular line with one end at the blocked circular aperture. Those who first opened the vault declared that the place smelled like the snake-house at a zoo.

The diary, which was apparently designed solely to cover an investigation of the dreaded van der Heyl house by the vanished Mr Typer, has been proved by handwriting experts to be genuine. The script shows signs of increasing nervous strain as it progresses towards the end, in places becoming almost illegible. Chorazin villagers—whose stupidity and taciturnity baffle all students of the region and its secrets—admit no recollection of Mr Typer as distinguished from other rash visitors to the dreaded house.

The text of the diary is here given verbatim and without comment. How to interpret it, and what, other than the writer's madness, to infer from it, the reader must decide for himself. Only the future can tell what its value may be in solving a generation-old mystery. It may be remarked that genealogists confirm Mr Typer's belated memory in the matter of *Adriaen Sleght*.

The Diary

April 17, 1908

Arrived here about 6 p.m. Had to walk all the way from Attica in the teeth of an oncoming storm, for no one would rent me a horse or rig, and I can't run an automobile. This place is even worse than I had expected, and I dread what is coming, even though I long at the same time to learn the secret. All too soon will come the night—the old Walpurgis Sabbat horror—and after that time in Wales I know what to look for. Whatever comes, I shall not flinch. Prodded by some unfathomable urge, I have given my whole life to the quest of unholy mysteries. I came here for nothing else, and will not quarrel with fate.

It was very dark when I got here, though the sun had by no means set. The storm-clouds were the densest I had ever seen, and I could not have found my way but for the lightning-flashes. The village is a hateful little backwater, and its few inhabitants no better than idiots. One of them saluted me in a queer way, as if he knew men. I could see very little of the landscape—just a small, swampy valley of strange brown weed-stalks and dead fungi surrounded by scraggly, evilly twisted trees with bare boughs. But behind the village is a dismal-looking hill on whose summit is a circle of great stones with another stone at the centre. That, without question, is the vile primordial thing V—— told me about at the N—— Sabbat.

The great house lies in the midst of a park all overgrown with curious-looking briars. I could scarcely break through, and when I did the vast age and decrepitude of the building almost stopped me from entering. The place looked filthy and diseased, and I wondered how so leprous a bulk could hang together. It is wooden; and though its original lines are hidden by a bewildering tangle of wings added at various dates, I think it was first built in the square colonial fashion of New England. Probably that was easier to build than a Dutch stone house—and then, too, I recall that Dirck van der Heyl's wife was from Salem, a daughter of the unmentionable Abaddon Corey. There was a small pillared porch, and I got under it just as the storm burst. It was a fiendish tempest—black as midnight, with rain in sheets, thunder and lightning like the day of general dissolution, and a wind that actually clawed at me.

The door was unlocked, so I took out my electric torch and went inside. Dust was inches deep on floor and furniture, and the place smelled like a mould-caked tomb. There was a hall reaching all the way through, and a curving staircase on the right.

I ploughed my way upstairs and selected this front room to camp out in. The whole place seems fully furnished, though most of the furniture is breaking down. This is written at eight o'clock, after a cold meal from my travelling-case. After this the village people will bring me supplies; though they won't agree to come any closer than the ruins of the park gate until (as they say) later. I wish I could get rid of an unpleasant feeling of familiarity with this place.

Later

I am conscious of several presences in this house. One in particular is decidedly hostile towards me—a malevolent will which is seeking to break down my own and overcome me. I must not countenance this for an instant, but must use all my forces to resist it. It is appallingly evil, and definitely non-human. I think it must be allied to powers outside Earth—powers in the spaces behind time and beyond the universe. It towers like a colossus, bearing out what is said in the Aklo writings. There is such a feeling of vast size connected with it that I wonder these chambers can contain its bulk—and yet it has no visible bulk. Its age must be unutterably vast—shockingly, indescribably so.

April 18

Slept very little last night. At 3 a.m. a strange, creeping wind began to pervade the whole region, ever rising until the house rocked as if in a typhoon. As I went down the staircase to see to the rattling front door the darkness took half-visible forms in my imagination. Just below the landing I was pushed violently from behind—by the wind, I suppose, though I could have sworn I saw the dissolving outlines of a gigantic black paw as I turned quickly about. I did not lose my footing, but safely finished the descent and shot the heavy bolt of the dangerously shaking door.

I had not meant to explore the house before dawn; yet now, unable to sleep again and fired with mixed terror and curiosity, I felt reluctant to postpone my search. With my powerful torch I ploughed through the dust to the great south parlour, where I knew the portraits would be. There they were, just as V—— had said, and as I seemed to know from some obscurer source as well. Some were so blackened and dust-clouded that I could make little or nothing of them, but from those I could trace I recognised that they were indeed of the hateful line of the van der Heyls. Some of the paintings seemed to suggest faces I had known; but just what faces, I could not recall.

The outlines of that frightful hybrid Joris—spawned in 1773 by old Dirck's youngest daughter—were clearest of all, and I could trace the green eyes and the serpent look in his face. Every time I shut off the flashlight that face would seem to glow in the dark until I half fancied it shone with a faint, greenish light of its own. The more I looked, the more evil it seemed, and I turned away to avoid hallucinations of changing expression.

But that to which I turned was even worse. The long, dour face, small, closely set eyes and swine-like features identified it at once, even though the artist had striven to make the snout look as human as possible. This was what V—— had whispered about. As I stared in horror, I thought the eyes took on a reddish glow, and for a moment the background seemed replaced by an alien and seemingly irrelevant scene—a lone, bleak moor beneath a dirty yellow sky, whereon grew a wretched-looking blackthorn bush. Fearing for my sanity, I rushed from that accursed gallery to the dust-cleared corner upstairs where I have my "camp".

Later

Decided to explore some of the labyrinthine wings of the house by daylight. I cannot get lost, for my footprints are distinct in the ankle-deep dust, and I can trace other identifying marks when necessary. It is curious how easily I learn the intricate windings of the corridors. Followed a long, outflung northerly "ell" to its extremity, and came to a locked door, which I forced. Beyond was a very small room quite crowded with furniture, and with the panelling badly worm-eaten. On the outer wall I spied a black space behind the rotting woodwork, and discovered a narrow secret passage leading downwards to unknown inky depths. It was a steeply inclined chute or tunnel without steps or hand-holds, and I wondered what its use could have been.

Above the fireplace was a mouldy painting, which I found on close inspection to be that of a young woman in the dress of the late eighteenth century. The face is of classic beauty, yet with the most fiendishly evil expression which I have ever known the human countenance to bear. Not merely callousness, greed, and cruelty, but some quality hideous beyond human comprehension seems to sit upon those finely carved features. And as I looked it seemed to me that the artist—or the slow processes of mould and decay—had imparted to that pallid complexion a sickly greenish cast, and the least suggestion of an almost imperceptibly scaly texture. Later I ascended to the attic, where I found several chests of strange books—many of utterly alien aspects in letters and in physical form alike. One contained variants of the Aklo formulae which I had never known to exist. I have not yet examined the books on the dusty shelves downstairs.

April 19

There are certainly unseen presences here, even though the dust bears no footprints but my own. Cut a path through the briars yesterday to the park gate where my supplies are left, but this morning I found it closed. Very odd, since the bushes are barely stirring with sprang sap. Again I have that feeling of something at hand so colossal that the chambers can scarcely contain it. This time I feel that more than one of the presences is of such a size, and I know now that the third Aklo ritual—which I found in that book in the attic yesterday—would make such beings solid and visible. Whether I shall dare to try this materialisation remains to be seen. The perils are great.

Last night I began to glimpse evanescent shadow-faces and forms in the dim corners of the halls and chambers—faces and forms so hideous and loathsome that I dare not describe them. They seem allied in substance to that titanic paw which tried to push me down the stairs the night before last, and must of course be phantoms of my disturbed imagination. What I am seeking would not be quite like these things. I have seen the paw again, sometimes alone and sometimes with its mate, but I have resolved to ignore all such phenomena.

Early this afternoon I explored the cellar for the first time, descending by a ladder found in a store-room, since the wooden steps had rotted away. The whole place is a mass of nitrous encrustations with amorphous mounds marking the spots where various objects have disintegrated. At the farther end is a narrow passage which seems to extend under the northerly "ell" where I found the little locked room, and at the end of this is a heavy brick wall with a locked iron door. Apparently belonging to a vault of some sort, this wall and door bear evidences of eighteenth-century workmanship and must be contemporary with the oldest additions to the house—clearly pre-Revolutionary. On the lock, which is obviously older than the rest of the ironwork, are engraved certain symbols which I cannot decipher.

V—— had not told me about this vault. It fills me with a greater disquiet than anything else I have seen, for every time I approach it I have an almost irresistible impulse to *listen* for something. Hitherto no untoward *sounds* have marked my stay in this malign place. As I left the cellar I wished devoutly that the steps were still there; for my progress up the ladder seemed maddeningly slow. I do not want to go down there again—and yet some evil genius urges me to try it *at night* if I would learn what is to be learned.

April 20

I have sounded the depths of horror—only to be made aware of still lower depths. Last night the temptation was too strong, and in the black small hours I descended once more into that nitrous hellish cellar with my flashlight, tiptoeing among the amorphous heaps to that terrible brick wall and locked door. I made no sound, and refrained from whispering any of the incantations I knew, but I listened with mad intentness.

At last I heard the sounds from beyond those barred plates of sheet iron, the menacing padding and muttering, as of gigantic night-things within. Then, too, there was a damnable slithering, as of a vast serpent or sea-beast dragging its monstrous folds over a paved floor. Nearly paralysed with fright, I glanced at the huge rusty lock, and at the alien, cryptic hieroglyphs graven upon it. They were signs I could not recognise, and something in their vaguely Mongoloid technique hinted at a blasphemous and indescribable antiquity. At times I fancied I could see them glowing with a greenish light.

I turned to flee, but found that vision of the titan paws before me, the great talons seeming to swell and become more tangible as I gazed. Out of the cellar's evil blackness they stretched, with shadowy hints of scaly wrists beyond them, and with a waxing, malignant will guiding their horrible gropings. Then I heard from behind me—within that abominable vault—a fresh burst of muffled reverberations which seemed to echo from far horizons like distant thunder. Impelled by this greater fear, I advanced towards the shadowy paws with my flashlight and saw them vanish before the full force of the electric beam. Then up the ladder I raced, torch between my teeth, nor did I rest till I had regained my upstairs "camp".

What is to be my ultimate end, I dare not imagine. I came as a seeker, but now I know that something is seeking me. I could not leave if I wished. This morning I tried to go to the gate for my supplies, but found the briars twisted tightly in my path. It was the same in every direction—behind and on all sides of the house. In places the brown, barbed vines had uncurled to astonishing heights, forming a steel-like hedge against my egress. The villagers are connected with all this. When I went indoors I found my supplies in the great front hall, though without any clue to how they came there. I am sorry now that I swept the dust away. I shall scatter some more and see what prints are left.

This afternoon I read some of the books in the great shadowy library at the rear of the ground floor, and formed certain suspicions which I cannot bear to mention. I had never seen the text of the Pnakotic Manuscripts or of the Eltdown Shards before, and would not have come here had I known what they contain. I believe it is too late now—for the awful Sabbat is only ten days away. It is for that night of horror that *they* are saving me.

April 21

I have been studying the portraits again. Some have names attached and I noticed one—of an evil-faced woman, painted some two centuries ago—which puzzled me. It bore the name of Trintje van der Heyl Slegth, and I have a distinct impression that I once met the name of Sleght before, in some significant connection. It was not horrible then, though it becomes so now. I must rack my brain for the clue.

The eyes of these pictures haunt me. Is it possible that some of them are emerging more distinctly from their shrouds of dust and decay and mould? The serpent-faced and swine-faced warlocks stare horribly at me from their blackened frames, and a score of other hybrid faces are beginning to peer out of shadowy backgrounds. There is a hideous look of family resemblance in them all, and that which is human is more horrible than that which is non-human. I wish they reminded me less of other faces—faces I have known in the past. They were an accursed line, and Cornelis of Leyden was the worst of them. It was *he* who broke down the barrier after his father had found that other key. I am sure that V—— knows only a fragment of the horrible truth, so that I am indeed unprepared and defenceless. What of the line before old Claes? What he did in 1591 could never have been done without generations of evil heritage, or some link with the outside. And what of the branches this monstrous line has sent forth? Are they scattered over the world, all awaiting their common heritage of horror? I must recall the place where I once so particularly noticed the name of Sleght.

I wish I could be sure that these pictures stay always in their frames. For several hours now I have been seeing momentary presences like the earlier paws and shadow-faces and forms, but closely duplicating some of the ancient portraits. Somehow I can never glimpse a presence and the portrait it resembles at the same time—the light is always wrong for one or the other, or else the presence and the portrait are in different rooms.

Perhaps, as I have hoped, the presences are mere figments of imagination, but I cannot be sure now. Some are female, and of the same hellish beauty as the picture in the little locked room. Some are like no portrait I have seen, yet make me feel that their painted features lurk unrecognised beneath the mould and soot of canvases I cannot decipher. A few, I desperately fear, have approached materialisation in solid or semi-solid form—and some have a dreadful and unexplained familiarity.

There is one woman who in fell loveliness excels all the rest. Her poisonous charms are like a honeyed flower growing on the brink of hell. When I look at her closely she vanishes, only to reappear later. Her face has a greenish cast, and now and then I fancy I can spy a suspicion of the squamous in its smooth texture. Who is she? Is she that being who must have dwelt in the little locked room a century and more ago?

My supplies were again left in the front hall—that, clearly, is to be the custom. I had sprinkled dust about to catch footprints, but this morning the whole hall was swept clean by some unknown agency.

April 22

This has been a day of horrible discovery. I explored the cobwebbed attic again, and found a carved, crumbling chest—plainly from Holland—full of blasphemous books and papers far older than any hitherto encountered here. There was a Greek *Necronomicon*, a Norman-French *Livre d'Eibon*, and a first edition of old Ludvig Prinn's *De Vermis Mysteriis*. But the old bound manuscript was the worst. It was in low Latin, and full of the strange, crabbed hand-writing of Claes van der Heyl, being evidently the diary or notebook kept by him between 1560 and 1580. When I unfastened the black-ened silver clasp and opened the yellowed leaves a coloured drawing fluttered out—the likeness of a monstrous creature resembling nothing so much as a squid, beaked and tentacled, with great yellow eyes, and with certain abominable approximations to the human form in its contours.

I had never before seen so utterly loathsome and nightmarish a form. On the paws, feet, and head-tentacles were curious claws—reminding me of the colossal shadow-shapes which had groped so horribly in my path—while the entity as a whole sat upon a great throne-like pedestal inscribed with unknown hieroglyphs of vaguely Chinese cast. About both writing and image there hung an air of sinister evil so profound and pervasive that I could not think it the product of any one world or age. Rather must that monstrous shape be a focus for all the evil in unbounded space, throughout the eons past and to come—and those elditch symbols be vile sentient ikons endowed with a morbid life of their own and ready to wrest them-selves from the parchment for the reader's destruction. To the meaning of that monster and of those hieroglyphs I had no clue, but I knew that both had been traced with a hellish precision and for no nameable purpose. As I studied the leering characters, their kinship to the symbols on that ominous lock in the cellar became more and more manifest. I left the picture in the attic, for never could sleep come to me with such a thing near by.

All the afternoon and evening I read in the manuscript book of old Claes van der Heyl; and what I read will cloud and make horrible whatever period of life lies ahead of me. The genesis of the world and of previous worlds, unfolded itself before my eyes. I learned of the city Shamballah, built by the Lemurians fifty million years ago, yet inviolate still behind its walls of psychic force in the eastern desert. I learned of the Book of Dzyan, whose first six chapters antedate the Earth, and which was old when the lords of Venus came through space in their ships to civilise our planet. And I saw recorded in writing for the first time that name which others had spoken to me in whispers, and which I had known in a closer and more horrible way—the shunned and dreaded name of *Yian-Ho.*

In several places I was held up by passages requiring a key. Eventually, from various allusions, I gathered that old Claes had not dared to embody all his knowledge in one book, but had left certain points for another. Neither volume can be wholly intelligible without its fellow; hence I have resolved to find the second one if it lies anywhere within this accursed house. Though plainly a prisoner, I have not lost my lifelong zeal for the unknown; and am determined to probe the cosmos as deeply as possible before doom comes.

April 23

Searched all the morning for the second diary, and found it about noon in a desk in the little locked room. Like the first, it is in Claes van der Heyl's barbarous Latin, and it seems to consist of disjointed notes referring to various sections of the other. Glancing through the leaves, I spied at once the abhorred name of Yian-Ho—of Yian-Ho, that lost and hidden city wherein brood eon-old secrets, and of which dim memories older than the body lurk behind the minds of all men. It was repeated many times, and the text around it was strewn with crudely drawn hieroglyphs plainly akin to those on the pedestal in that hellish drawing I had seen. Here, clearly, lay the key to that monstrous tentacled shape and its forbidden message. With this knowledge I ascended the creaking stairs to the attic of cobwebs and horror.

When I tried to open the attic door it stuck as never before. Several times it resisted every effort to open it, and when at last it gave way I had a distinct feeling that some colossal, unseen shape had suddenly released it—a shape that soared away on non-material but audibly beating wings. When I found the horrible drawing I felt that it was not precisely where I had left it. Applying the key in the other book, I soon saw that the latter was no instant guide to the secret. It was only a clue—a clue to a secret too black to be left lightly guarded. It would take hours—perhaps days—to extract the awful message.

Shall I live long enough to learn the secret? The shadowy black arms and paws haunt my vision more and more now, and seem even more titanic than at first. Nor am I ever long free from those vague, unhuman presences whose nebulous bulk seems too vast for the chambers to contain. And now and then the grotesque, evanescent faces and forms, and the mocking portrait-shapes, troop before me in bewildering confusion.

Truly, there are terrible primal arcana of Earth which had better be left unknown and unevoked; dread secrets which have nothing to do with man, and which man may learn only in exchange for peace and sanity; cryptic truths which make the knower evermore an alien among his kind, and cause him to walk alone on Earth. Likewise are there dread survivals of things older and more potent than man; things that have blasphemously straggled down through the eons to ages never meant for them; monstrous entities that have lain sleeping endlessly in incredible crypts and remote caverns, outside the laws of reason and causation, and ready to be waked by such blasphemers as shall know their dark forbidden signs and furtive passwords.

April 24

Studied the picture and the key all day in the attic. At sunset I heard strange sounds, of a sort not encountered before and seeming to come from far away. Listening, I realised that they must flow from that queer abrupt hill with the circle of standing stones, which lies behind the village and some distance north of the house. I had heard that there was a path from the house leading up that hill to the primal cromlech, and had suspected that at certain seasons the van der Heyls had much occasion to use it; but the whole matter had hitherto lain latent in my consciousness. The present sounds consisted of a shrill piping intermingled with a peculiar and hideous sort of hissing or whistling, a bizarre, alien kind of music, like nothing which the annals of Earth describe. It was very faint, and soon faded, but the matter has set me thinking. It is towards the hill that the long, northerly "ell" with the secret chute, and the locked brick vault under it, extend. Can there be any connection which has so far eluded me?

April 25

I have made a peculiar and disturbing discovery about the nature of my imprisonment. Drawn towards the hill by a sinister fascination, I found the briars giving way before me, *but in that direction only.* There is a ruined gate, and beneath the bushes the traces of an old path no doubt exist. The briars extend part-way up and all around the hill, though the summit with the standing stones bears only a curious growth of moss and stunted grass. I climbed the hill and spent several hours there, noticing a strange wind which seems always to sweep around the forbidding monoliths and which sometimes seems to whisper in an oddly articulate though darkly cryptic fashion.

These stones, both in colour and in texture, resemble nothing I have seen elsewhere. They are neither brown nor grey, but rather of a dirty yellow merging into an evil green and having a suggestion of chameleon-like variability. Their texture is queerly like that of a scaled serpent, and is inexplicably nauseous to the touch— being as cold and clammy as the skin of a toad or other reptile. Near the central menhir is a singular stone-rimmed hollow which I cannot explain, but which may possibly form the entrance to a long-choked well or tunnel. When I sought to descend the hill at points away from the house I found the briars intercepting me as before, though the path towards the house was easily retraceable.

April 26

Up on the hill again this evening, and found that windy whispering much more distinct. The almost angry humming came close to actual speech, of a vague, sibilant sort, and reminded me of the strange piping chant I had heard from afar. After sunset there came a curious flash of premature summer lightning on the northern horizon, followed almost at once by a queer detonation high in the fading sky. Something about this phenomenon disturbed me greatly, and I could not escape the impression that the noise ended in a kind of unhuman hissing speech which trailed off into guttural cosmic laughter. Is my mind tottering at last, or has my unwarranted curiosity evoked unheard-of horrors from the twilight spaces? The Sabbat is close at hand now. What will be the end?

At last my dreams are to be realised! Whether or not my life or spirit or body will be claimed, I shall enter the gateway! Progress in deciphering those crucial hieroglyphs in the picture has been slow, but this afternoon I hit upon the final clue. By evening I knew their meaning—and that meaning can apply in only one way to the things I have encountered in this house.

There is beneath this house—sepulchered I know not where—an ancient forgotten One Who will show me the gateway I would enter, and give me the lost signs and words I shall need. How long it has lain buried here, forgotten save by those who reared the stones on the hill, and by those who later sought out this place and built this house, I cannot conjecture. It was in search of this Thing, beyond question, that Hendrik van der Heyl came to New-Netherland in 1638. Men of this Earth know It not, save in the secret whispers of the fear-shaken few who have found or inherited the key. No human eye has even yet glimpsed It—unless, perhaps, the vanished wizards of this house delved further than has been guessed.

With knowledge of the symbols came likewise a mastery of the Seven Lost Signs of Terror, and a tacit recognition of the hideous and unutterable Words of Fear. All that remains for me to accomplish is the Chant which will transfigure that Forgotten One Who is Guardian of the Ancient Gateway. I marvel much at the Chant. It is composed of strange and repellent gutturals and disturbing sibilants resembling no language I have ever encountered, even in the blackest chapters of the *Livre d'Eibon*. When I visited the hill at sunset I tried to read it aloud, but evoked in response only a vague, sinister fumbling on the far horizon, and a thin cloud of elemental dust that writhed and whirled like some evil living thing. Perhaps I do not pronounce the alien syllables correctly, or perhaps it is only on the Sabbat—that hellish Sabbat for which the Powers in this house are without question holding me—that the great Transfiguration can occur.

Had an odd spell of fright this morning. I thought for a moment that I recalled where I had seen that baffling name of Sleght before, and the prospect of realisation filled me with unutterable horror.

April 28

Today dark ominous clouds have hovered intermittently over the circle on the hill. I have noticed such clouds several times before, but their contours and arrangements now hold a fresh significance. They are snake-like and fantastic, and curiously like the evil shadow-shapes I have seen in the house. They float in a circle around the primal cromlech, revolving repeatedly as though endowed with a sinister life and purpose. I could swear that they give forth an angry murmuring. After some fifteen minutes they sail slowly away, ever to the eastward, like the units of a straggling battalion. Are they indeed those dread Ones whom Solomon knew of old—those giant black beings whose number is legion and whose tread doth shake the earth?

I have been rehearsing the Chant that will transfigure the Nameless Thing; yet strange fears assail me even when I utter the syllables under my breath. Piecing all evidence together, I have now discovered that the only way to It is through the locked cellar vault. That vault was built with a hellish purpose, and must cover the hidden burrow leading to the Immemorial Lair. What guardians live endlessly within, flourishing from century to century on an unknown nourishment, only the mad may conjecture. The warlocks of this house, who called them out of inner Earth, have known them only too well, as the shocking portraits and memories of the place reveal.

What troubles me most is the limited nature of the Chant. It evokes the Nameless One, yet provides no method for the control of That Which is evoked. There are, of course, the general signs and gestures, but whether they will prove effective towards such a One remains to be seen. Still, the rewards are great enough to justify any danger, and I could not retreat if I would, since an unknown force plainly urges me on.

I have discovered one more obstacle. Since the locked cellar vault must be traversed, the key to that place must be found. The lock is far too strong for forcing. That the key is somewhere hereabouts cannot be doubted, but the time before the Sabbat is very short. I must search diligently and thoroughly. It will take courage to unlock that iron door, for what prisoned horrors may not lurk within?

Later

I have been shunning the cellar for the past day or two, but late this afternoon I again descended to those forbidding precincts.

At first all was silent, but within five minutes the menacing padding and muttering began once more beyond the iron door. This time it was louder and more terrifying than on any previous occasion, and I likewise recognised the slithering that bespoke some monstrous sea-beast—now swifter and nervously intensified, as if the thing were striving to force its way through the portal to where I stood.

As the pacing grew louder, more restless, and more sinister, there began to pound through it those hellish and unidentifiable reverberations which I had heard on my second visit to the cellar —those muffled reverberations which seemed to echo from far horizons like distant thunder. Now, however, their volume was magnified a hundredfold, and their timbre freighted with new and terrifying implications. I can compare the sound to nothing more aptly than to the roar of some dread monster of the vanished saurian age, when primal horrors roamed the Earth, and Valusia's serpent-men laid the foundation-stones of evil magic. To such a roar—but swelled to deafening heights reached by no known organic throat—was this shocking sound akin. Dare I unlock the door and face the onslaught of what lies beyond?

April 29

The key to the vault is found. I came upon it this noon in the little locked room—buried beneath rubbish in a drawer of the ancient desk, as if some belated effort to conceal it had been made. It was wrapped in a crumbling newspaper dated October 31, 1872; but there was an inner wrapping of dried skin—evidently the hide of some unknown reptile—which bore a Low Latin message in the same crabbed writing as that of the notebooks I found. As I had thought, the lock and key were vastly older than the vault. Old Claes van der Heyl had had them ready for something he or his descendants meant to do—and how much older than he they were

I could not estimate. Deciphering the Latin message, I trembled in a fresh access of clutching terror and nameless awe. "The secrets of the monstrous primal Ones," ran the crabbed text, "whose cryptic words relate the hidden things that were before man; the things no one of Earth should learn, lest peace be for ever forfeited; shall by me never suffer revelation. To Yian-Ho, that lost and forbidden city of countless eons whose place may not be told, I have been in the veritable flesh of this body, as none other among the living has been. Therein have I found, and thence have I borne away, that knowledge which I would gladly lose, though I may not. I have learnt to bridge a gap that should not be bridged, and must call out of the Earth That Which should not be waked nor called. And what is sent to follow me will not sleep till I or those after me have found and done what is to be found and done.

"That which I have awaked and borne away with me, I may not part with again. So is it written in the Book of Hidden Things. That which I have willed to be has twined its dreadful shape around me, and—if I live not to do the bidding—around those children born and unborn who shall come after me, until the bidding be done. Strange may be their joinings, and awful the aid they may summon till the end be reached. Into lands unknown and dim must they seeking go, and a house must be built for the outer guardians.

"This is the key to that lock which was given me in the dreadful, eon-old and forbidden city of Yian-Ho; the lock which I or mine must place upon the vestibule of That Which is to be found. And may the Lord of Yaddith succour me—or him—who must set that lock in place or turn the key thereof."

Such was the message—a message which, once I had read it, I seemed to have known before. Now, as I write these words, the key is before me. I gaze on it with mixed dread and longing, and cannot find words to describe its aspect. It is of the same unknown, subtly greenish frosted metal as the lock; a metal best compared to brass tarnished with verdigris. Its design is alien and fantastic, and the coffin-shaped end of the ponderous bulk leaves no doubt of the lock it was meant to fit. The handle roughly forms a strange, non-human image, whose exact outlines and identity cannot now be traced. Upon holding it for any length of time I seem to feel an alien, anomalous life in the cold metal—a quickening or pulsing too feeble for ordinary recognition.

Below the eidolon is graven a faint, eon-worn legend in those blasphemous, Chinese-like hieroglyphs I have come to know so well. I can make out only the beginning—the words: "My vengeance lurks . . ."—before the text fades to indistinctness. There is some fatality in this timely finding of the key—for tomorrow night comes the hellish Sabbat. But strangely enough, amidst all this hideous expectancy, that question of the Sleght name bothers me more and more. Why should I dread to find it linked with the van der Heyls?

Walpurgis-Eve—April 30

The time has come. I waked last night to see the key glowing with a lurid greenish radiance—that same morbid green which I have seen in the eyes and skin of certain portraits here, on the shocking lock and key, on the monstrous menhirs of the hill, and in a thousand other recesses of my consciousness. There were strident whispers in the air—sibilant whistlings like those of the wind around that dreadful cromlech. Something spoke to me out of the frore aether of space, and it said, "The hour falls." It is an omen, and I laugh at my own fears. Have I not the dread words and the Seven Lost Signs of Terror—the power coercive of any Dweller in the cosmos or in the unknown darkened spaces? I will no longer hesitate.

The heavens are very dark, as if a terrific storm were coming on—a storm even greater than that of the night when I reached here, nearly a fortnight ago. From the village, less than a mile away, I hear a queer and unwonted babbling. It is as I thought—these poor degraded idiots are within the secret, and keep the awful Sabbat on the hill.

Here in the house the shadows gather densely. In the darkness the sky before me almost glows with a greenish light of its own. I have not yet been to the cellar. It is better that I wait, lest the sound of that muttering and padding—those slitherings and muffled reverberations—unnerve me before I can unlock the fateful door.

Of what I shall encounter, and what I must do, I have only the most general idea. Shall I find my task in the vault itself, or must I burrow deeper into the nighted heart of our planet? There are things I do not yet understand—or at least, prefer not to understand—despite a dreadful, increasing, and inexplicable sense of bygone familiarity with this fearsome house. That chute, for instance, leading down from the little locked room. But I think I know why the wing with the vault extends towards the hill.

6 p.m.

Looking out of the north windows, I can see a group of villagers on the hill. They seem unaware of the lowering sky, and are digging near the great central menhir. It occurs to me that they are working on that stone-rimmed hollow place which looks like a long-choked tunnel entrance. What is to come? How much of the olden Sabbat rites have these people retained? That key glows horribly—it is not imagination. Dare I use it as it must be used? Another matter has greatly disturbed me. Glancing nervously through a book in the library I cam upon an ampler form of the name that has teased my memory so sorely: "Trintje, wife of Adriaen Sleght." The *Adriaen* leads me to the very brink of recollection.

Midnight

Horror is unleashed, but I must not weaken. The storm has broken with pandemoniac fury, and lightning has struck the hill three times, yet the hybrid, malformed villagers are gathering within the cromlech. I can see them in the almost constant flashes. The great standing stones loom up shockingly, and have a dull green luminosity that reveals them even when the lightning is not there. The peals of the thunder are deafening, and every one seems to be horribly *answered* from some indeterminate direction. As I write, the creatures on the hill have begun to chant and howl and scream in a degraded, half-simian version of the ancient ritual. Rain pours down like a flood, yet they leap and emit sounds in a kind of diabolic ecstasy.

"*Ia, Shub-Niggurath! The Goat with a Thousand Young!*"

But the worst thing is within the house. Even at this height, I have begun to hear sounds from the cellar. *It is the padding and muttering and slithering and muffled reverberations within the vault....*

Memories come and go. That name of *Adriaen Sleght* pounds oddly at my consciousness. Dirck van der Heyl's son-in-law ... his child old Dirck's granddaughter and Abaddon Corey's great-granddaughter....

Merciful God! *At last I know where I saw that name.* I know, and am transfixed with horror. All is lost. . . .

The key has begun to feel warm as my left hand nervously clutches it. At times that vague quickening or pulsing is so distinct that I can almost feel the living metal move. It came from Yian-Ho for a terrible purpose, and to me—who all too late know the thin stream of van der Heyl blood that trickles down through the Sleghts into my own lineage—has descended the hideous task of fulfilling that purpose. . . .

My courage and curiosity wane. I know the horror that lies beyond that iron door. What if Claes van der Heyl was my ancestor —need I expiate his nameless sin ? *I will not—I swear I will not !* . . . (the writing here grows indistinct) . . . too late—cannot help self— black paws materialise—am dragged away towards the cellar. . . .

THE CHALLENGE FROM BEYOND

As the mist-blurred light of the sapphire suns grew more intense, the outlines of the globe ahead wavered and dissolved to a churning chaos. Its pallor and its motion and its music all blended themselves with the engulfing mist – bleaching it to a pale steel-color and setting it undulantly in motion. And the sapphire suns, too, melted imperceptibly into the graying infinity of shapeless pulsation.

Meanwhile the sense of forward, outward motion grew intolerably, incredibly, cosmically swift. Every standard of speed known to earth seemed dwarfed, and George Campbell knew that any such flight in physical reality would mean instant death to a human being. Even as it was – in this strange, hellish hypnosis or nightmare – the quasi-visual impression of meteor-like hurtling almost paralyzed his mind. Though there were no real points of reference in the gray, pulsing void, he felt that he was approaching and passing the speed of light itself. Finally his consciousness did go under – and merciful blackness swallowed everything.

It was very suddenly, and amidst the most impenetrable darkness, that thoughts and ideas again came to George Campbell. Of how many moments – or years – or eternities – had elapsed since his flight through the gray void, he could form no estimate. He knew only that he seemed to be at rest and without pain. Indeed, the absence of all physical sensation was the salient quality of his condition. It made even the blackness seem less solidly black – suggesting as it did that he was rather a disembodied intelligence in a state beyond physical senses, than a corporeal being with senses deprived of their accustomed objects of perception. He could think sharply and quickly – almost preternaturally so – yet could form no idea whatsoever of his situation.

Half by instinct, he realized that he was not in his own tent. True, he might have awaked there from a nightmare to a world equally black; yet he knew this was not so. There was no camp cot beneath him – he had no hands to feel the blankets and canvas surface and flashlight that ought to be around him – there was no sensation of cold in the air – no flap through which he could glimpse the pale night outside . . . something was wrong, dreadfully wrong.

He cast his mind backward and thought of the fluorescent cube which had hypnotized him – of that, and all which had followed. He had known that his mind was going, yet had been unable to draw back. At the last moment there had been a shocking, panic fear – a subconscious fear beyond even that caused by the sensation of daemonic flight. It had come from some vague flash or remote recollection – just what, he could not at once tell. Some cell-group in the back of his head had seemed to find a cloudily familiar quality in the cube – and that familiarity was fraught with dim terror. Now he tried to remember what the familiarity and the terror were.

Little by little it came to him. Once – long ago, in connection with his geological life-work – he had read of something like that cube. It had to do with those debatable and disquieting clay fragments called the Eltdown Shards, dug up from pre-carboniferous strata in southern England thirty years before. Their shape and markings were so queer that a few scholars hinted at artificiality, and made wild conjectures about them and their origin. They came, clearly, from a time when no human beings could exist on the globe – but their contours and figurings were damnably puzzling. That was how they got their name.

It was not, however, in the writings of any sober scientist that Campbell had seen that reference to a crystal, disc-holding globe. The source was far less reputable, and infinitely more vivid. About 1912 a deeply learned Sussex clergyman of occultist leanings – the Reverend Arthur Brooke Winters-Hall – had professed to identify the markings on the Eltdown Shards with some of the so-called 'pre-human hieroglyphs' that were persistently cherished and esoterically handed down in certain mystical circles, and had published at his own expense what purported to be a 'translation' of the primal and baffling 'inscriptions' – a 'translation' still quoted frequently and seriously by occult writers. In this 'translation' – a surprisingly long brochure in view of the limited number of 'shards' existing – had occurred the narrative, supposedly of pre-human authorship, containing the now frightening reference.

As the story went, there dwelt on a world – and eventually on countless other worlds – of outer space a mighty order of worm-like beings whose attainments and whose control of nature surpassed anything within the range of terrestrial imagination. They had mastered the art of interstellar travel early in their career, and had peopled every habitable planet in their own galaxy – killing off the races they found.

Beyond the limits of their own galaxy – which was not ours – they could not navigate in person; but in their quest for knowledge of all space and time they discovered a means of spanning certain transgalactic gulfs with their minds. They devised peculiar objects – strangely energized cubes of a curious crystal containing hypnotic talismen and enclosed in space-resisting spherical envelopes of an unknown substance – which could be forcibly expelled beyond the limits of their universe, and which would respond to the attraction of cool solid matter only.

These, of which a few would necessarily land on various inhabited worlds in outside universe, formed the ether-bridges needed for mental communication. Atmospheric friction burned away the protecting envelope, leaving the cube exposed and subject to discovery by the intelligent minds of the world where it fell. By its very nature, the cube would attract and rivet attention. This, when coupled with the action of light, was sufficient to set its special properties working.

The mind that noticed the cube would be drawn into it by the power of the disc, and would be sent on a thread of obscure energy to the place whence the disc had come – the remote world of the worm-like space-explorers across stupendous galactic abysses. Received in one of the machines to which each cube was attuned, the captured mind would remain suspended without body or senses until examined by one of the sominant race. Then it would, by an obscure process of interchange, be pumped of all its contents. The investigator's mind would now occupy the strange machine while the captive mind occupied the interrogator's worm-like body. Then, in another interchange, the interrogator's mind would leap across boundless space to the captive's vacant and unconscious body on the transgalactic world – animating the alien tenement as best it might, and exploring the alien world in the guise of one of its denizens.

When done with exploration, the adventurer would use the cube and its disc in accomplishing his return – and sometimes the captured mind would be restored safely to its own remote world. Not always, however, were the sominant race so kind. Sometimes, when a potentially important race capable of space travel was found, the worm-like folk would employ the cube to capture and annihilate minds by the thousands, and would extirpate the race for diplomatic reasons – using the exploring minds as agents of destruction.

In other cases sections of the worm-folk would permanently occupy a transgalactic planet – destroying the captured minds and wiping out the remaining inhabitants preparatory to settling down in unfamiliar bodies. Never, however, could the parent civilization be quite duplicated in such a case, since the new planet would not contain all the materials necessary for the worm-race's arts. The cubes, for example, could be made only on the home planet.

Only a few of the numberless cubes sent forth ever found a landing and response on an inhabited world – since there was no such thing as *aiming* them at goals beyond sight or know-ledge. Only three, ran the story, had ever landed on peopled worlds in our own particular universe. One of these had struck a planet near the galactic rim 2000 billion years ago, while another had lodged 3 billion years ago on a world near the center of the galaxy. The third – and the only one ever known to have invaded the solar system – had reached our own earth 150,000,000 years ago.

Realizing that the changed individuals represented invading minds, the race's leaders had them destroyed – even at the cost of leaving the displaced minds exiled in alien space. They had had experience with even stranger transitions. Then, through a mental exploration of space and time, they formed a rough idea of what the cube was, they carefully hid the thing from light and sight, and guarded it as a menace. They did not wish to destroy a thing so rich in later experimental possibilities. Now and then some rash, unscrupulous adventurer would furtively gain access to it and sample its perilous powers despite the consequences – but all such cases were discovered, and safely and drastically dealt with.

Of this evil meddling the only bad result was that the worm-like outside race learned from the new exiles what had happened to the explorers on earth, and conceived a violent hatred of the planet and all its life-forms. They would have depopulated it if they could, and indeed sent additional cubes into space in the wild hope of striking it by accident in unguarded places – but that accident never came to pass.

The cone-shaped terrestrial beings kept the one existing cube in a special shrine as a relique and basis for experiments, till after aeons it was lost amidst the chaos of war and the destruction of the great polar city where it was guarded. When, 50 million years ago, the beings sent their minds ahead into the infinite future to avoid a nameless peril of inner earth, the whereabouts of the sinister cube from space were unknown.

This much, according to the learned occultist, the Eltdown Shards had said. What now made the account so obscurely frightful to Campbell was the minute accuracy with which the alien cube had been described. Every detail tallied: dimensions, consistency, hieroglyphed central disc, hypnotic effects. As he thought the matter over and over amidst the darkness of his strange situation, he began to wonder whether his whole experience with the crystal cube – indeed, its very existence – were not a nightmare brought on by some freakish subconscious memory of this old bit of extravagant, charlatanic reading. If so, though, the nightmare must still be in force; since his present apparently bodiless state had nothing of normality in it.

Of the time consumed by this puzzled memory and reflection, Campbell could form no estimate. Everything about his state was so unreal that ordinary dimensions and measurements became meaningless. It seemed an eternity, but perhaps it was not really long before the sudden interruption came. What happened was as strange and inexplicable as the blackness it succeeded. There was a sensation – of the mind rather than of the body – and all at once Campbell felt his thoughts swept or sucked beyond his control in tumultuous and chaotic fashion.

Memories arose irresponsibly and irrelevantly. All that he knew – all his personal background, traditions, experiences, scholarship, dreams, ideas, and inspirations – welled up abruptly and simultaneously, with a dizzying speed and abundance which soon made him unable to keep track of any separate concept. The parade of all his mental contents became an avalanche, a cascade, a vortex. It was as horrible and vertiginous as his hypnotic flight through space when the crystal cube pulled him. Finally it sapped his consciousness and brought on fresh oblivion.

Another measureless blank – and then a slow trickle of sensation. This time it was physical, not mental. Sapphire light, and a low rumble of distant sound. There were tactile impressions – he could realize that he was lying at full length on something, though there was a baffling strangeness about the feel of his posture. He could not reconcile the pressure of the supporting surface with his own outlines – or with the outlines of the human form at all. He tried to move his arms, but found no definite response to the attempt. But, there were little, ineffectual nervous twitches all over the area which seemed to mark his body.

He tried to open his eyes more widely, but found himself unable to control their mechanism. The sapphire light came in a diffused, nebulous manner, and could nowhere be voluntarily focused into definiteness. Gradually, though, visual images began to trickle in curiously and indecisively. The limits and qualities of vision were not those which he was used to, but he could roughly correlate the sensation with what he had known as sight. As this sensation gained some degree of stability, Campbell realized that he must still be in throes of nightmare.

He seemed to be in a room of considerable extent – of medium height, but with a large proportionate area. On every side – and he could apparently see all four sides at once – were high, narrowish slits which seemed to serve as combined doors and windows. There were singular low tables or pedestals, but no furniture of normal nature and proportions. Through the slits streamed floods of sapphire light, and beyond them could be mistily seen the sides and roofs of fantastic buildings like clustered cubes. On the walls – in the vertical panels between the slits – were strange markings of an oddly disquieting character. It was some time before Campbell understood why they disturbed him so – then he saw that they were, in repeated instances, precisely like some of the hieroglyphs on the crystal cube's disc.

The actual nightmare element, though, was something more than this. It began with the living thing which presently entered through one of the slits, advancing deliberately toward him and bearing a metal box of bizarre proportions and glassy, mirror-like surfaces. For this thing was nothing human – nothing of earth – nothing even of man's myths and dreams. It was a gigantic, pale-gray worm or centipede, as large around as a man and twice as long, with a disc-like, apparently eyeless, cilia fringed head bearing a purple central orifice. It glided on its rear pairs of legs, with its fore part raised vertically – the legs, or at least two pairs of them, serving as arms. Along its spinal ridge was a curious purple comb, and a fan-shaped tail of some gray membrane ended its grotesque bulk. There was a ring of flexible red spikes around its neck, and from the twistings of these came clicking, twanging sounds in measured, deliberate rhythms.

Here, indeed, was an *outré* nightmare at its height, capricious fantasy at its apex. But even this vision of delirium was not what caused George Campbell to lapse a third time into unconsciousness. It took one more thing – one final, unbearable touch – to do that. As the nameless worm advanced with its glistening box, the reclining man caught in the mirror-like surface a glimpse of what should have been his own body. Yet – horribly verifying his disordered and unfamiliar sensations – it was not his own body at all that he saw reflected in the burnished metal. It was, instead, the loathsome, pale-grey bulk of one of the great centipedes.

Pickman's Model

YOU needn't think I'm crazy, Eliot – plenty of others have queerer prejudices than this. Why don't you laugh at Oliver's grandfather, who won't ride in a motor? If I don't like that damned subway, it's my own business; and we got here more quickly anyhow in the taxi. We'd have had to walk up the hill from Park Street if we'd taken the car.

I know I'm more nervous than I was when you saw me last year, but you don't need to hold a clinic over it. There's plenty of reason, God knows, and I fancy I'm lucky to be sane at all. Why the third degree? You didn't used to be so inquisitive. Well, if you must hear it, I don't know why you shouldn't. Maybe you ought to, anyhow, for you kept writing me like a grieved parent when you heard I'd begun to cut the Art Club and keep away from Pickman. Now that he's disappeared I go around to the club once in a while, but my nerves aren't what they were.

No, I don't know what's become of Pickman, and I don't like to guess. You might have surmised I had some inside information when I dropped him – and that's why I don't want to think where he's gone. Let the police find what they can – it won't be much, judging from the fact that they don't know yet of the old North End place he hired under the name of Peters. I'm not sure that I could find it again myself – not that I'd ever try, even in broad daylight! Yes, I do know, or am afraid I know, why he maintained it. I'm coming to that. And I think you'll understand before I'm through why I don't tell the police. They would ask me to guide them, but I couldn't go back there even if I knew the way. There was something there – and now I can't use the subway or (and you may as well have your laugh at this, too) go down into cellars any more.

I should think you'd have known I didn't drop Pickman for the same silly reasons that fussy old women like Dr Reid or .Joe Minot or Bosworth did. Morbid art doesn't shock me, and when a man has the genius Pickman had I feel it an honour to know him, no matter what direction his work takes. Boston never had a greater painter than Richard Upton Pickman. I said it at first and I say it still, and I never swerved an inch, either, when he showed that *Ghoul Feeding*. That, you remember, was when Minot cut him.

You know, it takes profound art and profound insight into Nature to turn out stuff like Pickman's. Any magazine-cover hack can splash paint around wildly and call it a nightmare or Witches' Sabbath or a portrait of the devil, but only a great painter can make such a thing really scare or ring true. That's because only a real artist knows the actual anatomy of the terrible or the physiology of fear – the exact sort of lines and proportions that connect up with latent instincts or hereditary memories of fright, and the proper colour contrasts and lighting effects to stir the dormant sense of strangeness. I don't have to tell you why a Fuseli really brings a shiver while a cheap ghost-story frontispiece merely makes us laugh. There's something those fellows catch – beyond life – that they're able to make us catch for a second. Doré had it. Sime has it. Angarola of Chicago has it. And Pickman had it as no man ever had it before or – I hope to heaven – ever will again.

Don't ask me what it is they see. You know, in ordinary art, there's all the difference in the world between the vital, breathing things drawn from Nature or models and the artificial truck that commercial small fry reel off in a bare studio by rule. Well, I should say that the really weird artist has a kind of vision which makes models, or summons up what amounts to actual scenes from the spectral world he lives in. Anyhow, he manages to turn out results that differ from the pretender's mince-pie dreams in just about the same way that the life painter's results differ from the concoctions of a correspondence-school cartoonist. If I had ever seen what Pickman saw – but no! Here, let's have a drink before we get any deeper. Gad, I wouldn't be alive if I'd ever seen what that man – if he was a man – saw!

You recall that Pickman's forte was faces. I don't believe anybody since Goya could put so much of sheer hell into a set of features or a twist of expression. And before Goya you have to go back to the medieval chaps who did the gargoyles and chimeras on Notre Dame and Mont Saint-Michel. They believed all sorts of things – and maybe they saw all sorts of things, too, for the Middle Ages had some curious phases. I remember your asking Pickman yourself once, the year before you went away, wherever in thunder he got such ideas and visions. Wasn't that a nasty laugh he gave you? It was partly because of that laugh that Reid dropped him. Reid, you know, had just taken up comparative pathology, and was full of pompous 'inside stuff' about the biological or evolutionary significance of this or that mental or physical symptom. He said Pickman repelled him more and more every day, and almost frightened him toward the last – that the fellow's features and expression were slowly developing in a way he didn't like; in a way that wasn't human. He had a lot of talk about diet, and said Pickman must be abnormal and eccentric to the last degree. I suppose you told Reid, if you and he had any correspondence over it, that he'd let Pickman's paintings get on his nerves or harrow up his imagination. I know I told him that myself – then.

But keep in mind that I didn't drop Pickman for anything like this. On the contrary, my admiration for him kept growing; for that *Ghoul Feeding* was a tremendous achievement. As you know, the club wouldn't exhibit it, and the Museum of Fine Arts wouldn't accept it as a gift; and I can add that nobody would buy it, so Pickman had it right in his house till he went. Now his father has it in Salem – you know Pickman comes of old Salem stock, and had a witch ancestor hanged in 1692.

I got into the habit of calling on Pickman quite often, especially after I began making notes for a monograph on weird art. Probably it was his work which put the idea into my head, and anyhow, I found him a mine of data and suggestions when I came to develop it. He showed me all the paintings and drawings he had about; including some pen-and-ink sketches that would, I verily believe, have got him kicked out of the club if many of the members had seen them. Before long I was pretty nearly a devotee, and would listen for hours like a schoolboy to art theories and philosophic speculations wild enough to qualify him for the Danvers asylum. My hero-worship, coupled with the fact that people generally were commencing to have less and less to do with him, made him get very confidential with me; and one evening he hinted that if I were fairly close-mouthed and none too squeamish, he might show me something rather unusual – something a bit stronger than anything he had in the house.

'You know,' he said, 'there are things that won't do for Marlborough Street – things that are out of place here, and that can't be conceived here, anyhow. It's my business to catch the overtones of the soul, and you won't find those in a parvenu set of artificial streets on made land. Back Bay isn't Boston – it isn't anything yet, because it's had no time to pick up memories and attract local spirits. If there are any ghosts here, they're the tame ghosts of a salt marsh and a shallow cove; and I want human ghosts – the ghosts of beings highly organized enough to have looked on hell and known the meaning of what they saw.

'The place for an artist to love is the North End. If any æsthete, were sincere, he'd put up with the slums for the sake of the massed traditions. God, man! Don't you realize that places like that weren't merely *made*, but actually *grew*? Generation after generation lived and felt and died there, and in days when people weren't afraid to live and feel and die. Don't you know there was a mill on Copp's Hill in 1632, and that half the present streets were laid out by 1650? I can show you houses that have stood two centuries and a half and more; houses that have witnessed what would make a modern house crumble into power. What do moderns know of life and the forces behind it? You call the Salem witchcraft a delusion, but I'll wager my four-times-great-grandmother could have told you things. They hanged her on Gallows Hill, with Cotton Mather looking sanctimoniously on. Mather, damn him, was afraid somebody might succeed in kicking free of this accursed cage of monotony – I wish someone had laid a spell on him or sucked his blood in the night!

'I can show you a house he lived in, and I can show you another one he was afraid to enter in spite of all his fine bold talk. He knew things he didn't dare put into that stupid *Magnalia* or that puerile *Wonders of the Invisible World*. Look here, do you know the whole North End once had a set of tunnels that kept certain people in touch with each other's houses, and the burying ground, and the sea? Let them prosecute and persecute above ground – things went on every day that they couldn't reach, and voices laughed at night that they couldn't place!

'Why, man, out of ten surviving houses built before 1700 and not moved since I'll wager that in eight I can show you something queer in the cellar. There's hardly a month that you don't read of workmen finding bricked-up arches and wells leading nowhere in this or that old place as it comes down – you could see one near Henchman Street from the elevated last year. There were witches and what their spells summoned; pirates and what they brought in from the sea; smugglers; privateers – and I tell you, people knew how to live, and how to enlarge the bounds of life, in the old times!

This wasn't the only world a bold and wise man could know – faugh! And to think of today in contrast, with such pale-pink brains that even a club of supposed artists gets shudders and convulsions if a picture goes beyond the feelings of a Beacon Street tea-table!

'The only saving grace of the present is that it's too damned stupid to question the past very closely. What do maps and records and guidebooks really tell of the North End? Bah! At a guess I'll guarantee to lead you to thirty or forty alleys and networks of alleys north of Prince Street that aren't suspected by ten living beings outside of the foreigners that swarm them. And what do those Dagoes know of their meaning? No, Thurber, these ancient places are dreaming gorgeously and overflowing with wonder and terror and escapes from the commonplace, and yet there's not a living soul to understand or profit by them. Or, rather, there's only one living soul – for I haven't been digging around in the past for nothing!

'See here, you're interested in this sort of thing. What if I told you that I've got another studio up there, where I can catch the night-spirit of antique horror and paint things that I couldn't even think of in Marlborough Street? Naturally I don't tell those cursed old maids at the club – with Reid, damn him, whispering even as it is that I'm a sort of monster bound down the toboggan of reverse evolution. Yes, Thurber, I decided long ago that one must paint terror as well as beauty from life, so I did some exploring in places where I had reason to know terror lives.

'I've got a place that I don't believe three living Nordic men besides myself have ever seen. It isn't so very far from the elevated as distance goes, but it's centuries away as the soul goes. I took it because of the queer old brick well in the cellar – one of the sort I told you about. The shack's almost tumbling down, so that nobody else would live there, and I'd hate to tell you how little I pay for it. The windows are boarded up, but I like that all the better, since I don't want daylight for what I do. I paint in the cellar, where the inspiration is thickest, but I've other rooms furnished on the ground floor. A Sicilian owns it, and I've hired it under the name of Peters.

'Now if you're game, I'll take you there to-night. I think you'd enjoy the pictures, for as I said, I've let myself go a bit there. It's no vast tour – I sometimes do it on foot, for I don't want to attract attention with a taxi in such a place. We can take the shuttle at the South Station for Battery Street, and after that the walk isn't much.'

Well, Eliot, there wasn't much for me to do after that harangue but to keep myself from running instead of walking for the first vacant cab we could sight. We changed to the elevated at the South Station, and at about 12 o'clock had climbed down the steps at Battery Street and struck along the old waterfront past Constitution Wharf. I didn't keep track of the cross streets, and can't tell you yet which it was we turned up, but I know it wasn't Greenough Lane.

When we did turn, it was to climb through the deserted length of the oldest and dirtiest alley I ever saw in my life, with crumbling-looking gables, broken small-paned windows, and archaic chimneys that stood out half-disintegrated against the moon-lit sky. I don't believe there were three houses in sight that hadn't been standing in Cotton Mather's time – certainly I glimpsed at least two with an overhang, and once I thought I saw a peaked roof-line of the almost forgotten pre-gambrel type, though antiquarians tell us there are none left in Boston.

From that alley, which had a dim light, we turned to the left into an equally silent and still narrower alley with no light at all; and in a minute made what I think was an obtuse-angled bend toward the right in the dark. Not long after this Pickman produced a flashlight and revealed an antediluvian ten-panelled door that looked damnably worm-eaten. Unlocking it, he ushered me into a barren hallway with what was once splendid dark-oak panelling – simple, of course, but thrillingly suggestive of the times of Andros and Phips and the Witchcraft. Then he took me through a door on the left, lighted an oil lamp, and told me to make myself at home.

Now, Eliot, I'm what the man in the street would call fairly 'hard-boiled'. but I'll confess that what I saw on the walls of that room gave me a bad turn. They were his pictures you know – the ones he couldn't paint or even show in Marlborough Street – and he was right when he said he had 'let himself go'. Here – have another drink – I need one, anyhow!

There's no use in my trying to tell you what they were like, because the awful, the blasphemous horror, and the unbeliev-able loathsomeness and moral fetor came from simple touches quite beyond the power of words to classify. There was none of the exotic technique you see in Sidney Sime, none of the trans-Saturnian landscapes and lunar fungi that Clark Ashton Smith uses to freeze the blood. The back-grounds were mostly old churchyards, deep woods, cliffs by the sea, brick tunnels, ancient panelled rooms, or simple vaults of masonry. Copp's Hill Burying Ground which could not be many blocks away from this very house, was a favourite scene.

The madness and monstrosity lay in the figures in the foreground – for Pickman's morbid art was pre-eminently one of demoniac portraiture. These figures were seldom com-pletely human, but often approached humanity in varying degrees. Most of the bodies, while roughly bipedal, had a forward slumping, and a vaguely canine cast. The texture of the majority was a kind of unpleasant rubberiness. Ugh! I can see them now! Their occupations – well, don't ask me to be too precise. They were usually feeding – I won't say on what. They were sometimes shown in groups in cemeteries or underground passages, and often appeared to be in battle over their prey – or rather, their treasure-trove. And what damnable expressiveness Pickman sometimes gave the sight-less faces of this charnel booty! Occasionally the things were shown leaping through open windows at night, or squatting on the chests of sleepers, worrying at their throats. One canvas showed a ring of them baying about a hanged witch on Gallows Hill, whose dead face held a close kinship to theirs.

But don't get the idea that it was all this hideous business of theme and setting which struck me faint. I'm not a three-year-old kid, and I'd seen much like this before. It was the *faces*, Eliot, those accursed *faces*, that leered and slavered out of the canvas with the very breath of life! By God, man, I verily believe they *were* alive! That nauseous wizard had waked the fires of hell in pigment, and his brush had been a nightmare-spawning wand. Give me that decanter, Eliot!

There was one thing called *The Lesson* – heaven pity me, that I ever saw it! Listen – can you fancy a squatting circle of nameless doglike things in a churchyard teaching a small child how to feed like themselves? The price of a changeling, I suppose – you know the old myth about how the weird people leave their spawn in cradles in exchange for the human babes they steal. Pickman was showing what happens to those stolen babes – how they grow up – and then I began to see a hideous relationship in the faces of the human and non-human figures. He was, in all his gradations of morbidity between the frankly non-human and the degradedly human, establishing a sardonic linkage and evolution. The dog-things were developed from mortals!

And no sooner had I wondered what he made of their own young as left with mankind in the form of changelings, than my eye caught a picture embodying that very thought. It was that of an ancient Puritan interior – a heavily beamed room with lattice windows, a settle, and clumsy seventeenth century furniture, with the family sitting about while the father read from the Scriptures. Every face but one showed nobility and reverence, but that one reflected the mockery of the pit. It was that of a man young in years, and no doubt belonged to a supposed son of that pious father, but in essence it was the kin of the unclean things. It was their changeling – and in a spirit of supreme irony Pickman had given the features a very perceptible resemblance to his own.

By this time Pickman had lighted a lamp in an adjoining room and was politely holding open the door for me; asking me if I would care to see his 'modern studies'. I hadn't been able to give him much of my opinions – I was too speechless with fright and loathing – but I think he fully understood and felt highly complimented. And now I want to assure you again, Eliot, that I'm no mollycoddle to scream at anything which shows a bit of departure from the usual. I'm middle-aged and decently sophisticated, and I guess you saw enough of me in France to know I'm not easily knocked out. Remember, too, that I'd just about recovered my wind and got used to those frightful pictures which turned colonial New England into a kind of annexe of hell. Well, in spite of all this, that next room forced a real scream out of me, and I had to clutch at the doorway to keep from keeling over. The other chamber had shown a pack of ghouls and witches overrunning the world of our forefathers, but this one brought the horror right into our own daily life!

Gad, how that man could paint! There was a study called *Subway Accident*, in which a flock of the vile things were clambering up from some unknown catacomb through a crack in the floor of the Boylston Street subway and attacking a crowd of people on the platform. Another showed a dance on Copp's Hill among the tombs with the background of to-day. Then there were any number of cellar views, with monsters creeping in through holes and rifts in the masonry and grinning as they squatted behind barrels or furnaces and waited for their first victim to descend the stairs.

One disgusting canvas seemed to depict a vast cross-section of Beacon Hill, with antlike armies of the mephitic monsters squeezing themselves through burrows that honeycombed the ground. Dances in the modern cemeteries were freely pictured, and another conception somehow shocked me more than all the rest – a scene in an unknown vault, where scores of the beasts crowded about one who held a well-known Boston guidebook and was evidently reading aloud. All were pointing to a certain passage, and every face seemed so distorted with epileptic and reverberant laughter that I almost thought I heard the fiendish echoes. The title of the picture was *Holmes, Lowell and Longfellow Lie Buried in Mount Auburn*.

As I gradually steadied myself and got readjusted to this second room of deviltry and morbidity, I began to analyse some of the points in my sickening loathing. In the first place, I said to myself, these things repelled because of the utter inhumanity and callous cruelty they showed in Pickman. The fellow must be a relentless enemy of all mankind to take such glee in the torture of brain and flesh and the degradation of the mortal tenement. In the second place, they terrified because of their very greatness. Their art was the art that convinced – when we saw the pictures we saw the demons themselves and were afraid of them. And the queer part was, that Pickman got none of his power from the use of selectiveness or bizarrerie. Nothing was blurred, distorted, or conventionalized; outlines were sharp and life-like, and details were almost painfully defined. And the faces!

It was not any mere artist's interpretation that we saw; it was pandemonium itself, crystal-clear in stark objectivity.

That was it, by heaven! The man was not a fantaisiste or romanticist at all – he did not even try to give us the churning, prismatic ephemera of dreams, but coldly and sardonically reflected some stable, mechanistic, and well-established horror-world which he saw fully, brilliantly, squarely and unfalteringly. God knows what that world can have been, or where he ever glimpsed the blasphemous shapes that loped and trotted and crawled through it; but whatever the baffling source of his images, one thing was plain. Pickman was in every sense – in conception and in execution – a thorough, painstaking, and almost scientific *realist*.

My host was now leading the way down cellar to his actual studio, and I braced myself for some hellish effects among the unfinished canvases. As we reached the bottom of the damp stairs he turned his flashlight to a corner of the large open space at hand, revealing the circular brick kerb of what was evidently a great well in the earthen floor. We walked nearer, and I saw that it must be five feet across, with walls a good foot thick and some six inches above the ground level – solid work of the seventeenth century, or I was much mistaken. That, Pickman said, was the kind of thing he had been talking about – an aperture of the network of tunnels that used to undermine the hill. I noticed idly that it did not seem to be bricked up, and that a heavy disk of wood formed the apparent cover. Thinking of the things this well must have been connected with if Pickman's wild hints had not been mere rhetoric, I shivered slightly; then turned to follow him up a step and through a narrow door into a room of fair size, provided with a wooden floor and furnished as a studio. An acetylene gas outfit gave the light necessary for work.

The unfinished pictures on easels or propped against the walls were as ghastly as the finished ones upstairs, and showed the painstaking methods of the artist. Scenes were blocked out with extreme care, and penciled guide lines told of the minute exactitude which Pickman used in getting the right perspective and proportions. The man was great – I say it even now, knowing as much as I do. A large camera on a table excited my notice, and Pickman told me that he used it in taking scenes for backgrounds, so that he might paint them from photographs in the studio instead of carting his outfit around the town for this or that view. He thought a photograph quite as good as an actual scene or model for sustained work, and declared he employed them regularly.

There was something very disturbing about the nauseous sketches and half-finished monstrosities that leered around from every side of the room, and when Pickman suddenly unveiled a huge canvas on the side away from the light I could not for my life keep back a loud scream – the second I had emitted that night. It echoed and echoed through the dim vaultings of that ancient and nitrous cellar, and I had to choke back a flood of reaction that threatened to burst out as hysterical laughter. Merciful Creator! Eliot, I don't know how much was real and how much was feverish fancy. It doesn't seem to me that earth can hold a dream like that!

It was a colossal and nameless blasphemy with glaring red eyes, and it held in bony claws a thing that had been a man, gnawing at the head as a child nibbles at a stick of candy. Its position was a kind of crouch, and as one looked one felt that at any moment it might drop its present prey and seek a juicier morsel. But, damn it all, it wasn't even the fiendish subject that made it such an immortal fountain-head of all panic – not that, nor the dog face with its pointed ears, bloodshot eyes, flat nose, and drooling lips. It wasn't the scaly claws nor the mould-caked body nor the half-hoofed feet – none of these, though any one of them might well have driven an excitable man to madness.

It was the technique, Elliot – the cursed, the impious, the unnatural technique! As I am a living being, I never elsewhere saw the actual breath of life so fused into a canvas. The monster was there – it glared and gnawed and gnawed and glared – and I knew that only a suspension of Nature's laws could ever let a man paint a thing like that without a model – without some glimpse of the nether world which no mortal unsold to the Fiend has ever had.

Pinned with a thumb-tack to a vacant part of the canvas was a piece of paper now badly curled up – probably, I thought a photograph from which Pickman meant to paint a background as hideous as the nightmare it was to enhance. I reached out to uncurl and look at it when suddenly I saw Pickman start as if shot. He had been listening with peculiar intensity ever since my shocked scream had waked unaccustomed echoes in the dark cellar, and now he seemed struck with a fright which, though not comparable to my own, had in it more of the physical than the spiritual. He drew a revolver and motioned me to silence, then stepped out into the main cellar and closed the door behind him.

I think I was paralysed for an instant. Imitating Pickman's listening, I fancied I heard a faint scurrying sound somewhere, and a series of squeals or bleats in a direction I couldn't determine. I thought of huge rats and shuddered. Then there came a subdued sort of clatter which somehow set me all in gooseflesh – a furtive, groping kind of clatter, though I can't attempt to convey what I mean in words. It was like heavy wood falling on stone or brick – wood on brick – what did that make me think of?

It came again, and louder. There was a vibration as if the wood had fallen farther than it had fallen before. After that followed a sharp grating noise, a shouted gibberish from Pickman, and the deafening discharge of all six chambers of a revolver, fired spectacularly as a lion-tamer might fire in the air for effect. A muffled squeal or squawk, and a thud. Then more wood and brick grating, a pause, and the opening of the door – at which I'll confess I started violently. Pickman reappeared with his smoking weapon, cursing the bloated rats that infested the ancient well.

'The deuce knows what they eat, Thurber,' he grinned, 'for those archaic tunnels touched graveyard and witch-den and seacoast. But whatever it is, they must have run short, for they were devilish anxious to get out. Your yelling stirred them up, I fancy. Better be cautious in these old places – our rodent friends are the one drawback, though I sometimes think they're a positive asset by way of atmosphere and colour.'

Well, Elliot, that was the end of the night's adventure. Pickman had promised to show me the place, and heaven knows he had done it. He led me out of that tangle of alleys in another direction, it seems, for when we sighted a lamp-post we were in a half-familiar street with monotonous rows of mingled tenements blocks and old houses. Charter Street it turned out to be, but I was too flustered to notice just where we hit it. We were too late for the elevated, and walked back downtown through Hanover Street. I remember that walk. We switched from Tremont up Beacon, and Pickman left me at the corner of Joy, where I turned off. I never spoke to him again.

Why did I drop him? Don't be impatient. Wait till I ring for coffee. We've had enough of the other stuff, but I for one need something.

No – it wasn't the paintings I saw in that place; though I'll swear they were enough to get him ostracized in nine-tenths of the homes and clubs of Boston, and I guess you won't wonder now why I have to steer clear of subways and cellars. It was – something I found in my coat the next morning. You know, the curled-up paper tacked to that frightful canvas in the cellar; the thing I thought was a photograph of some scene he meant to use as a background for that monster. That last scare had come while I was reaching to uncurl it, and it seems I had vacantly crumpled it into my pocket. But here's the coffee – take it black, Eliot, if you're wise.

Yes, that paper was the reason I dropped Pickman; Richard Upton Pickman, the greatest artist I have ever known – and the foulest being that ever leaped the bounds of life into the pits of myth and madness. Eliot – old Reid was right. He wasn't strictly human. Either he was born in strange shadow, or he'd found a way to unlock the forbidden gate. It's all the same now, for he's gone – back into the fabulous darkness he loved to haunt. Here, let's have the chandelier going.

Don't ask me to explain or even conjecture about what I burned. Don't ask me, either, what lay behind that mole-like scrambling Pickman was so keen to pass off as rats. There are secrets, you know, which might have come down from old Salem times, and Cotton Mather tells even stranger things. You know how damned life-like Pickman's paintings were – how we all wondered where he got those faces.

Well – that paper wasn't a photograph of any background, after all. What it showed was simply the monstrous being he was painting on that awful canvas. It was the model he was using – and its background was merely the wall of the cellar studio in minute detail. But, by God, Eliot, *it was a photograph from life.*

MONSTER OF TERROR

*

WEST of Arkham the hills rise wild, and there are valleys with
deep woods that no axe has ever cut. There are dark narrow glens
where the trees slope fantastically, and where thin brooklets trickle
without ever having caught the glint of sunlight. On the gentler
slopes there are farms, ancient and rocky, with squat, moss-coated

cottages brooding eternally over old New England secrets in the lee of great ledges; but these are all vacant now; the wide chimneys crumbling and the shingled sides bulging perilously beneath low gambrel roofs.

The old folk have gone away, and foreigners do not like to live there. French-Canadians have tried it, Italians have tried it, and the Poles have come and departed. It is not because of anything that can be seen or heard or handled, but because of something that is imagined. The place is not good for imagination, and does not bring restful dreams at night. It must be this which keeps the foreigners away, for old Ammi Pierce has never told them of anything he recalls from the strange days. Ammi, whose head has been a little queer for years, is the only one who still remains, or who ever talks of the strange days; and he dares to do this because his house is so near the open fields and the travelled roads around Arkham.

There was once a road over the hills and through the valleys, that ran straight where the blasted heath is now; but people ceased to use it and a new road was laid curving far towards the south. Traces of the old one can still be found amidst the weeds of a returning wilderness, and some of them will doubtless linger even when half the hollows are flooded for the new reservoir. Then the dark woods will be cut down and the blasted heath will slumber far below blue waters whose surface will mirror the sky and ripple in the sun. And the secrets of the strange days will be one with the deep's secrets; one with the hidden lore of old ocean, and all the mystery of primal earth.

When I went into the hills and vales to survey for the new reservoir they told me the place was evil. They told me this in Arkham, and because that is a very old town full of witch legends I thought the evil must be something which grandmas had whispered to children through centuries. The name "blasted heath" seemed to me very odd and theatrical, and I wondered how it had come into the folklore of a Puritan people. Then I saw that dark westward tangle of glens and slopes for myself, and ceased to wonder at anything beside its own elder mystery. It was morning when I saw it, but shadow lurked always there. The trees grew too thickly, and their trunks were too big for any healthy New England wood. There was too much silence in the dim alleys between them, and the floor was too soft with the dank moss and mattings of infinite years of decay.

In the open spaces, mostly along the line of the old road, there were little hillside farms; sometimes with all the buildings standing, sometimes with only one or two, and sometimes with only a lone chimney or fast-filling cellar. Weeds and briars reigned, and furtive wild things rustled in the undergrowth. Upon everything was a haze of restlessness and oppression; a touch of the unreal and the grotesque, as if some vital element of perspective or chiaroscuro were awry. I did not wonder that the foreigners would not stay, for this was no region to sleep in. It was too much like a landscape of Salvator Rosa; too much like some forbidden woodcut in a tale of terror.

But even all this was not so bad as the blasted heath. I knew it the moment I came upon it at the bottom of a spacious valley; for no other name could fit such a thing, or any other thing fit such a name. It was as if the poet had coined the phrase from having seen this one particular region. It must, I thought as I viewed it, be the outcome of a fire; but why had nothing new ever grown over those five acres of grey desolation that sprawled open to the sky like a great spot eaten by acid in the woods and fields? It lay largely to the north of the ancient road line, but encroached a little on the other side. I felt an odd reluctance about approaching, and did so at last only because my business took me through and past it. There was no vegetation of any kind on that broad expanse, but only a fine grey dust or ash which no wind seemed ever to blow about. The trees near it were sickly and stunted, and many dead trunks stood or lay rotting at the rim. As I walked hurriedly by I saw the tumbled bricks and stones of an old chimney and cellar on my right, and the yawning black maw of an abandoned well whose stagnant vapours played strange tricks with the hues of the sunlight. Even the long, dark woodland climb beyond seemed welcome in contrast, and I marvelled no more at the frightened whispers of Arkham people. There had been no house or ruin near; even in the old days the place must have been lonely and remote. And at twilight, dreading to repass that ominous spot, I walked circuitously back to the town by the curving road on the south. I vaguely wished some clouds would gather, for an odd timidity about the deep skyey voids above had crept into my soul.

In the evening I asked old people in Arkham about the blasted heath, and what was meant by that phrase "strange days" which so many evasively muttered. I could not, however, get any good answers, except that all the mystery was much more recent than I had dreamed. It was not a matter of old legendry at all, but something within the lifetime of those who spoke. It had happened in the 'eighties, and a family had disappeared or was killed. Speakers would not be exact; and because they all told me to pay no attention to old Ammi Pierce's crazy tales, I sought him out the next morning, having heard that he lived alone in the ancient tottering cottage where the trees first begin to get very thick. It was a fearsomely ancient place, and had begun to exude the faint miasmal odour which clings about houses that have stood too long. Only with persistent knocking could I rouse the aged man, and when he shuffled timidly to the door I could tell he was not glad to see me. He was not so feeble as I had expected; but his eyes dropped in a curious way, and his unkempt clothing and white beard made him seem very worn and dismal.

Not knowing just how he could best be launched on his tales, I feigned a matter of business; told him of my surveying, and asked vague questions about the district. He was far brighter and more educated than I had been led to think, and before I knew it had grasped quite as much of the subject as any man I had talked with in Arkham. He was not like other rustics I had known in the sections where reservoirs were to be. From him there were no protests at the miles of old wood and farmland to be blotted out, though perhaps there would have been had not his home lain outside the bounds of the future lake. Relief was all that he showed; relief at the doom of the dark ancient valleys through which he had roamed all his life. They were better under water now—better under water since the strange days. And with this opening his husky voice sank low, while his body leaned forward and his right forefinger began to point shakily and impressively.

It was then that I heard the story, and as the rambling voice scraped and whispered on I shivered again and again despite the summer day. Often I had to recall the speaker from ramblings, piece out scientific points which he knew only by a fading parrot memory of professors' talk, or bridge over gaps where his sense of logic and continuity broke down. When he was done I did not wonder that his mind had snapped a trifle, or that the folk of Arkham would not speak much of the blasted heath. I hurried back before sunset to my hotel, unwilling to have the stars come out above me in the open; and the next day returned to Boston to give up my position. I could not go into that dim chaos of old forest and slope again, or face another time that grey blasted heath where the black well yawned deep beside the tumbled bricks and stones. The reservoir will soon be built now, and all those elder secrets will be safe forever under watery fathoms. But even then I do not believe I would like to visit that country by night—at least not when the sinister stars are out; and nothing could bribe me to drink the new city water of Arkham.

It all began, old Ammi said, with the meteorite. Before that time there had been no wild legends at all since the witch trials, and even then these western woods were not feared half so much as the small island in the Miskatonic where the devil held court beside a curious stone altar older than the Indians. These were not haunted woods, and their fantastic dusk was never terrible till the strange days. Then there had come that white noontide cloud, that string of explosions in the air, and that pillar of smoke from the valley far in the wood. And by night all Arkham had heard of the great rock that fell out of the sky and bedded itself in the ground beside the well at the Nahum Gardner place. That was the house which had stood where the blasted heath was to come—the trim white Nahum Gardner house amidst its fertile gardens and orchards.

Nahum had come to town to tell people about the stone, and dropped in at Ammi Pierce's on the way. Ammi was forty then, and all the queer things were fixed very strongly in his mind. He and his wife had gone with the three professors from Miskatonic University who hastened out the next morning to see the weird visitor from unknown stellar space, and had wondered why Nahum had called it so large the day before. It had shrunk, Nahum said, as he pointed out the big brownish mound above the ripped earth and charred grass near the archaic well-sweep in his front yard; but the wise men answered that stones do not shrink. Its heat lingered persistently, and Nahum declared that it had glowed faintly in the night. The professors tried it with a geologist's hammer and found it was oddly soft. It was, in truth, so soft as to be almost plastic; and they gouged rather than chipped a specimen to take back to the college for testing. They took it in an old pail borrowed from Nathum's kitchen, for even the small piece refused to grow cool. On the trip back they stopped at Ammi's to rest, and seemed thoughtful when Mrs. Pierce remarked that the fragment was growing smaller and burning the bottom of the pail. Truly, it was not large, but perhaps they had taken less than they thought.

The day after that—all this was in June of '82—the professors had trooped out. again in a great excitement. As they passed Ammi's they told him what queer things the specimen had done, and how it had faded wholly away when they put it in a glass beaker. The beaker had gone, too, and the wise men talked of the strange stone's affinity for silicon. It had acted quite unbelievably in that well-ordered laboratory; doing nothing at all and showing no occluded gases when heated on charcoal, being wholly negative in the borax bead, and soon proving itself absolutely non-volatile at any producible temperature, including that of the oxy-hydrogen blowpipe. On an anvil it appeared highly malleable, and in the dark its luminosity was very marked. Stubbornly refusing to grow cool, it soon had the college in a state of real excitement; and when upon heating before the spectroscope it displayed shining bands unlike any known colours of the normal spectrum there was much breathless talk of new elements, bizarre optical properties, and other things which puzzled men of science are wont to say when faced by the unknown.

Hot as it was, they tested it in a crucible with all the proper reagents. Water did nothing. Hydrochloric acid was the same. Nitric acid and even aqua regia merely hissed and spattered against its torrid invulnerability. Ammi had difficulty in recalling all these things, but recognized some solvents as I mentioned them in the usual order of use. There were ammonia and caustic soda, alcohol and ether, nauseous carbon disulphide and a dozen others; but although the weight grew steadily less as time passed, and the fragment seemed to be slightly cooling, there was no change in the solvents to show that they had attacked the substance at all. It was a metal, though, beyond a doubt. It was magnetic, for one thing; and after its immersion in the acid solvents there seemed to be faint traces of the Widmänstätten figures found on meteoric iron. When the cooling had grown very considerable, the testing was carried on in glass; and it was in a glass beaker that they left all the chips made of the original fragment during the work. The next morning both chips and beaker were gone without trace, and only a charred spot marked the place on the wooden shelf where they had been.

All this the professors told Ammi as they paused at his door, and once more he went with them to see the stony messenger from the stars, though this time his wife did not accompany him. It had now most certainly shrunk, and even the sober professors could not doubt the truth of what they saw. All around the dwindling brown lump near the well was a vacant space, except where the earth had caved in; and whereas it had been a good seven feet across the day before, it was now scarcely five. It was still hot, and the sages studied its surface curiously as they detached another and larger piece with hammer and chisel. They gouged deeply this time, and as they pried away the smaller mass they saw that the core of the thing was not quite homogeneous.

They had uncovered what seemed to be the side of a large coloured globule embedded in the substance. The colour, which resembled some of the bands in the meteor's strange spectrum, was almost impossible to describe; and it was only by analogy that they called it colour at all. Its texture was glossy, and upon tapping it appeared to promise both brittleness and hollowness. One of the professors gave it a sharp blow with a hammer, and it burst with a nervous little plop. Nothing was emitted, and all trace of the thing vanished with the puncturing. It left behind a hollow spherical space about three inches across, and all thought it probable that others would be discovered as the enclosing substance wasted away.

Conjecture was vain; so after a futile attempt to find additional globules by drilling, the seekers left again with their new specimen—which proved, however, as baffling in the laboratory as its predecessor. Aside from being almost plastic, having heat, magnetism, and slight luminosity, cooling slightly in powerful acids, possessing an unknown spectrum, wasting away in air, and attacking silicon compounds with mutual destruction as a result, it presented no identifying features whatsoever; and at the end of the tests the college scientists were forced to own that they could not place it. It was nothing of this earth, but a piece of the great outside; and as such dowered with outside properties and obedient to outside laws.

That night there was a thunderstorm, and when the professors went out to Nahum's the next day they met with a bitter disappointment. The stone, magnetic as it had been, must have had some peculiar electrical property; for it had "drawn the lightning," as Nahum said, with a singular persistence. Six times within an hour the farmer saw the lightning strike the furrow in the front yard, and when the storm was over nothing remained but a ragged pit by the ancient well-sweep, half-choked with a caved-in earth. Digging had borne no fruit, and the scientists verified the fact of the utter vanishment. The failure was total; so that nothing was left to do but go back to the laboratory and test again the disappearing fragment left carefully cased in lead. That fragment lasted a week, at the end of which nothing of value had been learned of it. When it had gone, no residue· was left behind, and in time the professors felt scarcely sure they had indeed seen with waking eyes that cryptic vestige of the fathomless gulfs outside; that lone, weird message from other universes and other realms of matter, force, and entity.

As was natural, the Arkham papers made much of the incident with its collegiate sponsoring, and sent reporters to talk with Nahum Gardner and his family. At least one Boston daily ·also sent a scribe, and Nahum quickly became a kind of local celebrity. He was a lean, genial person of about fifty, living with his wife and three sons on the pleasant farmstead in the valley. He and Ammi exchanged visits frequently, as did their wives; and Ammi had nothing but praise for him after all these years. He seemed slightly proud of the notice his place had attracted, and talked often of the meteorite in the succeeding weeks. That July and August were hot; and Nahum worked hard at his haying in the ten-acre pasture across Chapman's Brook; his rattling wain wearing deep ruts in the shadowy lanes between. The labour tired him more than it had in other years, and he felt that age was beginning to tell on him.

Then fell the time of fruit and harvest. The pears and apples slowly ripened, and Nahum vowed that his orchards were prospering as never before. The fruit was growing to phenomenal size and unwonted gloss, and in such abundance that extra barrels were ordered to handle the future crop. But with the ripening came sore disappointment, for of all that gorgeous array of specious lusciousness not one single jot was fit to eat. Into the finer flavour of the pears and apples had crept a stealthy bitterness and sickishness, so that even the smallest bites induced a lasting disgust. It was the same with the melons and tomatoes, and Nahum sadly saw that his entire crop was lost. Quick to connect events, he declared that the meteorite had poisoned the soil, and thanked Heaven that most of the other crops were in the upland lot along the road.

214

Winter came early, and was very cold. Ammi saw Nahum less often than usual, and observed that he had begun to look worried. The rest of his family too, seemed to have grown taciturn; and were far from steady in their church-going or their attendance at the various social events of the countryside. For this reserve or melancholy no cause could be found, though all the household confessed now and then to poorer health and a feeling of vague disquiet. Nahum himself gave the most definite statement of anyone when he said he was disturbed about certain footprints in the snow. They were the usual winter prints of red squirrels, white rabbits, and foxes, but the brooding farmer professed to see something not quite right about their nature and arrangement. He was never specific, but appeared to think that they were not as characteristic of the anatomy and habits of squirrels and rabbits and foxes as they ought to be. Ammi listened without interest to this talk until one night when he drove past Nahum's house in his sleigh on the way back from Clark's Corners. There had been a moon, and a rabbit had run across the road, and the leaps of that rabbit were longer than either Ammi or his horse liked. The latter, indeed, had almost run away until brought up by a firm rein. Thereafter Ammi gave Nahum's tales more respect, and wondered why the Gardner dogs seemed so cowed and quivering every morning. They had, it developed, nearly lost the spirit to bark.

In February the McGregor boys from Meadow Hill were out shooting woodchucks, and not far from the Gardner place bagged a very peculiar specimen. The proportions of its body seemed slightly altered in a queer way impossible to describe, while its face had taken on an expression which no one ever saw in a woodchuck before. The boys were genuinely frightened, and threw the thing away at once, so that only their grotesque tales of it ever reached the people of the countryside. But the shying of horses near Nahum's house had now become an acknowledged thing, and all the basis for a cycle of whispered legend was fast taking form.

People vowed that the snow melted faster around Nahum's than it did anywhere else, and early in March there was an awed discussion in Potter's general store in Clark's Corners. Stephen Rice had driven past Gardner's in the morning, and had noticed the skunk-cabbages coming up through the mud by the woods across the road. Never were things of such size seen before, and they held strange colours that could not be put into any words. Their shapes were monstrous, and the horse had snorted at an odour which struck Stephen as wholly unprecedented. That afternoon several persons drove past to see the abnormal growth, and all agreed that plants of that kind ought never to sprout in a healthy world. The bad fruit of the fall before was freely mentioned, and it went from mouth to mouth that there was poison in Nahum's ground. Of course it was the meteorite; and remembering how strange the men from the college had found that stone to be, several farmers spoke about the matter to them.

One day they paid Nahum a visit; but having no love of wild tales and folklore were very conservative in what they inferred. The plants were certainly odd, but all skunk-cabbages are more or less odd in shape and hue. Perhaps some mineral element from the stone had entered the soil, but it would soon be washed away. And as for the footprints and frightened horses—of course this was mere country talk which such a phenomenon as the aerolite would be certain to start. There was really nothing for serious men to do in cases of wild gossip, for superstitious rustics will say and believe anything. And so all through the strange days the professors stayed away in contempt. Only one of them, when given two phials of dust for analysis in a police job over a year and a half later, recalled that the queer colour of that skunk-cabbage had been very like one of the anomalous bands of light shown by the meteor fragment in the college spectroscope, and like the brittle globule found imbedded in the stone from the abyss. The samples in this analysis case gave the same odd bands at first, though later they lost the property.

The trees budded prematurely around Nahum's, and at night they swayed ominously in the wind. Nahum's second son Thaddeus, a lad of fifteen, swore that they swayed also when there was no wind; but even the gossips would not credit this. Certainly, however, restlessness was in the air. The entire Gardner family developed the habit of stealthy listening, though not for any sound which they could consciously name. The listening was, indeed, rather a product of moments when consciousness seemed half to slip away. Unfortunately such moments increased week by week, till it became common speech that "something was wrong with all Nahum's folks". When the early saxifrage came out it had another strange colour; not quite that of the skunk-cabbage, but plainly related and equally un-known to anyone who saw it. Nahum took some blossoms to Arkham and showed them to the editor of the *Gazette*, but that dignitary did no more than write a humorous article about them, in which the dark fears of rustics were held up to polite ridicule. It was a mistake of Nahum's to tell a stolid city man about the way the great, overgrown mourning-cloak butterflies behaved in connection with these saxifrages.

April brought a kind of madness to the country folk, and began that disuse of the road past Nahum's which led to its ultimate abandonment. It was the vegetation. All the orchard trees blossomed forth in strange colours, and through the stony soil of the yard and adjacent pasturage there sprang up a bizarre growth which only a botanist could connect with the proper flora of the region. No sane wholesome colours were anywhere to be seen except in the green grass and leafage; but everywhere were those hectic and prismatic variants of some diseased, under-lying primary tone without a place among the known tints of earth. The "Dutchman's breeches" became a thing of sinister menace, and the bloodroots grew insolent in their chromatic perversion. Ammi and the Gardners thought that most of the colours had a sort of haunting familiarity, and decided that they reminded one of the britle globule in the meteor. Nahum ploughed and sowed the ten-acre pasture and the upland lot, but did nothing with the land around the house. He knew it would be of no use, and hoped that the summer's strange growths would draw all the poison from the soil. He was prepared for almost anything now, and had grown used to the sense of some-thing near him waiting to be heard. The shunning of his house by neighbours told on him, of course; but it told on his wife more. The boys were better off, being at school each day; but they could not help being frightened by the gossip. Thaddeus, an especially sensitive youth, suffered the most.

In May the insects came, and Nahum's place became a night-mare of buzzing and crawling. Most of the creatures seemed not quite usual in their aspects and motions, and their nocturnal habits contradicted all former experience. The Gardners took to watching at night—watching in all directions at random for something—they could not tell what. It was then that they all owned that Thaddeus had been right about the trees. Mrs. Gardner was the next to see it from the window as she watched the swollen boughs of a maple against a moonlit sky. The boughs surely moved, and there was no wind. It must be the sap. Strangeness had come into everything growing now. Yet it was none of Nahum's family at all who made the next discovery. Familiarity had dulled them, and what they could not see was glimpsed by a timid windmill salesman from Bolton who drove by one night in ignorance of the country legends. What he told in Arkham was given a short paragraph in the *Gazette*; and it was there that all the farmers, Nahum included, saw it first. The night had been dark and the buggy-lamps faint, but around a farm in the valley which everyone knew from the account must be Nahum's, the darkness had been less thick. A dim though distinct luminosity seemed to inhere in all the vegetation, grass, leaves, and blossoms alike, while at one moment a detached piece of the phosphorescence appeared to stir furtively in the yard near the barn.

The grass had so far seemed untouched, and the cows were freely pastured in the lot near the house, but towards the end of May the milk began to be bad. Then Nahum had the cows driven to the uplands, after which this trouble ceased. Not long after this the change in grass and leaves became apparent to the eye. All the verdure was going grey, and was developing a highly singular quality of brittleness. Ammi was now the only person who ever visited the place, and his visits were becoming fewer and fewer. When school closed the Gardners were virtu-ally cut off from the world, and sometimes let Ammi do their errands in town. They were failing curiously both physically and mentally, and no one was surprised when the news of Mrs. Gardner's madness stole around.

It happened in June, about the anniversary of the meteor's fall, and the poor woman screamed about things in the air which she could not describe. In her raving there was not a single specific noun, but only verbs and pronouns. Things moved and changed and fluttered, and ears tingled to impulses which were not wholly sounds. Something was taken away—she was being drained of something—something was fastening itself on her that ought not to be—someone must make it keep off—nothing was ever still in the night—the walls and windows shifted. Nathum did not send her to the county asylum, but let her wander about the house as long as she was harmless to herself and others. Even when her expression changed he did nothing.

But when the boys grew afraid of her, and Thaddeus nearly fainted at the way she made faces at him, he decided to keep her locked in the attic. By July she had ceased to speak and crawled on all fours, and before that month was over Nahum got the mad notion that she was slightly luminous in the dark, as he now clearly saw was the case with the nearby vegetation.

It was a little before this that the horses had stampeded. Something had aroused them in the night, and their neighing and kicking in their stalls had been terrible. There seemed virtually nothing to do to calm them, and when Nahum opened the stable door they all bolted out like frightened woodland deer. It took a week to track all four, and when found they were seen to be quite useless and unmanageable. Something had snapped in their brains, and each one had to be shot for its own good. Nahum borrowed a horse from Ammi for his haying, but found it would not approach the barn. It shied, baulked, and whinnied, and in the end he could do nothing but drive it into the yard while the men used their own strength to get the heavy wagon near enough the hayloft for convenient pitching. And all the while the vegetation was turning grey and brittle. Even the flowers whose hues had been so strange were greying now, and the fruit was coming out grey and dwarfed and tasteless. The asters and golden-rod bloomed grey and distorted, and the roses and zinnias and hollyhocks in the front yard were such blasphemous-looking things that Nahum's oldest boy Zenas cut them down. The strangely puffed insects died about that time, even the bees that had left their hives and taken to the woods.

By September all the vegetation was fast crumbling to a greyish powder, and Nahum feared that the trees would die before the poison was out of the soil. His wife now had spells of terrific screaming, and he and the boys were in a constant state of nervous tension. They shunned people now, and when school opened the boys did not go. But it was Ammi, on one of his rare visits, who first realized that the well water was no longer good. It had an evil taste that was not exactly foetid nor exactly salty, and Ammi advised his friend to dig another well on higher ground to use till the soil was good again. Nahum, however, ignored the warning, for he had by that time become calloused to strange and unpleasant things. He and the boys continued to use the tainted supply, drinking it as listlessly and mechanically as they ate their meagre and ill-cooked meals and did their thankless and monotonous chores through the aimless days. There was something of stolid resignation about them all, as if they walked half in another world between lines of nameless guards to a certain and familiar doom.

Thaddeus went mad in September after a visit to the well. He had gone with a pail and had come back empty-handed, shrieking and waving his arms, and sometimes lapsing into an inane titter or a whisper about "the moving colours down there". Two in one family was pretty bad, but Nahum was very brave about it. He let the boy run about for a week until he began stumbling and hurting himself, and then he shut him in an attic room across the hall from his mother's. The way they screamed at each other from behind their locked doors was very terrible, especially to little Merwin, who fancied they talked in some terrible language that was not of earth. Merwin was getting frightfully imaginative, and his restlessness was worse after the shutting away of the brother who had been his greatest playmate.

Almost at the same time the mortality among the livestock commenced. Poultry turned greyish and died very quickly, their meat being found dry and noisome upon cutting. Hogs grew inordinately fat, then suddenly began to undergo loathsome changes which no one could explain. Their meat was of course useless, and Nahum was at his wits' end. No rural veterinary would approach his place, and the city veterinary from Arkham was openly baffled. The swine began growing grey and brittle and falling to pieces before they died, and their eyes and muzzles developed singular alterations. It was very inexplicable, for they had never been fed from the tainted vegetation. Then something struck the cows. Certain areas or sometimes the whole body would be uncannily shrivelled or compressed, and atrocious collapses or disintegrations were common. In the last stages— and death was always the result—there would be a greying and turning brittle like that which beset the hogs. There could be no question of poison, for all the cases occurred in a locked and undisturbed barn. No bites of prowling things could have brought the virus, for what live beast of earth can pass through solid obstacles? It must be only natural disease—yet what disease could wreak such results was beyond any mind's guessing. When the harvest came there was not an animal surviving on the place, for the stock and poultry were dead and the dogs had run away. These dogs, three in number, had all vanished one night and were never heard of again. The five cats had left some time before, but their going was scarcely noticed since there now seemed to be no mice, and only Mrs. Gardner had made pets of the graceful felines.

On the nineteenth of October Nahum staggered into Ammi's house with hideous news. The death had come to poor Thaddeus in his attic room, and it had come in a way which could not be told. Nahum had dug a grave in the railed family plot behind the farm, and had put therein what he found. There could have been nothing from outside, for the small barred window and locked door were intact; but it was much as it had been in the barn. Ammi and his wife consoled the stricken man as best as they could, but shuddered as they did so. Stark terror seemed to cling round the Gardners and all they touched, and the very presence of one in the house was a breath from regions unnamed and unnameable. Ammi accompanied Nahum home with the greatest reluctance, and did what he might to calm the hysterical sobbing of little Merwin. Zenas needed no calming. He had come of late to do nothing but stare into space and obey what his father told him; and Ammi thought that his fate was very merciful. Now and then Merwin's screams were answered faintly from the attic, and in response to an inquiring look Nahum said that his wife was getting very feeble. When night approached, Ammi managed to get away; for not even friendship could make him stay in that spot when the faint glow of the vegetation began and the trees may or may not have swayed without wind. It was really lucky for Ammi that he was not more imaginative. Even as things were, his mind was bent ever so slightly; but had he been able to connect and reflect upon all the portents around him he must inevitably have turned a total maniac. In the twilight he hastened home, the screams of the mad woman and the nervous child ringing horribly in his ears.

Three days later Nahum burst into Ammi's kitchen in the early morning, and in the absence of his host stammered out a desperate tale once more, while Mrs. Pierce listened in a clutching fright. It was little Merwin this time. He was gone. He had gone out late at night with a lantern and pail of water, and had never come back. He'd been going to pieces for days, and hardly knew what he was about. Screamed at everything. There had been a frantic shriek from the yard then, but before the father

221

could get to the door the boy was gone. There was no glow from the lantern he had taken, and of the child himself no trace. At the time Nahum thought the lantern and pail were gone too; but when dawn came, and the man had plodded back from his all-night search of the woods and fields, he had found some very curious things near the well. There was a crushed and apparently somewhat melted mass of iron which had certainly been the lantern; while a bent handle and twisted iron hoops beside it, both half-fused, seemed to hint at the remains of the pail. That was all. Nahum was past imagining, Mrs. Pierce was blank, and Ammi, when he had reached home and heard the tale, could give no guess. Merwin was gone, and there would be no use in telling the people around, who shunned all Gardners now. No use, either, in telling the city people at Arkham who laughed at everything. Thad was gone, and now Merwin was gone. Something was creeping and creeping and waiting to be seen and heard. Nahum would go soon, and he wanted Ammi to look after his wife and Zenas if they survived him. It must all be a judgment of some sort; though he could not fancy what for, since he had always walked uprightly in the Lord's ways so far as he knew.

For over two weeks Ammi saw nothing of Nahum; and then, worried about what might have happened, he overcame his fears and paid the Gardner place a visit. There was no smoke from the great chimney, and for a moment the visitor was apprehensive of the worst. The aspect of the whole farm was shocking—greyish withered grass and leaves on the ground, vines falling in brittle wreckage from archaic walls and gables, and great bare trees clawing up at the grey November sky with a studied malevolence which Ammi could not but feel had come from some subtle change in the tilt of the branches. But Nahum was alive, after all. He was weak, and lying on a couch in the low-ceiled kitchen, but perfectly conscious and able to give simple orders to Zenas. The room was deadly cold; and as Ammi visibly shivered, the host shouted huskily to Zenas for more wood. Wood, indeed, was sorely needed; since the cavernous fireplace was unlit and empty, with a cloud of soot blowing about in the chill wind that came down the chimney. Presently Nahum asked him if the extra wood had made him any more comfortable, and then Ammi saw what had happened. The stoutest cord had broken at last, and the hapless farmer's mind was proof against more sorrow.

Questioning tactfully, Ammi could get no clear data at all about the missing Zenas. 'In the well—he lives in the well—' was all that the clouded father would say. Then there flashed across the visitor's mind a sudden thought of the mad wife, and he changed his line of enquiry. "Nabby? Why, here she is!" was the surprised response of poor Nahum, and Ammi soon saw that he must search for himself. Leaving the harmless babbler on the couch, he took the keys from their nail beside the door and climbed the creaking stairs to the attic. It was very close and noisome up there, and no sound direction. Of the four doors in sight only one was locked, and on this he tried various keys of the ring he had taken. The third key proved the right one, and after some fumbling Ammi threw open the low white door.

It was quite dark inside, for the window was small and half-obscured by the crude wooden bars; and Ammi could see nothing at all on the wide-planked floor. The stench was beyond enduring, and before proceeding further he had to retreat to another room and return with his lungs filled with breathable air. When he did enter he saw something dark in the corner, and upon seeing it more clearly he screamed outright. While he screamed he thought a momentary cloud eclipsed the window, and a second later he felt himself brushed as if by some hateful current of vapour. Strange colours danced before his eyes; and had not a present horror numbed him he would have thought of the globule in the meteor that the geologist's hammer had shattered, and of the morbid vegetation that had sprouted in the spring. As it was he thought only of the blasphemous monstrosity which confronted him, and which all too clearly had shared the nameless fate of young Thaddeus and the livestock. But the terrible thing about the horror was that it very slowly and perceptibly moved as it continued to crumble.

Ammi would give me no added particulars of this scene, but the shape in the corner does not reappear in his tale as a moving object. There are things which cannot be mentioned, and what is done in common humanity is sometimes cruelly judged by the law. I gathered that no moving thing was left in that attic room, and that to leave anything capable of motion there would have been a deed so monstrous as to damn any accountable being to eternal torment. Anyone but a stolid farmer would have fainted or gone mad, but Ammi walked conscious through that low doorway and locked the accursed secret behind him. There would be Nahum to deal with now; he must be fed and tended, and removed to some place where he could be cared for.

Commencing his descent of the dark stairs, Ammi heard a thud below him. He even thought a scream had been suddenly choked off, and recalled nervously the clammy vapour which had brushed by him in that frightful room above. What presence had his cry and entry started up? Halted by some vague fear, he heard still further sounds below. Indubitably there was a sort of heavy dragging, and a most detestably sticky noise as of some fiendish and unclean species of suction. With an associative sense goaded to feverish heights, he thought unaccountably of what he had seen upstairs. Good God! What eldritch dream-world was this into which he had blundered? He dared move neither backward nor forward, but stood there trembling at the black curve of the boxed-in staircase. Every trifle of the scene burned itself into his brain. The sounds, the sense of dread expectancy, the darkness, the steepness of the narrow steps—and merciful Heaven!—the faint but unmistakable luminosity of all the woodwork in sight; steps, sides, exposed laths, and beams alike.

Then there burst forth a frantic whinny from Ammi's horse outside, followed at once by a clatter which told of a frenzied runaway. In another moment horse and buggy had gone beyond earshot, leaving the frightened man on the dark stairs to guess what had sent them. But that was not all. There had been another sound out there. A sort of liquid splash—water—it must have been the well. He had left Hero untied near it, and a buggy-wheel must have brushed the coping and knocked in a stone. And still the pale phosphorescence glowed in that detestably ancient woodwork. God! how old the house was! Most of it built before 1670, and the gambrel roof no later than 1730.

A feeble scratching on the floor downstairs now sounded distinctly, and Ammi's grip tightened on a heavy stick he had picked up in the attic for some purpose. Slowly nerving himself, he finished his descent and walked boldly towards the kitchen. But he did not complete the walk, because what he sought was no longer there. It had come to meet him, and it was still alive after a fashion. Whether it had crawled or whether it had been dragged by any external forces, Ammi could not say; but the death had been at it. Everything had happened in the last half-hour, but collapse, greying, and disintegration were already far advanced. There was a horrible brittleness, and dry fragments were scaling off. Ammi could not touch it, but looked horrifiedly into the distorted parody that had been a face. "What was it, Nahum—what was it?" he whispered, and the cleft, bulging lips were just able to crack out a final answer.

"Nothin' . . . nothin' . . . the colour . . . it burns . . . cold an' wet, but it burns . . . it lived in the well. . . . I seen it . . . a kind of smoke . . . jest like the flowers last spring . . . the well shone at night . . . Thad an' Merwin an' Zenas . . . everything alive . . . suckin' the life out of everything . . . in that stone . . . it must a' come in that stone . . . pizened the whole place . . . dun't know what it wants . . . that round thing them men from the college dug outen the stone . . . they smashed it . . . it was that same colour . . . jest the same, like the flowers an' plants . . . must a' ben more of 'em . . . seeds . . . seeds . . . they growed . . . I seen it the fust time this week . . . must a' got strong on Zenas . . . he was a big boy, full o' life . . . it beats down your mind an' then gets ye . . . burns ye up . . . in the well water . . . you was right about that . . . evil water . . . Zenas never come back from the well . . . can't git away . . . draws ye . . . ye know summ'at's comin' but tain't no use . . . I seen it time an' agin sence Zenas was took . . . whar's Nabby, Ammi? . . . my head's no good . . . dun't know how long sence I fed her . . . it'll git her ef we ain't keerful . . . jest a colour . . . her face is gittin' to hev that colour sometimes towards night . . . an' it burns an' sucks . . . it come from some place whar things ain't as they is here . . . one o' them professors said so . . . he was right . . . look out, Ammi, it'll do suthin' more . . . sucks the life out . . ."

But that was all. That which spoke could speak no more because it had completely caved in. Ammi laid a red checked tablecloth over what was left and reeled out the back door into the fields. He climbed the slope to the ten-acre pasture and stumbled home by the north road and the woods. He could not pass that well from which his horse had run away. He had looked at it through the window, and had seen that no stone was missing from the rim. Then the lurching buggy had not dislodged anything after all—the splash had been something else—something which went into the well after it had done with poor Nahum. . . .

When Ammi reached his house the horse and buggy had arrived before him and thrown his wife into fits of anxiety.

Reassuring her without explanations, he set out at once for Arkham and notified the authorities that the Gardner family was no more. He indulged in no details, but merely told of the deaths of Nahum and Nabby, that of Thaddeus being already known, and mentioned that the cause seemed to be the same strange ailment which had killed the livestock. He also stated that Merwin and Zenas had disappeared. There was considerable questioning at the police station, and in the end Ammi was compelled to take three officers to the Gardner farm, together with the coroner, the medical examiner, and the veterinary who had treated the diseased animals. He went much against his will, for the afternoon was advancing and he feared the fall of night over that accursed place, but it was some comfort to have so many people with him.

The six men drove out in a democrat-wagon, following Ammi's buggy, and arrived at the pest-ridden farmhouse about four o'clock. Used as the officers were to gruesome experiences, not one remained unmoved at what was found in the attic and under the red checked tablecloth on the floor below. The whole aspect of the farm with its grey desolation was terrible enough, but those two crumbling objects were beyond all bounds. No one, could look long at them, and even the medical examiner admitted that there was very little to examine. Specimens could be analysed, of course, so he busied himself in obtaining them— and here it develops that a very puzzling aftermath occurred at the college laboratory where the two phials of dust were finally taken. Under the spectroscope both samples gave off an unknown spectrum, in which many of the baffling bands were precisely like those which the strange meteor had yielded in the previous year. The property of emitting this spectrum vanished in a month, the dust therafter consisting mainly of alkaline phosphates and carbonates.

Ammi would not have told the men about the well if he had thought they meant to do anything then and there. It was getting towards sunset, and he was anxious to be away. But he could not help glancing nervously at the stony kerb by the great sweep, and when a detective questioned him he admitted that Nahum had feared something down there—so much so that he had never even thought of searching it for Merwin or Zenas. After that nothing would do but that they empty and explore the well immediately, so Ammi had to wait trembling while pail after pail of rank water was hauled up and splashed on the soaking ground outside. The men sniffed in disgust at the fluid, and towards the last held their noses against the foetor they were uncovering. It was not so long a job as they had feared it would be, since the water was phenomenally low. There is no need to speak too exactly of what they found. Merwin and Zenas were both there, in part, though the vestiges were mainly skeletal. There were also a small deer and a large dog in about the same state, and a number of bones of small animals. The ooze and slime at the bottom seemed enexplicably porous and bubbling, and a man who descended on hand-holds with a long pole found that he could sink the wooden shaft to any depth in the mud of the floor without meeting any solid obstruction.

Twilight had now fallen, and lanterns were brought from the house. Then, when it was seen that nothing further could be gained from the well, everyone went indoors and conferred in the ancient sitting-room while the intermittent light of a spectral half-moon played wanly on the grey desolation outside. The men were frankly nonplussed by the entire case, and could find no convincing common element to link the strange vegetable conditions, the unknown disease of livestock and humans, and the unaccountable deaths of Merwin and Zenas in the tainted well. They had heard the common country talk, it is true; but could not believe that anything contrary to natural law had occurred. No doubt the meteor had poisoned the soil, but the illness of persons and animals who had eaten nothing grown in that soil was another matter. Was it the well water? Very possibly. It might be a good idea to analyse it. But what peculiar madness could have made both boys jump into the well? Their deeds were so similar—and the fragments showed that they had both suffered from the grey brittle death. Why was everything so grey and brittle?

It was the coroner, seated near a window overlooking the yard, who first noticed the glow about the well. Night had fully set in, and all the abhorrent grounds seemed faintly luminous with more than the fitful moonbeams; but this new glow was something definite and distinct, and appeared to shoot up from the black pit like a softened ray from a searchlight, giving dull reflections in the little ground pools where the water had been emptied. It had a very queer colour, and as all the men clustered round the window Ammi gave a violent start. For this strange beam of ghastly miasma was to him of no unfamiliar hue. He had seen that colour before, and feared to think what it might mean. He had seen it in the nasty brittle globule in that aerolite two summers ago, had seen it in the crazy vegetation of the springtime, and had thought he had seen it for an instant that very morning against the small barred window of that terrible attic room where nameless things had happened. It had flashed there a second, and a clammy and hateful current of vapour had brushed past him—and then poor Nahum had been taken by something of that colour. He had said so at the last—said it was like the globule and the plants. After that had come the runaway in the yard and the splash in the well—and now that well was belching forth to the night a pale insidious beam of the same demoniac tint.

It does credit to the alertness of Ammi's mind that he puzzled even at that tense moment over a point which was essentially scientific. He could not but wonder at his gleaning of the same impression from a vapour glimpsed in the daytime, against a window opening on the morning sky, and from a nocturnal exhalation seen as a phosphorescent mist against the black and blasted landscape. It wasn't right—it was against Nature—and he thought of those terrible last words of his stricken friend, "It come from some place what things ain't as they is here . . . one o' them professors said so. . . ."

All three horses outside, tied to a pair of shrivelled saplings by the road, were now neighing and pawing frantically. The wagon driver started for the door to do something, but Ammi laid a shaky hand on his shoulder. "Duďn't go out thar," he whispered. "They's more to this nor what we know. Nahum said somethin' lived in the well that sucks your life out. He said it must be some'at growed from a round ball like one we all seen in the meteor stone that fell a year ago June. Sucks an' burns, he said, an' is jest a cloud of colour like that light out thar now, that ye can hardly see an' can't tell what it is. Nahum thought it feeds on everything livin' an' gits stronger all the time. He said he seen it this last week. It must be somethin' from away off in the sky like the men from the college last year says the meteor stone was. The way it's made an' the way it works ain't like no way o' God's world. It's summ'at from beyond."

So the men paused indecisively as the light from the well grew stronger and the hitched horses pawed and whinnied in increasing frenzy. It was truly an awful moment; with terror in that ancient and accursed house itself, four monstrous sets of fragments—two from the house and two from the well—in the woodshed behind, and that shaft of unknown and unholy iridescence from the slimy depths in front. Ammi had restrained the driver on impulse, forgetting how uninjured he himself was after the clammy brushing of that coloured vapour in the attic room, but perhaps it is just as well that he acted as he did. No one will ever know what was abroad that night; and though the blasphemy from beyond had not so far hurt any human of unweakened mind, there is no telling what it might not have done at that last moment, with its seemingly increased strength and the special signs of purpose it was soon to display beneath the half-clouded moonlit sky.

All at once one of the detectives at the window gave a short, sharp gasp. The others looked at him, and then quickly followed his own gaze upward to the point at which its idle straying had been suddenly arrested. There was no need for words. What had been disputed in country gossip was disputable no longer, and it is because of the thing which every man of that party agreed in whispering later on, that the strange days are never talked about in Arkham. It is necessary to premise that there was no wind at that hour of the evening. One did arise not long afterward, but there was absolutely none then. Even the dry tips of the lingering hedge-mustard, grey and blighted, and the fringe on the roof of the standing democrat-wagon were unstirred. And yet amid that tense, godless calm the high bare boughs of all the trees in the yard were moving. They were twitching morbidly and spasmodically, clawing in convulsive and epileptic madness at the moonlit clouds; scratching impotently in the noxious air as if jerked by some allied and bodiless line of linkage with subterrene horrors writhing and struggling below the black roots.

Not a man breathed for several seconds. Then a cloud of darker depth passed over the moon, and the silhouette of clutching branches faded out momentarily. At this there was a general cry; muffled with awe, but husky and almost identical from every throat. For the terror had not faded with the silhouette, and in a fearsome instant of deeper darkness the watchers saw wriggling at that tree-top height a thousand tiny points of faint and unhallowed radiance, tipping each bough like the fire of St. Elmo or the flames that come down on the apostles' heads of Pentecost. It was a monstrous constellation of unnatural light, like a glutted swarm of corpse-fed fireflies dancing hellish sarabands over an accursed marsh; and its colour was that same nameless intrusion which Ammi had come to recognize and dread. All the while the shaft of phosphorescence from the well was getting brighter and brighter, bringing, to the minds of the huddled men, a sense of doom and abnormality. It was no longer *shining* out; it was *pouring* out; and as the shapeless stream of unplaceable colour left the well it seemed to flow directly into the sky.

The veterinary shivered, and walked to the front door to drop the heavy extra bar across it. Ammi shook no less, and had to tug and point for lack of controllable voice when he wished to draw notice to the growing luminosity of the trees. The neighing and stamping of the horses had become utterly frightful, but not a soul of that group in the old house would have ventured forth for any earthly reward. With the moments the shining of the trees increased, while their restless branches seemed to strain more and more towards verticality. The wood of the well-sweep was shining now, and presently a policeman dumbly pointed to some wooden sheds and beehives near the stone wall on the west. They were commencing to shine, too, though the tethered vehicles of the visitors seemed so far unaffected. Then there was a wild commotion and clopping in the road, and as Ammi quenched the lamp for better seeing they realized that the span of frantic greys had broken their sapling and run off with the democrat-wagon.

The shock served to loosen several tongues, and embarrassed whispers were exchanged. "It spreads on everything organic that's been around here," muttered the medical examiner. No one replied, but the man who had been in the well gave a hint that his long pole must have stirred up something intangible. "It was awful," he added. "There was no bottom at all, just ooze and bubbles and the feeling of something lurking under there." Ammi's horse still pawed and screamed deafeningly in the road outside, and nearly drowned its owner's faint quaver as he mumbled his formless reflections. "It come from that stone—it growed down thar—it got everything livin'—it fed itself on 'em, mind and body—Thad an' Merwin, Zenas an' Nabby—Nahum was the last—they all drunk the water—it got strong on 'em—it come from beyond, what things ain't like they be here—now it's goin' home—"

At this point, as the column of unknown colour flared suddenly stronger and began to weave itself into fantastic suggestions of shape which each spectator later described differently, there came from poor tethered Hero such a sound as no man before or since ever heard from a horse. Every person in that low-pitched sitting-room stopped his ears, and Ammi turned away from the window in

horror and nausea. Words could not convey it—when Ammi looked
out again the hapless beast lay huddled inert on the moonlit ground
between the splintered shafts of the buggy. That was the last of
Hero till they buried him next day. But the present was no time
to mourn, for almost at this instant a detective silently called attention to something terrible in the very room with them. In the
absence of the lamplight it was clear that a faint phosphorescence
had begun to pervade the entire apartment. It glowed on the broad-
planked floor and the fragment of rag carpet, and shimmered over
the sashes of the small-paned windows. It ran up and down the
exposed corner-posts, coruscated about the shelf and mantel, and
infected the very doors and furniture. Each minute saw it strengthen,
and at last it was very plain that healthy living things must leave
that house.

Ammi showed them the back door and the path up through the
fields to the ten-acre pasture. They walked and stumbled as in a
dream, and did not dare look back till they were far away on the
high ground. They were glad of the path, for they could not have
gone the front way, by that well. It was bad enough passing the
glowing barn and sheds, and those shining orchard trees with their
gnarled, fiendish contours; but thank Heaven the branches did
their worst twisting high up. The moon went under some very
black clouds as they crossed the rustic bridge over, Chapman's
Brook, and it was blind groping from there to the open meadows.

When they looked back towards the valley and the distant Gardner place at the bottom they saw a fearsome sight. All the farm was
shining with the hideous unknown blend of colour : trees, buildings,
and even such grass and herbage as had not been wholly changed
to lethal grey brittleness. The boughs were all straining skyward,
tipped with tongues of foul flame, and lambent tricklings of the
same monstrous fire were creeping about the ridgepoles of the house,
barn and sheds. It was a scene from a vision of Fuseli, and over
all the rest reigned that riot of luminous amorphousness, that alien
and undimensioned rainbow of cryptic poison from the well—
seething, feeling, lapping, reaching, scintillating, straining, and
malignly bubbling in its cosmic and unrecognizable chromaticism.

Then without warning the hideous thing shot vertically up towards the sky like a rocket or meteor, leaving behind no trail and
disappearing through a round and curiously regular hole in the
clouds before any man could gasp or cry out. No watcher can ever
forget that sight, and Ammi stared blankly at the stars of Cygnus,

231

Deneb twinkling above the others, where the unknown colour had melted into the Milky Way. But his gaze was the next moment called swiftly to earth by the crackling in the valley. It was just that. Only a wooden ripping and crackling, and not an explosion, as so many others of the party vowed. Yet the outcome was the same, for in one feverish kaleidoscopic instant there burst up from that doomed and accursed farm a gleamingly eruptive cataclysm of unnatural sparks and substance; blurring the glance of the few who saw it, and sending forth to the zenith a bombarding cloudburst of such coloured and fantastic fragments as our universe must needs disown. Through quickly re-closing vapours they followed the great morbidity that had vanished, and in another second they had vanished too. Behind and below was only a darkness to which the men dared not return, and all about was a mounting wind which seemed to sweep down in black, frore gusts from interstellar space. It shrieked and howled, and lashed the fields and distorted woods in a mad cosmic frenzy, till soon the trembling party realized it would be no use waiting for the moon to show what was left down there at Nahum's.

Too awed even to hint theories, the seven shaking men trudged back towards Arkham by the north road. Ammi was worse than his fellows, and begged them to see him inside his own kitchen, instead of keeping straight on to town. He did not wish to cross the blighted wind-whipped woods alone to his home on the main road. For he had had an added shock that the others were spared, and was crushed forever with a brooding fear he dared not even mention for many years to come. As the rest of the watchers on that tempestuous hill had stolidly set their faces towards the road, Ammi had looked back an instant at the shadowed valley of desolation so lately sheltering his ill-starred friend. And from that stricken, far-away spot he had seen something feebly rise, only to sink down again upon the place from which the great shapeless horror had shot into the sky. It was just a colour—but not any colour of our earth or heavens. And because Ammi recognized that colour, and knew that this last faint remnant must still lurk down there in the well, he has never been quite right since.

Ammi would never go near the place again. It is forty-four years now since the horror happened, but he has never been there, and will be glad when the new reservoir blots it out. I shall be glad, too, for I do not like the way the sunlight changed colour around the mouth of that abandoned well I passed. I hope the water will always be very deep—but even so, I shall never drink it. I do not think I shall visit the Arkham country hereafter. Three of the men who had been with Ammi returned the next morning to see the ruins by daylight, but there were not any real ruins. Only the bricks of the chimney, the stones of the cellar, some mineral and metallic litter here and there, and the rim of that nefandous well. Save for Ammi's dead horse, which they towed away and buried, and the buggy which they shortly returned to him, everything that had ever been living had gone. Five eldritch acres of dusty grey desert remained, nor has anything ever grown there since. To this day it sprawls open to the sky like a great spot eaten by acid in the woods and fields, and the few who have ever dared glimpse it in spite of the rural tales have named it "the blasted heath".

The rural tales are queer. They might be even queerer if city men and college chemists could be interested enough to analyse the water from that disused well, or the grey dust that no wind seems to disperse. Botanists, too, ought to study the stunted flora on the borders of that spot, for they might shed light on the country notion that the blight is spreading—little by little, perhaps an inch a year. People say the colour of the neighbouring herbage is not quite right in the spring, and that wild things leave queer prints in the light winter snow. Snow never seems quite so heavy on the blasted heath as it is elsewhere. Horses—the few that are left in this motor age—grow skittish in the silent valley; and hunters cannot depend on their dogs too near the splotch of greyish dust.

They say the mental influences are very bad, too; numbers went queer in the years after Nahum's taking, and always they lacked the power to get away. Then the stronger-minded folk all left the region, and only the foreigners tried to live in the crumbling old homesteads. They could not stay, though; and one sometimes wonders what insight beyond ours their wild, weird stories of whispered magic have given them. Their dreams at night, they protest, are very horrible in that grotesque country; and surely the very look of the dark realm is enough to stir a morbid fancy. No traveller has ever escaped a sense of strangeness in those deep ravines, and artists shiver as they paint thick woods whose mystery is as much of the spirit as of the eye. I myself am curious about the sensation I derived from my one lone walk before Ammi told me his tale. When twilight came I had vaguely wished some clouds would gather, for an odd timidity about the deep skyey voids above had crept into my soul.

Do not ask me for my opinion. I do not know—that is all. There was no one but Ammi to question; for Arkham people will not talk about the strange days, and all three professors who saw the aerolite and its coloured globule are dead. There were other globules—depend upon that. One must have fed itself and escaped, and probably there was another which was too late. No doubt it is still down the well—I know there was something wrong with the sunlight I saw above the miasmal brink. The rustics say the blight creeps an inch a year, so perhaps there is a kind of growth or nourishment even now. But whatever daemon hatching is there, it must be tethered to something or else it would quickly spread. Is it fastened to the roots of those trees that claw the air? One of the current Arkham tales is about fat oaks that shine and move as they ought not to do at night.

What it is, only God knows. In terms of matter I suppose the things Ammi described would be called a gas, but this gas obeyed the laws that are not of our cosmos. This was no fruit of such worlds and suns as shine on the telescopes and photographic plates of our observatories. This was no breath from the skies whose motions and dimensions our astronomers measure or deem too vast to measure. It was just a colour out of space—a frightful messenger from unformed realms of infinity beyond all Nature as we know it; from realms whose mere existence stuns the brain and numbs us with the black extra-cosmic gulfs it throws open before our frenzied eyes.

I doubt very much if Ammi consciously lied to me, and I do not think his tale was all a freak of madness as the townsfolk had forewarned. Something terrible came to the hills and valleys on that meteor, and something terrible—though I know not in what proportion—still remains. I shall be glad to see the water come. Meanwhile I hope nothing will happen to Ammi. He saw so much of the thing—and its influence was so insidious. Why has he never been able to move away? How clearly he recalled those dying words of Nahum's—"can't git away—draws ye—ye know summ'at's comin' but tain't no use—" Ammi is such a good old man—when the reservoir gang gets to work I must write the chief engineer to keep a sharp watch on him. I would hate to think of him as the grey, twisted, brittle monstrosity which persists more and more in troubling my sleep.

IMPRISONED WITH THE PHARAOHS

by Houdini & H P Lovecraft

Mystery attracts mystery. Ever since the wide appearance of
my name as a performer of unexplained feats, I have encountered strange narratives and events which my calling has
led people to link with my interests and activities. Some of
these have been trivial and irrelevant, some deeply dramatic
and absorbing, some productive of weird and perilous experiences and some involving me in extensive scientific and
historical research. Many of these matters I have told and
shall continue to tell very freely; but there is one of which I
speak with great reluctance, and which I am now relating only
after a session of grilling persuasion from the publishers of this
magazine, who had heard vague rumours of it from other
members of my family.

The hitherto guarded subject pertains to my non-
professional visit to Egypt fourteen years ago, and has been
avoided by me for several reasons. For one thing, I am averse
to exploiting certain unmistakably actual facts and conditions
obviously unknown to the myriad tourists who throng about
the pyramids and apparently secreted with much diligence by
the authorities at Cairo, who cannot be wholly ignorant of
them. For another thing, I dislike to recount an incident in
which my own fantastic imagination must have played so
great a part. What I saw – or thought I saw – certainly did not
take place; but is rather to be viewed as a result of my then
recent readings in Egyptology, and of the speculations anent
this theme which my environment naturally prompted. These
imaginative stimuli, magnified by the excitement of an actual

event terrible enough in itself, undoubtedly gave rise to the culminating horror of that grotesque night so long past.

In January, 1910, I had finished a professional engagement in England and signed a contract for a tour of Australian theatres. A liberal time being allowed for the trip, I determined to make the most of it in the sort of travel which chiefly interests me; so accompanied by my wife I drifted pleasantly down the Continent and embarked at Marseilles on the P & O Steamer *Malwa*, bound for Port Said. From that point I proposed to visit the principal historical localities of lower Egypt before leaving finally for Australia.

The voyage was an agreeable one, and enlivened by many of the amusing incidents which befall a magical performer apart from his work. I had intended, for the sake of quiet travel, to keep my name a secret; but was goaded into betraying myself by a fellow-magician whose anxiety to astound the passengers with ordinary tricks tempted me to duplicate and exceed his feats in a manner quite destructive of my incognito. I mention this because of its ultimate effect – an effect I should have foreseen before unmasking to a shipload of tourists about to scatter throughout the Nile valley. What it did was to herald my identity wherever I subsequently went, and deprive my wife and me of all the placid inconspicuousness we had sought. Travelling to seek curiosities, I was often forced to stand inspection as a sort of curiosity myself!

We had come to Egypt in search of the picturesque and the mystically impressive, but found little enough when the ship edged up to Port Said and discharged its passengers in small boats. Low dunes of sand, bobbing buoys in shallow water, and a drearily European small town with nothing of interest save the great De Lesseps statue, made us anxious to get on to something more worth our while. After some discussion we decided to proceed at once to Cairo and the Pyramids, later going to Alexandria for the Australian boat and for whatever Greco-Roman sights that ancient metropolis might present.

The railway journey was tolerable enough, and consumed only four hours and a half. We saw much of the Suez Canal, whose route we followed as far as Ismailiya and later had a taste of Old Egypt in our glimpse of the restored fresh-water canal of the Middle Empire. Then at last we saw Cairo glimmering through the growing dusk; a winking constellation which became a blaze as we halted at the great Gare Centrale.

But once more disappointment awaited us, for all that we beheld was European save the costumes and the crowds. A prosaic subway led to a square teeming with carriages, taxicabs, and trolley-cars and gorgeous with electric lights shining on tall buildings; whilst the very theatre where I was vainly requested to play and which I later attended as a spectator, had recently been renamed the 'American Cosmograph'. We stopped at Shepheard's Hotel, reached in a taxi that sped along broad, smartly built-up streets; and amidst the perfect service of its restaurant, elevators, and generally Anglo-American luxuries the mysterious East and immemorial past seemed very far away.

The next day, however, precipitated us delightfully into the heart of the *Arabian Nights* atmosphere; and in the winding ways and exotic skyline of Cairo, the Bagdad of Harun-al-Rashid seemed to live again. Guided by our Baedeker, we had struck east past the Ezbekiyeh Gardens along the Mouski in quest of the native quarter, and were soon in the hands of a clamorous cicerone who – notwithstanding later developments – was assuredly a master at his trade.

Not until afterward did I see that I should have applied at the hotel for a licenced guide. This man, a shaven, peculiarly hollow-voiced and relatively cleanly fellow who looked like a Pharaoh and called himself 'Abdul Reis el Drogman', appeared to have much power over others of his kind; though subsequently the police professed not to know him, and to suggest that *reis* is merely a name for any person in authority, whilst 'Drogman' is obviously no more than a clumsy modification of the word for a leader of tourists parties – *dragoman*.

Abdul led us among such wonders as we had before only read and dreamed of. Old Cairo is itself a story-book and a dream – labyrinths of narrow alleys redolent of aromatic secrets; Arabesque balconies and oriels nearly meeting above the cobbled streets; maelstroms of Oriental traffic with strange cries, cracking whips, rattling carts, jingling money, and braying donkeys; kaleidoscopes of polychrome robes, veils, turbans, and tarbushes; water-carriers and dervishes, dogs and cats, soothsayers and barbers; and over all the whining of blind beggars crouched in alcoves, and the sonorous chanting of muezzins from minarets limned delicately against a sky of deep, unchanging blue.

The roofed, quieter bazaars were hardly less alluring. Spice, perfume, incense beads, rugs, silks, and brass – old Mahmoud Suleiman squats cross-legged amidst his gummy bottles while chattering youths pulverize mustard in the hollowed-out capital of an ancient classic column – a Roman Corinthian, perhaps from neighboring Heliopolis, where Augustus stationed one of his three Egyptian legions. Antiquity begins to mingle with exoticism. And then the mosques and the museum – we saw them all, and tried not to let our Arabian revel succumb to the darker charm of Pharaonic Egypt which the museum's priceless treasures offered. That was to be our climax, and for the present we concentrated on the mediaeval Saracenic glories of the Califs whose magnificent tomb-mosques form a glittering faery necropolis on the edge of the Arabian Desert.

At length Abdul took us along the Sharia Mohammed Ali to the ancient mosque of Sultan Hassan, and the tower-flanked Babel-Azab, beyond which climbs the steep-walled pass to the mighty citadel that Saladin himself built with the stones of forgotten pyramids. It was sunset when we scaled that cliff, circled the modern mosque of Mohammed Ali, and looked down from the dizzy parapet over mystic Cairo – mystic Cairo all golden with its carven domes, its ethereal minarets and its flaming gardens.

Far over the city towered the great Roman dome of the new museum; and beyond it – across the cryptic yellow Nile that is the mother of eons and dynasties – lurked the menacing sands of the Libyan Desert, undulant and iridescent and evil with older arcana.

The red sun sank low, bringing the relentless chill of Egyptian dusk; and as it stood poised on the world's rim like that ancient god of Heliopolis – Re-Harakhte, the Horizon-Sun – we saw silhouetted against its vermeil holocaust the black outlines of the Pyramids of Gizeh – the palaeogean tombs there were hoary with a thousand years when Tut-

Ankh-Amen mounted his golden throne in distant Thebes. Then we knew that we were done with Saracen Cairo, and that we must taste the deeper mysteries of primal Egypt – the black Kem of Re and Amen, Isis and Osiris.

The next morning we visited the Pyramids, riding out in a Victoria across the island of Chizereh with its massive lebbakh trees, and the smaller English bridge to the western shore. Down the shore road we drove, between great rows of lebbakhs and past the vast Zoological Gardens to the suburb of Gizeh, where a new bridge to Cairo proper has since been built. Then, turning inland along the Sharia-el-Haram, we crossed a region of glassy canals and shabby native villages till before us loomed the objects of our quest, cleaving the mists of dawn and forming inverted replicas on the roadside pools. Forty centuries, as Napoleon had told his campaigners there, indeed looked down upon us.

The road now rose abruptly, till we finally reached our place of transfer between the trolley station and the Mena House Hotel. Abdul Reis, who capably purchased our Pyramid tickets, seemed to have an understanding with the crowding, yelling and offensive Bedouins who inhabited a squalid mud village some distance away and pestiferously assailed every traveller; for he kept them very decently at bay and secured an excellent pair of camels for us, himself mounting a donkey and assigning the leadership of our animals to a group of men and boys more expensive than useful. The area to be traversed was so small that camels were hardly needed, but we did not regret adding to our experience this troublesome form of desert navigation.

The pyramids stand on a high rock plateau, this group forming next to the northernmost of the series of regal and aristocratic cemeteries built in the neighbourhood of the extinct capital Memphis, which lay on the same side of the Nile, somewhat south of Gizeh, and which flourished between 3400 and 2000 B.C. The greatest pyramid, which lies nearest the modern road, was built by King Cheops or Khufu about 2800 B.C., and stand more than 450 feet in perpendicular height. In a line southwest from this are successively the Second Pyramid, built a generation later by King Khephren, and though slightly smaller, looking even larger because set on higher ground, and the radically smaller Third Pyramid of King Mycerinus, built about 2700 B.C. Near the edge of the plateau and due east of the Second Pyramid, with a face probably altered to form a colossal portrait of Khephren, its royal restorer, stands the monstrous Sphinx – mute, sardonic, and wise beyond mankind and memory.

Minor pyramids and the traces of ruined minor pyramids are found in several places, and the whole plateau is pitted with the tombs of dignitaries of less than royal rank. These latter were originally marked by *mastabas*, or stone bench-like structures about the deep burial shafts, as found in other Memphian cemeteries and exemplified by Perneb's Tomb in the Metropolitan Museum of New York. At Gizeh, however, all such visible things have been swept away by time and pillage; and only the rock-hewn shafts, either sand-filled or cleared out by archaeologists, remain to attest their former existence. Connected with each tomb was a chapel in which priests and relatives offered food and prayer to the hovering *ka* or vital principle of the deceased. The small tombs have their chapels contained in their stone *mastabas* or superstructures, but the mortuary chapels of the pyramids, where regal Pharaohs lay, were separate temples, each to the east of its corresponding pyramid, and connected by a causeway to a massive gate-chapel or propylon at the edge of the rock plateau.

The gate-chapel leading to the Second Pyramid, nearly buried in the drifting sands, yawns subterraneously south-east of the Sphinx. Persistent tradition dubs it the 'Temple of the Sphinx'; and it may perhaps be rightly called such if the Sphinx indeed represents the Second Pyramid's builder Khephren. There are unpleasant tales of the Sphinx before Khephren – but whatever its elder features were, the monarch replaced them with his own that men might look at the colossus without fear.

It was in the great gateway-temple that the life-size diorite statue of Khephren now in the Cairo museum was found; a statue before which I stood in awe when I beheld it. Whether the whole edifice is now excavated I am not certain, but in 1910 most of it was below ground, with the entrance heavily barred at night. Germans were in charge of the work, and the war or other things may have stopped them. I would give much, in view of my experience and of certain Bedouin whisperings discredited or unknown in Cairo, to know what has developed in connection with a certain well in a transverse gallery where statues of the Pharaoh were found in curious juxtaposition to the statues of baboons.

The road, as we traversed it on our camels that morning, curved sharply past the wooden police quarters, post office, drug store and shops on the left, and plunged south and east in a complete bend that scaled the rock plateau and brought us face to face with the desert under the lee of the Great Pyramid. Past Cyclopean masonry we rode, rounding the eastern face and looking down ahead into a valley of minor pyramids beyond which the eternal Nile glistened to the east, and the eternal desert shimmered to the west. Very close loomed the three major pyramids, the greatest devoid of outer casing and showing its bulk of great stones, but the others retaining here and there the neatly fitted covering which had made them smooth and finished in their day.

Presently we descended towards the Sphinx, and sat silent beneath the spell of those terrible unseeing eyes. On the vast stone breast we faintly discerned the emblem of Re-Harakhte, for whose image the Sphinx was mistaken in a late dynasty; and though sand covered the tablet between the great paws, we recalled what Thutmosis IV inscribed thereon, and the dream he had when a prince. It was then that the smile of the Sphinx vaguely displeased us, and made us wonder about the legends of subterranean passages beneath the monstrous creature, leading down, down, to depths none might dare hint at – depths connected with mysteries older than the dynastic Egypt we excavate, and having a sinister relation to the persistence of abnormal, animal-headed gods in the ancient Nilotic pantheon. Then, too, it was I asked myself an idle question whose hideous significance was not to appear for many an hour.

Other tourists now began to overtake us, and we moved on to the sand-choked Temple of the Sphinx, fifty yards to the southeast, which I have previously mentioned as the great gate of the causeway to the Second Pyramid's mortuary chapel on the plateau. Most of it was still underground, and although we dismounted and descended through a modern passage to its alabaster corridor and pillared hall, I felt that Adul and the local German attendant had not shown us all there was to see.

After this we made the conventional circuit of the pyramid plateau, examining the Second Pyramid and the peculiar ruins of its mortuary chapel to the east, the Third Pyramid and its miniature southern satellites and ruined eastern chapel, the rock tombs and the honeycombings of the Fourth and Fifth dynasties, and the famous Campbell's Tomb whose shadowy shaft sinks precipitously for fifty-three feet to a sinister sarcophagus which one of our camel drivers divested of the cumbering sand after a vertiginous descent by rope.

Cries now assailed us from the Great Pyramid, where Bedouins were besieging a party of tourists with offers of speed in the performance of solitary trips up and down. Seven minutes is said to be the record for such an ascent and descent, but many lusty shieks and sons of shieks assured us they could cut it to five if given the requisite impetus of liberal *baksheesh*. They did not get this impetus, though we did let Abdul take us up, thus obtaining a view of unprecedented magnificence which included not only remote and glittering Cairo with its crowned citadel background of gold-violet hills, but all the pyramids of the Memphian district as well, from Abu Roash on the north to the Dashur on the south. The Sakkara step-pyramid, which marks the evolution of the low *mastaba* into the true pyramid, showed clearly and alluringly in the sandy distance. It is close to this transition-monument that the famed tomb of Perneb was found – more than four hundred miles north of the Theban rock valley where Tut-Ankh-Amen sleeps. Again I was forced to silence through sheer awe. The prospect of such antiquity, and the secrets each hoary monument seemed to hold and brood over, filled me with a reverence and sense of immensity nothing else ever gave me.

Fatigued by our climb, and disgusted with the importunate Bedouins whose actions seemed to defy every rule of taste, we omitted the arduous detail of entering the cramped interior pasages of any of the pyramids, though we saw several of the hardiest tourists preparing for the suffocating crawl through Cheops' mightiest memorial. As we dismissed and overpaid our local bodyguard and drove back to Cairo with Abdul Reis under the afternoon sun, we half regretted the omission we had made. Such fascinating things were whispered about lower pyramid passages not in the guide books; passages whose entrances had been hastily blocked up and concealed by certain uncommunicative archaeologists who had found and begun to explore them.

Of course, this whispering was largely baseless on the face of it; but it was curious to reflect how persistently visitors were forbidden to enter the Pyramids at night, or to visit the lowest burrows and crypt of the Great Pyramid. Perhaps in the latter case it was the psychological effect which was feared – the effect on the visitor of feeling himself huddled down beneath a gigantic world of solid masonry; joined to the life he has known by the merest tube, in which he may only crawl, and which any accident or evil design might block. The whole subject seemed so weird and alluring that we resolved to pay the pryamid plateau another visit at the earliest possible opportunity. For me this opportunity came much earlier than I expected.

That evening, the members of our party feeling somewhat tired after the strenuous programme of the day, I went alone with Abdul Reis for a walk through the picturesque Arab quarter. Though I had seen it by day, I wished to study the alleys and bazaars in the dusk, when rich shadows and mellow gleams of light would add to their glamour and fantastic illusion. The native crowds were thinning, but were still very noisy and numerous when we came upon a knot of revelling Bedouins in the Suken-Nahhasin, or bazaar of the coppersmiths. Their apparent leader, an insolent youth with heavy features and saucily cocked tarbush, took some notice of us, and evidently recognized with no great friendliness my competent but admittedly supercilious and sneeringly disposed guide.

Perhaps, I thought, he resented that odd reproduction of the Sphinx's half-smile which I had often remarked with amused irritation; or perhaps he did not like the hollow and sepulchral resonance of Abdul's voice. At any rate, the exchange of ancestrally opprobrious language became very brisk; and before long Ali Ziz, as I heard the stranger called when called by no worse name, began to pull violently at

Abdul's robe, an action quickly reciprocated and leading to a spirited scuffle in which both combatants lost their sacredly cherished headgear and would have reached an even direr condition had I not intervened and separated them by main force.

My interference, at first seemingly unwelcome on both sides, succeeded at last in effecting a truce. Sullenly each belligerent composed his wrath and his attire, and with an assumption of dignity as profound as it was sudden, the two formed a curious pact of honour which I soon learned is a custom of great antiquity in Cairo – a pact for the settlement of their difference by means of a nocturnal fist fight atop the Great Pyramid, long after the departure of the last moonlight sightseer. Each duellist was to assemble a party of seconds, and the affair was to begin at midnight, proceeding by rounds in the most civilized possible fashion.

In all this planning there was much which excited my interest. The fight itself promised to be unique and spectacular, while the thought of the scene on the hoary pile overlooking the antediluvian plateau of Gizeh under the wan moon of the pallid small hours appealed to every fibre of imagination in me. A request found Abdul exceedingly willing to admit me to his party of seconds; so that all the rest of the early evening I accompanied him to various dens in the most lawless regions of the town – mostly northeast of the Ezbekiyeh – where he gathered one by one a select and formidable band of congenial cutthroats as his pugilistic background.

Shortly after nine our party, mounted on donkeys bearing such royal or tourist-reminiscent names as 'Rameses,' 'Mark Twain,' 'J P Morgan,' and 'Minnehaha,' edged through street labyrinths both Oriental and Occidental, crossed the muddy and mast-forested Nile by the bridge of the bronze lions, and cantered philosophically between the lebbakhs on the road to Gizeh. Slightly over two hours was consumed by the trip, toward the end of which we passed the last of the returning tourists, saluted the last inbound trolley-car, and were alone with the night and the past and the spectral moon.

Then we saw the vast pyramids at the end of the avenue, ghoulish with a dim atavistical menace which I had not

244

seemed to notice in the daytime. Even the smallest of them held a hint of the ghastly – for was it not in this that they had buried Queen Nitocris alive in the Sixth Dynasty; subtle Queen Nitocris, who once invited all her enemies to a feast in a temple below the Nile, and drowned them by opening the water-gates? I recalled that the Arabs whisper things about Nitocris, and shun the Third Pyramid at certain phases of the moon. It must have been over her that Thomas Moore was brooding when he wrote a thing muttered about by Memphian boatmen:

> 'The subterranean nymph that dwells
> 'Mid sunless gems and glories hid –
> The lady of the Pyramid!'

Early as we were, Ali Ziz and his party were ahead of us; for we saw their donkeys outlined against the desert plateau at Kafrel-Haram; toward which squalid Arab settlement, close to the Sphinx, we had diverged instead of following the regular road to the Mena House, where some of the sleepy, inefficient police might have observed and halted us. Here, where filthy Bedouins stabled camels and donkeys in the rock tombs of Khephren's courtiers, we were led up the rocks and over the sand to the Great Pyramid, up whose time-worn sides the Arabs swarmed eagerly, Abdul Reis offering me the assistance I did not need.

As most travellers know, the actual apex of this structure has long been worn away, leaving a reasonably flat platform twelve yards square. On this eery pinnacle a squared circle was formed, and in a few moments the sardonic desert moon leered down upon a battle which, but for the quality of the ringside cries, might well have occurred at some minor athletic club in America. As I watched it, I felt that some of our less desirable institutions were not lacking; for every blow, feint, and defence bespoke 'stalling' to my inexperienced eye. It was quickly over, and despite my misgivings as to methods I felt a sort of proprietary pride when Abdul Reis was adjudged the winner.

Reconciliation was phenomenally rapid, and amidst the singing, fraternizing and drinking which followed, I found it difficult to realize that a quarrel had ever occurred. Oddly enough, I myself seemed to be more a centre of notice than the antagonists; and from my smattering of Arabic I judged that they were discussing my professional performances and escapes from every sort of manacle and confinement, in a manner which indicated not only a surprising knowledge of me, but a distinct hostility and scepticism concerning my feats of escape. It gradually dawned on me that the elder magic of Egypt did not depart without leaving traces, and that fragments of a strange secret lore and priestly cult-practices have survived surreptitiously amongst the fellaheen to such an extent that the prowess of a strange *hahwi* of magician is resented and disputed. I thought of how much my hollow-voiced guide Abdul Reis looked like an old Egyptian priest of Pharaoh or smiling Sphinx . . . and wondered.

Suddenly something happened which in a flash proved the correctness of my reflections and made me curse the denseness whereby I had accepted this night's events as other than the empty and malicious 'frame-up' they now showed themselves to be. Without warning, and doubtless in answer to some subtle sign from Abdul, the entire band of Bedouins precipitated itself upon me; and having produced heavy ropes, soon had me bound as securely as I was ever bound in the course of my life, either on the stage or off.

I struggled at first, but soon saw that one man could make no headway against a band of over twenty sinewy barbarians. My hands were tied behind my back, my knees bent to their fullest extent, and my wrists and ankles stoutly linked together with unyielding cords. A stifling gag was forced into my mouth, and a blindfold fastened tightly over my eyes. Then, as Arabs bore me aloft on their shoulders and began a jouncing descent of the pyramid, I heard the taunts of my late guide Adbul, who mocked and jeered delightedly in his hollow voice, and assured me that I was soon to have my 'magic powers' put to a supreme test which would quickly remove any egotism I might have gained through triumphing over all the tests offered by America and Europe. Egypt, he reminded me, is very old, and full of inner mysteries and antique powers not even conceivable to the experts of today, whose devices had so uniformly failed to entrap me.

How far or in what direction I was carried, I cannot tell; for the circumstances were all against the formation of any accurate judgment. I know, however, that it could not have been a great distance; since my bearers at no point hastened beyond a walk, yet kept me aloft a surprisingly short time. It is this perplexing brevity which makes me feel almost like shuddering whenever I think of Gizeh and its plateau – for one is oppressed by hints of the closeness to everyday tourist routes of what existed then and must exist still.

The evil abnormality I speak of did not become manifest at first. Setting me down on a surface which I reconized as sand rather than rock, my captors passed a rope around my chest and dragged me a few feet to a ragged opening in the ground, into which they presently lowered me with much rough hand-ling. For apparent eons I bumped against the stony irregular sides of a narrow hewn well which I took to be one of the numerous burial-shafts of the plateau until the prodigious, almost incredible depth of it robbed me of all bases of con-jecture.

The horror of the experience deepened with every dragging second. That any descent through the sheer solid rock could be so vast without reaching the core of the planet itself, or that any rope made by man could be so long as to dangle me in these unholy and seemingly fathomless profundities of nether earth, were beliefs of such grotesqueness that it was easier to doubt my agitated senses than to accept them. Even now I am uncertain, for I know how deceitful the sense of time becomes when one is removed or distorted. But I am quite sure that I preserved a logical consciousness that far; that at least I did not add any fullgrown phantoms of imagination to a picture hideous enough in its reality, and explicable by a type of cerebral illusion vastly short of actual hallucination.

All this was not the cause of my first bit of fainting. The shocking ordeal was cumulative, and the beginning of the later terrors was a very perceptible increase in my rate of descent. They were paying out that infinitely long rope very swiftly now, and I scraped cruelly against the rough and constricted sides of the shaft as I shot madly downward. My clothing was in tatters, and I felt the trickle of blood all over, even above the mounting and excruciating pain. My nostrils, too, were assailed by a scarcely definable menace: a creeping odour of damp and staleness curiously unlike anything I had ever smelled before, and having faint overtones of spice and incense that lent an element of mockery.

Then the mental cataclysm came. It was horrible – hideous beyond all articulate description because it was all of the soul, with nothing of detail to describe. It was the ecstasy of nightmare and the summation of the fiendish. The suddenness of it was apocalyptic and demoniac – one moment I was plunging agonizingly down that narrow well of million-toothed torture, yet the next moment I was soaring on bat-wings in the gulfs of hell; swinging free and swoopingly through illimitable miles of boundless, musty space; rising dizzily to measureless pinnacles of chilling ether, then diving gaspingly to sucking nadirs of ravenous, nauseous lower vacua. . . . Thank God for the mercy that shut out in oblivion those clawing Furies of consciousness which half unhinged my faculties, and tore harpy-like at my spirit! That one respite, short as it was, gave me the strength and sanity to endure those still greater sublimations of cosmic panic that lurked and gibbered on the road ahead.

It was very gradually that I regained my senses after that eldritch flight through stygian space. The process was infinitely painful, and coloured by fantastic dreams in which my bound and gagged condition found singular embodiment. The precise nature of these dreams was very clear while I was experiencing them, but became blurred in my recollection almost immediately afterwards, and was soon reduced to the merest outline by the terrible events – real or imaginary – which followed. I dreamed that I was in the grasp of a great and horrible paw; a yellow, hairy, five-clawed paw which had reached out of the earth to crush and engulf me. And when I stopped to reflect what the paw was, it seemed to me that it was Egypt. In the dream I looked back at the events of the preceding weeks, and saw myself lured and enmeshed little by little, subtly and insidiously, by some hellish ghoul-spirit of the elder Nile sorcery; some spirit that was in Egypt before ever man was, and that will be when man is no more.

I saw the horror and unwholesome antiquity of Egypt, and the grisly alliance it has always had with the tombs and temples of the dead. I saw phantom processions of priests with

248

the heads of bulls, falcons, cats, and ibises; phantom processions marching interminably through subterraneous labyrinths and avenues of titanic propylaea beside which a man is as a fly, and offering unnamable sacrifice to indescribable gods. Stone colossi marched in endless night and drove herds of grinning androsphinxes down to the shores of illimitable stagnant rivers of pitch. And behind it all I saw the ineffable malignity of primordial necromancy, black and amorphous, and fumbling greedily after me in the darkness to choke out the spirit that had dared to mock it by emulation.

In my sleeping brain there took shape a melodrama of sinister hatred and pursuit, and I saw the black soul of Egypt singling me out and calling me in audible whispers; calling and luring me, leading me on with the glitter and glamour of a Saracenic surface, but ever pulling me down to the age-mad catacombs and horrors of its *dead* and abysmal pharaonic heart.

Then the dream faces took on human resemblances, and I saw my guide Abdul Reis in the robes of a king, with the sneer of the Sphinx on his features. And I knew that those features were the features of Khephren the Great, who raised the Second Pyramid, carved over the Sphinx's face in the likeness of his own and built that titanic gateway temple whose myriad corridors the archaeologists think they have dug out of the cryptical sand and the uninformative rock. And I looked at the long, lean, rigid hand of Khephren; the long, lean, rigid hand as I had seen it on the diorite statue in the Cairo Museum – the statue they had found in the terrible gateway temple – and wondered that I had not shrieked when I saw it on Abdul Reis . . . That hand! It was hideously cold, and it was crushing me; it was the cold and cramping of the sarcophagus . . . the chill and constriction of unrememberable Egypt . . . It was nighted, necropolitan Egypt itself . . . that yellow paw . . . and they whisper such things of Khephren. . . .

But at this juncture I began to awake – or at least, to assume a condition less completely that of sleep than the one just preceding. I recalled the fight atop the pyramid, the treacherous Bedouins and their attack, my frightful descent by rope through endless rock depths, and my mad swinging and plunging in a chill void redolent of aromtic putrescence. I perceived that I now lay on a damp rock floor, and that my bonds were still biting into me with unloosened force. It was very cold, and I seemed to detect a faint current of noisome air sweeping across me. The cuts and bruises I had received from the jagged sides of the rock shaft were paining me woefully, their soreness enhanced to a stinging or burning acuteness by some pungent quality in the faint draft, and the mere act of rolling over was enough to set my whole frame throbbing with untold agony.

As I turned I felt a tug from above, and concluded that the rope whereby I was lowered still reached the surface. Whether or not the Arabs still held it, I had no idea; nor had I any idea how far within the earth I was. I knew that the darkness around me was wholly or nearly total, since no ray of moonlight penetrated my blindfold; but I did not trust my senses enough to accept as evidenc of extreme depth the sensation of vast duration which had characterized my descent.

Knowing at least that I was in a space of considerable extent reached from the surface directly above by an opening in the rock, I doubtfully conjectured that my prison was perhaps the buried gateway chapel of old Khephren – the Temple of the Sphinx – perhaps some inner corridor which the guides had not shown me during my morning visit, and from which I might easily escape if I could find my way to the barred entrance. It would be a labyrinthine wandering, but no worse than others out of which I had in the past found my way.

The first step was to get free of my bonds, gag, and blindfold; and this I knew would be no great task, since subtler experts than these Arabs had tried every known species of fetter upon me during my long and varied career as an exponent of escape, yet had never succeeded in defeating my methods.

Then it occurred to me that the Arabs might be ready to meet and attack me at the entrance upon any evidence of my probable escape from the binding cords, as would be furnished by any decided agitation of the rope which they probably held. This, of course, was taking for granted that my place of confinement was indeed Khephren's Temple of the Sphinx. The direct opening in the roof, wherever it might lurk, could not be beyond easy reach of the ordinary modern entrance near the Sphinx; if in truth it were any great distance at all on the surface, since the total area known to visitors is not at all enormous. I had not noticed any such opening during my daytime pilgrimage, but knew that these things are easily overlooked amidst the drifting sands.

Thinking these matters over as I lay bent and bound on the rock floor, I nearly forgot the horrors of abysmal descent and cavernous swinging which had so lately reduced me to a coma. My present thought was only to outwit the Arabs, and I accordingly determined to work myself free as quickly as possible, avoiding any tug on the descending line which might betray an effective or even problematical attempt at freedom.

This, however, was more easily determined than effected. A few preliminary trials made it clear that little could be accomplished without considerable motion; and it did not surprise me when, after one especially energetic struggle, I began to feel the coils of falling rope as they piled up about me and upon me. Obviously, I thought, the Bedouins had felt my movements and released their end of the rope; hastening no doubt to the temple's true entrance to lie murderously in wait for me.

The prospect was not pleasing – but I had faced worse in my time without flinching, and would not flinch now. At present I must first of all free myself of bonds, then trust to ingenuity to escape from the temple unharmed. It is curious how implicitly I had come to believe myself in the old temple of Khephren beside the Sphinx, only a short distance below the ground.

That belief was shattered, and every pristine apprehension of preternatural depth and demoniac mystery revived, by a circumstance which grew in horror and significance even as I formulated my philosophical plan. I have said that the falling rope was piling up about and upon me. Now I saw that it was continuing to pile, as no rope of normal length could possibly do. It gained in momentum and became an avalanche of hemp, accumulating mountainously on the floor and half burying me beneath its swiftly multiplying coils. Soon I was completely engulfed and gasping for breath as the increasing convulsions submerged and stifled me.

My senses tottered again, and I vainly tried to fight off a menace desperate and ineluctable. It was not merely that I was tortured beyond human endurance – not merely that life and breath seemed to be crushed slowly out of me – it was the knowledge of what those unnatural lengths of rope implied, and the consciousness of what unknown and incalculable gulfs of inner earth must at this moment be surrounding me. My endless descent and swinging flight through goblin space, then, must have been real, and even now I must be lying helpless in some nameless cavern world toward the core of the planet. Such a sudden confirmation of ultimate horror was insupportable, and a second time I lapsed into merciful oblivion.

When I say oblivion, I do not imply that I was free from dreams. On the contrary, my absence from the conscious world was marked by visions of the most unutterable hideousness. God! . . . If only I had not read so much Egyptology before coming to this land which is the fountain of all darkness and terror! This second spell of fainting filled my sleeping mind anew with shivering realization of the country and its archaic secrets, and through some damnable chance my dreams turned to the ancient notions of the dead and their sojournings in soul and body beyond those mysterious tombs which were more houses than graves. I recalled, in dream-shapes which it is well that I do not remember, the peculiar and elaborate construction of Egyptian sepulchers; and the exceedingly singular and terrific doctrines which determined this construction.

All these people thought of was death and the dead. They conceived of a literal resurrection of the body which made them mummify it with desperate care, and preserve all the vital organs in canopic jars near the corpse; whilst besides the body they believed in two other elements, the soul, which after its weighing and approval by Osiris dwelt in the land of the blest, and the obscure and portentous *ka* or life-principle which wandered about the upper and lower worlds in a horrible way, demanding occasional access to the preserved body, consuming the food offerings brought by priests and pious relatives to the mortuary chapel, and sometimes – as men whispered – taking its body or the wooden double always buried beside it and stalking noxiously abroad on errands peculiarly repellent.

For thousands of years those bodies rested gorgeously encased and staring glassily upward when not visited by the *ka*, awaiting the day when Osiris should restore both *ka* and soul, and lead forth the stiff legions of the dead from the sunken houses of sleep. It was to have been a glorious rebirth – but not all souls were approved, nor were all tombs inviolate, so that certain grotesque *mistakes* and fiendish *abnormalities* were to be looked for. Even today the Arabs murmur of unsanctified convocations and unwholesome worship in forgotten nether abysses, which only winged invisible *kas* and soulless mummies may visit and return unscathed.

Perhaps the most leeringly blood-congealing legends are those which relate to certain perverse products of decadent priestcraft – *composite mummies* made by the artificial union of human trunks and limbs with the heads of animals in imitation of the elder gods. At all stages of history the sacred animals were mummified, so that consecrated bulls, cats, ibises, crocodiles and the like might return some day to greater glory. But only in the decadence did they mix the human and animal in the same mummy – only in the decadence, when they did not understand the rights and prerogatives of the *ka* and the soul.

What happened to those composite mummies is not told of – at least publicly – and it is certain that no Egyptologist ever found one. The whispers of Arabs are very wild, and cannot be relied upon. They even hint that old Khephren – he of the Sphinx, the Second Pyramid and the yawning gateway temple – lives far underground wedded to the ghoul-queen Nitocris and ruling over the mummies that are neither of man nor of beast.

It was of these – of Khephren and his consort and his strange armies of the hybrid dead – that I dreamed, and that is why I am glad the exact dream-shapes have faded from my memory. My most horrible vision was connected with an idle question I had asked myself the day before when looking at the great carven riddle of the desert and wondering with what unknown depth the temple close to it might be secretly connected. That question, so innocent and whimsical then, assumed in my dream a meaning of frenetic and hysterical madness . . . *what huge and loathsome abnormality was the Sphinx originally carven to represent?*

My second awakening – if awakening it was – is a memory of stark hideousness which nothing else in my life – save one thing which came after – can parallel; and that life has been full and adventurous beyond most men's. Remember that I had lost consciousness whilst buried beneath a cascade of falling rope whose immensity revealed the cataclysmic depth of my present position. Now, as perception returned, I felt the entire weight gone; and realized upon rolling over that although I was still tied, gagged and blindfolded, *some agency had removed completely the suffocating hempen landslide which had overwhelmed me.* The significance of this condition, of course, came to me only gradually; but even so I think it would have brought unconsciousness again had I not by this time reached such a state of emotional exhaustion that no new horror could make much difference. I was alone . . . *with what?*

Before I could torture myself with any new reflection, or make any fresh effort to escape from my bonds, an additional circumstance became manifest. Pains not formerly felt were racking my arms and legs, and I seemed coated with a profusion of dried blood beyond anything my former cuts and abrasions could furnish. My chest, too, seemed pierced by a hundred wounds, as though some malign, titanic ibis had been pecking at it. Assuredly the agency which had removed the rope was a hostile one, and had begun to wreak terrible injuries upon me when somehow impelled to desist. Yet at the time my sensations were distinctly the reverse of what one might expect. Instead of sinking into a bottomless pit of despair, I was stirred to a new courage and action; for now I felt that the evil forces were physical things which a fearless man might encounter on an even basis.

On the strength of this thought I tugged again at my bonds, and used all the art of a lifetime to free myself as I had so often done amidst the glare of lights and the applause of vast crowds. The familiar details of my escaping process commenced to engross me, and now that the long rope was gone I half regained my belief that the supreme horrors were hallucinations after all, and that there had never been any terrible shaft, measureless abyss or interminable rope. Was I after all in the gateway temple of Khephren beside the Sphinx, and had the sneaking Arabs stolen in to torture me as I lay helpless there? At any rate, I must be free. Let me stand up unbound, ungagged, and with eyes open to catch any glimmer of light which might come trickling from any source, and I could actually delight in the combat against evil and treacherous foes!

How long I took in shaking off my encumbrances I cannot tell. It must have been longer than in my exhibition performances, because I was wounded, exhausted, and enervated by the experiences I had passed through. When I was finally free, and taking deep breaths of a chill, damp, evilly spiced air all the more horrible when encountered without the screen of gag and blindfolded edges, I found that I was too cramped and fatigued to move at once. There I lay, trying to stretch a frame bent and mangled, for an indefinite period, and straining my eyes to catch a glimpse of some ray of light which would give a hint as to my position.

By degrees my strength and flexibility returned, but my eyes beheld nothing. As I staggered to my feet I peered diligently in every direction, yet met only an ebony blackness as great as that I had known when blindfolded. I tried my legs, blood-encrusted beneath my shredded trousers, and found that I could walk; yet could not decide in what direction to go. Obviously I ought not to walk at random, and perhaps retreat directly from the entrance I sought; so I paused to note the direction of the cold, fetid, natron-scented air-current which I had never ceased to feel. Accepting the point of its source as the possible entrance to the abyss, I strove to keep track of this landmark and to walk consistently toward it.

I had a match-box with me, and even a small electric flashlight; but of course the pockets of my tossed and tattered clothing were long since emptied of all heavy articles. As I walked cautiously in the blackness, the draft grew stronger and more offensive, till at length I could regard it as nothing less than a tangible stream of detestable vapour pouring out of some aperture like the smoke of the genie from the fisherman's jar in the Eastern tale. The East . . . Egypt . . .

truly, this dark cradle of civilization was ever the wellspring of horrors and marvels unspeakable!

The more I reflected on the nature of this cavern wind, the greater my sense of disquiet became; for although despite its odour I had sought its source as at least an indirect clue to the outer world, I now saw plainly that this foul emanation could have no admixture or connection whatsoever with the clean air of the Libyan Desert, but must be essentially a thing vomited from sinister gulfs still lower down. I had, then, been walking in the wrong direction!

After a moment's reflection I decided not to retrace my steps. Away from the draft I would have no landmarks, for the roughly level rock floor was devoid of distinctive configurations. If, however, I followed up the strange current, I would undoubtedly arrive at an aperture of some sort, from whose gate I could perhaps work round the walls to the opposite side of this Cyclopean and otherwise unnavigable hall. That I might fail, I well realized. I saw that this was no part of Khephren's gateway temple which tourists know, and it struck me that this particular hall might be unknown even to archaeologists, and merely stumbled upon by the inquisitive and malignant Arabs who had imprisoned me. If so, was there any present gate of escape to the known parts or to the outer air?

What evidence, indeed, did I now possess that this was the gateway temple at all? For a moment all my wildest speculations rushed back upon me, and I thought of that vivid melange of impressions – descent, suspension in space, the rope, my wounds, and the dreams that were frankly dreams. Was this the end of life for me? Or indeed, would it be merciful if this moment *were* the end? I could answer none of my own questions, but merely kept on, till Fate for a third time reduced me to oblivion.

This time there were no dreams, for the suddenness of the incident shocked me out of all thought either conscious or subconscious. Tripping on an unexpected descending step at a point where the offensive draft became strong enough to offer an actual physical resistance, I was precipitated headlong down a black flight of huge stone stairs into a gulf of hideousness unrelieved.

That I ever breathed again is a tribute to the inherent vitality of the healthy human organism. Often I look back to that night and feel a touch of actual humour in those repeated lapses of consciousness; lapses whose succession reminded me at the time of nothing more than the crude cinema melodramas of that period. Of course, it is possible that the repeated lapses never occurred; and that all the features of that underground nightmare were merely the dreams of one long coma which began with the shock of my descent into that abyss and ended with the healing balm of the outer air and of the rising sun which found me stretched on the sands of Gizeh before the sardonic and dawn-flushed face of the Great Sphinx.

I prefer to believe this latter explanation as much as I can, hence was glad when the police told me that the barrier to Khephren's gateway temple had been found unfastened, and that a sizable rift to the surface did actually exist in one corner of the still buried part. I was glad, too, when the doctors pronounced my wounds only those to be expected from my seizure, blindfolding, lowering, struggling with bonds, falling some distance – perhaps into a depression in the temple's inner gallery – dragging myself to the outer barrier and escaping from it, and experiences like that . . . a very soothing diagnosis. And yet I know that there must be more than appears on the surface. That extreme descent is too vivid a memory to be dismissed – and it is odd that no one has ever been able to find a man answering the description of my guide, Abdul Reis el Drogman – the tomb-throated guide who looked and smiled like King Khephren.

I have digressed from my connected narrative – perhaps in the vain hope of evading the telling of that final incident; that incident which of all is most certainly an hallucination. But I promised to relate it, and I do not break promises. When I recovered – or seemed to recover – my senses after that fall down the black stone stairs, I was quite as alone and in darkness as before. The windy stench, bad enough before, was now fiendish; yet I had acquired enough familiarity by this time to bear it stoically. Dazedly I began to crawl away from the place whence the putrid wind came, and with my bleeding hands felt the colossal blocks of a mighty pavement. Once my head struck against a hard object, and when I felt of it I learned that it was the base of a column – a column of unbelievably immensity – whose surface was covered with gigantic chiseled hieroglyphics very perceptible to my touch.

Crawling on, I encountered other titan columns at incomprehensible distances apart; when suddenly my attention was captured by the realization of something which must have been impinging on my subconscious hearing long before the conscious sense was aware of it.

From some still lower chasm in earth's bowels were proceeding certain *sounds*, measured and definite, and like nothing I had ever heard before. That they were very ancient and distinctly ceremonial I felt almost intuitively; and much reading in Egyptology led me to associate them with the flute, the sambuke, the sistrum, and the tympanum. In their rhythmic piping, droning, rattling and beating I felt an element of terror beyond all the known terrors of earth – a terror peculiarly dissociated from personal fear, and taking the form of a sort of objective pity for our planet, that it should hold within its depths such horrors as must lie beyond these aegipanic cacophonies. The sounds increased in volume, and I felt that they were approaching. Then – and may all the gods of all pantheons unite to keep the like from my ears again – I began to hear, faintly and afar off, the morbid and millennial tramping of the marching things.

It was hideous that footfalls so dissimilar should move in such perfect rhythm. The training of unhallowed thousands of years must lie behind that march of earth's inmost monstrosities . . . padding, clicking, walking, stalking, rumbling, lumbering, crawling . . . and all to the abhorrent discords of those mocking instruments. And then – God keep the memory of those Arab legends out of my head! – the mummies without souls . . . the meeting-place of the wandering *kas* . . . the hordes of the devil-cursed pharaonic dead of forty centuries . . . the *composite mummies* led through the uttermost onyx voids by King Khephren and his ghoul-queen Nitocris . . .

The tramping drew nearer – Heaven save me from the sound of those feet and paws and hooves and pads and talons as it commenced to acquire detail! Down limitless reaches of sunless pavement a spark of light flickered in the malodorous wind and I drew behind the enormous circumference of a Cyclopic column that I might escape for a while the horror that was stalking million-footed toward me through gigantic hypostyles of inhuman dread and phobic antiquity. The flickers increased, and the tramping and dissonant rhythm grew sickeningly loud. In the quivering orange light there stood faintly forth a scene of such stony awe that I gasped from sheer wonder that conquered even fear and repulsion. Bases of columns whose middles were higher than human sight . . . mere bases of things that must each dwarf the Eiffel Tower to insignificance . . . hieroglyphics carved by unthinkable hands in caverns where daylight can be only a remote legend . . .

I *would not* look at the marching things. That I desperately resolved as I heard their creaking joints and nitrous wheezing above the dead music and the dead tramping. It was merciful that they did not speak . . . but God! *their crazy torches began to cast shadows on the surface of those stupendous columns. Hippopotami should not have human hands and carry torches . . . men should not have the heads of crocodiles . . .*

I tried to turn away, but the shadows and the sounds and the stench were everywhere. Then I remembered something I used to do in half-conscious nightmares as a boy, and began to repeat to myself, 'This is a dream! This is a dream!' But it was of no use, and I could only shut my eyes and pray . . . at least, that is what I think I did, for one is never sure in visions – and I know this can have been nothing more. I wondered whether I should ever reach the world again, and at times would furtively open my eyes to see if I could discern any feature of the place other than the wind of spiced putrefaction, the topless columns, and the thaumatropically grotesque shadows of abnormal horror. The sputtering glare of multiplying torches now shone, and unless this hellish place were wholly without walls, I could not fail to see some boundary or fixed landmark soon. But I had to shut my eyes again when I realized how many of the things were assembling – and when I glimpsed a certain object walking solemnly and steadily *without any body above the waist.*

A fiendish and ululant corpse-gurgle or death-rattle now

split the very atmosphere – the charnel atmosphere poisonous with naftha and bitumen blasts – in one concerted chorus from the ghoulish legion of hybrid blasphemies. My eyes, perversely shaken open, gazed for an instant upon a sight which no human creature could even imagine without panic, fear and physical exhaustion. The things had filed cere-monially in one direction, the direction of the noisome wind, where the light of their torches showed their bended heads – or the bended heads of such as had heads. They were worshipping before a great black fetor-belching aperture which reached up almost out of sight, and which I could see was flanked at right angles by two giant staircases whose ends were far away in shadow. One of these was indubitably the staircase I had fallen down.

The dimensions of the hole were fully in proportion with those of the columns – an ordinary house would have been lost in it, and any average public building could easily have been moved in and out. It was so vast a surface that only by moving the eye could one trace its boundaries . . . so vast, so hideously black, and so aromatically stinking . . . Directly in front of this yawning Polyphemus-door the things were throwing objects – evidently sacrifices or religious offerings, to judge by their gestures. Khephren was their leader; sneering King Khephren *or the guide Abdul Reis*, crowned with a golden pshent and intoning endless formulae with the hollow voice of the dead. By his side knelt beautiful Queen Nitocris, whom I saw in profile for a moment, noting that the right half of her face was eaten away by rats or other ghouls. And I shut my eyes again when I saw what objects were being thrown as offerings to the fetid aperture or its possible local deity.

It occurred to me that, judging from the elaborateness of this worship, the concealed deity must be one of considerable importance. Was it Osiris or Isis, Horus or Anubis, or some vast unknown God of the Dead still more central and supreme? There is a legend that terrible altars and colossi were reared to an Unknown One before even the known gods were worshipped. . . .

And now, as I steeled myself to watch the rapt and sepulchral adorations of those nameless things, a thought of escape flashed upon me. The hall was dim, and the columns heavy with shadow. With every creature of that nightmare throng absorbed in shocking raptures, it might be barely possible for me to creep past to the far-away end of one of the staircases and ascend unseen; trusting to Fate and skill to deliver me from the upper reaches. Where I was, I neither knew nor seriously reflected upon – and for a moment it struck me as amusing to plan a serious escape from that which I knew to be a dream. Was I in some hidden and unsuspected lower realm of Khephren's gateway temple – that temple which generations have persistently called the Temple of the Sphinx? I could not conjecture, but I resolved to ascend to life and consciousness if wit and muscle could carry me.

Wriggling flat on my stomach, I began the anxious journey toward the foot of the left-hand staircase, which seemed the more accessible of the two. I cannot describe the incidents and sensations of that crawl, but they may be guessed when one reflects on what I had to watch steadily in that malign, wind-blown torchlight in order to avoid detection. The bottom of the staircase was, as I have said, far away in shadow, as it had to be to rise without a bend to the dizzy parapeted landing above the titanic aperture. This placed the last stages of my crawl at some distance from the noisome herd, though the spectacle chilled me even when quite remote at my right.

At length I succeeded in reaching the steps and began to climb; keeping close to the wall, on which I observed decorations of the most hideous sort, and relying for safety on the absorbed, ecstatic interest with which the monstrosities watched the foul-breezed aperture and the impious objects of nourishment they had flung on the pavement before it. Though the staircase was huge and steep, fashioned of vast porphyry blocks as if for the feet of a giant, the ascent seemed virtually interminable. Dread of discovery and the pain which renewed exercise had brought to my wounds combined to make that upward crawl a thing of agonizing memory. I had intended, on reaching the landing, to climb immediately onward along whatever upper staircase might mount from there; stopping for no last look at the carrion abominations that pawed and genuflected some seventy or eighty feet below – yet a sudden repetition of that thunderous corpse-gurgle and death-rattle chorus, coming as I had nearly gained the top of the flight and showing by its ceremonial rhythm that it was not an alarm of my discovery, caused me to pause and peer cautiously over the parapet.

The monstrosities were hailing something which had poked itself out of the nauseous aperture to seize the hellish fare proffered it. It was something quite ponderous, even as seen from my height; something yellowish and hairy, and endowed with a sort of nervous motion. It was as large, perhaps, as a good-sized hippopotamus, but very curiously shaped. It seemed to have no neck, but five separate shaggy heads springing in a row from a roughly cylindrical trunk; the first very small, the second good-sized, the third and fourth equal and largest of all, and the fifth rather small, though not so small as the first.

Out of these heads darted curious rigid tentacles which seized ravenously on the excessively great quantities of unmentionable food placed before the aperture. Once in a while the thing would leap up, and occasionally it would retreat into its den in a very odd manner. Its locomotion was so inexplicable that I stared in fascination, wishing it would emerge farther from the cavernous lair beneath me.

Then it *did emerge* . . . it *did* emerge, and at the sight I turned and fled into the darkness up the higher staircase that rose behind me; fled unknowingly up incredible steps and ladders and inclined planes to which no human sight or logic guided me, and which I must ever relegate to the world of dreams for want of any confirmation. It must have been a dream, or the dawn would never have found me breathing on the sands of Gizeh before the sardonic dawn-flushed face of the Great Sphinx.

The Great Sphinx! God! That idle question I asked myself on that sun-blest morning before . . . *what huge and loathsome abnormality was the Sphinx originally carven to represent?* Accursed is the sight, be it in dream or not, that revealed to me the supreme horror – the unknown God of the Dead, which licks its colossal chops in the unsuspected abyss, fed hideous morsels by soulless absurdities that should not exist. The five-headed monster that emerged . . . that five-headed monster as large as a hippopotamus . . . the five-headed monster – *and that of which it is the merest forepaw* . . .

But I survived, and I know it was only a dream.

BEYOND THE WALL OF SLEEP

I HAVE often wondered if the majority of mankind ever pause to reflect upon the occasionally titanic significance of dreams, and of the obscure world to which they belong. Whilst the greater number of our nocturnal visions are perhaps more than faint and fantastic reflections of our waking experiences—Freud to the contrary with his puerile symbolism—there are still a certain remainder whose immundane and ethereal character permits of no ordinary interpretation, and whose vaguely exciting and disquieting effect suggests possible minute glimpses into a sphere of mental existence no less important than physical life, yet separated from that life by an all but impassable barrier. From my experience I cannot doubt but that man, when lost to terrestrial consciousness, is indeed sojourning in another and uncorporeal life of far different nature from the life we know, and of which only the slightest and most indistinct memories linger after waking. From those blurred and fragmentary memories we may infer much, yet prove little. We may guess that in dreams life, matter, and vitality, as the earth knows such things, are not necessarily constant; and that time and space do not exist as our waking selves comprehend them. Sometimes I believe that this less material life is our truer life, and that our vain presence on the terraqueous globe is itself the secondary or merely virtual phenomenon.

It was from a youthful revery filled with speculations of this sort that I arose one afternoon in the winter of 1900-01, when to the state psychopathic institution in which I served as an intern was brought the man whose case has ever since haunted me so unceasingly. His name, as given on the records, was Joe Slater, or Slaader, and his appearance was that of the typical denizen of the Catskill Mountain region; one of those strange, repellent scions of a primitive Colonial peasant stock whose isolation for nearly three centuries in the hilly fastnesses of a little-traveled countryside has caused them to sink to a kind of barbaric degeneracy, rather than advance with their more fortunately placed brethren of the thickly settled districts. Among these odd folk, who correspond exactly to the decadent element of "white trash" in the South, law and morals are non-existent; and their general mental status is probably below that of any other section of the native American people.

Joe Slater, who came to the institution in the vigilant custody of four state policemen, and who was described as a highly dangerous character, certainly presented no evidence of his perilous disposition when I first beheld him. Though well above the middle stature, and of somewhat brawny frame, he was given an absurd appearance of harmless stupidity by the pale, sleepy blueness of his small watery eyes, the scantiness of his neglected and never-shaven growth of yellow beard, and the listless drooping of his heavy nether lip. His age was unknown, since among his kind neither family records nor permanent ties exist; but from the baldness of his head in front, and from the decayed condition of his teeth, the head surgeon wrote him down as a man of about forty.

From the medical and court documents we learned all that could be gathered of his case: This man, a vagabond, hunter and trapper, had always been strange in the eyes of his primitive associates. He had habitually slept at night beyond the ordinary time, and upon waking would often talk of unknown things in a manner so bizarre as to inspire fear even in the hearts of an unimaginative populace. Not that his form of language was at all unusual, for he never spoke save in the debased patois of his environment; but the tone and tenor of his utterances were of such mysterious wildness, that none might listen without apprehension. He himself was generally as terrified and baffled as his auditors, and within an hour after awakening would forget all that he had said, or at least all that had caused him to say what he did; relapsing into a bovine, half-amiable normality like that of the other hill-dwellers.

As Slater grew older, it appeared, his matutinal aberrations had gradually increased in frequency and violence; till about a month before his arrival at the institution had occurred the shocking tragedy which caused his arrest by the authorities. One day near noon, after a profound sleep begun in a whisky debauch at about five of the previous afternoon, the man had roused himself most suddenly, with ululations so horrible and unearthly that they brought several neighbors to his cabin—a filthy sty where he dwelt with a family as indescribable as himself. Rushing out into the snow, he had flung his arms aloft and commenced a series of leaps directly upward in the air; the while shouting his determination to reach some "big, big cabin with brightness in the roof and walls and floor and the loud queer music far away." As two men of moderate size sought to restrain him, he had struggled with maniacal force and fury, screaming of his desire and need to find and kill a certain "thing that shines and shakes and laughs." At length, after temporarily felling one of his detainers with a sudden blow, he had flung himself upon the other in a demoniac ecstasy of blood-thirstiness, shrieking fiendishly that he would "jump high in the air and burn his way through anything that stopped him."

Family and neighbors had now fled in a panic, and when the more courageous of them returned, Slater was gone, leaving behind an unrecognizable pulp-like thing that had been a living man but an hour before. None of the mountaineers had dared to pursue him, and it is likely that they would have welcomed his death from the cold; but when several mornings later they heard his screams from a distant ravine they realized that he had somehow managed to survive, and that his removal in one way or another would be necessary. Then had followed an armed searching-party, whose purpose (whatever it may have been originally) became that of a sheriff's posse after one of the seldom popular state troopers had by accident observed, then questioned, and finally joined the seekers.

*　　*　　*

On the third day Slater was found unconscious in the hollow of a tree, and taken to the nearest jail, where alienists from Albany examined him as soon as his senses returned. To them he told a simple story. He had, he said, gone to sleep one afternoon about sundown after drinking much liquor. He had awaked to find himself standing bloody-handed in the snow before his cabin, the mangled corpse of his neighbor Peter Slader at his feet. Horrified, he had taken to the woods in a vague effort to escape from the scene of what must have been his crime. Beyond these things he seemed to know nothing, nor could the expert questioning of his interrogators bring out a single additional fact.

That night Slater slept quietly, and the next morning he wakened with no singular feature save a certain alteration of expression. Doctor Barnard, who had been watching the patient, thought he noticed in the pale blue eyes a certain gleam of peculiar quality, and in the flaccid lips an all but imperceptible tightening, as if of intelligent determination. But when questioned, Slater relapsed into the habitual vacancy of the mountaineer, and only reiterated what he had said on the preceding day.

On the third morning occurred the first of the man's mental attacks. After some show of uneasiness in sleep, he burst forth into a frenzy so powerful that the combined efforts of four men were needed to bind him in a strait-jacket. The alienists listened with keen attention to his words, since their curiosity had been aroused to a high pitch by the suggestive yet mostly conflicting and incoherent stories of his family and neighbors. Slater raved for upward of fifteen minutes, babbling in his backwoods dialect of green edifices of light, oceans of space, strange music, and shadowy mountains and valleys. But most of all did he dwell upon some mysterious blazing entity that shook and laughed and mocked at him. This vast, vague personality seemed to have done him a terrible wrong, and to kill it in triumphant revenge was his paramount desire. In order to reach it, he said, he would soar through abysses of emptiness, *burning* every obstacle that stood in his way. Thus ran his discourse, until with the greatest suddenness he ceased. The fire of madness died from his eyes, and in dull wonder he looked at his questioners and asked why he was bound. R. Barnard unbuckled the leather harness and did not restore it till night, when he succeeded in persuading Slater to don it of his own volition, for his own good. The man had now admitted that he sometimes talked queerly, though he knew not why.

Within a week two more attacks appeared, but from them the doctors learned little. On the *source* of Slater's visions they speculated at length, for since he could neither read nor write, and had apparently never heard a legend or fairy-tale, his gorgeous imagery was quite inexplicable. That it could not come from any known myth or romance was made especially clear by the fact that the unfortunate lunatic expressed himself only in his own simple manner. He raved of things he did not understand and could not interpret; things which he claimed to have experienced, but which he could not have learned through any normal or connected narration. The alienists soon agreed that abnormal dreams were the foundation of the trouble; dreams whose vividness could for a time completely dominate the waking mind of this basically inferior man. With due formality Slater was tried for murder, acquitted on the ground of insanity, and committed to the institution wherein I held so humble a post.

*   *   *

I have said that I am a constant speculator concerning dream-life, and from this you may judge of the eagerness with which I applied myself to the study of the new patient as soon as I had fully ascertained the facts of his case. He seemed to sense a certain friendliness in me, born no doubt of the interest I could not conceal, and the gentle manner in which I questioned him. Not that he ever recognized me during his attacks, when I hung breathlessly upon his chaotic but cosmic word-pictures; but he knew me in his quiet hours, when he would sit by his barred window weaving baskets of straw and willow, and perhaps pining for the mountain freedom he could never again enjoy. His family never called to see him; probably it had found another temporary head, after the manner of decadent mountain folk.

By degrees I commenced to feel an overwhelming wonder at the mad and fantastic conceptions of Joe Slater. The man himself was pitiably inferior in mentality and language alike; but his glowing, titanic visions, though described in a barbarous disjointed jargon, were assuredly things which only a superior or even exceptional brain could conceive. How, I often asked myself, could the stolid imagination of a Catskill degenerate conjure up sights whose very possession argued a lurking spark of genius? How could any backwoods dullard have gained so much as an idea of those glittering realms of supernal radiance and space about which Slater ranted in his furious delirium? More and more I inclined to the belief that in the pitiful personality who cringed before me lay the disordered nucleus of something beyond my comprehension; something infinitely beyond the comprehension of my more experienced but less imaginative medical and scientific colleagues.

And yet I could extract nothing definite from the man. The sum of all my investigation was, that in a kind of semi-corporeal dream-life Slater wandered or floated through resplendent and prodigious valleys, meadows, gardens, cities, and palaces of light, in a region unbounded and unknown to man; that there he was no peasant or degenerate, but a creature of importance and vivid life, moving proudly and dominantly, and checked only by a certain deadly enemy, who seemed to be a being of visible yet ethereal structure, and who did not appear to be of human shape, since Slater never referred to it as a *man*, or as aught save a *thing*. This *thing* had done Slater some hideous but unnamed wrong, which the maniac (if maniac he were) yearned to avenge.

From the manner in which Slater alluded to their dealings, I judged that he and the luminous *thing* had met on equal terms; that in his dream existence the man was himself a luminous *thing* of the same race as his enemy. This impression was sustained by his frequent references to *flying through space* and *burning* all that impeded his progress. Yet these conceptions were formulated in rustic words wholly inadequate to convey them, a circumstance which drove me to the conclusion that if a true dream world indeed existed, oral language was not its medium for the transmission of thought. Could it be that the dream soul inhabiting this inferior body was desperately struggling to speak things which the simple and halting tongue of dullness could not utter? Could it be that I was face to face with intellectual emanations which would explain the mystery if I could but learn to discover and read them? I did not tell the older physicians of these things, for middle age is skeptical, cynical, and disinclined to accept new ideas. Besides, the head of the institution had but lately warned me in his paternal way that I was overworking; that my mind needed a rest.

It had long been my belief that human thought consists basically of atomic or molecular motion, convertible into ether waves of radiant energy like heat, light and electricity. This belief had early led me to contemplate the possibility of telepathy or mental communication by means of suitable apparatus, and I had in my college days prepared a set of transmitting and receiving instruments somewhat similar to the cumbrous devices employed in wireless telegraphy at that crude, pre-radio period. These I had tested with a fellow-student, but achieving no result, had soon packed them away with other scientific odds and ends for possible future use.

Now, in my intense desire to probe into the dream-life of Joe Slater, I sought these instruments again, and spent several days in repairing them for action. When they were complete once more I missed no opportunity for their trial.

At each outburst of Slater's violence. I would fit the transmitter to his forehead and the receiver to my own, constantly making delicate adjustments for various hypothetical wave-lengths of intellectual energy. I had but little notion of how the thought-impressions would, if successfully conveyed; arouse an intelligent response in my brain, but I felt certain that I could detect and interpret them. Accordingly I continued my experiments, though informing no one of their nature.

*   *   *

It was on the twenty-first of February, 1901, that the thing occurred. As I look back across the years I realize how unreal it seems, and sometimes half wonder if old Doctor Fenton was not right when he charged it all to my excited imagination. I recall that he listened with great kindness and patience when I told him, but afterward gave me a nerve-powder and arranged for the half-year's vacation on which I departed the next week.

That fateful night I was wildly agitated and perturbed, for despite the excellent care he had received, Joe Slater was unmistakably dying. Perhaps it was his mountain freedom that he missed, or perhaps the turmoil in his brain had grown too acute for his rather sluggish physique; but at all events the flame of vitality flickered low in the decadent body. He was drowsy near the end, and as darkness fell he dropped off into a troubled sleep.

I did not strap on the straitjacket as was customary when he slept, since I saw that he was too feeble to be dangerous, even if he woke in mental disorder once more before passing away. But I did place upon his head and mine the two ends of my cosmic "radio," hoping against hope for a first and last message from the dream world in the brief time remaining. In the cell with us was one nurse, a mediocre fellow who did not understand the purpose of the apparatus, or think to inquire into my course. As the hours wore on I saw his head droop awkwardly in sleep, but I did not disturb him. I myself, lulled by the

270

rhythmical breathing of the healthy and the dying man, must have nodded a little later.

The sound of weird lyric melody was what aroused me. Chords, vibrations, and harmonic ecstasies echoed passionately on every hand, while on my ravished sight burst the stupendous spectacle of ultimate beauty. Walls, columns, and architraves of living fire blazed effulgently around the spot where I seemed to float in air, extending upward to an infinitely high vaulted dome of indescribable splendor. Blending with this display of palatial magnificence, or rather, supplanting it at times in kaleidoscopic rotation, were glimpses of wide plains and graceful valleys, high mountains and inviting grottoes, covered with every lovely attribute of scenery which my delighted eyes could conceive of, yet formed wholly of some glowing, ethereal plastic entity, which in consistency partook as much of spirit as of matter. As I gazed, I perceived that my own brain held the key to these enchanting metamorphoses; for each vista which appeared to me was the one my changing mind most wished to behold. Amidst this elysian realm I dwelt not as a stranger, for each sight and sound was familiar to me; just as it had been for uncounted eons of eternity before, and would be for like eternities to come.

Then the resplendent aura of my brother of light drew near and held colloquy with me, soul to soul, with silent and perfect interchange of thought. The hour was one of approaching triumph, for was not my fellow-being escaping at last from a degrading periodic bondage; escaping for ever, and preparing to follow the accursed oppressor even unto the uttermost fields of ether, that upon it might be wrought a flaming cosmic vengeance which would shake the spheres? We floated thus for a little time, when I perceived a slight blurring and fading of the objects around us, as though some force were recalling me to earth—where I least wished to go. The form near me seemed to feel a change also, for it gradually brought its discourse toward a conclusion, and itself prepared to quit the scene, fading from my sight at a rate somewhat less rapid than that of the other objects. A few more thoughts were exchanged, and I knew that the luminous one and I were being recalled to bondage, though for my brother of light it would be the last time. The sorry planet shell being well-nigh spent, in less than an hour my fellow would be free to pursue the oppressor along the Milky Way and past the hither stars to the very confines of infinity.

* * *

A well-defined shock separates my final impression of the fading scene of light from my sudden and somewhat shamefaced awakening and straightening up in my chair as I saw the dying figure on the couch move hesitantly. Joe Slater was indeed awaking, though probably for the last time. As I looked more closely, I saw that in the sallow cheeks shone spots of color which had never before been present. The lips, too, seemed unusual, being tightly compressed, as if by the force of a stronger character than had been Slater's. The whole face finally began to grow tense, and the head turned restlessly with closed eyes.

I did not rouse the sleeping nurse, but readjusted the slightly disarranged headbands of my telepathic "radio," intent to catch any parting message the dreamer might have to deliver. All at once the head turned sharply in my direction and the eyes fell open, causing me to stare in blank amazement at what I beheld. The man who had been Joe Slater, the Catskill decadent, was now gazing at me with a pair of luminous, expanding eyes whose blue seemed subtly to have deepened. Neither mania nor degeneracy was visible in that gaze, and I felt beyond a doubt that I was viewing a face behind which lay an active mind of high order.

At this juncture my brain became aware of a steady external influence operating upon it. I closed my eyes to concentrate my thoughts more profoundly, and was rewarded by the positive knowledge that *my long-sought mental message had come at last*. Each transmitted idea formed rapidly in my mind, and though no actual language was employed, my habitual association of conception and expression was so great that I seemed to be receiving the message in ordinary English.

"Joe Slater is dead," came the soul-petrifying voice of an agency from beyond the wall of sleep. My opened eyes sought the couch of pain in curious horror, but the blue eyes were still calmly gazing, and the countenance was still intelligently animated. "He is better dead, for he was unfit to bear the active intellect of cosmic entity. His gross body could not undergo the needed adjustments between ethereal life and planet life. He was too much an animal, too little a man; yet it is through his deficiency that you have come to discover me, for the cosmic and planet souls rightly should never meet. He has been in my torment and diurnal prison for forty-two of your terrestrial years.

"I am an entity like that which you yourself become in the freedom of dreamless sleep. I am your brother of light, and have floated with you in the effulgent valleys. It is not permitted me to tell your waking earth-self of your real self, but we are all roamers of vast spaces and travelers in many ages. Next year I may be dwelling in the Egypt which you call ancient, or in the cruel empire of Tsan Chan which is to come three thousand years hence. You and I have drifted to worlds that reel about the red Arcturus, and dwelt in the bodies of the insect-philosophers that crawl proudly over the forth moon of Jupiter. How little does the earth self know life and its extent! How little, indeed, ought it to know for its own tranquillity!

"Of the oppressor I cannot speak. You on earth have unwittingly felt its distant presence—you who without knowing idly gave the blinking beacon the name of *Algol, the Demon-Star*. It is to meet and conquer the oppressor that I have vainly striven for eons, held back by bodily encumbrances. Tonight I go as a Nemesis bearing just and blazingly cataclysmic vengeance. *Watch me in the sky close by the Demon-Star.*

"I cannot speak longer, for the body of Joe Slater grows cold and rigid, and the coarse brains are ceasing to vibrate as I wish. You have been my only friend on this planet—

the only soul to sense and seek for me within the repellent form which lies on this couch. We shall meet again—perhaps in the shining mists of Orion's Sword, perhaps on a bleak plateau in prehistoric Asia, perhaps in unremembered dreams tonight, perhaps in some other form an eon hence, when the solar system shall have been swept away."

At this point the thought-waves abruptly ceased, and the pale eyes of the dreamer—or can I say dead man?—commenced to glaze fishily. In a half-stupor I crossed over to the couch and felt of his wrist, but found it cold, stiff, and pulseless. The sallow cheeks paled again, and the thick lips fell open, disclosing the repulsively rotten fangs of the degenerate Joe Slater. I shivered, pulled a blanket over the hideous face, and awakened the nurse. Then I left the cell and went silently to my room. I had an instant and unaccountable craving for a sleep whose dreams I should not remember.

* * *

The climax? What plain tale of science can boast of such a rhetorical effect? I have merely set down certain things appealing to me as facts, allowing you to construe them as you will. As I have already admitted, my superior, old Doctor Fenton, denies the reality of everything I have related. He vows that I was broken down with nervous strain, and badly in need of the long vacation on full pay which he so generously gave me. He assures me on his professional honor that Joe Slater was but a low-grade paranoiac, whose fantastic notions must have come from the crude hereditary folk-tales which circulated in even the most decadent of communities. All this he tells me—yet I cannot forget what I saw in the sky on the night after Slater died. Lest you think me a biased witness, another pen must add this final testimony, which may perhaps supply the climax you expect. I will quote the following account of the star *Nova Persei* verbatim from the pages of that eminent astronomical authority, Professor Garrett P. Serviss:

"On February 22, 1901, a marvelous new star was discovered by Doctor Anderson of Edinburgh, *not very far from Algol*. No star had been visible at that point before. Within twenty-four hours the stranger had become so bright that it outshone Capella. In a week or two it had visibly faded, and in the course of a few months it was hardly discernible with the naked eye."